Acclaim for the *Shelter* series

"Rob Gittins is a highly acclaimed dramatist whose work has been enjoyed by millions in TV and radio dramas. In *Gimme Shelter*, his first novel, he has advanced his skills in a compelling story of modern times. He takes us into the violent and murky criminal world of witness protection, where boundaries between good and evil are ill-defined. *Gimme Shelter* is an extraordinary achievement."

Nicholas Rhea

"Visceral, strongly visual and beautifully structured… powerful, quirky characters."

Andrew Taylor

"No one could guess that *Gimme Shelter* is Rob Gittins's first novel because his hand is so sure in developing characters as complex as they are convincing, in managing a plot chock full of surprising twists and in maintaining a tension that keeps the reader totally absorbed… Gittins's gritty story introduces the reader to a dangerous and troubled part of society, and his murky, damaged and at times violent characters are as vividly (and disturbingly) portrayed as those of Elmore Leonard."

Susanna Gregory

"An unflinching debut… as vicious and full of twists as a tiger in a trap."

Russell James

"A major new crime writer has given us the definitive interpretation of 'page turnability' and created characters that step effortlessly off the page and into the memory. This is a book that will haunt the reader long after the covers are closed."

Katherine John

SHELTER ME

For Alison and Dai

SHELTER ME

ROB GITTINS

The characters in this book are entirely
fictional and are not intended to bear any
resemblance to anyone living or dead.

First impression: 2020

© Rob Gittins & Y Lolfa Cyf., 2020

This book is subject to copyright and may not be reproduced
by any means except for review purposes without the
prior written consent of the publishers.

The publishers wish to acknowledge the support
of the Books Council of Wales

Cover design: Matthew Tyson
Cover image: den-belitsky/istockphoto,
Media Whalestock/shutterstock

Paperback ISBN: 978 1 912631 22 3
Hardback ISBN: 978 1 78461 924 4

Published and printed in Wales
on paper from well maintained forests by
Y Lolfa Cyf., Talybont, Ceredigion SY24 5HE
e-mail ylolfa@ylolfa.com
website www.ylolfa.com
tel 01970 832 304
fax 832 782

PROLOGUE

GREENLAND, 1997

IT SHOULD NEVER have happened. It was just the one rogue element, a single aberration in the firmament.

But it did happen.

That was all that mattered.

They'd been travelling north for what seemed like days, the horizon ahead an unbroken kaleidoscope of crystal – the effect hypnotic, almost hallucinatory. The young girl on the sled closed her eyes for the third time in as many minutes, turned her face towards the sun, and for the third time in as many minutes again, began to doze. Sleep had come in fits and starts for longer than she could remember, the daylight – constant at this time of year – continually tricking her body into believing it needed no rest.

Then, suddenly, she heard it.

'*Harru! Harru!*'

The young girl's eyes jerked open as her sled suddenly swung left, then right a moment later as a second cry sounded.

'*Atsuk! Atsuk!*'

Ahead, far ahead, she saw her father's sled moving towards a musk ox that had just been spotted heading for the glimpsed sanctuary of a bay.

But they were still hundreds of metres away from their quarry and so the hunter on whose sled she was travelling immediately cut loose two of their dogs, and then another pair. The dogs joined two other dogs now cut loose from her father's sled too. The snow was deep, but the dogs still closed fast on their panicked kill, urged on all the while by the cries of the hunters behind them:

Huughuaq!

Huughuaq!

Go faster!

Go faster!

But they were closing too fast. Something was wrong: the animal was holding back, and the young girl soon saw why.

As the hunters drew closer, she could see that the creature wasn't alone. She was accompanied by her small calf, its eyes wide: black, frightened holes. Panicked by the fast-closing dogs she'd probably mistaken for wolves, the musk ox had tried to pick up speed, but then stopped as her calf fell on the snow behind her. She tried to get back to it, but by then the dogs were in between them and had cut the mother off from her baby.

The musk ox pawed the frozen snow, snarling and lashing out at the dogs, but they held their ground as they waited for the hunters on the sleds to catch up. For those few moments, it was stalemate.

The young girl joined the rest of the hunters huddled around the lead sled a moment later, growing anxious now. But her father then gave a small nod across at her and she relaxed. The young girl hadn't been on that many trips with him up to that point, but she still knew what he was saying to her with that silent signal.

The musk ox was with her calf. That meant the dogs would now be called back, that the kill would not take place. Mother and calf would be released to travel on, as the hunters would travel on in turn. Perhaps later when her small charge was fully grown, their paths would cross again and then there would be a very different outcome, but for now both would be spared.

Then something went wrong. Without warning, one of the dogs suddenly sprang forward and, before anyone could stop what was happening, the rogue dog leapt at the frightened calf. That sole act of individual madness acted as a signal to the other dogs, who all now sprang forward too, tearing away at the small creature as the trapped mother roared and pawed at the air a few metres away.

The young girl's father was the first to reach the suddenly maddened dogs, beating them away with his whip handle, the rest of the hunters joining him. Between them they quelled the unexpected attack in moments, but it was too late.

The cowed dogs retreated, still maintaining their makeshift barricade barring the crazed mother's way to the calf as the hunters inspected their victim, but it was already clear there was no hope. The calf was alive but weakening by the moment, although it still snarled and scratched at the hunter's approach: something of the mother's spirit extant, perhaps.

Meanwhile, the musk ox was scooping up snow from the ground, perhaps feeding a sudden thirst, perhaps readying herself for one last desperate, doomed assault on her persecutors. Then she paused as she saw her calf try to stand, probably in some similarly desperate and doomed attempt to return to its mother. Then the calf's eyeballs rolled back, exposing the whites of its eyes, and the small animal fell back onto the snow.

The girl looked across at her father, fearful, already knowing in her heart what would happen next.

Her calf had been the mother's passport to survival.

With it gone, the mother was a legitimate kill once more.

Tears began to prick the young girl's eyes as her father looked back at her in turn. All it took on his part was another simple glance – he really didn't need to put it into words.

The young girl was warm because of a polar bear shot on a previous hunting trip. Fragments of that bear's hide were still being used to patch the young girl's boots. She'd been fed the previous winter courtesy of that same kill. Did she really imagine they could pass up this new opportunity, whatever the circumstances that had brought it about?

The young girl turned and walked towards the trapped musk ox, who was now just standing still. She knew her calf was gone and it seemed to have crushed the life out her too. Now and again her eyes still darted across the horizon as if searching for some sort of escape, but of course there was none.

So the musk ox just rested her head against the edge of an ice-cold berg and waited.

A few metres away the father watched his now silent daughter, growing ever more troubled. When he'd first accompanied his own father on similar trips in the past, he would never have dreamt of making the same plea he'd just witnessed in his daughter's eyes.

But times were changing now and changing fast. A few months before, back in their home town, he'd watched as a wave swept onto the shore by a calving glacier washed a small handful of anchored boats up onto a nearby road. The boats belonged to a family recently arrived from the south, who were so busy trying to salvage their pleasure craft they forgot all about their dogs tied up on the shore, and the dogs all drowned. Years before, no one would have dreamt of behaving that way, as years before, no Inuit child would ever have looked at their father with a request, silent or otherwise, that a kill be set free.

The hunter looked out over the ice towards the dogs, all now huddled together a short distance from the doomed musk ox. Maybe even the actions of that one rogue dog that day bore witness to those same changing times. Dogs usually acted as one, following the dictates of the pack. For one to break away like that was strange, unsettling. The hunter made a mental note to identify that one dog and later, once they'd returned from their trip, to take it to one side and kill it.

Those few metres away, the dogs had now lost interest in their quarry and were starting to lick away at the various wounds the musk ox had managed to inflict as they'd encircled her.

As if she knew the end was near and her fate now inevitable, the musk ox herself bent forward, then sank down into the snow. Or maybe she'd just caught sight of another of the hunters now securing her calf's leg with a length of rope, getting ready to drag the small carcass back to the sled.

The father kept watching his child. The simple truth was that his daughter was beginning to absorb other cultures and other influences and it didn't matter how many trips similar to this one he took her on. She was changing now; caught, like so many others, between two cultures: neither Inuit nor Dane. She was becoming part of a new race, was already beginning to sound different – even look different – as she tried, like so many of her generation, to find a balance between very different worlds.

The father took a bow from the back of his sled and approached the musk ox. As the hunter approached, the creature raised her head, not looking at him now, but at the watching girl. But there was no last appeal in those eyes. She simply gave the young girl the sort of stare she would have given any another species in the food chain, the same appraising stare her father was now giving the musk ox in turn.

The animal understood, the hunter reflected, even if his daughter did not. Predator and kill. It was still the one constant, irrespective of those changing times. One constant in a landscape that was fast becoming anything but.

The hunter released a single arrow and the musk ox sank back onto the snow, dead now along with her calf.

Alasie, the young girl, moved away while the actual killing took place. Partly to distract herself and partly because she loved to do so, she began to sing, softly, her small voice wafting over the white landscape, almost providing a requiem accompaniment to the second of the lives that was now ending just a few metres away from her.

But then she turned back and joined the rest of the hunters, beginning to play her full part in all they had to do next. Maybe she was just paying tribute to old superstitions, but the hunter – her father, Imaneq – preferred to think that the Inuit side of her character still prevailed.

So for the next few hours, father, daughter and the rest of the hunters all worked in silence, laying the musk ox out on her back, cutting her skin open from the umbilicus to her neck, stretching the skin out on the snow before folding it and packing it carefully in a gunny sack on one of the sleds. Then the large creature's limbs were sliced from the rest of her body and the dismembered and disrobed parts were packed on the sled too.

All the time strict silence was observed, another of the old superstitions – although Imaneq still preferred to think of them as something more. According to everything he'd ever been taught and still believed, all hunted animals could hear and understand everything humans said to each other, even after death. So for the next day at least and until they reached their destination, not a word would pass anyone's lips.

When they returned home, other rituals would similarly be observed, just as they'd done with a kill from the previous year. The flayed hide of that kill – a she-bear – had been brought into the house and placed in a box for the dogs to sleep on. As the meat was eaten, all the bones had been collected and placed on the windowsill with the head of the bear so its soul would have no difficulty in reaching its home.

Nothing would be needlessly discarded or wasted. Years before Imaneq had stood as a small boy with his grandfather, already by then a nonagenarian. It wasn't a musk ox that had just been killed that day by him and nine other hunters, but two minke whales – the first their home community had trapped and killed in more than twenty years – and the age-old practice of flensing and carving was taking place under the old man's watchful eyes.

Within a matter of hours all that remained of the great mammals, six and nine metres long respectively, were ten equal piles of skin, blubber, fins and large blocks of blood-red meat. One pile would be going to each of the hunters and their families, with nothing again going to waste. Even the giant backbones would be dragged to the eagerly waiting huskies, who would then fight each other for their share.

The hunter still remembered hunching down next to his grandfather, who'd offered him a slice of thick whale skin cut with a pocket knife, and he could still remember too the salty crunch and taste the oily sheen of lipids from the small fillets seared on a hot skillet. The next year he'd accompanied him on a walrus hunt and watched as his aged relation examined the slit stomach of the 400 kg behemoth they'd just killed, fishing around in the bloody mass with his knife before extracting a scallop and popping it into his mouth.

But what he remembered most was his grandfather's extraordinary memory. He could sketch the coastline for miles around in the snow, not missing out a single bay or inlet. Before the old man had died, Imaneq had asked him how he managed to keep all that inside his head, but according to his grandfather, it was simple. The old man never forgot anything, he told his grandson, because he'd never learnt to read or write.

That night, the night of the unexpected kill courtesy of that one rogue dog, they feasted on the first of the meat from their prey. Later, with Alasie sleeping as fitfully as they all slept in the constant sunlight, as fitfully as they would all sleep until darkness crept across the land once more, he opened one of the newspapers he'd brought with him from home and as he did so,

Imaneq's eyes fell on a single advertisement standing out among the rest.

The hunter traced the outline of the words with his fingers, reading as he did so a notice for young children with an interest in song to join a new choir that had been established back in their home town.

Imaneq looked across at the sleeping Alasie and then leant forward with his pocket knife – the same knife bequeathed to him by his nonagenarian grandfather – and smoothly excised the notice from the paper. Then he placed the notice next to his sleeping daughter so she'd see it when she woke.

Maybe that was his way of trying to make up to his daughter for some of the clear distress of the day, he now silently reflected. And he went to his own sleep shaking his head more than a little sadly at the thought.

Later, much later, he would think back to that moment and to spotting that simple notice in the paper as he rested after their exertions on the ice cap.

And Imaneq would wish more than anything he'd wished for before that he'd been born blind.

2

UK, 1997

O NE HOUR TO go. All the preparations had been made.
The team assembled in that pressure cooker of an office had been carefully hand-picked, and they had to be. Most officers could handle what might be called the 'normal' kind of criminals, such as robbers and arsonists, even murderers and rapists.

But many of those same officers simply couldn't deal with paedophiles.

Across the packed room, the lean young Detective Sergeant, James Delaney, reviewed his case notes for a third and then a fourth time, searching for potential banana skins, knowing what would happen should he or any of his team get any part of the upcoming operation even slightly wrong.

And just in case that had somehow slipped his mind, he'd had those highest of stakes forcibly pointed out to him by his ball-breaker of a senior officer, DCI Gill Adams, just half an hour previously.

And an hour before that.

And for the past few days and weeks as well.

And all DCI Adams's warnings were very much justified, Delaney knew that – as he'd also made clear time and again to his team. There were risks here, real risks: of that, every officer in that room was only too well aware. But there was a real prize on offer here as well.

It wasn't unusual for sex offenders to fantasise about children and there wasn't in reality too much the police could do about it. What those sex offenders were writing to each other might be distasteful at best, disgusting at worst, but may not in itself be a crime. It could just be the depraved ramblings of a few noxious inadequates. Or even, as one particularly noxious inadequate had claimed in the past, a writing exercise for his evening class.

But now they had a clear indication that two of the paedophiles in question had moved on from simple talk – had taken, in fact, the crucial next step. And today was the day all the intense and increasingly animated discussion that Delaney and his team had monitored for weeks might bear fruit. The day when all his team's covert surveillance might just pay off.

The problem, the ever-present problem, being that all the compelling detail they'd painstakingly assembled from phone calls and the newly established internet chat rooms wasn't enough. They still needed evidence – and incontrovertible evidence too. They needed to put before a court absolute proof that these two sickos really had physically targeted a young and vulnerable child as opposed to merely talking about doing so, and that would then be that. Michael Thomas and Douglas Leonard would be off the streets for the next 15 years at least.

It wouldn't be the first experience of life behind bars for either man, and the sad truth was that it probably wouldn't be the last. Most men would have taken the savage beatings they'd already both suffered inside as a clear hint that they should mend their ways, but in common with most paedophiles, these two simply didn't seem able to stop.

Which was the lesson spelt out by the chilling statistics again and again. Rapists tired of their activity; murderers too. Career criminals eventually also usually drifted into retirement, be that voluntarily or at the hands of the law. But paedophiles never tired of their predilections. And they never retired. No matter their age or even any physical disability brought on by all those savage beatings, they simply kept on offending until death. Whether that betokened evil in its most unalloyed form, or a sickness for which there was no cure, wasn't an issue for Delaney or the rest of his team, and it didn't interest any of them too much either, in truth. It just made it all the more imperative they present enough evidence to a jury to return these men where they belonged, which was behind bars.

'Guv.'

Delaney looked up as a female DC handed him the latest set of photographs collated by the specialist unit carrying out the covert surveillance on both men. Delaney spread them out on the desk in front of him, adding them to the latest evidence they'd assembled, evidence that had prompted this hasty assembly of specialist officers in the first place.

In the first, taken just one day previously, Leonard could be seen leaving a pet shop, a newly purchased dog lead in hand.

In the second – an hour or so later – Thomas was seen leaving a local electronics shop having just purchased some lengths of speaker cable.

In the third, taken less than an hour after the first image of him had been captured on camera, Thomas was featured again, this time visiting a cobbler's to acquire some spare laces.

It might all have seemed innocuous enough taken one by one, but every officer in that room knew the significance of those very different purchases. Both men had made that crystal clear in their exchanges with the other.

With his dog lead in hand, Leonard would now approach a target child, pretending he'd lost his small puppy and asking for the child's help in finding it.

Meanwhile Thomas would have fashioned the cable and laces into ties that would make it look as if either he or Leonard were holding hands with their target child rather than restraining her or him. Neither man was all that fussy if past form was anything to go by. Age was the key attraction here, not gender.

But despite the curious nature of the purchases, despite the corroborating evidence of the two men's recorded and filed phone calls and internet exchanges, it was all, as any half-decent defence barrister would definitely point out, pure supposition. A belligerent Leonard would simply insist he was about to visit a local pound to choose a dog. An aggrieved Thomas would show any jury before whom he was arraigned details of a hi-fi system he intended to build, showing them at the same time a pair of boots with rotted laces. And in the absence of any other evidence – sad fantasies aside – both men would probably walk free.

'On the move.'

Across the room another DC, male this time and hunched over a monitor, issued the terse, almost curt, statement, the tension in the room rising palpably as he did so. On the monitor before him the two men, plastic bags in hand and both wearing hoodies, could now be seen leaving Leonard's small flat, taking a left along the street and then a right, heading for the local park.

The bags, Delaney strongly suspected, contained the tools of their trade, including the dog lead and speaker cable. The hoodies were a necesary precaution, something both men had taken to wearing on all their excursions lately. A local vigilante group had already identified the two men as past sex offenders and had pasted their mugshots on railings outside the local school.

Monitoring the moving men all the while, Delaney checked on the position of the plain-clothes officers in and around the park. Between them, they were in clear sight of all the usual attractions, including the children's playground and a boating lake. Wherever the two men made their move – and Delaney had absolutely no doubt that they would – they'd be in view of at least two, if not more, of his officers. Once they made a direct approach to any playing child, those same officers would be on them in seconds.

Delaney focused on the hunched, shuffling figure of Leonard, his hands now gripping his bag tight, as if he was transporting holy relics rather than the monuments to twisted depravity that were actually inside.

Another specialist unit in a different force had first come across him some 20 years before. Leonard had snatched a three-year-old girl off the street and had then subjected her to a four-hour period of abuse. But then, rather than abandoning the deeply traumatised child, he'd taken her home. Leonard, affecting troubled shock, had told her parents he'd found her wandering around in the street near his house in what was clearly a terrible state.

The grateful parents had quickly befriended their very own Good Samaritan and a relationship had developed, as Leonard had always intended it would, although not even he could have foreseen he'd actually end up renting a room from them too.

Leonard went on to abuse his helpless victim from the age of three to six, before she finally plucked up the courage to speak out to a sympathetic teacher at school. That had earned Leonard the first of his prison sentences, a sentence he'd actually served in full, despite his being a model prisoner – which wasn't all that difficult, in truth. Temptations of the kind that interested Leonard were non-existent in the Scrubs.

But there were plenty of temptations now.

Delaney watched Leonard and Thomas turn into the park, where both men were instantly confronted with at least a dozen potential victims, as children played on the swings and slides just inside the main entrance.

Delaney kept watching as the men split up and circled the playground for a while. Then Leonard approached one small child in particular who'd chased after a football, momentarily cutting him off from the rest of his friends. A flurry of surveillance shots captured the moment of the approach. A more intense and even more damning flurry of shots captured Leonard as he reached out his hand to physically detain the boy as he tried to move back to rejoin his friends.

And that was it. That really should be more than enough. That and the tools of his trade should now be enough to convince even the most sceptical of jurors.

Delaney instantly dispatched the prearranged signal and the plain-clothes officers dotted around the park moved in. Thomas was the first to be apprehended, Leonard a close second. Their bags were confiscated, their hoodies removed.

Only the first figure wasn't Thomas.

And the second wasn't Leonard.

Two local crackheads stood revealed before the now disbelieving officers instead.

A later debriefing back in the local station would establish they'd both been offered a substantial amount of cash for the simple act of walking from a local flat and circling a local park. They'd been promised a bonus if they actually managed to engage one of the children playing there in conversation. They'd no idea what it was about and didn't care.

All they could see was a windfall, which the two aggrieved crackheads were already beginning to suspect they wouldn't actually now receive.

A mile or so away across the city, the passers-by couldn't help themselves. One by one each and every one of them smiled as the small girl passed by, hand in hand with her clearly adoring father – and no wonder.

The beautifully behaved child had a serene, almost dreamlike expression on her face. She looked as if she was almost walking on air – and in a sense she was, thanks to the alcopops that she'd just been all but force-fed, but the indulgently approving passers-by didn't know that, of course.

They also had no way of knowing that one of her small hands was also virtually welded to her adult companion right now, courtesy of specially designed ties.

Now and again the young girl did try to ask where they were going, but as she couldn't actually force open her lips – courtesy of the superglue she'd been told was lip balm to prevent her lips burning in the sun – she made no sound.

The adult helped the young girl into a car where another adult – another man – was waiting. Then the young girl was driven away, silent screams now beginning to reverberate inside her head as she finally regained sufficient of her senses to realise that something was very badly wrong here.

The young girl's increasingly distraught parents, frantically searching the nearby adventure playground from which she seemed to have just disappeared, were feeling exactly the same.

Meanwhile, those few miles away across the city, the expression on Delaney's face as he stared at the ever more agitated but basically harmless crackheads in the park said it all: he was also experiencing the same sense of blind panic as the parents of the young girl who was soon to be reported missing, along with the same terrible fear that they were already too late to stop a genuine atrocity as opposed to the grotesque charade that had just been acted out before them.

And Delaney was to be proved right. It was too late for the young child who'd just been abducted from that adventure playground, and it was too late for her parents, who would never see her alive again.

It was also to signal an inglorious end to the promising young Detective Sergeant's career as well. But that was the last thing on Delaney's mind right now, as he kept staring at the monitor before him. He didn't see the crackheads, now arguing volubly with the PC charged with detaining them. He didn't see the rest of the ever more panicked officers as they trawled the rest of the park in their doomed efforts to find out where the crackheads' paymasters might be right now. He didn't even see the staring eyes of his ball-breaker of a DCI, her silent glare confirming more eloquently than any later disciplinary tribunal could, that his career in that particular force was now very much over.

All Delaney saw was the innocent life he'd just sacrificed.

PART ONE

THE TIME BETWEEN

TWO WINTERS

3

UK, PRESENT DAY

UNDER NORMAL CIRCUMSTANCES, DCI Masters – Head of the local Murder Squad – simply wouldn't want to know.

Outside agencies were habitually excluded from most crime scenes his unit encountered. Sometimes, indeed, he even excluded those in his own department. Masters was renowned in his home city of Cardiff and beyond for ploughing his own determinedly individual furrow.

So for Ros Gilet – Acting Head of the local Protected Persons Unit – to receive a call from him, asking her to attend the scene of a double killing, was something of a surprise.

Ros listened as Masters spat out a characteristically curt and bare-bones summary of the murders that had just taken place. Then she cut the call, snatching up her keys from a table in her small and functional first-floor apartment before heading down the single flight of stairs and outside towards her designated parking space and her car, as chaotically parked as ever.

On the way, and using a mobile also snatched up from that same small table, she contacted Conor, her newly promoted second-in-command.

Five minutes after receiving Masters's phone call, Ros had picked up Conor from his rather more upmarket apartment nearby and the two officers were travelling west out of the city along a feeder road leading to a man-made abomination some town planner had attempted to dignify by christening a retail park, in the shadow of which squatted an immaculately maintained new-build housing estate.

One hour previously, Jo Edwards, in her mid thirties and mother to the two small boys at that moment sleeping inside, had closed the front door of her new-build house on that same immaculately maintained estate. And as she did so, Jo stood on the step and exhaled a silent sigh of relief.

Tom, her husband, had been checking and double-checking the central heating boiler for the whole of the last hour. It still wasn't igniting properly, despite his having worked on it every spare moment of every evening for the last week. What had started as mild amusement on the family's part at Tom's characteristically single-minded refusal to accept that the task was beyond him had quickly mutated into an all too familiar irritation. But Jo – and indeed Steven and Callum, their two boys: aged five and three respectively – knew better than to let that irritation show. Once provoked, Tom's legendary sulks could scale the upper reaches of epic.

Jo drove the short distance to her friend Angie's house. Angie was booked in for her latest IVF session the next day and both Angie and her husband, Josh, knew this new attempt was probably make or break. They were at the limit of their borrowing already. Another failure could dash their already fragile hopes for good.

Jo was away from home for less than an hour. She'd made all the right noises and said all the right things, but she was already beginning to feel more than a little awkward in Angie's company. Like most young mothers, even the most innocuous of conversations tended to touch on her two sons – what they'd been doing, what they hadn't been doing, what they should have been doing. Everyday stuff, but Jo could see it in her friend's eyes. She'd have given the world to be able to reciprocate with similar everyday stuff of her own. She'd already indeed given most of what she and Josh owned in the world to do so, but it hadn't been enough. Despite herself – and Angie didn't normally possess a sour bone in her body – Jo could almost see the bitterness building inside her towards those blessed with the babies she craved.

But as Jo returned along the newly resurfaced road, she could see their front drive was empty.

Which was odd. Very odd.

It meant Tom had gone out in his own car while she'd been away at Angie's, but where the hell would he have gone? And more to the point, why?

Briefly, Jo felt a sudden surge of anger as she remembered it was late opening at one of the DIY stores on the retail park nround the corner. If Tom had nipped out even for a few moments to get some part or other for the boiler, leaving their two boys alone, then fuck his sulks. OK, Callum and Steven might have been sleeping and Tom would have made sure that the doors and all the windows were secured and locked, but this was still a total no-no and Tom would be told that in no uncertain terms. Jo didn't blow her top often but when she did, her rages could also scale the heights.

It was as Jo let herself in a moment later that a second and infinitely more sickening possibility suddenly assaulted her.

Had something happened? Had one of the boys had some sort of accident? Had Tom had to bundle them both into the car and drive them to the nearest surgery a mile or so away, or even down to the A & E unit in the nearby hospital, locally known as The Heath?

Now feeling sick to the pit of her stomach, Jo dashed upstairs, poking her head into first Steven's room and then Callum's, the relief ebbing out of her, making her knees literally go weak as she saw both boys still sleeping in their beds, the night light on in Callum's room as usual, the light spilling through partly open curtains into Steven's, things looking pretty much as she'd left them that hour or so before.

Jo retraced her steps back downstairs to the hall, which was when, for the first time, she heard it. Music, sounding softly on the CD player in the sitting room. Previously, all Jo had heard was her own blood rushing in her ears as she'd charged up the stairs, but now she not only registered the music, she recognised the song that was playing too. It was a song she and Tom had heard on their first date together, a song that Tom had chosen to have played at their wedding.

Their song, in fact.

Jo, ever more bewildered, kept listening as the song finished and then began again, clearly on some sort of repeat cycle.

Then she looked back towards the stairs again.

And felt something deep inside her stomach turn to ice.

Just over ten minutes after receiving Masters's call, Ros was making her way along that newly resurfaced road, a very different scene greeting her to the one Jo had seen a short time before.

The same neat homes were still in evidence, as were the same front lawns and hedges, all trimmed to within an inch of their lives. Here and there, Ros glimpsed the odd jarring note – a trampoline in one garden, a climbing frame in another – but even they seemed to be sited in the exact centre of each of the uniform lawns. Little, it was already clear, would dare threaten the fearful symmetry here.

For Ros and Conor, every nook and cranny of that street and the surrounding gardens was now cast into jagged relief by the flashing blue lights from the three attending police cars and two attending ambulances.

Outside Jo's house, Ros saw Masters. He was talking to a shaken-looking woman Ros recognised as one of the force's Family Liaison Officers: Amy Manson, a raw new recruit who seemed to be fast regretting her recent appointment, if her whey-faced expression right now was anything to go by.

Ros felt a sudden stab of sympathy. Ros wasn't a great deal older than Amy herself. In Ros's few years in her present department, her first and only posting so far, she'd seen more than her fair share of the kind of horror that had greeted that new recruit inside the house behind them. Ros had coped with each and every one of those horrors – but given all that had happened to her in her short life, maybe she'd had a head start when it came to that sort of thing.

By Ros's side, Conor also registered the new presence by Masters's side. He also registered the look on her face: an expression that bore the most eloquent of testimonies to the fact she was already hopelessly out of her depth, and Conor couldn't help but sympathise. He'd only been in the Protection Unit a few years. During that time, he'd also witnessed a fair few difficult situations, but right now as Conor looked at the upstairs windows of the house before them, he also had to confess to feeling more than a little out of his depth too.

Jo had taken the stairs two at a time after hearing the song. At the top there was a dog-leg kink that led up onto the landing. She'd lost count of the number of times she'd banged her shins on it and she did so again now, hard. This time she never even noticed.

Jo now knew why that feeling had crept over her as she'd stood in the hallway a moment before, listening to that song end and then begin again, still wondering where the hell Tom had gone and why. In truth, she'd known something was wrong the second she turned away from Steven and Callum's rooms. She just hadn't allowed her brain to formalise it into anything like coherent thought. But it was only a temporary impasse, delaying the inevitable.

It was the way her boys were arranged. Jo couldn't put it any other way. She'd seen both her sons sleeping thousands of times. She'd seen them assume a seemingly infinite number of ever more contorted positions. Just a few years before, as a new mother, she'd actually tried to rearrange her eldest, Steven, in particular; straightening his twisted limbs, certain that he must be in pain – he had to be: what human being could sleep with his legs and arms in that sort of position? She'd only succeeded in waking her infuriated and totally unharmed son along the way, of course, as a long-suffering Tom had pointed out more than once.

Since then, Jo had let each of the two boys sleep however they wished, and they had: sometimes on one side of the bed, sometimes on the other; sometimes half in and half out of those beds, occasionally out completely, finishing the night in a crumpled but still-sleeping heap on the floor. She'd seem them resemble starfish, crabs and species of marine life that hadn't been created yet and probably never would.

But she'd never seen either of them sleep in the way they were sleeping right now.

They were both identically positioned. Steven and Callum each had their arms under their duvets and were lying flat on their backs, their eyes closed and their faces pointing up towards the ceiling. A couple of toys were lying on the beds next to them, which was another jarring element in the tableau. Callum took toys to sleep with him but Steven was already growing beyond such distractions. He'd started primary school recently and was very much in thrall to all the older kids, meaning these days he was more likely to sneak a small torch and comics featuring various superheroes into bed with him at night.

Jo paused at Callum's door, the night light still illuminating him. He was in the exact same position she'd seen him in just a few moments before.

Peaceful.

Way, way, too peaceful.

She hesitated a moment more, then turned and crossed the small landing to Steven's room before hesitating again at the slightly open doorway, now seeing her eldest son in the exact same position he'd been in a few moments previously as well.

She stayed there for what couldn't have been more than a second or so, but felt like an eternity; as if she knew that she was hovering somehow, suspended between one life and a different life completely, some instinct already warning her that to actually walk in through either of those doors would be to lift a lid on a future that should never be permitted to exist.

But then she moved into the room of her firstborn. She stood above him for a moment, listening, but could hear nothing. Nothing at all. Steeling herself all the while, Jo reached out her hand and touched his forehead. Then she turned back towards the door and back out onto the landing.

She stood there for a second longer.

Then she started to scream.

Lynne Maher hadn't heard any screams. She'd heard a whisper instead. But it had still chilled her to the bone.

In common with many of her colleagues in the Comms Department, Lynne had endured her fair share of hoax calls. Some were malicious, usually prompted by spite aimed at neighbours or exes. Some weren't malicious at all, just thinly disguised cries for help from varying degrees of lost souls.

Or even, in the case of one rather lovely old lady called (somewhat magnificently, Lynne had always thought) Elsie Borstal, from an even more lost soul in the grip of obvious dementia. Elsie had once racked up a local record in Lynne's department: 22 calls in the course of a single shift.

But this call – this woman – was different.

It had been a quiet evening up to then. The 300 or so CCTV cameras that were all sited at one end of the long room hadn't shown anything too alarming. The radio operators who were seated beside Lynne had been kept fairly busy, dispatching officers in vehicles and on foot to the scenes of various disturbances and incidents, but it had all been pretty low-key stuff.

A scuffle outside a city-centre pub that was never going to threaten any actual injury to anyone, given the clearly intoxicated state of the largely incoherent combatants.

Another drunk in a Chinese restaurant, who couldn't understand why the bewildered staff wouldn't serve him the Indian takeaway he'd ordered and which he'd quite obviously set his heart on, and who was stoutly refusing to leave until they did so.

Timewasters, some of the other officers called them, but Lynne didn't. In her book she and her colleagues were providing a service, helping the public in whatever way they could. Yes, sometimes that might mean acting as glorified nursemaids, but if they didn't, who would?

But for Lynne, these were really just diversions because she was an emergency call handler. She was seated beside the radio operators, so if she was busy on another call then one of the other handlers could immediately step in. They were called on only rarely, much to Lynne's private relief. In common with most of her other emergency colleagues, Lynne's telephone manner, honed over the years, was soothing, reassuring – almost motherly. Some of the other dispatchers, more used to liaising with harassed police officers than members of the public in extremes of panic and distress, were anything but.

'Police emergency, how can I help?'

As Lynne answered, she glanced at a number and an approximate location that had just illuminated on the screen before her. Lynne swiftly identified the location as one not far from the small terraced house she shared with her husband Bryan, an ex-police officer himself, invalided out of the force some two years previously following a minor stroke. Bryan had recovered, but his days on active duty were over. But he still lived his old life, vicariously, through his wife's often-forensic reporting of the calls she'd taken during the course of her latest shift. Most provoked considerable amusement. Something in the way this latest caller paused before responding was already telling her this one would not.

Silence at the start of an emergency call wasn't unusual. Most people never call 999 in their lives. Of the ones who do, malicious callers or those with dementia aside, the vast majority probably only ever use the service once. The circumstances that provoke the call are usually daunting enough; it isn't surprising that people need a moment to organise their thoughts and control their often raging emotions.

'It's my husband.'

The woman's voice was soft, almost inaudible. Lynne adjusted her earpiece, boosting the volume.

'What's happened to him?'

For a moment there was silence again and when she next spoke, Lynne's caller seemed to have gone off on a tangent.

'They're not waking up.'

Lynne paused. The caller had just gone from a *he* to a *they* but Lynne didn't challenge her, just maintained the same low soothing tone.

'Could you give me your name and address, please?'

'He's killed them.'

On the other end of the line, Lynne stilled.

'He's killed both of them.'

Lynne looked up, caught the eye of the Duty Inspector, a tall, stick-thin veteran and former colleague of her husband called Alex James. On the other end of the line the caller's voice dipped in volume even more.

'My beautiful boys.'

Alex moved over to her quickly, alerted by Lynne's silent signal. As he did so, Lynne was already typing out a running incident log which was being automatically sent on, even as she was typing it, to one of the nearby radio dispatchers. Lynne glanced at the screen again. Her caller was using a mobile and even though the location of the cell tower receiving and transmitting her call was showing clearly on the screen, she could still be on any one of a handful of local streets. Lynne stabbed at a quick, hopefully educated, guess.

'Are you on Castleton Way?'

'Cory Avenue.'

Lynne typed into her log, still talking all the while.

'Please stay on the line for me, caller – there's someone on their way to you now, but let's me and you just keep talking till they get to you, OK?'

The call sign of the police response car that had been allocated the emergency call appeared on screen. Lynne checked the location again. To her relief, she could see it was no more than a quarter of a mile away, maybe less – and as if by way of confirmation, the pink symbol of the police car suddenly jumped. They'd now turned off Castleton Way onto Jo's actual street.

'Are you outside, caller? If you are, can you see a police car? It should be approaching you right now.'

The same, almost inaudible voice responded.

'Yes.'

At the same time a message flashed up on Lynne's screen.

Officers at scene.

Operating almost on automatic pilot, Lynne finished typing out the last details of the call. Alex James immediately called his Duty Force Gold Commander, who in turn alerted the Head of the local Murder Squad, DCI Masters, that they had a potential double killing on their hands.

Back at her desk, Lynne picked up her next call – or tried to, but for a few moments her fingers didn't seem to be obeying the signals sent out by her brain. She just stared at the emergency call that was coming in, not immediately answering. A couple of the nearby radio dispatchers looked over at her, puzzled.

But then Lynne shook her head, forcing her mind back to the task in hand and clearing the tears she hadn't even been aware had filled her eyes in the last few moments. She made herself concentrate on the next call, from a young man who'd phoned a few times in the last couple of weeks to tell her he was going to kill himself. So far he hadn't carried out his threat, but that didn't mean he wouldn't.

Lynne took the young man's details, checking on his location and dispatching another police car to him at the same time, but all the time her mind wrestled with her previous caller, the few chilling words the still unnamed woman had spoken to her reverberating inside Lynne's head.

As Ros walked into the neighbour's house, Jo was standing by the sink in the kitchen, an untouched coffee mug at her side.

Jo's neighbour, an older lady, was filling the kettle with water to make more drinks that wouldn't be touched.

The husband of the house was outside, talking to a few of their neighbours. More were joining them all the while, summoned by those same blue lights still flashing up and down the suburban street, and all watching as scene-of-crime tape was rolled out, cordoning Jo's house off from the rest.

No one could keep still either inside or outside that identikit house on that identikit street right now. Ros had seen it time and again at the scene of countless other atrocities. No one stopped moving or talking, everyone taking refuge in activity – any kind of activity, it didn't matter how aimless or pointless. As if by their constant movement they might somehow still avert the evil that had so obviously visited their quiet backwater that evening. As if it would then pass over their heads and move on.

At the same time the same questions, to which there were at present no answers, were being asked over and over again, as well as the same answering refrain taken up by each new arrival in turn. Because something like this – whatever *this* was, because no one was really sure yet – simply did not happen; not here, not amongst this community, not on this street. At the same time too, they all stared at the scene-of-crime tape being unfurled by the uniformed officers in front of them in flat contradiction of everything they were saying, cocooning the house across the recently tarmacked road from the rest, the air around it growing more and more rancid with exhaust fumes from the idling ambulances and police cars nearby – and from something else Ros had smelt on more occasions than she also cared to remember: the sharp acid of collective anxiety.

Inside the house Ros approached the young mother, who was still just standing by the sink. The young and now even more nervous Family Liaison Officer was at Ros's side, just in case Jo remembered her. Amy had introduced herself when she'd first arrived but Ros could already see it in Jo's eyes. Sometimes a Family Liaison Officer becomes the one constant in a seemingly never-ending sea of darkness, someone to cling onto when everything and everyone else has been lost. That was never going to happen in this case and Masters knew that as well as Ros did, which was the main reason for his call. There were other reasons too – of that Ros was only too well aware, but now wasn't the time or place to go into them. Right now only one thing mattered, and that was the young woman standing in front of her.

'Jo, I'm Ros. I'm working with the local police.'

Ros didn't say any more. It wouldn't go in anyway. Ros could have given the young mother her name, rank and number along with her entire life history and none of it would have registered. Jo just looked back at Ros in turn and spoke one word in reply.

'Hi.'

That was it. And it wasn't just the simple, instinctive response, it was the tone: the same tone that had so freaked the young FLO standing next to Ros and wishing she wasn't.

Jo was calm. Eerily so. Amy had no idea what she'd be doing in similar circumstances, but one thing she was sure of was that she wouldn't be standing at a sink, coffee mug by her side, nodding at a stranger and speaking back to her that simple greeting.

But she probably would. Ros had seen that time and again as well. The more extraordinary the event, the more ordinary the response. Everything had now been deadened inside Jo as her brain had gone into survival mode, ensuring that none of the pictures she'd just seen across the road in the upstairs bedrooms of her home were before her eyes right now.

They'd return, of course, but now, had she been so bidden, Jo would probably have picked up that coffee and tipped it down the sink before rinsing the mug and drying it with one of the tea towels neatly stacked by her side on the nearby worktop.

Like the neighbours milling outside, their numbers still swelling all the while, Jo was doing one thing and one thing only right now, and that was going through the motions.

Ten minutes later, Ros and Conor were inside one of the first responder police pool cars with Masters, parked outside Jo's house. Officially, all lines of enquiry were open regarding the likely perpetrator of the double killing that had taken place inside. Unofficially, all eyes were on one man: the still-missing father.

'We've tried his mobile six times. It's going straight to his voicemail, meaning he's probably turned it off.'

Ros cut in.

'Call tracker?'

Masters nodded back. He'd already thought of that and acted on it. Call tracking was a means of tracing a phone whether it was switched on or not. It was standard practice when a life was at risk, and with two small boys lying dead in their beds and a father now missing, that was clearly the situation Masters and Murder Squad were facing, one way or the other.

The only question was whether the risk to Tom Edwards's life was from a person or persons unknown who'd entered his house that night, killed his two boys and abducted him.

Or from himself.

The expression on Masters's face once again said it all. No one else was involved here: Masters was sure of it. For reasons unknown to them as yet, Tom Edwards had murdered his two sons and then driven away, leaving his returning wife to discover their bodies.

If he was typical of the breed – that breed being men who kill their own children – he'd now be looking to take his own life.

Ros looked back at the house, still being sealed off by scene-of-crime officers.

If he wasn't dead already, of course.

Suddenly, with Ros and Masters now outside, and without any warning, Jo pushed herself away from the sink and headed for the front door as Amy, the hapless FLO, stared after her, caught unawares by the unexpected exit.

Jo moved through the open front door towards the ever-expanding knot of neighbours gathered outside on the thin strip of recently weeded pavement.

The crowd parted as she approached. No one spoke because no one knew what to say. Some even moved further away from her. No one yet knew exactly what had happened behind the closed front door of the house opposite, but the local rumour mill was already going into overdrive.

Jo paused, staring across the street at a house that up to a short time before had been a home, but which would never be again. Then Jo tore her eyes away from the upstairs windows in front of her and looked down at the ground.

Another of Jo's neighbours was a keen gardener. When they'd first moved in, he'd offered to help Tom stock and tend to their new flowerbeds. The neighbour loved having projects, as his indulgent wife always called them. Jo had always smiled to herself at the thought that they might be a project, but Tom had never seemed all that amused. He hadn't acted on the offer either.

When the police had first arrived, turning from Castleton Way onto their small and hitherto unremarkable side street, their helpful neighbour had been taking advantage of the long summer evening to trim and shape his front hedge with his trusty and much-loved pair of hedge shears. He'd been vaguely aware of Jo standing outside the door of her own house – waiting for someone, it seemed – but hadn't taken too much notice either of her or the police car that approached a few moments later. They often had cars passing through the estate on what most of the grateful residents assumed were precautionary patrols.

Then the car stopped outside Jo's house, which was strange. Usually they just drove straight on. One of the officers went inside while the other stayed by the front door with Jo, which was even stranger. Moments later, the officer who'd gone inside was back out again and his agitation was obvious.

The neighbour had placed his shears down, carefully, on the edge of one of his flowerbeds and then went inside to alert his wife that something seemed to be happening across the road. In all the excitement since, he'd forgotten about them. Now, in the company of his neighbours, he watched as Jo leant down and picked them up.

Jo looked across at a parked police car and at the officers visible inside, including the woman who'd just spoken to her back in her neighbour's kitchen and an older officer too, the man who seemed to be in charge. Then, and without any sort of warning once again, Jo crossed to the parked car and began smashing the hedge shears down onto its roof.

The officers were out of the car in seconds but Jo didn't even see them. She just kept smashing the shears, which weren't going to trim many hedges from that point, down onto the vehicle.

Ros was the first to react, nodding at Conor before moving towards Jo.

'Get a blanket.'

Conor nodded back, heading towards Ros's car as Ros herself approached Jo. Ros reached out her hand, snatching it back as Jo turned and waved the hedge shears in her face, Jo's own face now an unrecognisable snarl. But as the shears connected with air where Jo had expected Ros's head or upper arm, she was momentarily unbalanced and Ros snaked out her hands again, gripping Jo's wrists as she did so. Then Ros stood, no more than half a metre away, not speaking, just staring deep into Jo's eyes, not letting go of her hands for an instant.

Jo's eyes fixed on those of her unexpected captor. Slowly, her breathing slowed. Still staring at Ros, the rage in those eyeballs began to fade. Then Ros and Jo stood facing each other, silent for a few moments longer as Conor approached, blanket in hand.

Ros placed it, gently, around Jo's shoulders. Then she steered her, with the shears still in her hand, back towards Ros's own car, parked as haphazardly as ever further down the street.

Masters had never exactly been the sensitive type. Over the years, indeed, his information-gathering techniques had bordered on the positively barbaric. One particularly useful lead in an especially tricky case had been acquired after two lowlife drug dealers had been bound together back to back, thick rope securing their hands and feet, before being doused with paraffin.

Then Masters had wafted a portable flamethrower in front of their terrified eyes, threatening to turn them at any moment into human torches unless they told him precisely and immediately what he wanted to know.

It was far from an empty threat. When one of the drug dealers had debated just that little bit too long whether he could actually offer up the quarry Masters was seeking, he'd first heard a click as the flamethrower was ignited and then smelt flesh beginning to burn. It took a second or so for him to realise it was his own body that was sizzling. By that time his companion was blurting out the whereabouts of the quarry in question, but it was still too late for him to avoid needing skin grafts.

On another notorious occasion a bent copper on Masters's own force called Donovan Banks had been shown the folly of his ways by being hauled onto the guard rail of a balcony above a ten-storey drop onto a concrete path below. For a moment the copper, soon to become bent in more ways than one, simply refused to believe what was about to happen. He'd witnessed the attack on the drug dealers at first hand but they'd been criminals, lowlifes from the other side of the tracks. Yes, he might have erred in the line of duty but he was still a fellow police officer holding the thin blue line. Two seconds or so later Banks had all his fond illusions literally smashed as his still-disbelieving head hit the concrete path below, closely followed by the rest of his soon-to-be-broken body.

But on another occasion Masters had displayed a different side to his character, which had been all the more astonishing given all Ros had witnessed from him in both a personal and professional capacity up to then.

It had been sparked by yet another atrocity, but this one hadn't been instigated by Masters. This was the work of a Ukrainian psychopath known only by his surname, Yaroslav, whose path had crossed that of Ros and Masters with quite devastating consequences for another member of Masters's Murder Squad – an innocent officer and his equally innocent, pregnant wife. Both had been murdered, as had their unborn child. When Ros and Masters discovered the officer's body, his arms had been wrapped around the bloodied foetus, which had been forcibly extracted from the mother's body while she was still alive. In darker moments – and there'd been plenty of those, both before and since – Ros could still see the mother's eviscerated stomach sliced open from pelvis to chest.

In the hours that followed, Masters and Ros had drifted through a succession of late-night bars. They'd barely spoken, hadn't even referred once to the grotesque evil they'd just uncovered. There was no need for words that night, and there were none anyway that would have seemed even remotely appropriate. Ros and Masters just traversed some subterranean landscape instead, beneath all normal communication.

At some point that same night they'd ended up in Ros's anonymous new-build apartment by the side of an old, restored waterway, a mile or so from the city centre. They'd spent the night together there, although nothing actually happened between them. Nothing had since, and probably never would. Masters had just talked about a son and a wife from whom he was estranged. Up to that point, neither Ros nor indeed anyone else on Masters's own squad had known anything about his life outside the force.

Ros had listened but hadn't reciprocated with any personal insights of her own. She never did.

A lid had been lifted on Masters that night. It was of course slammed shut the very next morning, but albeit briefly, a very different kind of man had been on view. And Ros was now seeing that different man again as Masters leant close to Jo, who was standing by the door of Ros's small car, her neighbour's hedge shears still in her hand.

'We can only go in that house once. The one time that really counts, anyway. Because that's when we see the most. Every time we go in there after that, we don't see those rooms like we saw them that first time – we see what we saw the last time we were there and the time before that.'

Jo just stared back at him, blank. Was any of this going in, Ros wondered? She doubted it, and she could see Masters doubted it too. That didn't stop him trying though, and for that – in time – Jo would be grateful. She might look right now as if all Masters's words were simply washing over her, and in a sense they were, but in another more atavistic sense every syllable was being stored somewhere so deep inside it would feel as if the words had never been said. Until something resembling strength returned, and then maybe Jo would be able to access what she was now hearing. And, maybe, take comfort from it too.

'And that's not just my officers; that's forensics, scene-of-crime, the pathologist, every single person who's about to walk into that house, into those rooms. They all have to do the same: they have to look at everything you saw with nothing in the way.'

Jo's eyes were still blank. The scream that had filled her universe a short time before was still blotting everything else out, making all Masters was saying to her right now even more important. No one, as Ros knew only too well, should ever hang on to a scream.

'Every one of those people is either here or will be in the next few minutes. Right now we're just waiting for the last one to arrive, the pathologist, and the reason we're waiting for her is because she's the best, the very best, the one who's going to be able to look at your two boys and tell us exactly what happened to them and how, and once she's done that we're going to be a hell of a lot closer to working out who did this and why.'

Which was when Jo finally spoke.

'I want to see them.'

Masters hesitated only a second or two before calmly nodding back at her.

'You will.'

Jo stared at him.

'I promise.'

Jo's eyes searched his. Masters held her stare all the while as further down the street another car pulled up, allowed through the police cordon by the uniformed officers. From inside stepped a slim man in his thirties, later to be identified as Jo's family GP. He looked confused and lost, making him yet another member of an overwhelming majority on that street right now.

Jo kept staring into Masters's eyes. Ros knew what he was saying to her with that silent stare and so did Jo. He was telling her the truth, but not the truth Jo wanted to hear. She would see her sons again before their bodies were laid to rest but it wouldn't be where she'd last seen them; sleeping but not sleeping, surrounded by all that was familiar but not, in a place they'd been loved but which in two extinguished heartbeats had come to resemble hell on earth. Jo's next and final sight of her two beloved boys would be in the morgue.

Jo kept staring at Masters for a moment longer, then she put the hedge shears down on the tarmac drive. Then she half-turned away from him and away from her house, looking instead at a street she'd lived on and people she'd lived amongst for the last two years.

One second later, Jo's legs gave way.

A few minutes later, Ros followed Conor, Masters and his newly arrived pathologist of choice, an Iraqi émigrée called Maha Najafi, up the stairs of the Edwards family house to the first-floor landing.

Ros and Conor were there at Ros's request. Jo's family GP had already administered a sedative to his patient and she would be comatose for the next few hours at least, giving Ros time to see what she'd seen, to experience in some small part what she'd endured. Depending how the investigation panned out, Ros could be spending days if not weeks with Jo from now on. If she was going to get through to her in any way at all, she knew she was going to have to walk at least some distance in her shoes.

Jo and her husband Tom's bedroom was at the front. A large picture window looked out over the obligatory well-tended patch of front lawn and the normally quiet street. The two upstairs rooms at the rear of the property, looking out over a larger and equally well-tended patch of back lawn, were the bedrooms formerly inhabited by the boys.

The first room Masters, Maha, Conor and Ros came to was the bedroom of the eldest, Steven; the first room Jo herself had visited before turning and checking on Callum next door. Like Jo, all three hesitated before heading inside, not a reflex response this time but to allow a scene-of-crime officer to take photographs from the door. A volley of shots of both the room and the small body in the bed sounded as the four of them continued to hover for a few moments. Then they moved in.

The first thing Ros noticed was the strong similarity between Steven and Jo. They both had the same colour hair, the same cut of the jawline. Steven's face was clearly exposed in the light filtering in through the partly open curtains. So was that how he normally slept, Ros wondered: with the curtains slightly parted, or had his killer opened those curtains to give the mother a better view of her dead child?

Maha moved to the bed, conducting her preliminary investigations all the while. Later, a much more exhaustive forensic procedure would take place. Now it was all about those all-important first impressions, as well as the seemingly redundant but essential formality of certifying that each of the boys was actually dead so their bodies could be removed.

Ros looked round some more. Steven's room bore testimony to a life already in transition. Toys were still in evidence: some stacked on shelves, some tucked away in half-open drawers. But so were posters of footballers, all from the same team: not Cardiff, Steven's local team, but a more successful team – at least in recent years – some forty miles to the west in Swansea. And there were other posters too, one featuring a new boy band; fresh heroes Steven had clearly started to admire and emulate, but would admire and emulate no more.

Steven was still in the position Jo had found him in – that position now being captured from every angle by the scene-of-crime photographer as Maha continued her silent preliminary investigations. The young boy was still on his back, his head facing upward towards the ceiling, his arms under the duvet: a sick parody of peaceful sleep – although it had been enough, at first glance, anyway, to almost convince and reassure his mother.

Was that deliberate, Ros wondered? Had that also been carefully designed to afford Jo that initial sense that all was fine, followed by the crashing realisation that it really was not?

By Steven's bed was a beaker, half-filled with what looked like lemon squash. Maha nodded across at it and the photographer took shots of it, again from various angles, but no one picked it up. It was left, like everything else, exactly where the officers had found it.

Callum's room was next door and more chaotic than Steven's. Here, toys were out on every surface, some also littering the floor, although an attempt had been made to organise the chaos. Toy trucks were lined up alongside each other, model aeroplanes had been arranged on top of a chest of drawers. On the walls, scrawled paintings and drawings were tacked up.

The way Callum was positioned was a mirror image of his elder sibling. He didn't share Steven's close physical similarity to his mother. Maybe Callum favoured the father – Ros hadn't seen any photographs of Tom yet so didn't know. But like Steven, Callum was also lying on his back, his face pointing upward towards the ceiling in the same position that, at first glance, anyway, would have reassured Jo, staring in from the half-open door as the night light illuminated her younger son's face.

Maha nodded back at Masters as she bent over the smaller figure in the second bedroom. By his side was another glass, half-filled again what looked like lemon squash. Once again no one touched it, but the scene-of-crime photographer took the same volley of snaps from the usual different angles.

Maha finally spoke, although it was already all too clear to the others what had happened here. The two boys had been asphyxiated. Someone – and Ros at least was still keeping an open mind as to who – had placed something over the faces of both boys and had held it there until each of those boys had stopped breathing.

Masters, Maha, Conor and Ros moved back out onto the landing past a bathroom, its door partly open once again, and on into the parents' bedroom.

The room, like the rest of the house, was ultra-tidy, making the bed stand out even more. Much in the manner of hotels trying to emulate a more upmarket look, cushions were propped against the pillows. A thin folded throw in a contrasting colour to the white duvet was positioned two-thirds of the way down the bed, stretching from one side to the other. But on one side of the bed, one of the cushions was missing.

Ros, Masters, Conor and Maha looked at each other, the same thought now in all their minds.

Was that the murder weapon? A simple cushion? And if so, where was it? If it had been used to kill the two children in the bedrooms opposite, it would provide the most damning of evidence.

But another matter was now on Ros's mind too. Why didn't they wake up? These were two young and presumably healthy kids. Someone has just put a cushion over each of their faces: aren't they going to struggle or yell? And whoever did this couldn't have killed them both at the same time, so what did the other do: just lie there, waiting his turn while his brother was being killed?

Ros paused, those two beakers half-filled with what looked like lemon squash by the side of the beds now before her eyes.

Across the room, Masters wasn't looking at those two half-filled beakers. Masters was looking at Ros.

He'd never really understood why witnesses – or clients, as her department habitually called them – always responded to Ros in the undeniable way they did. Still in her twenties, no significant other, she wasn't a woman blessed with what might be called soft edges. A buttoned-up anal retentive was how Masters had described her in the past, sometimes to her face. On those occasions, Ros had done what she'd always done when faced with Masters in full flow: just eyed him coolly, not rising for a moment to the bait.

There was a mystery at the heart of Ros that Masters had never been able to penetrate and which – until recently, anyway – he had suspected he never would. Which offended his professional pride. He spent his life solving mysteries. Why he should have been unable to fully comprehend this one, he didn't know. It was a loose end and Masters didn't like loose ends.

In more private moments, Masters occasionally dwelt on the unwilling acknowledgement that perhaps part of this was personal too. For reasons he didn't fully understand, Masters had always wanted to get to know more about the enigmatic Ros.

But Ros would get to know Jo. Starting the moment those sedatives she'd just been administered loosened their grip, Ros would make a connection that no one else in his department or in any other police department would or could make, and Jo would open up to Ros in ways she'd never have done with even supposedly specially trained officers, such as the hapless Amy.

Maybe Ros just had the knack. Or maybe it was something else. That something else Masters had never been able to properly fathom. That mystery he'd never been able to totally solve.

But there was another reason he'd summoned Ros to this house that evening. Yes, with her two children dead and her husband missing, Jo was very definitely at risk and a person in need of protection right now. But there was more to his decision to involve Ros than that.

Masters knew that the next couple of days were going to be critical. If Jo was going to say anything or do something that was going to make some sort of sense out of all this – even if anything she might say or do right now would probably make no sense to her at all – it would be in that next 24 to 48 hours. And if anyone was going to elicit that sort of response from the shell of a young woman they'd all just had the misfortune to encounter, it was going to be the small, slight officer tasked with her protection.

Ten minutes later, Ros was outside Jo's house and back in her car. A search by scene-of-crime officers had found a cushion discarded in the sitting room downstairs. It had been photographed and recorded but left where it was, along with the two beakers of what looked like lemon squash found in the bedrooms upstairs. The bodies of the boys were now both encased in body bags – or Human Remains Pouches, to give them their official title – and were being brought out of the house to be placed in a waiting ambulance for transportation on to the morgue.

The press had been kept back courtesy of a hastily erected police cordon, but that hadn't stopped a news crew from a satellite TV station chartering a small helicopter, which was now hovering above the street, feeding images of the dead bodies being loaded into the rear of the waiting ambulance back to the studio that had dispatched it.

Ros looked out at the ambulance, the whole street now reverberating to the sound of the hovering helicopter. But Ros wasn't seeing the helicopter, the bodies in those HRPs or the tense neighbours staring at the confirmation of their worst collective fears and the obvious evidence that evil had indeed stalked their well-tended slice of suburban heaven that night.

Ros was seeing another body, female this time: another victim, another life cut short.

Another scene of almost medieval barbarity.

Ros kept watching as the ambulance doors were closed and the emergency vehicle began to move towards the police cordon, which was now being lifted by uniformed officers to allow its passage. The helicopter, still hovering overhead, followed.

The ambulance passed the neighbours, their silent stares framing the same silent question that had been in Ros's mind ever since she'd arrived on that neat suburban street. The same question that had been in her mind as a small child, witnessing that equally brutal murder all those years before.

Why?

4

Twenty minutes after leaving Masters, Conor and Maha, Ros parked her car in a small car park round the corner from a normal-looking High Street.

Opposite, an all-night petrol station had just opened a catering concession and was doing a roaring trade in cut-price burgers and hotdogs. Already at least two of the local fast-food outlets had given up the unequal battle and closed their doors. The traditional wisdom was that no business could afford to sell food at the prices the petrol station was charging, and they were probably right. It all depended, as the perhaps understandably bitter owners of those former fast-food outlets had pointed out, on your definition of food.

Ros looked out of the side window at another motorist parked a few metres along the road, his mouth smeared with ketchup and grease, wondering if and when Jo would next enjoy any kind of food, dubious or otherwise.

Already the portents were clear. Ros had seen that many times before too. Despite the best efforts of all sorts of agencies, including her own, Jo's will would soon become fixed on one point, and one only. Enduring an existence that was no more than a living death, consciously or unconsciously Jo would soon be mentally ticking down the days until she joined her murdered children and her present trials were over.

The still-sedated Jo had been transferred to one of the local safe houses, this one larger than normal as all the smaller flats and nondescript bungalows were currently occupied. It had been a more than usually busy time lately, as a recent memo sent around the various Protection Units in the country had confirmed. Admissions were now running at more than three thousand annually and Ros's own unit in the Welsh capital was definitely contributing more than its fair share to that seemingly ever-expanding total. So Jo now had the sole run of a large four-bedroomed detached property on the outskirts of an estate on the other side of Cardiff; not far in terms of distance from her old home, but a world away from her more usual surroundings in terms of well-tended hedges and neatly trimmed lawns.

The interior was a million miles removed from her former home too. If Jo had the eyes to take it in, she'd see a well-used sofa in the sitting room covered in the kind of flowery fabric that had gone out of fashion a good couple of decades before. In the kitchen she'd see wooden chairs and a table pockmarked with white rings, where hundreds of hot drinks had rested. In the fridge she'd find a bottle of long-life milk and little else – although some sort of food would have been ordered in, perhaps from the same sort of outlet in the same type of all-night petrol station Ros could still see across the road.

This locale was also host to more of a floating population than Jo would have been used to; a place people passed through rather than somewhere where they stocked flowerbeds and mowed lawns. Tomorrow, after the unit doctor – who was also staying in the house right now – had given her another shot of the same sedative, they might consider another move, but for now this would be Jo's new home.

A few metres away, the now-sated motorist wiped his ketchup and grease-smeared mouth with his sleeve, opened his window and dropped an empty carton onto the pavement, watched all the while by a couple of hungry gulls. As he started his engine, the bolder of the gulls swooped down onto the discarded wrapping, the other setting up a discordant screech of protest.

Ros opened her driver's door and moved the other way along the street towards a one-storey building, picking her way through more discarded food wrappers already picked clean by other circling gulls.

As always, nothing outside the anonymous-looking building gave any indication as to what went on inside. It wasn't the sort of place that advertised what might be called its 'wares', but it had never needed to. Word of mouth had always been enough.

Ros pressed the buzzer, waited for the more or less cursory security check to take place via the wall-mounted camera, then moved inside, past the security desk and under the first of the monitors playing constant adult DVD fare. Stripping off her clothes, she shrugged herself into the white robe hanging up in one of the lockers in the changing room, which was communal, for obvious reasons. Given the nature of the club and all that happened there, there was little point in segregating the sexes.

A couple of other people, one male and in his thirties, one female and approaching her late sixties, were also changing but Ros didn't take any notice of them and they didn't of her. Closing her locker, she put the key into the pocket of her robe and moved through a small bar where a florid barman was munching – as he always was, or so it seemed – on a large slice of pizza.

Ros moved on through the bar, which was hosting just the one couple so far, but the evening was still relatively young for the club's habitual clientele. Then she turned into an adjoining corridor which led down to the showers, slipped off her robe and slid into the warm waters of an oversized Jacuzzi.

As she did so, Ros looked up at a glitterball just a few metres away. On party nights – nights to be resolutely avoided – it would spin ceaselessly, reflecting myriad coloured shafts of light off a small army of sweating bodies, but tonight it was still. But it didn't matter. Still or stationary, it always entranced her. They had done, for reasons she still didn't fully understand, ever since she was a small child.

Ros had always thought they were a relatively modern invention, but recently she'd discovered they'd already become a mainstay in nightclubs in America by the 1920s. A 1927 silent film from Germany, *Berlin: Symphony of a Metropolis*, featured another early example in its impressionistic early-twentieth-century tribute to the life of its titular city, and Ros had even found a reference to one in the description of a ballroom dance in Boston at the end of the nineteenth century.

Almost a hundred years later, Madonna would use a two-ton example embellished with two million dollars' worth of Swarovski crystals for her *Confessions* tour, but for Ros the original was still the best. That single spinning mirrored ball, catching a million different faces – or so it seemed – with each and every turn; each face distinct, but somehow merging with the others, a fluid wave of humanity. And even when no one else was in the club, when the glitterball was still as it was now – no music playing, just the odd stray sound percolating in from the street outside – she'd still stare up at it, transfixed.

Then the waters around her started to ripple as first one new body entered the Jacuzzi and then another. Ros came back to the moment to see two new arrivals, a couple in their early forties, settling on a small seat directly opposite, their robes hanging on hooks next to Ros's own.

Ros had seen them before. She'd received the same silent invitation before as well, always from the woman. The man, so far as she could see, never initiated any approach – he left that to his companion. But Ros closed her eyes and stretched out some more, a clear – if unspoken – signal that the invitation was on this occasion declined; a signal that was instantly respected.

Club rules were simple. Everything was always a matter of individual choice. Attendance inside the club didn't constitute any kind of contract. No one joined in with anything if they chose not to do so. There were even cubicles along the corridor specifically for those of a more reserved persuasion. They had doors attached to the outside constructed in two sections, an upper and a lower. If either part of those double doors was closed, then the inhabitants of that cubicle at that time wanted and were guaranteed absolute privacy.

Across the Jacuzzi, Ros heard a small gasp. The woman had now turned to her partner instead and had straddled him. With her back arched away from Ros, he'd entered her, a gentle bucking motion causing the waters to ripple now around the giant tub. Ros barely registered the rippling waters, the evening's horror and all it had brought back now before her eyes instead.

Aged five, Ros's world had literally exploded in front of her.

At the time she was living a totally normal – even nondescript – life, in a totally normal family in a definitely nondescript small town. She was the youngest of three girls with a mother who looked after them full-time. Her father ran his own small transport company from a local lorry yard. But in a single instant everything changed when her sister was gunned down inches from Ros's frozen stare.

Without even beginning to realise his true vocation at the time, Ros's middle sister, Di, had just married an undercover cop following a whirlwind romance. It was a genuine love match and the cop wanted out of his former life. That decision set in train a chain of events that led to the discovery of his real identity by his criminal colleagues. The killing of his wife on the day he was to be introduced to her family was intended to be the start of a wholesale reprisal for his treachery that would eventually claim every member of his new family.

The undercover cop was known to the family at the time only by his Christian name, Emmanuel; a name Ros later learnt meant 'God is with us'. But wherever God might have been, he was definitely not with Ros's family that day and didn't prove to be with Emmanuel Ocon either. It took time, almost twenty years in fact, but his hunters finally tracked down Emmanuel and killed him too.

The original killing of Ros's sister actually turned out to be a case of mistaken identity. The gunman in question had been pursuing the middle sister but because of the strong family resemblance, killed the eldest one instead. Not that it made much difference. It still condemned Ros and what remained of her forever-fractured family to life inside the protection programme.

For years Ros and her family remained hidden, buried inside a web of fake identities and everyday lies. Then, when Ros was in her late teens and still living inside that programme, she'd made the decision, a decision she still didn't totally understand, to become a protection officer herself. But maybe the fact she didn't understand it was the whole point. Maybe by making that decision, she was taking the first step in trying to do so. And maybe by journeying through similar experiences played out in the lives of others, she might one day come to understand her own. The only problem being, that day still hadn't dawned and Ros was already beginning to wonder if it ever would.

The complication, of course, was that Ros was still living inside the programme she now helped to run. She would continue to do so until either she died or the threat against her was judged to be over. But given the nature of the people who'd first pursued her unknowing sister all those years before, that threat was still very much alive.

Ros opened eyes she didn't even know she'd closed to see thin red wisps of liquid snaking their way across the water, momentarily clinging to her skin. The woman's back was bleeding now, from a scratch inflicted by her lover's fingernails.

Ros closed her eyes again as more past horrors washed in front of them.

A few months before, Ros had been in a new restaurant down in the Bay, a distant view of the Senedd across the water, a mini-iPad in place of a menu in front of her. It was a neat marketing gimmick that had made the place briefly fashionable. Diners made their selection via their portable devices and their food was then delivered courtesy of an automated trolley. The restaurateurs claimed it was an attempt to introduce a note of informality into the evening, to allow diners chance to get to know each other, undisturbed even by waiters. It also of course saved on wages.

Some diners found it quirky and fun. Others found it soulless and dehumanising. Ros had mentally declared herself in the former category the only night she'd been there, but maybe that was due more to the fact that within ten minutes of sitting down she'd found her hand taken by her male companion for that evening, an officer she'd been working with from Masters's Murder Squad, called Hendrix.

For the next few moments, Ros's hand had remained in his hand, which was something of a novelty for her. Human contact of that kind was an unfamiliar experience – something that would have sounded very odd to anyone who could have seen her right now, lying naked in the outsize Jacuzzi of a sex club.

But the contact she was experiencing in that restaurant that night was tender, chaste, almost coy in a sense, while the encounters that took place inside this single-storey building were anything but. Contact in here was industrial, between damaged souls seeking something, even if none of them could probably identify exactly what. Then again, Ros had never asked any questions of those different men or women of different races, creeds and colours, and they had asked none of her. It wasn't that kind of place and neither they nor Ros, at least up to that night in that strange and now-closed restaurant, were that kind of people.

But then the restaurant door had opened behind them. Conor had appeared and then, tentative and hesitant, had approached. He was clearly reluctant to intrude but he had his instructions. Ros had issued those instructions herself. So he tried to keep his eyes averted from the hand still enveloping that of his senior officer and spoke just four words.

'That Category A again.'

It was a simple sentence but it was one that would see Ros out of that restaurant and into her small car less than thirty seconds later. A simple sentence that would a short time later condemn any possible relationship that might have developed that night to the same fate as all other relationships in her life so far.

The Category A in question was a man in his late sixties, and a client. He'd been picked up in connection with a serious crime he'd freely admitted committing, but a short time later the necessity for any investigation into that crime had been removed when he opened the front door of his small and anonymous house to find a gun pointing back at him. A moment or so later he was lying on the floor, blood pumping from a massive head wound, before his heart quickly gave up its unequal struggle to keep beating.

Ros had walked into the hallway of the Category A's house and looked down at his dead body. Then she'd looked up at the blood streaked all over the ceiling and walls, blood that on one of those walls spelt out some numbers. No one could know the exact sequence of events as no witnesses to the shooting ever came forward, but the scene-of-crime officers could only assume that the assassin had dipped the gun into the victim's blood and had then used that to scrawl a date high on the wall behind his body.

The day and the month was that day and that month, the day and month that the Category A had died. But the year was wrong. Instead of the current year, the following one was picked out, provoking the usual gallows humour among the investigating officers about the IQ of the modern hired assassin.

Ros hid her emotions as always. It helped that Masters wasn't attending this investigation – he was away on one of his rare holidays, for which Ros muttered grateful, if silent, thanks. She listened to the speculation as to what might have happened and why. She didn't even flinch as she looked down at the dead body on the floor and she certainly didn't tell any of the other officers milling around the narrow hallway that the victim and Category A in question was her own father.

Ros just kept looking at that date daubed on the wall in her father's blood, recognising for what it was.

A prediction.

The date the last remaining member of her family – herself – was destined to die too.

Ros had already felt the coldest of chills creep over her as she stepped into that house a few moments before.

Now that chill had turned arctic.

Ros left the club ten minutes later. Ten minutes after that, she pulled into a parking space outside her first-floor apartment.

The parking space was sandwiched between two flower beds and bordered by no automotive neighbour – unlike most of the spaces in the complex, which were of the more traditional variety, one next to the other. Months of chaos courtesy of Ros's habitually inaccurate parking had led the rest of the long-suffering residents to lobby the management company for a dedicated parking space for her, sited well away from the rest.

While she waited for her neighbours' ever more agitated requests to be considered, Ros had taken refresher driving courses and had even practised using computer simulations, but nothing had worked. Whenever and wherever Ros parked, her small car still seemed to slew itself across two spaces and even, on one notorious occasion which seemed to defy the laws of physics, across three. Which was when Ros had finally been granted her dubious exclusivity.

Ros got out of and locked her car. Across the yard was the glorified hut that housed the on-site concierge but that seemed empty at the moment, for which relief Ros also muttered silent thanks. He'd once spent a whole hour showing her his family tree on the grounds of a superficial similarity in their surnames, totally unaware that Ros's surname was only the latest in a long line of fictions her handlers had invented for her while she was growing up.

Keeping her eyes averted from the windows of the hut just in case the concierge suddenly returned, having found some new branch of their supposedly potentially-mutual family tree, Ros headed for a blue door at the end of the courtyard and held her pass key up to the electronic reader before heading inside and up the single flight of stairs.

Ros slotted her key into the lock of the door to her apartment and swung it open. Dumping her bag on the floor, she turned towards the small kitchen-diner that led out to a balcony looking down onto the water.

At the very far end of the hall a large man with a pockmarked face looked back at her.

For a moment blood pounded in Ros's ears. For that moment, the whole world seemed to stand still. Everything seemed to have shrunk down to two souls in one small space: herself and this intruder. Which was when the man with the pockmarked face moved to one side, and the more familiar face of that on-site concierge appeared behind him.

'The damp man.'

Ros kept staring at the apparition, not even hearing the concierge for a moment. As well as a pockmarked face, her visitor had the most extraordinary eyebrows: thick, black and bushy, meeting above his nose in a single sweep.

The concierge nodded at Ros again.

'You had a letter. About the moisture?'

Monobrow, at his side, nodded in turn. When he spoke, his voice was surprisingly high-pitched, his tone sage.

'Always a problem in modern builds. You've got insulation to comply with building regs, fair enough. But the downside is rubbish ventilation in terms of draughts.'

Monobrow nodded towards the kitchen.

'You've got fans and extractors, but I'm guessing they're probably only used when you're cooking?'

Then Monobrow nodded towards the rest of the rooms, all sited off the small hallway.

'And your windows all open, of course they do, but you're probably like everyone else who lives here – out for most of the day, maybe most of the evenings too – so the air's trapped inside for hours on end.'

Much in the manner of a prosecuting barrister unfolding a killer punch, Monobrow nodded back at Ros.

'Add to that the fact that new concrete and plaster sweats for at least couple of years, and that's it.'

Ros finally found her voice.

'That's what?'

She simply couldn't take her eyes off his eyebrows.

Or brow.

'Humidity.'

Monobrow looked round her small flat some more with the same practised eye.

'Have you noticed any mould spores lately? Inside a wardrobe, maybe, or on the inside of any of the kitchen cupboards? You wipe them down and they disappear, then the next day they're back again?'

Monobrow crossed to and opened a kitchen cupboard that Ros could never remember opening in all the years she'd been there. Sure enough, a telltale black covering coated the exposed wall at the rear.

The concierge stepped in.

'Shouldn't the damp course have stopped that, then?'

Monobrow's mouth twisted into an expression of scorn.

'Do you know in Holland, they don't even have damp courses? Even in brand new houses? They build their homes with their foundations in water and they don't get damp walls.'

Monobrow shook his head.

'Dutch architects fall about laughing when you talk about stuff like that. And in America they don't have them either – try walking the streets of New York: look anywhere you like, you won't see a single injection hole.'

Ros still couldn't take her eyes off his eyebrows as he rode more and more insistently on what was becoming only too clear was a habitual hobby horse.

'When a wall warms up after a cool night, air moves out. When it cools down, air moves back. Next thing you know the render's flaking away and then –'

'So you can sort it?'

The concierge stepped in again, curt. There were 80 apartments in Ros's block and he was already getting the feeling he was going to hear this a few times before the night was over.

Monobrow nodded.

'I'm going to need access to the apartment six or seven times over the next few weeks, but I'm assuming you won't have any problem with that?'

Monobrow turned and looked back at the watching Ros as Ros's mobile pulsed, a single name illuminated on the display.

Ros stared at the name on the display, then nodded back.

'No problem at all.'

Then, equally quickly, she moved out onto her balcony to take her call.

Masters, as ever, didn't waste any time in preliminaries.

'We've found Tom Edwards.'

Ros didn't waste any words either.

'Alive?'

Masters answered and Ros looked down onto the waterway below.

For the first time since they'd discovered the bodies of those two small boys, they'd had some good news.

5

MATTHEW BAXTER WAS a lucky man. Matthew, always abbreviated to Matt, ran three garages in different but always affluent parts of his home city. It was all a long way from his early days trying to knock out cheap Toyotas with dodgy warranties on that locally renowned thoroughfare for equally dubious motor dealers, City Road.

But even then Matt had been lucky. His easy charm secured him more than enough sales to satisfy his boss at the time, an overweight colossus of a man of Greek extraction – at least until the colossus in question fulfilled all his doctor's dire predictions by suffering a massive heart attack one day while attempting the simple manoeuvre of switching on the air conditioning in his office during that summer's only heatwave.

It wasn't much of a manoeuvre. The air conditioning switch, sited just behind an equally outsize TV, wasn't that difficult to reach. But it was clearly too much for a heart already overburdened by having to haul around the sort of excess weight that would have attracted penalties had it been airline baggage. A giant crash heard more than two streets away heralded the end of the useful life of the outsize TV as Matt's boss crashed down onto it. Half an hour later an attending paramedic confirmed the end of any sort of life for the outsize Greek as well.

Matt was a tower of strength to his former boss's widow in the dark days that followed. In truth he'd been something of a comfort to her in the days and weeks before that too, all of which was down to that easy charm. The same charm that had also persuaded many young mums in the area to take out loans at exorbitant rates of interest for cars that would spend more time back in the showroom's repair bay than out on the open road, though a lot of those young mums didn't seem to mind. It meant they'd spend time in the repair bay too, and a few other places besides – and always with Matt.

That easy charm again.

The outsize Greek turned out to be well insured and his new widow suddenly found herself in receipt of a substantial windfall. Matt became even more of a tower of strength to her. Within six months Matt had moved the business out from City Road to a purpose-built unit just off a roundabout leading out of Roath towards the motorway. The new unit was passed each day by yet more, rather richer, young mums on regular runs to and from the local school. Business boomed, as did Matt's extra-curricular activities. Three months later Matt and the Greek widow married in a small ceremony, in a secluded hotel renowned for its fine dining and distant views of a city that had become something of a playground for a lucky man called Matthew Baxter, who'd always insisted on the snappier abbreviation of Matt.

But there was a price to pay. His new wife, a woman called Eleanor who also preferred the snappier abbreviation of Ellie, was well aware of her new husband's weakness for the opposite sex. She herself was ample first-hand evidence of that, which had been fine when it came to keeping her company on the occasional lonely afternoon, and which had very definitely boosted the sales figures of her late husband's formerly struggling business. But none of that was going to continue now Matt and Ellie were man and wife, as she made abundantly clear the night before their wedding.

It was a deal Matt agreed to without the slightest hesitation. It was an agreement he broke without the slightest hesitation when faced with his first temptation, in the form of a smiling new waitress on the night of the wedding itself. But there was little risk involved, as Matt saw it. The waitress had been warned, on pain of losing her job, not to fraternise with the guests. Matt had been warned, on pain of losing a bride who held all the purse strings, not to misbehave. So both parties to the brief but passionate coupling that took place a few yards from the rear kitchen door while the rest of the wedding guests were being diverted by a local oompah band had their own reasons for keeping that coupling strictly to themselves. Matt, in short, began married life in exactly the same way he'd ended life as a single man, and so it continued. He just became a little more careful, that's all.

Business continued to boom, meaning he opened a second showroom, and then a third. It was all a long way from those early days selling motors most of which were so old, a grinning Matt would tell his punters, they had to be insured against fire, theft and Vikings.

Each new opening gave him access to another new clutch of young mums on school runs. Unlike his former employer, Matt remained whippet-slim, and no wonder. Unlike that former employer, Matt was exercising regularly and with considerable commitment. As he was doing on the night he inadvertently crossed paths with Tom Edwards.

Matt had found the picturesque beauty spot some months before. He'd taken a wrong turn while delivering a hot hatch to an even hotter young mum who lived in one of the upmarket villages leading out from Cardiff into the Vale. All of a sudden, Matt found himself on an open headland at the end of a single-track and little-used lane with a view of the Bristol Channel in the distance.

Turning back, Matt mentally filed the remote location away. He had a feeling it might prove useful at some point in the future – as indeed it had.

Many times, in fact.

Tonight's punter was a young physical education student who had wanted to know if not having power steering on her vehicle of choice would prove a problem. She didn't want to complete her daily commute to college with aching arms. Matt had suggested a test drive after her training finished for the evening along a winding lane and a little-used track he knew.

The student completed the various manoeuvres with ease. She completed some more manoeuvres a short time later, meaning she was probably destined to wake up the next morning with the aching limbs she'd feared, but that was going to be nothing to do with the test drive.

It was as Matt and his new conquest were relaxing after what had proved to be some pretty demanding exertions that he saw it. Another car parked at the far end of the headland, facing not towards the sea but back towards the winding lane. Matt had occasionally seen other vehicles there before so he didn't take much notice at first.

Until his young companion saw the hosepipe.

'The what?'

Matt looked at the puzzled girl, who was looking back across the headland, shielding her eyes against the now lowering sun.

'Can't you see it?'

But Matt still barely gave the car, which must have arrived while they'd been otherwise engaged, so much as a passing glance. All he was looking at was the digital clock on the dash, which was telling him he really should be getting back. It wasn't unusual for him to have to work late – he was in a service industry, after all, and frequently had to conduct test drives after hours. But there was late and there was taking the piss. Another half hour and he'd be straying dangerously from the former into the latter.

Casually, Matt took the car keys from his pocket, hoping his companion would take the hint and start getting dressed. She lived in Cathays, which was on the other side of the city. That was going to add another 20 minutes to the journey home, so he really could do with making a start.

'It's coming out of the exhaust.'

Which was when Matt stopped. Now she had his attention.

Matt looked across to the other car, registering for the first time that its engine was running. He could now see a dim shape hunched over the steering wheel. And he could also now see that the hosepipe, which was indeed attached to the exhaust, ran over the boot before feeding into the rear passenger window.

Matt's student was taking a degree in Physical Education and while her body was stunning and finely honed, her mind was obviously less so. She was still staring, puzzled, at the strange apparition a few metres away when the more quick-witted Matt was already halfway across the clearing towards the car.

Matt yanked at the driver's door but it didn't give an inch. The slumped driver inside, who was male and around Matt's own age, had either deadlocked the door or it was fitted with the sort of automatic device that secured the doors once the driver started the engine. There'd been a spate of carjackings at traffic lights in the last few years and more and more manufacturers were fitting them. They'd thwarted many a would-be opportunist thief in the past, and in some extreme cases had proved a literal life saver. Right now they were proving the opposite.

Matt couldn't see if the driver was breathing, meaning it may be already too late, but he picked up a large rock anyway. Yelling back at the still-staring student to call an ambulance, he smashed the rock into the rear passenger window just below the narrow aperture created by the pipe. The window refused to buckle under the first blow, but succumbed on the second and safety glass showered the rear seat. Matt reached his hand inside and flipped the lock on the driver's door, wrenched it open, then dragged the driver out.

The driver, who was still breathing but already lapsing into unconsciousness, began mumbling, but Matt wasn't really taking in what he was saying. For now, all he was interested in was getting some much-needed air into the man's lungs. He laid the driver out on the grass, making sure his airways were clear, desperately trying to remember a few stray tips from a first-aid course he'd once attended.

A few metres away across the open headland the student was now on the phone to the emergency services, but she was panicking, unable to tell them where she actually was – though this didn't matter too much as the emergency response handler was already triangulating her position from the signal being received from her mobile via nearby transmission masts. But the student was able to give the registration number of the vehicle she was in and that of the other vehicle on that open headland, which even she could now see seemed to be the scene of some sort of suicide bid.

The emergency handler duly passed on all the details, including the registration numbers of the vehicles involved.

The registration of the car the student was test driving didn't ring any sort of bells, but the other car's did.

And a few miles away across the city, Masters looked at his mobile as the automatic alert came through.

Ten minutes later paramedics were loading the driver into the back of an ambulance, now on an oxygen feed. Masters was with Matt and the student, as was Ros, who had parked her small car next to Masters's more exotic chariot of choice, a Bentley Continental GT Speed – the second the Head of the local Murder Squad had owned, his first having been destroyed in a close encounter with a local harbour wall some months previously.

Usually Matt would have spent some time in rapt appreciation of the rather beautiful machine before him. Under normal circumstances, he'd have discussed with the owner some fine point of detail regarding its performance or design, mentally filing away that owner's name and hopefully his contact details, as a potential punter. Tonight Matt did none of those things, and that wasn't simply down to his understandable shock at having just pulled a near-dead body from the inside of a fume-filled car. Through the rear window of the Bentley, Matt could see the Breitling clock in the middle of the car's piano-black dashboard.

Time was ticking on now, and fast. He'd already received a call from his concerned wife, wanting to know where he was – a call he'd diverted to his answerphone. He was going to have to come up with a swift and convincing-sounding story to explain what was obviously going to be a late arrival home, which wasn't going to be easy as the owner of that upmarket vehicle wasn't exactly giving him too much time to think right now.

'What did he say?'

It was the third time Matt had been asked exactly the same question. Three times Matt had supplied exactly the same answer. He didn't know. The driver was out of it. Yes, he was mumbling something, but that's all it was: just random, disconnected stuff; not even words, not really – none of it made any sense, anyway.

Which was when Ros stepped in.

'Not to you.'

'What?

Matt stared at the slim twenty-something woman. Masters and Ros had both shown him their warrant cards when they'd first approached and now, slowly, Matt started to take them in. The man was from Murder Squad, the much younger woman was from a Protection Unit. And, for the first time, Matt started to wonder what the hell a failed suicide bid had to do with Murder Squad or a Protection Unit?

Ros held his stare.

'It might have sounded like he was rambling, and he might have been, but we've got to make sure – so just tell us exactly what he said, even if it didn't make any sense to you.'

Matt paused, his mind now beginning to work overtime, becoming intrigued despite himself and very definitely despite the advancing lateness of the hour.

'So who is he?'

The eyes of the lean, rangy officer opposite just bored back into his.

'What's he done?'

Then Matt hesitated. Something in the way he was being stared at right now was telling him the male officer was starting to lose patience. Something was also telling him that was something he really wouldn't like to encourage, and so Matt began to dredge his memory.

'It was just words. I kept saying to him, "It's all right, it's all right, I've got you," and all he kept saying was, "free".'

'Free?'

Matt nodded.

'I thought he was telling me to get him free or something and I kept saying, "I am, look – I'm here, I'm getting you free, you're going to be OK."'

'And he didn't say anything else?'

Matt paused again. Slowly, mists were clearing. Slowly, the mayhem of the last half hour was beginning to order itself, coagulating into something approaching coherence as both Ros and Masters knew it would, one of the reasons the attending patrol officers had been told on pain of terminal danger to their careers not to let the chief witness to this particular suicide bid out of their sights until they'd both got there.

Both Ros and Masters knew there was a real possibility they may not get too much out of Tom Edwards himself now. He'd probably survive, thanks to Matt's swift intervention, but that didn't mean he hadn't already inflicted the sort of damage on himself that would render any subsequent interviews useless. Wannabe suicides who had been interrupted in that way in the past frequently suffered all sorts of side effects, from psychosis to paralysis. So while Tom Edwards would in all likelihood come round, what sort of state he'd be in when he did was now in the lap of the gods. Making the evidence of the only independent witness to what could become his last coherent words all the more important right now.

Matt remained silent for a few moments more, now not even seeing the Breitling clock on the dashboard of the Bentley.

'They.'

Suddenly and almost from nowhere, it came back: another word he'd taken as just more inconsequential rambling at the time, but now he was thinking about all this some more, the driver had said it at least twice.

Masters nodded, grimly encouraging. Now it wasn't just the one word that Matt had recalled, but a second as well.

'They're free.'

Matt shrugged again.

'I didn't know what he was talking about. I didn't think he did. I just kept telling him it was OK, but then he said it again.'

Matt nodded once more.

'"They're free."'

The eyes of the owner of the upmarket dream motor were still boring into him.

'But nothing else, I swear.'

Ros looked at Masters, who looked back at her.

Tom Edwards might well not have said anything else.

But it was enough.

Ros walked across to the edge of the headland and looked out over the sea.

Behind her, Masters was now mining the second of their new chief witnesses, Matt's hapless girlfriend, just in case she could add anything. She'd claimed not to have heard a thing, but then so had Matt at the start.

Ros kept staring out over the sea, not seeing the tide – which was now on the turn – or the seagulls circling above the rocks, or even a distant tanker on the horizon, heading out to sea. All Ros could see, and all she knew she would see for the foreseeable future, were two small bodies, each lying in the very centre of an immaculately made bed.

It was happening more and more often. Each week yet another instance scarred the local and national news. Two days previously a father in Glasgow had stabbed his wife and twin sons to death just hours before the boys would have celebrated their seventh birthday. According to local newspaper reports, the father had become increasingly depressed following a string of business failures. No one could know for certain if that had led him to the triple killing, and no one ever would. After murdering his family, he'd ended his own life courtesy of a fistful of prescription pills.

A month before that, a father in Leeds had strangled his wife and small daughter. He'd placed their dead bodies on the marital bed, then lain down next to them and set fire to the mattress. The forensic report still couldn't decide if he'd died due to smoke inhalation or from his extensive burns. The few neighbours who'd been interviewed had all expressed the hope that it was the latter and that his death had been as painful as possible. The family were described by those same neighbours, in one of the starkest examples of unconscious irony Ros could recall, as 'perfect'. To do something like that to them had to be the work of a monster. But what he was and why he did it, again, no one would ever know. Like the Scottish father a few weeks later, the one in Leeds had made sure of it.

There were different words for the phenomenon. 'Familicide' was one that had crept into use lately. But no matter the nomenclature, it all added up to pretty much the same thing. The violent death of an entire family at the hands of one its members, almost always the father.

Those fathers would almost always, again, be white and middle class. They would all have failed in some way, sometimes having lost a job or a business, or suffered the collapse – impending or otherwise – of a marriage. But sometimes that failure would be more long-standing, deriving from feelings of powerlessness as a child, perhaps. In those cases, that usually resulted in the fathers trying to exert strict control over their own households as they sought to create an idealised version of the family they themselves had never experienced.

There were different types too, according to the research Ros had seen. Some were termed 'livid' or 'coercive' killers, some were called 'civil' or even 'reputable' killers instead. The former were driven by rage and by their controlling abuse, more often than not prompting a wife to attempt to leave with their children, leading the father to reassert his power in a final paroxysm of violence. The latter were motivated by a perverse sense of altruism. The father, and usually again only the father, would be aware of some impending crisis that was about to devastate the family. Murdering them became the father's way of protecting them from the upcoming hardship and suicide his way of protecting himself from the inevitable shame.

Connected to that was another uncomfortable statistic. Ros was well aware of the unpalatable truth that a young child was much more likely to be murdered by a parent than a stranger. On average, a child in the UK is killed by one of their relatives every ten days. Statistically, and incredible as it had always seemed to Ros, it was actually more dangerous leaving a child with a spouse than a complete stranger out on the street.

Behind her, Ros was dimly aware of a car now approaching, but she didn't look round. She was still looking out over the sea, the image of those two small bodies remaining imprinted on her eyes.

The difference in this case, of course, was that the man who'd been pulled from that car on that headland and who was now being rushed into the nearest A & E wasn't a charred hulk in an incinerated room, lying next to a family who may or may not have been perfect but who definitely didn't deserve the fate he'd visited on them. He also wasn't a man whose life had been poisoned out of him by the sudden ingestion of prescription painkillers. Tom Edwards had certainly attempted to tread that well-worn path but he hadn't succeeded, thanks to the chance intervention of the couple whose ragged recollections were still being harvested by the insistent Masters just a few metres away.

Tom Edwards had survived. He hadn't intended to do so, but now he'd broken a crucial mould. In every other case Ros had ever read about, all the police had to rely on by way of an explanation was hearsay and the often dubious testimony of bewildered friends, colleagues and neighbours.

But in the case of Tom Edwards all that might be just about to change.

A few metres away, Matt was taking rather more notice of that approaching car. There was a distinctive burble to the exhaust that struck a note of immediate panic deep inside him. And, as it grew louder and as he saw uniformed police officers begin to move down the track to intercept it, panic began to spiral towards barely concealed hysteria as he saw a woman in her mid thirties with a shock of blonde hair exit the now halted vehicle.

Distantly and in a tone he recognised only too well, he heard her yell at the officers, telling them that she knew her husband was here because she'd put a tracker on the slimy little shit's phone, now would someone kindly tell her what the fuck was going on!

Which was when she looked beyond the harassed officers attempting to protect a crime scene, saw Matt himself, and immediately behind Matt saw the young, pretty and suddenly very nervous-looking student.

From the look on Ellie's face, Matt could see she'd already worked out exactly what might have been going on.

Masters nodded at the officers protecting the scene, a silent signal dispatched and understood. One of them lifted the tape and Ellie ducked underneath. Briefly, she looked down at the ground as she approached and it might have been Matt's guilty conscience, but it looked to him as if she was already searching for some kind of weapon.

'I can explain.'

This opening gambit sounded pathetic even to his ears.

Ellie didn't even dignify that with a reply, just looked across at the student, who was now looking even more nervous.

Matt tried again.

'It's not how it looks.'

Which, even to his ears again, almost rivalled his first statement in the ultra-feeble stakes.

'We were on a test drive – we were mixing it up, country roads and the bypass – then we turned in here, which is when we saw that motor.'

Matt didn't get any further. Whether Ellie was actually looking for a weapon or not suddenly became a moot point because she didn't need one anyway. Her right hand balled into a sudden fist before snaking out and catching Matt clean on the bridge of his nose. Matt catapulted back into the student and both ended up on the grass in a position neither had yet assumed that evening, and they'd assumed a few. Not much of the young student was now visible beneath the larger bulk of

Matt, but there was enough for Ellie, who proceeded to stamp on her and her new husband as she yelled at the pair of them at the top of her voice.

Masters moved back towards the police tape, leaving the parties to the domestic unfolding behind him to sort matters out as they wished. Or not. Masters didn't really care too much either way. He was pretty confident he'd extracted from the hapless Matt and the student all they knew regarding their rescue of Tom Edwards, so that concluded all official business on that headland that evening.

As for the more unofficial business, Masters had a pretty shrewd idea what the slimy snake-oil salesman and the slinky student had been doing out there that night. Masters was a naturally gifted investigator, but you didn't really need to be christened Sherlock to work that out. A deserted clearing, an older man, a nubile young woman – it all led to one obvious conclusion.

Masters opened the door of his Bentley, the keyless entry system sanctioning his entrance, and looked out over the same stretch of water that was still claiming Ros's attention at the far end of the headland.

It had always been an irony, and one not lost on the Head of the local Murder Squad, that despite his own proven talents in the investigative stakes, Masters had missed every sign when his own wife began to cheat on him. At work there was little anyone could put past him. In his private life he'd proved something of a babe in arms. And despite a fabled volcanic temper, when Masters finally found out about her affair, he didn't actually do very much about it aside from saying goodbye to an uncomprehending small son and moving out of the family home. His wife remarried after the subsequent divorce. The last Masters had heard, she was a leading light on a social scene frequented by dentists in Bath, her new partner being something of a locally renowned orthodontist.

Masters hadn't thought about his ex-wife in years. He occasionally thought about his son, or more accurately felt a heaviness settle on his stomach at key times like Christmas or his birthday, and knew he was thinking about him. But that aside, the breakdown of his marriage hadn't left him with too many regrets.

But it had left him with a positive hatred for and distrust of cheats. And whenever he picked up gossip on the office grapevine about this officer straying from the marital fold or that officer playing away from home, the officers in question were always removed from his team.

So when Masters had seen the vengeful-looking blonde approach the police cordon a few moments before, he'd had little hesitation in giving a signal to the uniformed officers to let her through. And he hadn't even thought about intervening in the ensuing physical exchange – an exchange that seemed destined to continue for some time to come, if the angry shouts and yells still sounding behind him were anything to go by.

It was all quite comforting in a sense. No matter what evidence there might occasionally be to the contrary, it seemed that somewhere there was still some force for good at work; that a universe still existed somewhere in which lowlifes received their just desserts.

For most of the time, Masters's world was painted the very darkest shade of black.

For one brief moment, light had been restored.

6

T HE BRIEFING WAS scheduled for the next morning.

It should have been held in Murder Squad's new offices, built on reclaimed wasteland fringing the old Cardiff Docks. They'd only moved there relatively recently, decamping from their old offices in a large Victorian house sited in a leafy suburb of the city some three or so miles away. The house had sported two palm trees outside, a clear act of faith on the part of some long-deceased romantic from decades before – but a faith that had proved justified as the years ticked by. The palm trees in question were now over six metres tall and still growing.

The suburb hadn't only been home to Masters and the city's elite Murder Squad, but also to a vibrant mix of students, young professionals and media workers, attracting an eclectic array of cafés and coffee shops to spring up in turn. A local arts centre established in another act of faith some few decades before had also benefited from the influx and was now similarly vibrant.

But then a number cruncher in some accounts department somewhere had done some calculations and come to the conclusion that it made a lot more sense to concentrate most local police departments in just the one location. To back up his recommendations, the number cruncher in question had produced a flow chart detailing all the benefits that would ensue, along with a breakdown of the reduced rates and rent that could be offered by the local Council if those various police departments agreed to the move, meaning there wouldn't only be improvements in efficiency but actual cost savings too.

The number cruncher was happy. The local Council were happy. The local office supply companies were more than happy at all those orders for new desks and chairs. The only people not happy were the police, who now had to leave their vibrant suburb with its cafés, restaurants and coffee shops, not to mention the now buzzing and vibrant local arts centre, and decamp miles out of the city centre to a former dock which still looked to them like a present-day wasteland.

Masters had endured the move for as long as his patience permitted, which in his case wasn't long at all. Within a matter of weeks, briefings were being held back in that eclectic and vibrant suburb in a multiplying succession of rented spaces, making a mockery of the savings clawed back by the original move.

That very morning the increasingly harassed number cruncher in question was making a visit to Masters's offices on the former dockside to demonstrate a newly designed meeting space constructed inside something called a Pod. It was the number cruncher's view that once the troublesome Masters saw this new space laid out before him, no more charges for additional rented spaces in vibrant suburbs would be assaulting his increasingly belaboured budget.

The Pod had been erected the previous evening. The meeting was fixed for nine in the morning. At a quarter to nine that morning, driving the two miles from his city-centre office with a view of the railway station, dwarfed by new office developments on one side and a distant mountain range on the other, the number cruncher smelt it before he saw it. Something borne on the wind blowing in from the water. An uneasy harbinger of trouble. A few seconds later he saw an unmistakable pall of smoke hanging over the whole of the Bay.

For a moment he wondered whether it was a film shoot. A prime-time TV soap had recently decamped to a new studio that had opened up in another of the purpose-built units on the site, and had been known to stage various high-octane stunts involving exploding cars and lots of fake blood. Then he pulled up outside the new police offices and saw the fire engines – and they weren't props from a film set, they were real.

A grinning fireman approached and wanted to know if someone had been destroying evidence again. But the number cruncher wasn't listening. All he was looking at was the clear seat of the fire, a space at the rear of the building into which other firemen were currently pumping a large quantity of damping foam, extinguishing what had clearly been an intense blaze. A blaze which had turned something that had formerly been called a Pod into a charred and sodden wreck.

Then he saw Masters.

Everyone else outside that evacuated building was either looking at the last of the flames still flickering behind the smashed windows or at the smoke floating ever higher across the Bay.

But Masters was standing by what looked to be a brand-new Bentley and was staring, unblinking, at the number cruncher.

And Masters held his stare until the number cruncher – as both he and Masters knew he would – blinked first.

One hour later, and with the newly constructed and newly incinerated Pod out of commission for the next month at least, Masters was holding his latest briefing three miles away in the back room of a small café called the Fat Pig. A few metres along the opposite side of the street could be seen a large Victorian house which sported two palm trees outside.

As Ros closed the door behind her, she looked back into the front room of the small café. Stick-thin media-types occupied most of the haphazard collection of wooden tables and mismatched wooden benches. Irony had clearly also been on the menu when the premises were being christened.

Masters didn't waste time in apologies for the delayed start to the briefing. He also didn't waste time in reflecting on minor victories recently achieved. The day's cabaret, such as it was, was now behind them.

'Tom Edwards is still being treated for the effects of carbon monoxide poisoning.'

Masters eyed the file on the table in front of him.

'The consultant doesn't anticipate any lasting damage and expects to release him for interview either sometime later today or tomorrow. Needless to say, given the evidence so far collected in Steven and Callum's bedrooms, he remains our prime suspect. He's not been arrested, but only because right now he's under the guard of two of our officers. The moment the consultant gives us the nod, he'll be read his rights.'

Masters extracted two pieces of paper from the file.

'We already have the medical and social statements.'

Those papers contained a brief life history of the two young victims, detailing where they were born, what they weighed at the time of their deaths, and a list of any illnesses they'd suffered in their short lives. Its primary purpose was ammunition. Should any slippery defence brief attempt to argue sometime in the future that the deaths may be due to something other than sinister causes, they'd be produced.

When she'd first heard of such statements, in another case involving the torture and murder of a never-to-be-forgotten family called the Kincaids, it seemed incredible to Ros that they should ever be needed. The same went for another and much-regretted fatality on her watch, a young and unfortunate former member of a notorious Manchester gang, called Gina Bell. Plain common sense dictated otherwise in both those cases, and in this case too. How could anyone even attempt to argue Steven and Callum's deaths could in any way have been natural? Years of sitting in Crown Courts listening to highly paid barristers argue black was white and night was day had disabused Ros of all such fond illusions.

'We've also had a report from the head teacher of Steven and Callum's school.'

By Ros's side, Conor looked at another sheet of paper now taken from the file by Masters. Copies had already been emailed around the various other agencies, including the Protection Unit, and Conor had scanned it before he came in. The head teacher had clearly been genuinely rocked by all that had happened. She described Steven and Callum as lovely boys from a lovely family. They'd never been in trouble in any of their classes, had never indeed even been late for any of those classes in all the time they'd attended the school. They'd been model pupils, in fact.

Perfect. Maybe too perfect.

'Report from the family doctor.'

Masters held up another sheet of paper, the contents of which had also already been circulated. The children had been registered with the practice but had barely been seen, a couple of routine injections aside. The mother, Jo, had brought the boys in on both occasions. The doctor in question had never seen the father as he never seemed to have fallen ill.

'Report from Tom Edwards's employer.'

From the few snatches of conversation she'd managed to have so far with the still largely sedated Jo, Ros already knew that Tom Edwards worked for a small company specialising in garden machinery and supplies. The company's premises boasted a showroom and workshop, and Tom had been employed to oversee the workshop bookings as well as to deal with any customers who wandered in to look at the lawnmowers and strimmers on display. As trade was inevitably seasonal, the company had branched out in the last year into mobility aids such as motorised scooters and rollators, and Tom Edwards had been looking after those too.

What Ros didn't know – because Jo hadn't told her, because Jo didn't know – was that the business had been struggling lately and her husband had recently been placed on part-time hours. The hope was that his hours would increase again as business hopefully picked up. According to the owner of the company, Tom Edwards had taken the news of his downgrading calmly, with no histrionics or complaints. Despite the inevitable knock to his weekly income and with two children and a wife to support, he'd taken it well, in fact.

Maybe too well.

Tom Edwards's employer had proffered one further insight into the man he'd taken on to run his showroom and workshop. He was a willing worker. He was steady and reliable. But somehow people didn't warm to him. Tom Edwards did his job and he did it competently. But he didn't seem to possess that spark that endeared many of his other workers to their customers. There just seemed to be something missing.

'Statement from Jo Edwards's mother.'

Another sheet of paper joined the others in front of Masters. Both Ros and Conor had scanned this one too. Initially Jo's mother, Ann, had believed her daughter had landed something of a catch, as she'd somewhat anachronistically termed her new son-in-law. Tom Edwards was charm personified, kind and considerate – a real gentleman, in fact.

Ann had credited his service background, as he'd previously served five years in the Army. Rumours, perhaps instigated by Edwards himself in an attempt to impress his new family, suggested that the otherwise unremarkable soldier had been something of a high-flyer in his previous life and career – although in what capacity had always been oddly vague. Not that it made any difference. Ann had been as smitten in her own way as her daughter. She'd always been a leading light in various local charities and after meeting her daughter's new boyfriend had enthusiastically debated with her coffee morning friends the return of National Service.

But that wasn't the full picture and it was only in the last year or so that Ann had realised there was another side to him, as her statement made clear. In public, he never let down his guard. In private, his more controlling character revealed itself, although never overtly. He never laid a finger on Jo or on the boys, for example, but he still ruled the household with a rod of iron.

If Tom Edwards got his way, he'd be his usual smiling self. If he didn't, he'd withdraw behind a wall of silence and the boys in particular would buckle in moments. They understood traditional punishment; they even understood screaming and shouting – plenty of their friends endured that from their own harassed parents, and plenty of teachers in school had been known to shout at misbehaving kids as well. But silence was something else.

Her mother said that now and again Jo had tried to hold out against him, particularly when those silences were sparked by something unreasonable in her view, such as insisting both boys had to be in bed by 6 p.m. even in the height of summer. But she never seemed to succeed. Tom Edwards had something of an implacable will when it came to imposing his wishes on others, principally his family. His silent treatment of them continued until they came back in line. Once they did so, Tom Edwards reverted to the kind and considerate perfect gentleman he presented to the rest of the world.

Masters brought out another slim document from the file in front of him. Ros hadn't seen this one. Neither had anyone else in the room. This wasn't from a member of the family or anyone closely associated with them. This was from a local heating engineer.

'A week or so ago, Tom Edwards decided to bleed all their radiators. It should have been a routine job but something went wrong. One radiator in particular didn't seem to have any air inside but it still wasn't getting hot. Edwards, with the help of a manual from the internet, decided to investigate further. Within days the boiler was in bits. After they'd been without hot water for over three days, Jo finally called in a local plumber.'

Masters tapped the file.

'Edwards came home to find the plumber fixing the considerable mess he'd created. Only he didn't accept he'd made any mess. He told the plumber he'd done some more research and the boiler simply needed a new ignitor as the old one was faulty. The plumber told Edwards the ignitor was fine and functioning completely normally. The problem lay elsewhere, but he wasn't going to be able to identify exactly where until he'd reassembled the boiler that Tom had so comprehensively dismantled.'

Masters paused again.

'Edwards didn't reply. In fact he never spoke another word to him. He just stared at him instead. The plumber doesn't seem to be a man given to the metaphorical, but he told us that his eyes seemed to freeze somehow. As if his pupils had turned to stone. The plumber became more and more uncomfortable, which was when Jo – who'd clearly been growing ever more nervous too – stepped in and suggested he leave. The plumber collected his tools, then Jo followed him out to his van, where she paid him for his call-out.'

Masters paused again.

'The plumber saw Jo once more after that. He'd been asked to call into a neighbour's house a couple of days later to sort out some problem. As he came back out to his van to collect some tools, Jo was returning with her kids from school. The plumber tried asking about the heating and Jo seemed about to respond but then one of the boys – the eldest, he thought – put his hand on his mother's arm, which looked to him like a clear signal she should not reply. The other boy kept glancing towards the house. Jo turned and, without saying another word, led the boys back inside.'

Masters didn't even glance down at the piece of paper, all this committed now to memory.

'Half an hour later and having completed his job at their neighbour's, the plumber came back out of the house to find Tom Edwards standing by the front door, staring at him again. The plumber got the same feeling he'd first experienced when he was standing by Tom Edwards's dismantled boiler. He's aware this might sound like hindsight given all that's happened and what Tom Edwards seems to have done, but he describes the look in his eyes as pure evil.'

Then Masters brought out another file no one else in that room had seen till that point, a single word printed at the top.

'Lorazepam.'

Masters passed copies of this new file around the room.

'A Class C, Schedule 4 Controlled Drug under the Misuse of Drugs Regulations 2001, sometimes sold under the brand name Ativan, Lorazepam is a benzodiazepine medication aimed at the short-term treatment of anxiety disorders, acute seizures and, sometimes, insomnia. It's also occasionally used to sedate aggressive patients.'

Masters paused.

'Needless to say, Lorazepam is strictly a prescription drug. The Edwards family doctor has confirmed that no member of the family had ever been prescribed it. So why two empty bottles of liquid Lorazepam should have been found in the boot of Tom Edwards's car is something of a puzzle. The drug had been mixed with the water that was found in the tumblers by the side of the two boys' beds. Roughly half had been drunk in both instances.'

Masters paused again, all this seeming to take its toll now even on him.

'There could have been a potential complication in that Lorazepam isn't particularly soluble. It certainly wouldn't have fooled any suspicious adult who expected a glass of clear water and was faced with more of a milky substance instead. But two already sleepy boys, one aged five and the other aged three, would probably have proved more malleable, particularly when faced with a clearly determined father.'

Masters fell silent and didn't say anything else for a few moments.

He didn't need to.

It was already only too obvious how both boys had remained compliant throughout their killing.

Ros kept looking at the file, her mind back in Jo's house once again, where the previous evening another piece in the jigsaw had slotted into place.

'It's harder than you think.'

The previous evening, Ros had been standing next to Maha Najafi in the second of the small children's bedrooms in what from now on would be Jo Edwards's former home. The cushion still assumed to be from Jo and Tom's bed remained on the floor of the downstairs sitting room. It wouldn't be touched until Maha had formed a clear picture of the sequence of events that had taken place in the house, at which point she'd personally supervise its removal, taking care not to disturb or contaminate anything that could provide any crucial evidence.

Masters, staring out of the window onto the rear garden, turned to look back at her, as did Conor on the other side of the room.

'What is?'

'To suffocate someone.'

Ros eyed Maha as she in turn stared at the pillows left on Callum's bed.

Maha had come to the UK as a refugee some two decades before, although for a time it had seemed unlikely that she and her family would ever leave their temporary refuge in Lebanon.

Maha, a teenager at the time, had been the eldest of four children, living with their mother on the streets in Beirut. Every day for months her mother would stand in line at the makeshift offices of one of the hard-pressed refugee border agencies, waiting for the help she needed so they could begin the new life she'd promised her children.

One morning in that office, after receiving yet more hollow assurances of assistance she was increasingly certain would never materialise, her mother had taken a small bottle out of her bag. Maha and the rest of her siblings had assumed it was water but rather than drinking it, their mother poured the contents over her upper body and head. The next moment she set light to the fuel that had by now soaked through her clothes and matted her hair to her scalp. She died in hospital two days after her last, desperate attempt to make herself and her family count in some way.

One day later, Maha and her siblings landed in Gatwick as the hard-pressed border agency fast-tracked their case. Two years on, Maha began her medical studies. Five years later she graduated, dedicating her new qualification and new life to her mother. Ten years on from that graduation she was in a small suburban house that had previously housed the two dead boys in the upstairs bedrooms, determined – as with everything she now encountered in both her professional and personal life – to make the next few moments count.

Masters's brief delay in instituting the normal scene-of-crime procedure was to prove more than justified. Nothing escaped Maha's forensic attention, particularly where the loss of innocents was concerned. That imparted to cases such as these something of the status of a crusade.

Maha kept eyeing the rest of the cushions on the parents' bed, visible through the partly open door, almost as if they were talking to her. Perhaps they were.

'You have to get something over the nose and the mouth at the same time. If you don't block the air supply to both, it takes too long. And even if you do manage to get something fully over the nose and mouth, you really have to press down hard.'

Maha appraised Callum's bed.

'But a bed's soft. So even though you're pressing hard, you're doing it into a yielding surface. The more you press, the more it yields. Yes, there's a point at which it compacts, but it's still a pretty inefficient way of killing someone.'

Masters broke in, beginning to grow uneasy. This was already sounding like the start of some defence strategy to him.

'Meaning?'

'Meaning we're not only looking for the murderer's DNA on that cushion downstairs, we're probably looking for the same DNA on the underside of each child's head.'

Ros, Masters and Conor all stared at her for a moment before comprehension began to dawn, Ros the first to give voice to it.

'You mean if Tom Edwards did this, he cupped his hand behind their heads and then pressed down onto that?'

Maha nodded as Conor turned away, suddenly unable to deal with this, his foot knocking against a small toy alarm clock as he did so. Everyone stilled as Minnie Mouse emerged from inside and began singing a bouncy song, urging anyone in that room to wake up, telling them that the day was just beginning and that it was going to be fun, so come on Sleepyhead, get out of bed, it's a brand new morning.

Masters reached out a hand and switched it off.

Across the room, Conor had stared at the now silent toy clock.

Conor had looked after all sorts in the Protection Unit, from career criminals to gangland villains. He'd even overseen the safe welfare of cop killers in the past. Right now, he'd have chosen any of those charges over this particular case.

Conor had also been in Murder Squad at one time. Back then, Masters was his senior officer. At that time and with a recent marriage to a high-flying surgeon, life couldn't really get any better. But then Conor's life and career began to go off the rails. He made the fatal mistake of trying to keep up with Francesca, his high-flying wife, who was several rungs above him both socially and financially. A couple of lucky wins at poker convinced him he could do so, for a time at least. For that brief period, he lived a surgeon's lifestyle on a lowly DC's salary, matching her holiday for holiday, encouraging her ambitions for ever larger and more expensive apartments.

It was doomed and so was he. Several unlucky nights at the poker table really should have told him that, but he'd ploughed on, convinced he could reverse the rising tide that was now threatening to swamp him. Already the strain was beginning to tell on his marriage. One disciplinary offence too many saw him transferred out of the glamour department of Murder Squad into the backwater, or so he'd seen it at the time, of the Protection Unit, an outfit he regarded with the sort of contempt matched only by his disdain for his new immediate senior officer, Ros.

One night changed everything. It should have been the final nail in the coffin: Ros had just come across incontrovertible evidence of his considerable gambling debts. He was now in the sort of position that could put him and his new department at intense professional risk. In his situation, many officers had succumbed to temptation, negotiating favours for minor and not-so-minor villains in exchange for financial help. Had he had some sort of out-of-body experience at that moment, he'd have pronounced his own inevitable capitulation to the dark side as just a matter of time.

By rights, Ros should have marched him straight down to the nearest duty officer. Moments later he should have been clearing his desk and preparing for an extended period of leave while the disciplinary machine swung into action. It wouldn't have taken long. His career would be in freefall – followed closely by his marriage, in all probability. Within a few short days he fully expected to lose the lot.

But none of that had happened. Instead Ros had taken him down to a small path overlooking one of the newly restored waterways along which water taxis plied their trade. And Ros had started talking about herself and about a case from years before that still haunted her, telling him how she felt about it then and now. Along the way she'd lifted a lid on some of the more extreme emotions he'd ever heard or could ever have expected to hear from a woman he'd never imagined laying herself bare in that way. And it was, as he'd reflected many times since, like listening to some kindred spirit where he'd previously believed none existed.

And Conor had reciprocated, not because he thought it might help him rescue a career he'd already consigned to oblivion, but because he too wanted to drag it all out of him, to say the unsayable, to give voice to everything which up to now had remained unsaid and would probably always have remained unsaid had it not been for that extraordinary encounter in those most unlikely of circumstances.

From that moment on, Conor's lot in life had improved. He extricated himself from the financial pit into which he'd fallen just in time to rescue his marriage. Francesca had returned from a trip abroad with the same intention seemingly in view. He didn't know what had provoked her new resolve and some instinct had told him not to enquire too deeply. They'd both reached a stage in their relationship where after spiralling so far apart there appeared to be no common ground left, they both wanted to rescue what they'd previously shared together, and that was all that mattered.

The future. Not the past.

And lately the unthinkable had happened. Francesca had actually started dropping small hints about children. Nothing too explicit, and they hadn't had a proper conversation about yet. It had been just half-hints and allusions, but Conor knew his wife. He knew she was circling around a major decision that would turn their lives upside down. And Conor felt a massive surge of excitement every time he thought about it.

It would involve lots of changes, Conor knew that. Their flat would have to go for a start, small kids and open-plan living with lots of high and unprotected balconies and walkways being something of a clear no-no. It would probably mean a drop in income too, at least for a while. Knowing his wife, she would probably work up to the last minute but not even Francesca could carry out full surgical procedures through childbirth, and it was always possible that sort of experience might change her totally. She might decide she didn't want to go back to work, that she wanted from that point on to devote her considerable powers of concentration to raising their child.

Conor had been careful not to push this along too quickly, to engage Francesca too openly in the internal debate she was clearly conducting. This was still a fragile issue and the last thing he wanted to do was crush it at too early a stage. Conor wanted a child, not a half-formed notion destined to wither before it had chance to bloom.

Conor pushed one foot in front of the other, heading down the stairs after Ros, Maha and Masters and coming out onto a small suburban street where hushed groups of people stared out from their own pieces of heaven onto a scene that had come straight out of hell.

Conor had experienced a lot in his time in both Murder Squad and the Protection Unit. Strong emotions had been provoked by all sorts of encounters. He'd felt rage – sometimes uncontrollable rage – he'd been scarred by grief and he'd plumbed emotional depths he wasn't even aware existed. He'd seen some of the most terrible things his fellow man could do and just when he thought he'd seen the absolute worst, another depth revealed itself.

Conor turned to look back at the house behind him. In his time in the police he'd become aware of things inside himself he didn't want to acknowledge existed, but no matter what extremes he'd encountered and experienced, he could never imagine – in a million lifetimes – being in the sort of state in which he'd pick up a cushion from a bed he shared with his wife, cross a narrow landing and suffocate the life out of first one small son and then another.

Conor had met many twisted characters in his time and had occasionally recognised an uneasy kinship with some of them. But there was no kinship here. Whoever had done this had very definitely crossed the line from something human into something that was not.

And for the first time since his high-flying wife had hesitantly, shyly even, broached the subject of bringing another life into the world, Conor wasn't experiencing dizzying exultation anymore.

Now all he was feeling was fear.

7

T HE FIRST THING Ros did on returning from Masters's briefing was to take Jo out of the safe house.

There was no fresh appointment to keep, no new interview for her client to endure. In truth, she probably wouldn't be a client for much longer now Tom Edwards had been apprehended, but for now Ros still wanted to get her outside into what passed for fresh air. She did the same with any new entrant to the protection programme. They were all there for a multitude of reasons, a myriad variety of circumstances dictating their sudden and always enforced move from the world they'd previously known to a world they couldn't even begin to recognise. But all virtually without exception shared the same reaction.

Most closed down or retreated into a cocoon, went to ground in one way or another. And at some point, usually very early on in the process, Ros made sure they did something simple and everyday. Something they'd have done without thinking in the world that had suddenly been denied to them.

Take a walk.

Buy a paper.

Go and see a film.

Or in this case, take a totally ordinary bus ride into the city centre for a cup of coffee.

Jo didn't ask where they were going. Most didn't. She didn't even demur when Ros laid out her clothes for her, a simple shirt and jeans, topped off with a black jacket and contrasting pink scarf. Like almost every client under Ros's care, Jo was inside a bubble right now, propelled from one point to the next by hands she didn't even see, doing things she no longer understood.

But it didn't matter. She'd still see people out on the street and hear snatches of conversation, and while none of it would go in and she wouldn't even begin to be able to describe anyone she'd seen or tell you what anyone was talking about, that didn't matter either. Some of it, at some level, would sink in. Some part of her would absorb the one thing she craved right now, even if she was a million miles from understanding that too.

Normality.

The ordinary and the everyday.

A reminder, however subliminal, that life was going on. The life to which one day she might hopefully return.

Ros steered Jo past the large new development in the centre of the city that had been passed a couple of hours before by the number cruncher on his way to that fateful reunion with his Pod. At one time it had been the site of the city's bus depot as well as its train station, making the whole area a fully functioning transport hub. Now there were just office blocks, office blocks and more of the same.

Normally Ros would have given the multiplying monstrosities the widest of berths but on the ground floor of one of them, a concession had recently opened. The food was OK and the coffee passed muster but that wasn't the attraction. Along one wall was sited a whole array of private cubicles, each one hosting up to four people on two benches that faced each other. It was a private retreat looking out onto a street where office workers, train commuters and shoppers surged and eddied. So the OK food and the coffee that passed muster didn't matter. As a private setting inside a public space, the place was perfect.

Jo settled herself on one of the benches, Ros seated herself opposite. A waitress with dyed hair approached and immediately embarked on a smiling declamation of that day's specials. Ros ordered for them both, sticking to coffee and eschewing the food. The waitress passed on the order to another waitress who sported a multi-coloured fringe. Which was when Jo spoke for the first time since they'd left the safe house that morning – although it didn't betoken much in the way of a breakthrough. She just asked where she could find the toilets.

Ros watched as Jo levered herself up off the bench and headed away across the tiled floor, her head bowed. The various office workers, train commuters and shoppers parted almost unconsciously as she moved by them. Some instinct seemed to be telling them she was a woman apart right now. Or maybe they could sense something else, something they really didn't want to investigate too deeply.

Ros had been there herself. She'd spent most of her childhood in the same sort of stasis. Going through the motions, being part of the world she moved amongst, while remaining above and beyond everything and everyone she came into contact with. Life lived behind a constant veil.

She'd overheard colleagues in the Protection Unit speculate occasionally about the lack of any significant other in her life and she'd heard various theories propounded as to why that might be. She was a buttoned-up bitch in love with one thing and one thing only, and that was her job. Or she was a closet dyke.

None of those colleagues – so far, anyway – had hazarded anything even remotely near the truth, for which relief she proffered silent and heartfelt thanks once again.

It was a truth and a character trait she had shared with her late sister, Di. To form a relationship meant letting someone in, and she knew that once that process started, it didn't stop. Love meant trust so far as she was concerned, otherwise it wasn't love at all. And so Ros was caught in a classic Catch-22. How could she trust someone and how could anyone trust her, when from the start of any prospective relationship every word Ros would tell them was a lie? Who she was, where she came from, who her parents were; all that was a carefully constructed fiction repeated so many times by her that she'd almost come to accept it as fact.

Only it wasn't. It was an invention, a smokescreen behind which she hid. And on the very few, occasions anyone had grown close to Ros in the past, they'd always sensed it. They always knew she was holding something back and they always tried to find out what that might be, not out of any malevolent intent but because they were genuinely interested, because they cared.

At which point Ros did what she always did. She broke it off, cutting off all future contact at the same time. She ended it usually before it had even properly begun, leading those colleagues inside the Protection Unit to speculate ever more luridly on why she remained a woman alone.

The waitress with the multi-coloured fringe appeared before Ros again this time with the coffees, double-checking at the same time that they really didn't want any food, because they did have some ultra-tempting specials on offer today? Ros struggled back a declining smile, that smile instantly wiping as out of the corner of her eye she caught the flash of a pink scarf moving past an incoming press of more office workers, train commuters and shoppers, heading outside.

Ros was out of the café in seconds. She looked round at a scene that might still be ordinary and everyday but which now seemed to be positively fecund with danger.

Scaffolding rose in front of her, clinging to the side of another half-completed office block, each floor open to the elements, innumerable access points dotted around the so-called security perimeter as diggers moved in and out, platforms were manoeuvred into position and construction workers went about their tasks at the same time. If she'd picked up one of the many hard hats Ros could see lying around inside, Jo would be virtually indistinguishable from them in seconds. Ros looked up, scanning the gaping floors, searching for one face in amongst at least dozens she could see right now.

Then the sound of a train's air horn snapped her round in the opposite direction and now Ros stared at the city's main rail station. A ceaseless hub at this time of the day, trains arriving and departing every few moments from a multitude of different platforms, most stopping to pick up passengers, some speeding straight through. All Jo had to do was get through the ticket barrier – and at peak times Ros had seen those barriers left open and passengers waved through onto the platforms by hard-pressed station staff – and she'd be on any of those platforms and in literal touching distance of any of those trains in a heartbeat that could stop beating just a moment later.

All the time she scanned the square and the crowds, Ros frantically punched numbers into her phone, a pre-arranged code to alert not only her own Protection Unit but also the city's emergency services.

More images flooded Ros's eyes. A large river flowed through the city, traversed by a footbridge just a few metres away from where Ros was standing. Within seconds of leaving that coffee shop, Jo could have hauled herself up onto the small wall overlooking that surging water. The local police had seen many casualties go into the river at that point, usually drunken sports fans celebrating a famous victory in the nearby stadium or drowning their sorrows after a bitter defeat. Few made it out again. Their bodies were usually found a day or so later, washed up on the dockside a mile or so downriver.

And all those clear and present dangers didn't even begin to include the buses, taxi cabs, private cars and motorbikes that sped round the packed city streets, roaring from one red light to another, each one a potential instrument of death if anyone was of the mind to throw themselves in front of it.

Then Ros stopped suddenly as another image flashed before her eyes.

For that one moment she saw it all again: the police lights, the inquisitive neighbours, the seemingly never-ending succession of well-tended lawns.

The frail woman with those hedge shears in her hand.

Within ten minutes, Ros was back there.

The house looked exactly the same. The police tape was still in place, but to all intents and purposes the dwelling matched each of the houses on either side of it on that well-tended street. Only one thing jarred, and that was the smashed kitchen window at the rear of the ground floor and the now-open door beside it.

Ros moved through the gaping door, on into the kitchen and up the stairs. The house was as quiet as it had been that first time she'd been there.

Quiet as the grave.

Ros paused on the landing, then moved into the eldest boy's room. Steven's bedroom.

That looked just as it had before as well. Nothing had been touched and the room still bore testimony to the same young life in transition. The same toys were still in evidence, some stacked on shelves, some tucked away in half-open drawers. The same posters of footballers were there too, as were the other posters as well – including the one featuring the new boy band, fresh heroes who were heroes no more.

Everything was exactly the same, in fact, aside from one further single jarring note. On Steven's bed, Jo now lay; just where her eldest son had lain, arranged in exactly the same manner: lying flat on her back, her eyes closed, face pointing up towards the ceiling.

Ros stood in the doorway. If Jo sensed her presence, she didn't betray it by so much as a single flutter of the eyelids. She just lay there, perhaps in some desperate attempt to feel what her son had felt, to endure what he'd endured, to claim some sort of kinship with all he and Callum might have suffered that night.

Ros hesitated a moment, then sat down beside Jo on the bed. Again, Jo stayed exactly where she was, still giving no hint she was even aware of Ros's presence.

They stayed like that for a few moments longer.

Then Jo spoke.

'This is my fault.'

Ros looked at her. Up to that point, Jo had hardly spoken in the whole time she'd been under Ros's care; had hardly, indeed, moved – one of the reasons Ros had decided on that trip to the coffee shop in the first place. Ever since they'd taken her into the safe house, Jo had wrapped her new surroundings around her like a cloak, seeking out ever smaller spaces to inhabit, choosing the smallest bedroom in which to sleep, the smallest chair in which to enfold herself.

She wouldn't even look outside the window, let alone consider taking a walk in the small garden to the rear. The Protection Unit doctor had diagnosed a mild and probably temporary form of agoraphobia – which, contrary to popular belief, isn't actually a fear of large outside spaces or crowds, but is more accurately defined as the fear of not being able to be saved. The fear of being afraid, in fact; the kind of generalised panic that may most likely to occur in places where a sufferer would naturally feel isolated – in the middle of a vast expense of desert or buried deep inside some dense and inaccessible forest. But in truth it was just as likely to happen in a street packed full of people.

Ros had overseen many clients like Jo. She'd coached them all in the cover stories they'd have to present to the world from that moment on. All had the same expressions on their faces, as if the world around them had suddenly twisted into some sort of alien entity, as if everything they'd previously known and trusted had in one bewildering instant turned against them with the vengeance of a thousand furies – and for good reason. Because it usually had.

'I'd brought the boys back from swimming.'

Jo paused.

'Neither of them liked it very much but at least they could use the showers down there so they didn't have to go to school in the morning all skanky.'

Jo shook her head.

'We still hadn't got any hot water – that fucking boiler.'

Jo paused, struggling some more.

'I knew I should just have kept quiet. I knew Tom would fix it eventually – he always did – I just had to keep my head down and in another day or so he'd work out what he'd done wrong, what any half-decent plumber could have told him in five minutes if only he'd let them, and then everything would be back to normal.'

On the bed Jo paused again and this time Ros, cautiously, prompted her.

'So what happened?'

Jo looked across at her, her eyes focusing on Ros, almost as if she was seeing her for the first time.

'All of a sudden I just came out with it. I stood there in that kitchen, the boys under their duvets upstairs, and I told him I wasn't happy.'

She shook her head.

'Not just about the boiler, not just about the boys having to use the showers at the swimming pool. About everything. Him.'

Ros just looked at her as Jo fell silent again, just waiting.

'I told him to lighten up – that's all I wanted, that was all the kids wanted: just relax, let some light in, what did it matter if he couldn't do this job or that job? No one cared.'

Jo paused as more involuntary memories crowded in, more involuntary associations being made.

'That's what was keeping us safe, wasn't it? Him being all buttoned-up like that? That was his way of keeping everything under control, keeping everything inside in check?'

Ros remained silent. Jo didn't want answers anyway and they both knew it. She was just talking out, or trying to talk out, demons that were never going to be exorcised anyway.

'He couldn't bend, could he? He couldn't bend because the minute he did that's when he'd break, and he knew that and I should have known it too.'

Jo looked up at the ceiling for a moment.

Then she looked back at Ros, ever bleaker.

'Now he's done it, hasn't he?'

Ros held her stare.

'Now he's punished me.'

8

L ATER THAT SAME day, the hospital consultant examined and discharged Tom Edwards, pronouncing him fit for police interview. His two constant companions, Masters's officers from Murder Squad, took immediate charge of him, reading him his rights as they escorted him down a hospital corridor. Within half an hour he was in an interview room in Murder Squad Headquarters: a room with walls and a door though no windows; a room that bore no resemblance to anything that might be called a Pod.

Prior to Tom Edwards being brought in, various checks had been carried out, principally on his finances. In a box file again found in the boot of his car, officers had found a whole collection of recent bank statements, all of which painted the clearest of pictures. Tom Edwards was drowning in debt. Those same statements revealed that he'd always lived life close to the financial edge; had always, indeed, borrowed as much as he'd been able in order to acquire, among other things, a home for his family that was just slightly above his means.

Taking the charitable view, that betokened a man who wanted to provide the best for his kith and kin. To take a less charitable stance, it suggested a man to whom appearances were everything.

But the various and extended gambles, be they calculated or otherwise, that Tom Edwards had taken with his family finances seemed to have paid off until recently at least. He'd just about managed to keep himself and that family afloat. But lately with the downgrading of his job and the resultant reduction in income, he'd sunk into trouble. He'd been maintaining the same level of spending as before, perhaps because, as Masters and his investigating team of officers already strongly suspected, to admit to his wife and his two boys that he could no longer provide for them as he had before would have been unsupportable. So Tom Edwards left the family home he ruled with a rod of iron at the same time each morning and returned the same time each night irrespective of whether he was actually working that day or not. Tom Edwards, in short, was a control freak, although when the two officers brought him in for his first police interview he looked as if he'd have difficulty controlling a simple bowel movement.

Leaving Jo in the care of Conor, Ros watched the interview via a one-way mirror. Aside from the paleness of his skin and the slight sheen of sweat that seemed to be permanently on his forehead, Tom Edwards looked ordinary. There was no other word to describe him. In a street you'd have passed him a thousand times without a second glance and with absolutely no clue as to what he was capable of doing. Maybe, Ros silently reflected, the same was true for a thousand other multiple killers as well.

As soon as the regulation spiel about the interview being recorded and his rights was completed, Masters, sitting opposite Tom Edwards and the duty brief, plunged straight in, no preamble.

'Have you read your wife's statements concerning the night you were found in your car?'

Edwards hesitated momentarily almost as if he was scanning the question for a virus. Then he nodded, slightly.

Masters nodded back at him.

'For the record.'

Edwards hesitated again, then spoke, his response almost inaudible to the human ear, but the recording picked it up clearly enough.

'Yes.'

'And what do you remember of the events of that night?'

Edwards's watery blue eyes focused, briefly, on the officer on the opposite side of the table, then looked away. Ros sympathised. Stronger men than Tom Edwards had found it difficult to maintain eye contact with the Head of the local Murder Squad.

'I don't understand.'

'Did anything unusual happen?'

Tom Edwards hesitated fractionally again.

'Not really.'

'Just a normal sort of evening?'

'I suppose.'

Masters hadn't mentioned the children yet and Ros wouldn't have expected him to, at least not this early in the interview. The last thing any of them wanted was for Edwards to retreat into a shell. Masters let the silence stretch and then stretch some more.

'I remember going for a drive.'

'Was that usual? Going for a drive at that time in the evening?'

'No.'

'Maybe that's why you remember it.'

It wasn't a question, more of a statement, but Edwards nodded anyway.

'Maybe.'

'And do you remember why you went for that drive?'

Edwards hesitated, his eyes focusing briefly on Masters again before looking away once more. Then he nodded again.

'I was feeling depressed.'

'Any particular reason?'

Like having just ended the lives of your two small boys, Ros reflected silently again. She might even have said it out loud had she been in that room with Tom Edwards right now. Which was perhaps one of the reasons Masters was conducting this interview and not her.

'I don't know, not really.'

Edwards struggled for a moment, then continued.

'Maybe it's the time of year.'

'What about this time of year?'

Edwards hesitated again, whether out of a genuine reluctance to open up or for effect, Ros couldn't decide. It didn't matter. Masters would extract the information anyway.

'It's the summer. It always gets to me like that.'

'Because?'

The answer came back prompt, almost rehearsed. Maybe it was.

'It was this time of year when my Dad died. It's a long time ago now, but –'

Edwards paused for a moment, then shrugged.

'It's like a trigger. Something seems to happen inside.'

Masters had tensed halfway through that and on the other side of the glass Ros did too, and for the same reason. Both officers could already see the line any future defence barrister might take. Either consciously or unconsciously, Edwards was planting all the tent poles for a trade or plea bargain, probably involving diminished responsibility.

'Why did you drive to that headland?'

'I didn't know I had.'

Masters just let the silence stretch once again.

'I remember driving away from the house. Next thing I knew I was there.'

'And you'd never been there before?'

'No.'

'You're sure?'

'Yes.'

Masters looked down at notes in front of him.

'Have you ever heard of ANPR – Automatic Number Plate Recognition?'

Edwards's eyes widened slightly as if he could almost see the trap opening up before him.

'One of our cameras flagged you as you drove to that exact same spot a week ago.'

Edwards hesitated again.

'I don't remember.'

Smoothly, Masters changed tack.

'A generous gesture on your employer's part, wasn't it?'

'What was?'

'Allowing you to keep the car when your hours had been reduced so drastically?'

Edwards didn't reply.

'Other employers might have taken it off you.'

Edwards hesitated, then nodded once more, this time just the slightest inclination of the head.

'How did your wife take all that? Was she worried? It was quite a drop in income.'

'She didn't know.'

'Why not?'

'Because I didn't want to worry her.'

'So you didn't tell her?'

'No.'

'Is your marriage a good one, Mr Edwards?'

For the first time, Tom Edwards looked Masters straight in the eye and held it for a moment at least, and when he answered, his voice was firm.

'Yes.'

'Even though you didn't tell her about your working hours being cut?'

'I told you why.'

'Did you tell her about feeling depressed?'

'No.'

'Did you not want to worry her about that too?'

'Why would I want to worry about her about anything?'

'Who bought the Lorazepam?'

Edwards hesitated again at the sudden change of subject and Masters leant closer across the table.

'We found two empty bottles in the boot of your car. Your wife has no idea how they got there. The name on the labels on the bottles – the intended recipient – wasn't anyone in the family, but we've already matched the fingerprints we found on the bottles and they're yours.'

'I bought them.'

'From?'

'An old Army friend.'

'Where?'

'At a reunion. We got talking. I told him how I was feeling. The time of the year. All that. He was having treatment for PTSD. He thought it might help.'

'You talked to him about all that even though you hadn't talked to your wife.'

'It's easier sometimes, isn't it? Talking to someone who's not so close.'

Smoothly once more, not giving Edwards time to settle, Masters changed tack again.

'What happened when your wife went out that night?'

'I don't understand.'

'Do you remember anything unusual happening just before she went out?'

'Not really. She just said she was going out to see a friend.'

'And what did she do just before she went out? Anything out of the ordinary that you can remember?'

Edwards hesitated again. This time his attempt to ransack his memory seemed genuine.

'She just put the boys to bed.'

It was the first time there'd been any reference to Tom Edwards's two children and it had been made, as Masters had always intended, by Edwards himself.

'So she settled them down for the night, read them a story, that sort of thing?'

Edwards nodded back.

'That sort of thing.'

'Did Jo – your wife – always do that?'

'We took it in turns. That night was her turn.'

'You remember that?'

'What?'

'You remember it was her turn to settle your two boys that night even though you don't seem to remember anything else?'

Tom Edwards just stared back across the table, his expression as blank as ever.

'It must have been her turn or she wouldn't have done it.'

'And did you go and check on them after she left the house?'

'No.'

'So when you left the house yourself a short while later you did that without seeing them again.'

'I must have done.'

'Then you went for your drive?'

'I already said.'

'Did you hurt your children before you went out for your drive?'

The reply was instant. Once again, Edwards didn't falter for a second.

'No.'

Masters didn't falter either.

'Did you put the Lorazepam into the beakers of water that we found by their beds?'

'No.'

'Did you make them drink it?'

'No.'

'So why were your fingerprints on those beakers?'

'I don't know.'

Masters pressed on.

'We found a cushion on the floor of the downstairs sitting room. The cushion matched others we found on your and your wife's bed. Your DNA was found in a loose pattern on one side of the cushion consistent with your having held it with your open palm.'

Edwards didn't reply.

'Steven and Callum's DNA was also found on the other side of the cushion. Those spreads of DNA were consistent with the cushion being placed over each of their mouths and noses and held there.'

Edwards still didn't reply.

'Your DNA was also found on the back of both boys' heads, consistent with your having cupped their heads in one of your hands while you pressed down onto each of their faces.'

There was still just silence from Edwards, a silence Masters let stretch once again until it was obvious that this time Edwards wasn't going to break it.

'They're free.'

Edwards looked back at him, but remained silent.

'That's what you said when you were found in your car. According to the witness who found you, you said your children were free.'

Edwards just kept looking at him.

'What did you mean when you said that?'

For a moment Ros expected the same silence to endure. For that same moment she feared it would last until the end of what was already proving something of an abortive interview.

But then and somewhat unexpectedly, Tom Edwards spoke.

'Because it's true.'

'Meaning they were in a better place, that they weren't in any sort of pain, that they weren't suffering any more?'

'No.'

'Then what did you mean?'

Edwards looked back at Masters and for the first time in the course of the interview something actually shone in his eyes. For the very first time there was something that resembled genuine emotion.

But there was something more than that too. Something Masters hadn't remotely expected.

Something that immediately and alternately felt as if it had set the head of the local Murder Squad on fire, at the same time as chilling him to the bone.

On the other side of the glass, Ros wasn't now looking at the man who'd unexpectedly provoked all that.

Ros was looking at Masters.

Because from her vantage point, she could see something shining in Masters's eyes now too.

Some might have called it a copper's nose, but it was a faculty Masters had possessed for years before he'd joined the force. Some might also have called it God-given, but Masters had never counted himself as part of that hopeful flock. The only other word that seemed to fit was intuition and, Masters being Masters, he'd made a special study of the phenomenon in an attempt to understand it better.

That special study had taken place, as did most studies of a similar kind, at Masters's regular weekly retreat. Every Tuesday evening Masters attended a local chess club. He'd first become interested in the ancient game courtesy of a frustrated Grandmaster in his old school. The Grandmaster had had the ability but lacked the application to make the grade professionally and had turned to earning his crust as a perennially disappointed maths teacher. Masters had been something of a protégé at one time and the failed Grandmaster in question had once harboured hopes of fulfilling his own destiny by proxy.

But then Masters discovered something much more interesting, namely the criminal mind. For a short period it was a close-run thing whether Masters would spend his life as one of its leading lights or simply one of its more acute and empathetic students, but then he joined his local police force. The police gained an unconventional if brilliant recruit at the same time that the criminal world lost something of a potential legend.

The chess club had come into Masters's life at a time when his career was on one of its habitual rocks. Masters had always battled what the force's psychiatrists had termed anger issues. They'd manifested themselves many times over the years over the course of innumerable investigations. The only saving grace so far as Masters's hard-pressed employers were concerned was that almost every one of those investigations ended in a result. Masters, by fair means or foul – albeit usually the latter – more often than not removed yet another high-level villain from the streets with each high-profile case slotted away in some filing cabinet with a nice big tick on the cover. So Masters was well worth keeping so far as those hard-pressed employers were concerned. Indeed, to maintain the local force's clear-up rate, it was essential that they did hang on to him.

The only problem being the growing litany of casualties – some physical, some emotional – that littered each and every one of those cases. Some viewed it as collateral damage, others as a PR nightmare.

When that rogue DC by the name of Banks, first name Donovan, was summarily dispatched by Masters over a ten-storey drop, the force stepped in again. That the DC more than deserved that punishment, and his subsequent incarceration in a specialist hospital devoted to spinal injuries, wasn't in doubt. He was a more than usually bad apple who had cost the lives of total innocents. But his punishment was still very much a step too far, which was when Masters himself had mentioned the chess club.

In truth, Masters had attended the club for some time. It was composed of a similar ragbag collection of life's casualties, all of whom certainly shared a keen interest in the Four Knights Game and the King's Indian Defence. But they were all there for similar, if tacit, therapy too. Some were old lags, some ex-university professors, some were still career criminals. But all sought out the club and the company of its members as a bulwark against a world they barely understood and which certainly didn't understand them.

The weekly debates that were initiated over those chessboards were wide-ranging. No one could predict what one or other of the members would propose as a topic of debate from one week to the next. But whatever it was, each of those members left every session stimulated and calmed in equal measure. The force's psychiatrists didn't understand it, but once alerted to it, they didn't care. All they knew was that it seemed to be working. Masters hadn't had an anger issue in all the months he'd been keeping his weekly date with some of the unlikeliest co-therapists those same psychiatrists could imagine. A couple of them had even contemplated writing a paper about it, but knew they probably never would.

That intuitive facility, the subject of the previous week's collective debate, had been defined in various journals that Masters had consulted as the ability to acquire knowledge without the use of reason, or perhaps more accurately without necessarily utilising an individual's more usual powers of deduction. The word itself, Masters had further discovered, derived from the Latin term *intueri*, commonly translated as to look inside or to contemplate, providing an individual with beliefs or conclusions that might otherwise be difficult to justify. It also derived – so psychologists asserted – from the right-hand side of the brain, which has always been associated with intuitive processes such as aesthetics.

Masters had warmed to his theme in front of his now rapt audience, hunched over their chess pieces, explaining that he'd next consulted various writers who'd dealt with the phenomenon, finding perhaps the most interesting – if one of the most flawed – in the writings of Carl Jung. The famed psychologist saw individuals in whom intuition was dominant as acting not on the basis of any sort of rational judgment, but on sheer intensity of perception. To Jung, those inclined to the intuitive persuasion were more likely to be mystics, prophets or cranks, often cursed by an overpowering desire to escape any given situation before it became a trap, a characteristic that held true for their love life as well as the more everyday world of work.

Masters had looked round the silent room at that point and he could see his own response to that mirrored in each pair of eyes that looked back at him.

Bollocks.

Did that then make him a mystic, a prophet or a crank? Yes, it was occasionally difficult to defend some of the wilder pursuits on which he'd dispatched members of his team in the past. His immediate senior officers, not unreasonably, had occasionally asked for reasons why they should sanction the sometimes considerable expenses incurred, not to mention deal with the occasionally all-too-public flak and pressure from office suits and number crunchers. Not unreasonably, they hadn't been too impressed by a treatise on empathetic instinct.

But there was always that same problem for those senior officers: the quite remarkable success rate delivered by the intuitive Masters. Time and again he seemed to simply sense the correct and relevant avenue to explore, the one course of inquiry that would deliver a genuine miscreant to book.

So was there a similar intuition at work inside everyone, Masters wanted to know?

The intuition that led a wife to investigate a husband's phone records, some nameless instinct driving her on, telling her he was up to something on those evenings and weekends away on business, fearful of finding out what it might be but unable to stop herself.

The intuition that led a parent to track a teenage child, knowing somehow that that child was in danger, often of his or her own volition.

The intuition that made an employer hire one employee over another with seemingly identical qualities, somehow just knowing he or she was the one without quite knowing how or why.

The same intuition that, somehow and without his conscious mind apparently intruding on the process at all, seemed to enable Masters to fix on the one guilty party in a room packed full of other suspects, sometimes despite all available evidence to the contrary.

The same intuition that was at work right now.

Back in that interview room and with Ros still staring at him from the other side of the one-way glass, Masters kept his eyes fixed on Tom Edwards.

For a moment, Masters wondered if something else was going on here. Was all he was experiencing right now a recognition of a fellow soul in torment, perhaps? Masters had never acted against a child in the way Tom Edwards had certainly acted against his children, despite all his stonewalling. But Masters had given in to overpowering impulses from time to time and had inflicted suffering on a scale to rival that of the man sitting opposite him too. That might have been in the name of what most would call the greater good, but there were many – some, indeed, in Masters's own chess club – who'd questioned whether that sort of suffering could ever be justified. Whether the means, if extreme enough, could ever justify the ends.

In truth, Masters didn't really know. He also didn't actually know what he was about to say. But suddenly he knew exactly what was behind all this and he knew in that instant too that they'd got this wrong. They'd got it wrong and they'd got the man with the nondescript face and the watery eyes sitting opposite him right now wrong as well. Perhaps it would have been better if they hadn't. Perhaps it would have been easier all round if Tom Edwards had been just another white, middle-aged male who'd simply snapped.

But all that was for later.

This was now.

Edwards looked up at the one-way mirror behind which Ros still stood, almost as if he could see her. Across the desk, Masters kept looking into Edwards's watery blue eyes almost as if he was staring into his soul.

Moments ticked down, the silence stretching until it felt like it really would break. Edwards could almost feel his eyes being wrenched back from that one-way mirror as if they were being forced back to meet the eyes of his interviewer.

Which was when Masters nodded at him again.

'They were free as in out of danger? They were safe now?'

Tom Edwards didn't reply.

He didn't need to.

'They were safe from you?'

Edwards just kept staring back at him, the expression on his face Masters's reply.

9

Two hours later and Masters was in Ros's office, which was housed in an anonymous unit on a business park.

A sign outside read *Mega-Bed Sale*; the sign left behind by the unit's previous tenants, the *B* now missing and the other letters clinging on for dear life. And Masters was staring at the slight, diminutive figure in front of him, trying to battle an all too familiar and rising irritation.

It wasn't the first time Ros had stoutly refused a request from the Head of the local Murder Squad and it wouldn't, as both he and she strongly suspected, be the last. It also wasn't the first time he'd tried to persuade her otherwise, and on each of the previous occasions he'd had the same marked lack of success.

A definition of madness that Masters had once read, and had indeed once debated with fellow devotees at his chess club, involved an individual doing the same thing over and over again whilst expecting totally different results from those exact same actions. Whether that was true or not had occupied Masters and his collection of amateur philosophers all that evening and into the small hours of the following morning. For not the first time, Masters recalled that particular exchange of views as he kept staring at the young woman standing before him.

Tom Edwards had finally started talking after his extended silence. And it didn't help his present mood that all Tom Edwards had said was still reverberating inside Masters's head.

'She was next.'

Masters had stared at Edwards from the other side of the interview desk.

'That was the idea. Right from the start. The kids: Steven, then Callum. Then Jo.'

Edwards hesitated and Masters supplied the prompt.

'And then you?'

A simple nod was all Edwards managed by way of an answer and this time Masters didn't insist on a spoken response. Something, that same intuition again perhaps, was already telling him this interview was on a knife edge. One false move either way, the introduction of one single discordant note, and Tom Edwards would scuttle back into his shell.

'So what happened?'

Edwards looked beyond Masters and for a moment Masters almost pitied him the pictures that were all too obviously dancing before his eyes. Masters had seen the results of his handiwork that night and that had been bad enough. But Edwards had performed those executions. His hands had been on warm flesh that had then turned cold.

'After the boys, I thought it'd be easier. One – two – what's another one? I'd put myself in a tunnel. Three steps, that's all it was. Three steps and then it would all be over.'

'That would still have left you.'

Edwards looked across the table and for a moment anger flashed behind his eyes.

'And how hard do you think that would have been? I'd killed my sons, I was going to kill my wife, how difficult do you think it would have been after I'd done that to them?'

Masters didn't respond. He didn't need to. It wasn't really a question and even if it had been, there would only ever have been one answer.

'So what happened?'

Edwards struggled.

'Jo was only supposed to be gone a few minutes. That's what she said, anyway. She was going to visit a friend: she only lived a few streets away; it was just a quick call. Her friend had an appointment with some doctor or someone the next day, and she just wanted to pop in and say good luck.'

'But?'

Masters supplied the prompt again.

'After half an hour she still wasn't back.'

Edwards leant closer over the small table.

'I tried, so hard, to keep myself in there, in that tunnel. I kept walking round the house, counting down the minutes, telling myself to just hang on, that it'd soon be over. One hit as she was coming through the door, that's all it'd take. I had my tools with me: one hit from one of those heavy spanners or the hammer and if that didn't kill her, it'd knock her out at least and then I could make sure.'

Edwards looked up, his eyes now orbs of silent appeal.

'Either way, if I did it right, she wouldn't know anything about it.'

Then Edwards tailed off again.

'I just couldn't do it. Maybe I could have done if she'd come back when she said, maybe then I'd still have been OK; but the longer it went on, just being there, in that house –'

Edwards tailed off again and this time his whole body shuddered.

'I'd put on some music. It was on when I was upstairs. I kept listening to it: it helped, blotted everything else out, I suppose, but even that stopped working. I didn't even hear it any more, all I could hear was the boys breathing and then not breathing and it was like that was the loudest sound I could hear: the sound of them not making any sound at all.'

Edwards looked past Masters, almost as if he'd forgotten he was there.

'Suddenly I just couldn't stomach it. Not anymore. I wasn't in that tunnel any more, I couldn't just keep counting and make it all right. I couldn't do to Jo what I'd done to Steven and to Callum so I walked out, got in the car and drove away. It was the coward's way out, I knew it was. If I loved Jo like I should, like I kept telling myself I loved her, then I'd have stayed. I'd have put her out of her misery as well, spared her all I'd spared my boys – but I didn't.'

Silence descended again like a shroud. Masters let it settle for a few moments. Now there was nothing in the world but the two of them. Everything outside had muted to a distant hum.

Then Masters spoke.

'Spared her what?'

Masters leant closer over the table.

'You said you'd spared the boys whatever it was you felt you had to protect them from, you were about to take yourself out of the frame as well, you were going to do the same to Jo, but you couldn't.'

Masters kept staring at him.

'There isn't anyone in the world who wouldn't understand why you couldn't do that, but what was it?'

Masters looked at the silent Tom Edwards.

'What was so bad it was better you ended all their lives that night, as well as your own?'

Tom Edwards looked back at Masters. But that's all he did. For the rest of the interview, and despite Masters approaching the same question from more than a dozen different angles, Tom Edwards didn't say another single word.

But in a sense, he didn't need to. Masters now knew there was something a lot bigger going on here than a suburban tragedy executed by some lowlife inadequate.

It wasn't that same intuition at work again.

It was there for anyone to see in Edwards's eyes.

Two hours later, that made it even more important in Masters's eyes that he coaxed the right response out of Ros.

'You've already got a relationship with her. I'd be starting from scratch. I'd have to caution her and put her in a police interview room. You can chat to her over a cup of tea.'

Ros just kept staring back at him, coolly.

'I'm not asking you to break the sanctity of the confessional and anyway even if I was, you're hardly the local priest.'

Masters attempted the semblance of a smile – an attempt that wasn't met with any semblance of an answering smile from Ros.

'Jo Edwards is my client.'

'She's also the wife of a murder suspect.'

Ros just stared back at him again.

This had happened on almost every investigation they'd conducted together and probably always would. There was always a time when she received a visit like this from her opposite number in Murder Squad.

She'd forge a relationship with a client and Masters would then put pressure on her to use that to provide information of some sort. And not just information either. On one notorious occasion in the past, one of Ros's clients, an equally notorious gangland leader who'd turned Queen's evidence, was found to suffer from nightmares. Masters had requested spy surveillance be installed in his bedroom to record his night-time ramblings in the hope they'd provide even more information than they were currently excavating in their daily interviews. Ros's answer had been the same. That hadn't exactly impressed Masters then, and this new refusal wasn't remotely impressing him now either.

'Tom Edwards has gone back into his shell. He came out of that shell briefly to say why he killed his boys. In his mind it was a kinder fate than the one they actually faced.'

Masters hunched closer.

'But what actually set him off on that trail of destruction? We don't know, and we don't know because there's something he's keeping back: something he's not saying, something that's terrifying him. And whatever that is is the real reason he did what he did that night.'

Masters nodded at her again as Ros stared back at him, as calm and cool as ever.

'All I'm asking is that you try and find out if she knew or even suspected what it is that might have terrified him so badly that he saw the death of himself and his family as a blessing, not a curse.'

Masters held up Tom Edwards's phone.

'We've been through his phone and his computer. So far we've found just a few faces on both of them. Are they anything to do with all this? Again, we don't know – how can we? – but does Jo?'

Ros kept looking at him.

It was the same old – very old – problem. Two police departments, two very different ends in view. For Masters and his merry band of brothers most cases were simple, even if the investigations usually proved anything but. Get a villain into court, get a conviction, move on, get another villain into court: the cycle of life in Murder Squad.

But there was always a necessary precondition. They had to actually get the villain into court. Then they had to persuade that court that the villain in question should be sent down. And for that they needed the witness – sometimes just the one, sometimes more than one, but they always needed at least one.

Ros tried to not get involved in the actual cases. She tried on most occasions not to even know anything about them – but that usually proved impossible, as it had already proved in the case of

Jo Edwards and her two dead boys. Her job was to assess the risk to any new client and then work out how best to minimise that risk. She certainly wasn't supposed to be some sort of glorified support service for Murder Squad, meaning Ros and Masters were usually on a collision course from the start.

It didn't exactly help interdepartmental relations that in the majority of cases the vast majority of Ros's clients weren't exactly innocent victims themselves. Jo Edwards might well be, but many others were seriously heavyweight criminals, most only turning Queen's evidence to secure themselves a lighter sentence when their various crimes finally came to court. Which meant, more often than not, that Ros was keeping lowlifes safe. Turning a blind eye to all they'd done, in Masters's jaundiced and oft-repeated view.

A few years before, relations between those who used witnesses to put villains away and those who tried to make sure those witnesses lived long enough to do so had deteriorated almost to the point of open warfare breaking out. Then the decision had been made to make the whole protection procedure more open and inclusive, encouraging officers from other departments to apply for secondments so as to give other units in the same force an understanding of the pressures they were under and the conflicting claims and counter-claims they continually had to juggle. Conor was one such beneficiary of that new type of transfer, although at the time he'd felt it to be anything but any sort of benefit.

It was abandoned almost as quickly as it had started. For the vast majority of officers like Masters, witnesses were a means to an end. They were plugged into a system at a certain point, discarded when that system had no further use for them. The problem being that those witnesses were also people with hopes and dreams and fears. Masters and Murder Squad saw them as the former, Ros had to deal with them as the latter.

Chalk and cheese, as Ros had reflected on countless occasions in the past and doubtless would do again. No point in even trying to square that age-old circle.

All the time, Masters was swiping through more images on Tom Edwards's phone.

'There are people here he's been in touch with over the past year or so – mostly male, some old oppos from his time in the Army, and there's some women on here too.'

Masters's voice was deepening in tone and intensity.

'We don't know who they are or how they fit into all this, but we will. We'll find out and we'll do it, but we'll do it a fuck of a lot quicker with a bit of old-fashioned co-operation.'

Masters was right about one thing and Ros knew it. He would find out. Masters had a well-deserved reputation for getting exactly what he wanted, as everyone in his department and outside it knew only too well. Which was why the human stonewall he was now encountering was all the more frustrating.

But then Ros realised that Masters had stopped talking. For a moment she thought he'd actually, albeit reluctantly, abandoned this latest attempt to recruit her onto Team Masters.

But then Ros realised he was just staring at the screen on Tom Edwards's mobile phone, zooming in on the image. And the expression on his face was one she'd never seen before. Because now Masters looked as if he'd seen a literal ghost.

Ros moved to his side and stared at the new image herself.

The image now filling the screen was of one single face.

And as she stared at it, suddenly Ros was back there again.

Back in her own private nightmare.

The five-year-old Ros raced to the front door, just a few feet behind her much older sister, Braith. The bell pressed from outside was already ringing for a second time and they were placing bets as they made for the door, trying to second-guess what it was that had brought the middle sister, Di, back this time. She'd already returned twice, the first time for her purse, the second for her phone.

Braith won the race. Later again, Ros would wonder whether it would have made any difference, whether what happened a moment later wouldn't have happened at all if a little girl had opened the door, as opposed to her grown-up sister.

A man stared back at Braith – a man who looked quite ordinary, in truth; quite everyday. Apart from the gun he was holding in his hand. As Ros stared out from the small hallway of their family home, it was all she could focus on. Everything else seemed to melt away.

With a still lost-looking Masters now staring at her, Ros took Tom Edwards's mobile phone from him.

Carefully, her fingers betraying no hint of the inner turmoil she was experiencing, Ros zoomed in on the face before her too, studying each feature in its every detail, even though she was already absolutely sure who it was she was looking at right now.

Then an uncomprehending Ros looked back at the equally uncomprehending Masters.

The man paused for a moment. Then the nozzle of the gun kicked upwards and Braith, perhaps acting on some unconscious compulsion to protect her younger sister, moved in front of the hovering Ros, who was just a few feet behind.

As Braith half-turned, the bullet exploded from the gun, smashing into her face, her brains exploding out of the back of her skull, blood running down over her neck, staining the dress Braith had picked out for the family party that night.

Ros looked up and saw the man still standing in the doorway for a moment – making sure she was dead, perhaps – then the gunman was gone.

Then she looked down the hallway at bits of her sister's brain now beginning to slide, snail-like, down the wallpaper leading up to the first-floor landing.

Back in her first-floor office, the sun was now throwing shadows across the *Mega-Bed Sale* sign outside, a sign which Ros could now see was in clear danger of losing its *M* as well as its *B*.

Ros couldn't work out what her mother was doing at first.

What she was yelling was clear enough – 999! 999! – and Ros, as if in some sort of trance, moved to the phone. But her eyes didn't leave her mother, now bent over the body of her sister.

Ros kept staring at her as a voice on the other end of the line asked what service she wanted, which was when Ros turned back to the receiver and told the operator that her sister had been shot.

As she said it, her mother moaned – which was when Ros had heard the sound of a car pulling up outside. Then, all of a sudden, Di's new husband appeared. The man they hadn't actually met up to that point, although they'd seen pictures of him; the man they only knew as Emmanuel.

Ros kept watching as Emmanuel knelt next to her sister, checking her wrists, trying to find any evidence of a pulse.

Masters might as well not have been there.

Tom Edwards had been similarly wiped from her mind.

All Ros could see was the face she'd seen all those years before, framed in the hallway of her old family home.

Ros looked away, then looked back, almost as if to break some sort of spell, but it made no difference.

Emmanuel Ocon stared back at her once again.

10

*E*VERY LOVE STORY *is a ghost story.*
*   I read that somewhere but I didn't understand it.*
At least not at the time.
But then it happened.
Then a lover became a ghost, and then I understood.
Because love haunts you.
It haunts you like a ghost.
And it haunts you long after the lover is gone.

PART TWO

TOUCHDOWN ON

A WHITE PLANET

11

GREENLAND, PRESENT DAY

MORE THAN TWENTY years after the failed paedophile sting and the end of his career with the UK police force, James Delaney – now in his mid forties but still sporting the same spare, almost ascetic frame – stepped into a graveyard overlooking a wide expanse of water packed full of giant icebergs.

By his side was a young female companion, Cecilie Lynge, her grey-blue eyes an almost perfect match for the steel blue sea below. Cecilie was a fellow officer in the national police force of Greenland, one of the twelve police districts of the *Rigspolitiet*, the Danish national police service. Both officers had made the journey up from the Commissioner's office in the capital, Nuuk, the previous afternoon.

Delaney looked down onto the bay and from out of nowhere a picture suddenly flashed before his eyes of another graveyard; this one mystical, almost beautiful. But maybe he'd been looking at it through eyes that at the time shouldn't entirely have been trusted.

Delaney had still been in his twenties. After leaving the UK, he'd spent a few aimless years wandering through South and then North America before, on an impulse, taking a flight from the Canadian Arctic to Qaanaaq, one of the northernmost settlements of Greenland. It was the first time he'd visited the country that was to become his home.

The pilot of the tiny Cessna Skymaster had been dressed in a formal white shirt, a relic from his days, improbably, as a concierge in Washington Heights. He'd swabbed the windscreen with a roll of paper towels before take-off. There'd been no control tower, or at least none that Delaney could see. After the small plane had scrabbled into the air, the pilot had climbed to twelve thousand feet in a blue expanse of sky streaked with high cloud, its engine straining all the while.

As they neared a distant ice cap and journey's end, the pilot pushed the plane into a steep descent. Delaney and the rest of his fellow passengers could see they were now just a couple of hundred metres over a dark and glassy sea, skimming icebergs as they continued their descent.

Which was when the flock of birds hit the small plane.

The birds were later identified as lesser auks. At the time they were just black streaks outside the windows. The pilot immediately jerked the aircraft to the left, taking what avoiding action he could. At the same time, they entered a giant ice-covered fjord where Delaney caught his first glimpse of the airstrip bulldozed into the tundra, a red smoke flare indicating the direction of the wind.

But the sudden manoeuvre meant the plane was approaching too fast and as the wheels crashed down onto the ice, the Cessna lurched dangerously, first to the left again and then to the right, before fishtailing down the makeshift runway. There was a crushing, grinding noise as rock hit metal and the plane flipped into a sideways skid, dragging its tail through the packed snow on either side of the landing strip before finally coming to a halt, the nose now pointing skyward again.

There hadn't actually been time to be scared. The pilot just jumped from his seat yelling at his passengers to get out, that the plane could explode at any moment. Delaney and his fellow travellers needed no second invitation.

Which was when, crawling outside into the numbing wind blasting off the frozen fjord, putting more and more distance between himself and the stricken aircraft – the stench of fuel, trickling all the while from its ruptured fuel tank, in his nostrils – Delaney saw it. A hundred metres or so across the runway: a small cemetery planted with white crosses. The rest of the passengers saw it at the same time, and almost as one everyone began smiling at each other, survivor's euphoria perhaps beginning to infuse them all at the same time.

Delaney kept looking out over this new graveyard, sited above the wide expanse of water. It may not have possessed the savage beauty of that final resting place in Qaanaaq, but it still possessed an undeniable charm as a steady procession of glaciers floated below it, out to the open sea.

The world's most productive glacier was out in that bay: the Sermeq Kujalleq, flowing down from the inland ice sheet and calving roughly 10% of all icebergs in the water between Greenland and Canada. It pushed twenty billion tons of ice into the fjord every year. The biggest ones, up to one thousand metres high, would run aground and lie on the bottom of the bay sometimes for years until they were dislodged by even larger bergs, pushing into them from behind. All would eventually float away, most heading north.

But one iceberg, over a hundred years before, had turned west and had ended up on the Canadian side of the Davis Strait, where the currents flowed south. It floated all the way down to the Grand Banks of Newfoundland, where it met a transatlantic liner on its maiden voyage. The year was 1912. And over 1,500 people lost their lives.

Of course, no one could be certain that the berg that sank *Titanic* came from that one glacier. But the town was and still is called Ilulissat, which translates as 'iceberg'. And given its name, perhaps it was always going to claim the most famous berg in the world as its own.

But it wasn't just the constant procession of icebergs that assaulted the senses of any newly arrived visitor. Even at that distance, high up above the town, you could hear the dogs – 8,000 of them, or so it was said, although no one had ever done anything like a forensically accurate count – each and every one of them howling almost constantly, as they always did at this time of the year.

In the winter, from November to April, they'd be used for transport. But in the summer, and it was now the height of midsummer, there was nothing for the dogs to do. So they just lay chained up on the ground all day and night and howled. Tourists often asked how the locals could get used to it, but those same locals didn't understand the question. You might as well have asked how they got used to the sun or the moon. How do you get used to a simple fact of life? You just get on with it. And so the locals got on with their lives, while the visitors continued with their holiday.

'The shared bus dropped her off at about six o'clock.'

Delaney and Cecilie paused as they came up to a small gate in a fence that led to more graves beyond.

'From the stop to her house would have been about a twenty-minute walk.'

Delaney nodded out across the water below them towards a distant strip of land.

'Which would have taken her across the headland?'

Cecilie nodded back. Her companion, her senior in age by some fifteen or so years as well as in rank, had clearly done his homework.

'It was a walk she'd done hundreds of times. Not just coming home from school – or choir practice, which she'd had that night – but also after visiting family or playing with friends.'

Cecilie opened the narrow gate, the two officers squeezing through the small gap one after the other.

'By seven o'clock she hadn't arrived, but her mother wasn't that worried at first as she was sometimes late after choir practice.

Alasie often used to stop off to collect things on her way home if she had a project to do.'

Delaney picked his way carefully between two well-tended graves.

'She was only thirteen but she was always doing that little extra, according to all her teachers.'

Delaney suddenly turned as a great crash sounded below them, yet another berg just calved from the glacier about to begin its own journey out into the open sea.

The ferry ride up from the capital the previous day had been nothing out of the ordinary, meaning it had been every bit as extraordinary as all trips along that stretch of coastline always tended to be. With no roads between towns or villages in his adopted country, ferry journeys were commonplace. Delaney's fellow travellers, as always, were anything but. On that particular trip, Delaney and Cecilie had been under the care of a jaunty Swedish captain on one of his habitual twelve-hour shifts at the helm, who'd kept himself awake by smoking cheroots and listening to heavy metal. Some respite from the constant drumming of the bass notes from the wheelhouse had been provided by a Danish opera singer of voluptuous physical proportions who had been blessed with an equally prodigious voice. As she demonstrated at that lunchtime's onboard karaoke entertainment, which had previously threatened only one participant: a Filipino barman intent on working his way through the greatest hits of all the classic crooners, missing each and every note along the way.

Delaney turned back and followed Cecilie as she moved on.

'By half past seven, her mother was worried. By then she'd retraced Alasie's route home, had even walked down to where the bus had stopped, but she still hadn't seen her. She started calling all her friends, but none of them had seen her since they'd left choir. She called the hall where the choir was rehearsing in case she was still there for some reason, but she wasn't in the hall either. That's when she went to the police. There were only two officers on duty at the time but they started an immediate search. Over the evening almost everyone in the town joined in, including Alasie's father, Imaneq, who had now come back from work, but they didn't find her for another twelve hours.'

Delaney kept looking out over the water. Even with the distance of all those years, it all still felt horribly immediate and all too real.

The biting cold, the heavy snow that began to fall later in the evening, according to all the reports, the panic in the parents' voices as they called their daughter's name over and over again.

The silence that was their only reply.

'She was found around ten the next morning. One of the local dog handlers had shot two of his dogs the night before.'

Cecilie paused again, the smooth flow of her briefing halting momentarily, and Delaney looked at her, surprised. For dogs to be shot was standard practice, either when they were of no more use for hunting due to age, or at the first sign of any kind of illness. The biggest cull, admittedly, would have come some few months before that when only the dogs worth feeding throughout the summer would be retained, but dogs could be shot at any time. But it wasn't the fate of two dogs that had momentarily ambushed the new recruit.

'He'd left the carcasses outside his house with the rest of the trash to be taken away. Which was why no one had seen her before. Whoever killed Alasie had hidden her body beneath them.'

Cecilie took another file from her bag.

'That morning one of her schoolfriends came forward: a boy, Tobias Lundblad. He was in Alasie's class in school. He said he'd seen Alasie on her way home from choir after the bus had dropped her off, making him the last person to see her alive.'

'Why hadn't he been interviewed before?'

'He'd been in the local hospital all night. He'd been playing down by the water and decided to go swimming, but he'd stayed in too long. When he finally arrived home, he was hypothermic. His mother threw a comforter over him but it wasn't enough, he was already ice-cold and beginning to turn blue. When he began slurring his speech, she rushed him to the doctor, so he was being treated while the rest of his friends and classmates were being questioned.'

'And did he talk to her? When he saw her that previous night?'

'According to his statement, she was singing when he saw her walking along the headland, but she stopped the minute she saw him. He said she looked embarrassed. Children that age would be, I suppose.'

Cecilie didn't register the slight freeze that had now stilled her senior officer's face.

'According to Lundblad, he just walked on. Then, as he came out beside the bay, he heard her starting to sing again.'

Cecilie put away the file, scanned the graveyard, pausing as she spotted what she was looking for, at the far end just in front of another white fence.

'A few moments later she must have been snatched off the track, presumably by someone who'd been waiting for her. He beat her around the head with the butt of a gun. When she was found she had five deep gashes in her skull. Then he raped her before shooting her twice in the chest as she lay on the ground. Maybe he shot her after he raped her because she recognised him, we don't know.'

Cecilie paused again.

'But if he was that intent on covering his tracks, it was odd that he then just dropped his gun. It was found just off the track: a US Army-issue, Colt .45 pistol. It was manufactured in the Lake Cross Armoury in 1942 and shipped to US forces in

Europe sometime after that. But that's when the trail ran cold. With so many weapons in circulation at that time, there was never going to be any record of who that particular gun had been issued to, and anyway any one of the servicemen stationed up at Kangerlussuaq could have sold it to on to some local or just lost it or something.'

Delaney nodded. Kangerlussuaq, or to use its Danish name at the time, Søndre Strømfjord, had been a US airbase during the Second World War and an American presence had later been maintained there throughout the Cold War as well. During the Korean War, a large hospital on the base had also received American soldiers too badly hurt to be sent home. They might have received more effective treatment back in the US, but their injuries were considered too corrosive from a public relations point of view and so they were dispatched to that particular outpost of the frozen north, where they remained largely out of sight.

Delaney himself had found a job there when he'd first arrived in the country, helping to maintain the miles of steaming pipes that serviced the underground missile sites, taking walks in his spare time along the river that flowed through the centre of the base. An American civilian who'd also come to work on the airbase had grown homesick and Delaney had given him enough money for his airfare home in exchange for his dogs, his sled and small shack. For a few months and to the amusement of his new companions, Delaney toyed with the dream of a new life as a latter-day explorer, touring far-flung communities, absorbing himself in the ancient ways of the hunter.

Before reality, as it always did, kicked in.

'They took too much on trust.'

Delaney looked at his junior officer, Cecilie's tone suddenly strident, vehement even.

'Lundblad?'

She nodded.

'No one wanted to believe it. Another thirteen year old? And a local boy as well?'

Cecilie shook her head.

'Imagine if something like that happened now? Would everyone shake their heads and say, "It's impossible, we know this boy – we know his family"?'

Delaney looked out over the bay. It wasn't the first time he'd heard similar sentiments. Over the years there'd been a growing chorus of dark mutterings against the now-adult Tobias Lundblad.

Cecilie rolled on.

'It wouldn't matter what age he was or where he came from, no one now would let him go, not until they were 100% sure he didn't even know what a gun looked like, let alone where to get hold of one and how to use it.'

Delaney remained silent as, unbidden, another memory floated in front of his eyes, an infamous image from his own country caught on CCTV: two small boys escorting a toddler from a crowded shopping centre only to savagely kill him a few moments later, the small boy stoned to death on a railway line by boys who were little more than children themselves.

'Why did he go for a swim like that? Why that particular afternoon? What happened to suddenly make him want to plunge into ice-cold water and stay there till he almost died?'

Cecilie quietened. Then she nodded down at a grave, now just a few feet away in the shadow of that white fence. Delaney read the simple inscription on the granite slab.

In Loving Memory of Alasie Kalia.

That was it. Nothing about the way she'd died or the manner of her passing. Not even a date of birth or death. Just a simple testament to a life cut short with no explanation as to how or why. The sun was now full on it and the black granite slab seemed to be almost sparkling as light played on its surface, marking it out from the graves on either side. But that wasn't the only thing marking it out.

All the other headstones in that row were pitted, their inscriptions faded over time. One on the end had really suffered the double ravages of the weather and decades of neglect, but even those which had been tended more carefully were showing definite signs of age.

But Alasie's headstone wasn't showing any sign of age, and for good reason. It had been replaced a month or so ago. The local stonemason who replaced it had been contacted by letter by a member of the family and asked to carry out the work. The letter specified the grade of granite he was to use as well as the words he was to inscribe. He quoted a price, which was agreed and he was paid in cash in advance.

Delaney kept looking down at the headstone, the sunlight still playing directly onto it.

After he'd installed it, the stonemason had got in touch with the family to make sure everything was in order and that they were pleased with his handiwork. But they knew nothing about it. The name and address he'd been given was false. He started asking round in the town but no matter how hard he tried, he kept coming up against the same brick wall. No one, be that family or otherwise, knew anything about the commissioning of the new headstone. Which was when the uneasy stonemason had notified the local police.

Delaney kept staring down at the headstone as he maintained his silent vigil. All this meant that years after Alasie Kalia was killed, someone had gone to a lot of trouble to put a new headstone on her grave and that same someone seemed to have gone to an equal amount of trouble to make sure no one knew who they were.

Delaney kept looking down at Alasie's grave.

So what was this? A late attack of conscience on the part of a killer? Or the work of someone else, someone who'd perhaps found out something about that killer all these years later?

Delaney turned, looking out over the bay again as another berg calved from the Sermeq Kujalleq with another great crash and began its journey from the inland ice sheet down into the fjord and out into the open sea.

The problem was that this new puzzle now had to take its place in a whole landscape of other puzzles, all of which demanded even more immediate answers.

Including, and this was one of the most puzzling of all, a text that had arrived for him the previous evening from the Commissioner's office back in Nuuk.

Not to mention the small, slight female figure which had just appeared at the far end of the graveyard.

TWO DAYS EARLIER, and three hours after first staring at that bombshell photo on Tom Edwards's phone, Ros had been sitting at a table in a famed local landmark, a converted church down in the Bay.

The church in question was something of a city institution, built by an organisation called the Norwegian Church Abroad, part of the Church of Norway. Briefly threatened by demolition some years before, a Norwegian support group in Bergen had raised a quarter of a million pounds for its renovation, preserving many of its original features including the pulpit and central chandelier.

In recent times the church had become something of a place of refuge and reflection for Ros. At the moment it was scoring highly on the former count but the latter was proving more of a problem. Ros's whole world had just been blasted apart, as it had similarly exploded on at least one other occasion too. On both occasions the same man had been responsible.

'The photo's been dated.'

Masters, sitting opposite her, flicked through a report that had just been forwarded through on his own phone.

'It's definitely no more than a couple of days old.'

Ros hardly heard him. She just kept looking at the face on the screen looking back at her. She'd only seen that face twice in her whole life, and those sightings had been twenty years apart, but it was as if every feature had been burned into her eyes.

'That's not some miracle of carbon dating, by the way.'

Masters hesitated.

'That's down to one of the other people in the picture.'

Masters looked up from his report to a still silent Ros, who was totally floundering now.

Emmanuel Ocon had been her sister's husband.

He was the reason her family had been destroyed.

Not that he'd escaped the mayhem himself. Emmanuel had also been killed by the same forces that had moved so implacably and ruthlessly against her totally ordinary and innocent family.

Or so Ros had believed. Until a few hours earlier, when she'd stood with Masters in her first-floor office, looking at an all too familiar face on the screen of a mobile phone.

Across the same table, pictures from the past were beginning to open up in front of Masters's eyes too and it was, unusually, a part of the past he'd shared with Ros. There were precious few such memories like that, despite the years they'd spent working together on a multiplying number of cases. Battles and disputes were commonplace. That sort of shared experience was not.

Ros had asked Masters to be with her the last time she'd seen Emmanuel, in a small semi-detached house on the outskirts of the city. He hadn't quite known why at the time. Ros hadn't told him too much and certainly hadn't told him this was to be the first meeting between her sister and her husband in over twenty years.

Masters had pieced most of it together subsequently. He understood that some sort of family reunion had been taking place, but it wasn't like any reunion he'd ever seen before. Tension almost dripped from the walls. The four family members assembled for that most curious of gatherings barely looked at each other, which was yet another mystery to add to what had fast become a growing number.

Masters had looked around the room as they all waited for their visitor to arrive. The father seemed quiet, maybe too quiet; the mother anything but. She didn't seem too mobile but her body was still a bag of nerves, eyes darting everywhere.

She looked hunted, as if she was waiting for some unseen and inevitable blow to strike.

The other daughter – Ros's sister, a woman he'd been introduced to as Di – seemed rather more cool and collected, although when Masters stood as the doorbell rang and moved to answer the door with Ros herself by his side, he could see she was trembling.

Masters's presence had been part of the larger unspoken agreement made in the aftermath of the fate suffered at Masters's hands by the bad apple, Donovan Banks. The betrayal Banks had set in train justified that fate in Masters's view, and Ros had found it difficult to disagree. They'd never actually spoken about it, and Ros had certainly not said a word to the officers who came along to mount the subsequent investigation.

So as far as Masters was concerned, the message was received and well understood. Ros wasn't going to do anything to nail Masters, so in return, Masters would help Ros out too. He hadn't quite understood how and in what way, much as he hadn't understood what that strange gathering of lost souls in that small suburban house was all about, and his cautious attempts at the time to find out even a little more about it all had been met with the usual and characteristic stonewall from his sparky colleague from the Protection Unit. Ros just made it all too clear that if he didn't want to be there then he didn't have to be.

But Masters had wanted to be there, and for reasons he once again couldn't entirely explain. Maybe it was simply because for the first time Masters felt as if he was on the brink of some sort of breakthrough with her. But nothing, as he'd reflected on more than one occasion both previously and since, was ever quite that simple with Ros.

As Ros, and her elder sister now too, had moved towards the door, Masters had seen the bag-of-nerves mother looking at him, curious. Her eyes had said it all. Clearly, she couldn't work out the relationship between himself and her youngest daughter. She wasn't alone. Masters had ducked her stare and followed the two women out into the hall.

As the front door opened Masters had seen a fit middle-aged man with slightly greying hair standing in the doorway, his head slightly bowed.

And then some instinct had awoken. Masters's whole body had tensed as he almost literally smelt danger.

Then he'd seen the blood beginning to stain the front of the man's coat. As his insides began to spill out onto the front step, the man had half-turned and Masters had realised that sometime in the last few seconds he'd been hit by a bullet, designed to explode just after impact. The bullet had entered his body in the middle of his back and exploded deep inside his stomach, forcing his intestines, liver and kidneys out from beneath the ruptured skin.

A second later another bullet had ended the life of Ros's sister, Di: the long-lost lover he'd returned to meet.

Back in the Norwegian Church, Ros kept looking at Masters.

'You saw the whole thing.'

Ros's eyes drilled down into Masters's own eyes.

'You saw what happened to him.'

Ros kept staring at him, willing him to contradict the evidence of that single photograph on the phone before them, and perhaps more importantly the world it had just opened up.

Masters just looked back at her, without replying. He didn't need to. From the few nuggets he'd managed to piece together in the last year or so, Ros had been scarred by illusion, double-dealing and treachery all her life. So was this really so surprising? Her whole life, ever since she'd been a small child, had been built on shifting sands. Was it really going to be such a shock to now discover more of the same?

Yes, Masters had been there that day and yes, like her, Masters had taken everything that had happened on face value. Her sister had been rushed into an ambulance that had arrived within minutes, but she was quite clearly already beyond any help any medic could proffer. The husband was still alive at the time but given the extent of his injuries, which both Ros and Masters had seemingly witnessed at such close quarters, it was absolutely no surprise to them to learn that he'd died in a different ambulance on his way to the nearest A & E.

Only Emmanuel had quite clearly not died. Whatever trickery had taken place literally before their eyes was something to be investigated later, so far as Masters was concerned. For now, there was only one priority for him and that wasn't ghosts, albeit real-life ghosts from the past. It was the present that was much more on his mind.

'Di.'

Ros cut across again, her mind still working at its trademark hundred miles an hour.

'That's all we were thinking about, getting her to hospital.'

Ros didn't finish. She didn't need to. Di's heart – incredible as it had seemed to Masters, who had witnessed at first hand the assassin's bullet blasting into her brain – had still been beating. But that bullet had still killed her. Even if somehow Di had survived, there would have been nothing left of the sister Ros had only just been reacquainted with after two decades apart. This had all been confirmed by an exhausted surgeon as he walked back into the relatives' room a short time later, his scrubs stained with blood and his face telling Ros and Masters all they needed to know.

Ros hadn't spoken either. She'd just nodded back at him and then, without even looking at Masters, had left the hospital and returned to that same small semi-detached house to tell her mum and dad the news they already knew in their hearts.

Somewhere during the course of that same night they'd received the news that Emmanuel had also died, but that had scarcely registered. Masters dimly remembered some arrangements being referred to for his body to be repatriated to the land of his birth, a holiday island in the Indian Ocean where he'd first met a girl called Di on a beach, in an encounter that was to change not only his life and hers but the lives of the rest of her family as well.

Back in the present day, Masters looked at the wracked figure of Ros, her fingers now cradling a large mug of untouched coffee.

Of that family there was now just the one sole, surviving member. Ros's mum had died of what were euphemistically called 'natural causes' a year or so after Di's murder, but no one believed her death to be anything but a direct result of that. Her heart had simply been broken by the latest killing and, seeing all around her a world that only promised more heartbreak and pain, she'd simply slipped away one otherwise uneventful night in her sleep.

That had left Ros and her father, a still proud man called Macklyn, who had once commanded his own transport business and patrolled his lorry yard like a mini-Colossus, but his and Ros's mutual past had caught up with him too.

Now the former family of five had shrunk to just the one.

'He was a man who'd reinvented himself time and again. He'd presented one face to you and your family, another to his employers, another to his associates. He was at least three different men to three different sets of people.'

Ros kept looking at him, Masters's tone alerting her to what was to come. Or maybe it was her own finely honed instincts, her ever-present awareness of the approach of imminent danger.

Masters nodded back at Ros.

'A chameleon, forever shifting shape.'

Masters didn't say another word. Once more, he didn't need to. His eyes were now telling Ros all she needed to know and somewhere deep inside she felt another world collapse, while her face remained poker-still as always.

But something had changed now and changed forever, and she knew it.

Which was when Ros stood, turned for the door and walked out of the converted church without even a backward glance.

One hour later, Ros and Masters were walking by the Bay. Behind them on the water, speedboats were performing some sort of display, a curtain-raiser to a powerboat race that was taking place at the weekend.

To their side, police tape cordoned off a stretch of water by an upmarket hotel. A reveller on a stag night had decided to crown a whole day's drinking by attempting to jump into the bay from a tenth-floor window. His intention was to swim to an equally upmarket restaurant just visible on the other side of the breakwater. His companions were already piling into taxis to head for that same spot and he thought he'd surprise them by getting there first.

His neck snapped in two the minute his head hit the water but he didn't feel a thing. He'd already passed out due to his legs fracturing as they too smashed into the shallow and debris-strewn silt. The rest of the stag party arrived at the restaurant completely oblivious to the frantic activity taking place outside the hotel they'd just left.

During the course of the evening their companion was missed but they just assumed he'd gone to his room to sleep off the effects of their collective and already prodigious drinking. They all raised a glass to him and toasted his absence at about the same time the local pathologist was confirming his death a mile or so away in the city morgue.

Ros looked out over the water at the scene of a totally needless and completely pointless death. Then she looked back at Masters, more victims of totally needless and completely pointless deaths before her eyes now too.

'How long have you known?'

Ros stopped as her mind flashed back to every case they'd ever worked on together. Dozens – if not hundreds – of investigations.

Had Masters really known all that time?

Had he journeyed with her through each and every one of them, knowing all the time her deepest, darkest secret?

Ros seized onto a name as a possibility presented itself.

'Jukes.'

Jukes, or to give him his full title, DCI Jukes, had been Ros's senior officer in the Protection Unit, although he was always more the consummate politician than the career cop. But maybe, as Ros had reflected on many occasions in the past, he'd had to be. No one rose to what had been Jukes's exalted rank without being able to sup with princes and dance with devils. Ros hadn't seen too many princes grace the corridors of the Protection Unit during his time in charge but she'd seen plenty of devils and Jukes had battled many demons there too.

But his last battle had been against the most dangerous and insidious one of all – the devil inside – and it was a battle that Jukes had disastrously and ignominiously lost.

Masters shook his head, his old opposite number in the Protection Unit and a former colleague in one other unit as well before his eyes now too. Masters had always been aware of Jukes's particular failings. At one time, when the two of them had first met as rookie cops, it had been prostitutes. Jukes's first few visits had all followed the usual time-honoured pattern, but he soon wanted something different. A two-girl booking initially provided some extra spice but then he'd investigated the local S&M scene, although most of the stuff he'd been offered had been pretty tame, apparently – little more than ordinary working girls with a whip.

Deep down, and Masters had seen it in him from the start, Jukes had always needed to refine the thrill, push whatever boundary he'd previously transgressed. In idle moments Masters sometimes wondered just where that would lead his somewhat tortured colleague. Not even Masters could have predicted it would lead him into a five-year campaign targeting pre-pubescent girls in train carriages.

'Jukes never knew. To be honest I don't think he ever cared enough to try and find out anyway.'

Ros cut across.

'So?'

Ros's eyes never left his face as Masters's reply came back, prompt.

'Just under a year.'

Inside Ros's head, the next connection was made equally promptly.

'So it was Macklyn?'

Masters nodded. Ros's late father had indeed been the all-important key.

Ros's next question came hard on the heels of the previous one, and it wouldn't be the last question either – that was already all too obvious.

'How?'

But Masters paused, growing impatient. Inquests and explanations would come. Apart from anything else, he had little doubt that Ros would make sure of it. But for now, and so far as he was concerned, there were more pressing matters to resolve. Matters that didn't only involve Masters and his current and ongoing investigation but ones that now, and as was only too obvious, had entrapped Ros as well.

'I want to bring you into Murder Squad.'

Ros stared at him again.

'You'll have the same rank you have now. Same conditions of employment, nothing will change. To all intents and purposes, it'll be a secondment – much as Conor's move across to you – at the start, anyway. We can even spin the same line we spun back then if you like: hands across the ocean, one department observing at first hand the inner workings of another, all in the interests of building a closer working relationship. No one's going to care too much anyway, in truth.'

Ros kept staring at him.

'So far as the Protection Unit's concerned, Conor can move up to take temporary charge. He can still report to you if you want to keep tabs on him, but you and I both know there'd be no need. You've turned him into the officer I never could. I don't know how you did it, but Conor's the real deal now, so there'd be no problem leaving him to oversee things for a while.'

Ros's eyes, once again, still hadn't left his face.

'We take joint charge of the investigation into the present-day whereabouts of the man we both know as Emmanuel Ocon. Somewhere along the way, I'll find out his connection to Tom Edwards. Once I find that, I'm going to be a hell of a lot closer to finding out why a totally ordinary if somewhat anally retentive suburban husband, the archetypal Mondeo man, ended the life of his two children and only just bottled out of doing the same to his wife.'

Masters nodded at the still staring Ros.

'I'll find out what spooked him so badly he couldn't see any other way out, and if I find that out then I might save his life and the life of his wife along the way. I don't care too much about the first; but so far as Jo's concerned, it'd be some small victory, at least.'

Masters leant closer.

'And how many other people like Jo are there? How many other Tom Edwards? So far, as well as Emmanuel, there's more than fifty other faces on that phone of his. We'll identify each and every one but that's going to take time, and my guess is that each time we do identify and then find one, we're going to find the same kind of character as Tom Edwards: a frightened little man who can't even begin to tell us what he's frightened of, because whatever it is terrifies them far more than anything I can ever threaten them with.'

Masters hunched closer still.

'Steven and Callum's lives were ended in moments. What demons drove Tom Edwards to do that, and what the fuck has Emmanuel Ocon, or whatever he calls himself now, got to do with it?'

Then Masters paused.

'And we do something else as well.'

Ros just kept looking at him.

'I saw photos of that wall, that date – those numbers on that wallpaper, daubed in your father's blood.'

Involuntarily, the same picture flashed before Ros's eyes. Once again she could see herself walking into the hallway, looking up at the blood streaked all over the ceiling and walls, blood that on one of those walls spelt out that sequence of numbers.

As if she was back there again, Ros listened once more to the banter among the attending officers about the intelligence of this particular hired assassin. Ros had realised immediately that this wasn't a mistake but a prediction. The pursuers who'd sanctioned the original hit on her family had waited more than two decades to find and eliminate their last victim, and that date scrawled on the wall was a message.

On that day, exactly one year on from the death of her father, they'd be coming after her too.

The sole remaining child.

The use of the gun and her father's blood would also have been deliberate, all intended to raise echoes of the original shooting of Braith, a promise that what happened before had not only happened again, but would happen once more too.

Ros had hidden her emotions then as she was hiding them now. She'd just kept looking at that date, daubed in her father's blood.

Back out on the quayside, Masters nodded at her once more.

'We might just stop another murder.'

Ros looked back at him. Masters didn't need to say what he said next, but he did.

'Yours.'

Ros kept looking back at him, still not replying.

'And it might finally explain what happened.'

Masters kept looking at her. It was the one thing that would guarantee her acceptance of his offer and he knew it.

'To you and to your family.'

Ros looked out over the water again.

'All those years ago.'

ONE HOUR AFTER she'd first appeared at the far end of that graveyard overlooking Disko Bay, the small, slight new arrival who had been introduced to Delaney and Cecilie as a visiting Detective Sergeant from the UK, Ros Gilet, approached a small house bolted onto rocks.

What exactly Ros was doing in Greenland hadn't been properly explained to Delaney. She'd visited the country once before; he'd been told that much, although that seemed to have been as a private individual and not on any sort of police business. She was here now apparently to oversee the possible transfer of the small girl they were about to visit into an international protection programme.

But there was obviously much more to her sudden appearance than that. It was equally obvious to Delaney that he wasn't going to be told any more for now though, so while Cecilie returned to Nuuk, Delaney and his new companion made the visit that was actually the main purpose of this trip in the first place.

Inside that small house was a family that had suffered the violent loss some years before of a daughter called Alasie Kalia, whose grave – and new headstone – they'd just visited.

A family who, in the last few days, had also suffered the equally violent loss of a husband and father called Imaneq.

As the two officers approached the small house, Ros felt her nostrils flare as she inhaled air bleached sour from kitchen scraps sourced from the bars and cafés in the town to feed the sled dogs chained outside.

As Delaney knocked on the door, she looked around, taking in drying clothes flapping on makeshift washing lines, the arms of the shirts and the legs of the trousers almost frozen stiff. All around them children played.

A moment later the door was opened by a wary-eyed middle-aged woman, affording Ros and Delaney their first sighting of the mother of the murdered girl whose grave had been recently and puzzlingly graced by that new headstone. A bereaved mother who had also just become a widow.

Dorthe Kalia didn't speak a single word, just nodded at the two officers before turning and leading them inside past piles of winter clothing, mittens, polar bear pants and caribou skins and on into a small room where her youngest daughter, Desna, eleven years old, was waiting.

Ros glanced down at the file in her hand, then back at Desna, sibling to a murdered sister she'd never known. The young girl seemed far away, barely focusing on the new arrivals. Her unblinking eyes seemed to be fixed on a very different and distant landscape instead.

Despite all appearances to the contrary, Desna Kalia actually was aware of the man sitting opposite and the woman at his side. She also understood why they were there. Desna and her family had endured many similar visits since she'd returned those few nights before and told her shocked mother all she'd seen.

The days since had passed in a blur as she'd retraced her steps, time and again, back to that clearing, as the local police had removed her father's body and as neighbours had gathered in small knots up and down their small settlement and held inquests in hushed tones on what might have happened and what it all might mean.

Even their dogs had cowered outside, not howling as they always did as strangers approached, hoping for a new source of food. As one, the pack hunkered down, keeping silent, their eyes averted from the new arrivals.

Desna also understood all the questions she'd been asked, and which she assumed she'd now be asked again. She was the only one who'd seen her father's attackers, after all, and even if all she could remember were vague, large, shapes, she knew that there might be something in those hazy images that might help find them.

The problem being that all the time she was being talked to, all she was seeing was the face of her mother. One hour after she'd told her all she'd seen in that clearing, Desna and Dorthe had been standing outside their small house. Down in the harbour, a ferry was docking. Two kayakers were out on the water – they'd been keeping pace with it for the last few moments of its trip and the ferry's klaxon suddenly sounded a warning to them to get out of the way.

Which was when both mother and daughter saw it. A hunter on that same quayside had just driven his dogsled through a flock of Arctic gulls. The birds all flew from the path of the approaching sled but one remained, not through stubbornness or defiance but because its foot had frozen to the ice. The dogsled missed the bird, but the danger was far from over. The gull was struggling to escape the grip of the ice but couldn't, and the other gulls began to return. They circled for a few moments around their trapped companion before attacking and killing it, beating at each other with their wings as they competed for a taste of the unexpected feast.

Dorthe turned away from the now cannibalised bird, and looked back at her daughter. She didn't say a word. She didn't need to. Her eyes were now telling her daughter all she needed to be told.

Don't do or say anything.

This is what will happen if you do.

They will return and they will devour you.

Desna had no idea if her mother's silent warning extended to these new visitors as well. All she had to go on were her instincts, but she couldn't even trust them now. She hadn't sensed danger that evening, at least not until it was almost too late. She would never have followed that trail into those woods if she had.

So for now, Desna just maintained her unblinking stare.

Across the room from Desna, Ros glanced down at the report in her hand again. It was a report she'd read only once on the flight in from Iceland, but its every detail was still imprinted in front of her.

Which was something that happened time and again. Whether that was some kind of overidentification at work, or just the by-product of an overactive imagination, she didn't know. All Ros did know was that the more acute the horror, the more visceral the crime scene outlined in any report, the more vividly Ros's imagination seemed to recreate it.

As if it wasn't a second-hand report, simple words on a page. As if she herself had been there and had seen it all too.

A low and distant drumming on the ice-packed road told him they'd arrived. He checked his watch. Their timing was exact as he'd been told it would be. These people prided themselves on attention to detail. It had been expensive flying them in from Denmark but if tonight's objective was achieved, and he had no reason to doubt it would, then it would be more than justified.

He looked out over the impacted snow. The days when one could trust in the natural discretion and reserve of the men in this country were long gone, it seemed. Along with so many other things.

The low drumming was louder now, more intense. They'd come in via the heliport the previous evening and had quickly identified and taken charge of the truck he'd sourced. Should anyone be watching – and there were always plenty of curious eyes around – they stacked some cameras and audio equipment in the rear of the truck. Another documentary crew shooting yet more footage for an ever-multiplying number of channels broadcasting a seemingly endless supply of wallpaper.

They'd taken a quick tour of the town a short time earlier, looking for a spot such as this. They'd driven past a succession of front-loaders which up to a few days earlier had been retrieving ice for the town's domestic water supply, past the Kommune offices and grocery and clothing stores. Then they'd taken one of the roads that led nowhere apart from a dead end, before turning off the track.

The drumming was now close at hand and he tensed as the large truck now appeared before him. He remained tense as the driver's door opened and a figure in a dark suit, unmistakably Danish somehow, emerged. Two other figures, also Danes, were visible in the back.

'Move your car off the road.'

He stared back, blank for a moment.

'We don't want anyone wondering what it's doing parked here late at night, no one inside.'

He did as he was told. They were right – he should have thought of it himself. Cars such as his would be easily identified. That task complete, he climbed into the passenger seat of the truck and nodded as his contact made brief introductions. The men in the back made little effort to hide their lack of interest in him. They were interested in one thing and one thing only right now, and that was the night's sport.

Then, suddenly, they heard it. Another drumming sound, only this time the sound was more high-pitched, tinnier somehow, a constant whine from a two-stroke engine sounding clear in the still night air, as well as an occasional misfire. The lead figure in the front of the vehicle nodded at the two men behind, and spoke just the one word.

'Now.'

The men exited, almost casually. Seconds later a large metal barrier, taken from the back of the truck and concealed inside the bags containing the cameras and audio equipment, was unfolded in sections and laid across the small road. Whether they'd brought it with them from Denmark or sourced it locally, he didn't know. In truth, he didn't care. His mouth was dry now, his heart pounding.

The sound of the approaching motorbike was louder. The spot had been carefully chosen. Once the rider swung round the corner he'd be virtually upon the obstruction. He'd then have two choices: continue on and smash into it, or wrench his bike to the left or right and plunge into one of the two ditches lining the side of the track.

A moment later the motorcyclist rounded the corner at speed, clearly keen to get home; the speed he was travelling meaning he didn't even have the luxury of choice as a moment later he hit the metal barrier full on. A moment later again and the two men were hauling a bloodied figure from beside the stricken motorbike before throwing him into one of the back seats of the truck.

Sitting in the front seat beside the driver, he looked round, making sure the rider recognised him. The rider's eyes were open and he was breathing heavily through his mouth, his nose clearly broken. Small shards of stone could be seen embedded in his face. One of the men produced a roll of heavy-duty tape and secured the casualty's arms and legs, pinning them to his body while the other removed and folded up the barrier from the track before putting it back behind the rear seats.

All the time, the driver himself just stared straight ahead, seemingly taking no notice of all that was taking place behind.

Their tasks completed, the two men climbed in the back of the vehicle, one each side of the now-trussed motorcyclist. Then the driver accelerated away, hard, the tail of the lumbering truck fishtailing as he did so.

The two men in the rear seat turned to their hapless captive and for the next few moments all that could be heard was a succession of blows and muffled grunts.

They drove for another few minutes, passing no other vehicle. The driver swung off the track onto another even narrower track and followed it all the way down to an open clearing. Then the driver stopped the engine and nodded at his two companions, still either side of the now moaning body in the back.

Now there wasn't even a single word by way of an instruction. Just a simple nod.

The two men removed the tape and pulled at their captive, who suddenly fought to stay in the vehicle. However bad the last few minutes had been, some instinct was telling him a worse ordeal now lay ahead. He kicked a feeble leg out at them, but one of the men just snapped it between his hands, as casually as you'd snap the neck of an ailing dog, before hauling him by his now broken leg down into the snow, where the other man kicked him hard in the stomach. The motorcyclist lay on the ground, curled into a broken ball, and started to make urgent choking noises.

The first of the men, the one who'd just broken his leg with his bare hands, next lined up the captive's head and took a kick at it in the manner of a footballer lining up a penalty. The crack echoed around the clearing, sending a fox – watching from a few metres away – bolting for cover. None of the three visitors from overseas even glanced its way. They hauled their captive to his feet instead, streams of vomit now pouring from his nostrils. Some of the vomit spattered onto the suit of one of the attackers which earned the captive a karate-style chop across the throat at which point he began to fit, his back arching as he did so. The next moment he was curled up again in agony as he was kicked in the testicles.

One of the men next brought out an iron bar from the truck and used it to hit him about the head and body. The sound of unprotected bones being broken echoed around the clearing, sending other animals to follow the lead of the fox, all scuttling for cover.

After a few more moments of vicious beating, they paused. Their victim opened a bruised eye, looked across at the man who'd arranged all this, the only man he knew of all those assembled in the remote clearing, and whispered just one word.

'Please.'

The driver crossed to him, yanking open his mouth, and what he saw inside didn't seem to please him because he nodded back at his two large companions.

'There's a rope in the back. String him up and cut him open, let's get this over with.'

The captive tried to scream but no sound emerged, which was when the only man the captive recognised finally made his intervention, speaking the only word he'd uttered since the beating started.

'Enough.'

The driver looked back at him.

The man who had just spoken hesitated, making sure the captive registered his hesitation. Then he nodded, albeit a little reluctantly, back at his watching companion.

The driver turned back to the captive, who was now keening softly, leaning close to his bloodied head before yanking it back. He spoke for a minute, no more. His captive probably didn't understand a single word that was being said by that time, but he nodded anyway. Then he closed his eyes.

The two men who'd administered the beating waited for a few moments, but then their faces clouded as those eyes remained closed and an all too familiar realisation dawned.

The night's sport was over.

Ros looked across the room at the silent Desna. The girl had found her father's smashed, abandoned motorbike that night. No attempt had been made to conceal the tyre tracks leading away from the scene of what was clearly some kind of accident and she had followed those tyre tracks on into the woods.

Desna arrived just in time to witness the final part of the beating, but sensibly had concealed herself in the undergrowth while it was taking place. A short time later the vehicle that had made the tyre tracks left, with three or four men inside.

Desna moved out from her hiding place and walked into the clearing and up to the body that had now been left for the returning animals to devour. By morning, and as the departing men knew only too well, little would be left.

Desna looked down at her father's mutilated body but she actually felt little at that moment. Later, unaccustomed emotions would swamp her, but she'd known little of regret or loss up to that point in her life, even though her parents had endured more than their share of both. And anyway, her father – already approaching late middle age when she'd been born – had always seemed a distant figure to her. Other children had fathers who played with them, took part in their games, but hers never had. Not because he didn't care: she understood that. He'd just always been more like an aged grandfather than the more normal sort of parent all her other friends seemed to have.

So Desna looked down at the broken and bleeding body that was once her living, breathing, if somewhat distant, father for a moment longer.

Then she returned home.

Across the room, Delaney already knew this was hopeless.

The facts here were simple enough, even though all his instincts were already telling him that nothing else about this killing was likely to be simple at all.

Twenty years before, a young girl, Alasie Kalia, had been murdered by a person or persons unknown. In the last month a new headstone had been placed on her grave, also by a person or persons unknown.

Then, a few nights ago, her father had been murdered too – perhaps again by those same person or persons unknown.

So did Imaneq Kalia, the now murdered father of the long-dead Alasie, know something about that new headstone?

Had he discovered the identity of that mystery donor and had that discovery cost him his life?

And now there was Desna, the only surviving child of this stricken family; a child clearly at risk and the ostensible reason for his new companion's presence in that house right now.

Had Desna seen something she wasn't telling them? Was there something locked behind those frightened young eyes that might threaten this young girl now too?

But all that was for another time, if at all, and he knew it. For now, Delaney and Ros were going to have to leave this house, having secured absolutely nothing in the way of any extra eyewitness testimony from either Desna or her mother.

Dorthe Kalia watched, still silent as the two police officers made their preparations to leave.

Why had Imaneq done it? That's what she couldn't understand. Hadn't they trotted out the same mantra time and again, to each other and to everyone else?

Keep quiet.

Stay silent.

Keep your head down.

And they'd done that. They'd done everything they were told. Everything that would guarantee their safety and the safety of their family.

From time to time the pressure became almost unbearable, of course it did; at the usual times of the year, like birthdays or the anniversary of Alasie's killing. Then that certain silence would settle over the room. Neither she nor Imaneq needed to say anything. One look would tell each of them all they needed to know.

But it passed, it always did. They got through the day, survived whatever had sparked that most difficult of silences and moved on. And most important of all, their family remained out of harm's reach.

Maybe it was Desna coming along all those years later. They'd acted so quickly with their second daughter, a much smaller child at the time, who had idolised Alasie virtually from birth. They'd spirited her well out of harm's way before anyone in the town could possibly have known what they were doing or could act to prevent it, even changing her name to further distance her from her former family.

The rumours had circulated for years. Young Inuit girls – most around twelve or thirteen – would suddenly disappear; spirited abroad, some said, for purposes unimaginable. The problem being, those purposes could be imagined and only too clearly, and it chilled every parent in the town to their core. Alasie may not have disappeared – her fate had been more brutal. But both Dorthe and Imaneq were convinced she'd fallen foul somehow of the same evil trade and were determined it wouldn't ensnare their remaining daughter too.

But then, all those years later, along had come Desna.

Maybe Imaneq had relaxed his guard. He always said she was a late gift from the gods and for the first few years after her unexpected birth they'd both simply luxuriated in her. But as she grew closer to Alasie's age, the age at which they'd lost the sister she would never know, Dorthe could see it in her husband's eyes. And if she was honest, she knew it from the leaden feeling in her own stomach too. As well as in everything they were saying to each other without saying anything at all. That certain silence again.

Was that why? Had it finally become completely impossible all of a sudden? Or had he been lulled into a false sense of security through their being left alone all these years?

Dorthe didn't know, and she couldn't ask anyone either. They'd already had the starkest possible demonstration of the folly of raising heads above a still forbidden parapet.

So the lesson remained a simple one.

From now to her dying day, Dorthe would stay silent.

Ros stole a last look back at the silent young Desna from the door. One element of Ros's cover story was true. She would indeed oversee her transfer back to the UK. But Ros would stay on in Greenland, and the reason for that was that single photograph she'd seen a few days before on Tom Edwards's phone.

That photograph of Emmanuel Ocon standing over the newly butchered body of Imaneq Kalia, posed like a hunter over a trophy kill.

What the hell was that all about? And why had it been sent to Tom Edwards – and it had to have been sent to him, because how else would he – could he – have acquired it?

Had it been a warning of some kind? A silent instruction not to speak out along, with a visual reminder of the dangers of doing so? But speak out about what? And who posed the obvious and implicit danger to him if he did?

Was it the man from Ros's past looking out at the camera? Or was there another explanation for Emmanuel's presence in that photo? Despite the apparent hunter-like pose, was that not the full story? Was Emmanuel not the aggressor in all this but next in line for the same sort of treatment?

But above everything else floated the biggest question of all.

How had Emmanuel survived what had happened to him those few years before?

How?

Ros and Delaney returned from Ilulissat courtesy of a cargo Twin Otter that had been delivering flat-pack houses to a local contractor and which occasionally made its services available to the police if the pilot had an empty leg to fly.

Along the way, the amused pilot of the Twin Otter had spluttered and snorted as he related the story of his latest delivery, which had been sourced – like most houses in Greenland – from a kit manufacturer just outside Copenhagen. Everything inside the pack had been as detailed in the inventory, the chimney, the stovepipe, the walls, the doors and windows. The only thing that was missing, to the homeowner's bemusement, were the nails.

Emerging from the airport into a shower, Ros and Delaney had transferred to a Toyota pick-up taxi, its driver mercifully silent this time, and had been driven back into Nuuk.

Ros looked out of the window at the rainwashed streets as they drove on. Unlike Ilulissat, Nuuk – Greenland's capital – was well below the Arctic Circle. It boasted a population of around sixteen thousand people, about a third of the country's population. Two languages dominated: Greenlandic and Danish. The old Danish name for Nuuk was Godthaab, which meant Good Hope.

Early impressions had always counted for everything for Ros and when she'd visited Greenland that one time before, as a largely itinerant teen, those first impressions were clear. Never, in her opinion, had a town been more spectacularly misnamed.

The taxi sped on, passing the former site of the infamous and now demolished Block P, a vast concrete structure some two hundred metres long, housing around three hundred and twenty residential apartments. It had been erected as part of the Danish-inspired strategy of decanting Greenlanders from their traditional fishing villages into modern housing schemes beloved by most other European countries at that time. Incredible as it had seemed to Ros when she'd visited back then, Block P had actually housed fully 1% of all Greenland's population and had been hailed as the shape of housing in the future.

It had been an unmitigated disaster. Doors weren't wide enough for residents to enter wearing their usual full winter clothes, storage space inside was virtually non-existent and any hunting or fishing equipment usually ended up hanging from windows and doors. Blood and guts regularly clogged the drainage system since the only place to clean fish was the bathtub. Architecturally and culturally misconceived, it was one of the starkest examples of inappropriate design imposed from a distance, and a far cry from the archetypal gable-roofed timber dwellings that more traditionally peppered the landscape.

The vista kept unfolding before Ros's eyes. In defence of the local planners, some genuinely stylish modern buildings seemed to have recently graced the landscape. A public swimming pool with its roof shaped, appropriately enough, like a giant wave clearly allowed swimmers a matchless view of the fjord and fells that stretched out just behind its panoramic windows, while the newly built University of Greenland and the Greenland Institute of Natural Resources were two other institutions that had also steered away from the more usual box-like structures.

But then Ros tensed as the traffic ahead of them suddenly ground to a halt. She looked sideways at Delaney, but he remained as silent as he'd largely been since the moment they'd met.

So Ros just looked out of the window and waited for the sudden bottleneck to clear.

Maybe it was the presence of the visitor from his old country sitting by his side, or the wall of silence he'd encountered from Dorthe and Desna Kalia. But an old and all too familiar unsettling feeling was seeping through Delaney right now – although, unlike Ros, it was nothing to do with their surroundings.

Delaney looked, unseeing, out of the window. One month earlier he'd given a talk to a party of visiting police officers from France about a hunting trip he'd taken a few weeks before. A small clutch of polar bears had been the quarry that day. The animals had first been spotted a day or so before on the other side of a river of melted ice and the hunt had been postponed while either the bears moved closer or the channel of ice froze over again, allowing the hunters access to their prey.

With Delaney was an inmate from a local Home for Convicts called Kaju Olsen. He'd been convicted three years previously of the murder of another hunter in a drunken fight. Whatever Kaju and Delaney managed to catch or kill on that trip would be used to feed not only themselves, but other convicts. Any excess would be sent to other places of incarceration in Greenland or overseas to another similar institution at Herstedvester in Denmark. If it proved a particularly spectacular haul, then some of it might also be taken down to the local trading station.

Delaney had been in the country for many years now, but the contradictions still pressed powerfully on him, as he'd made clear to his audience. To those overseeing Kaju's imprisonment, this trip remained an excellent way of maintaining the hunting traditions of convicts as well as making it possible for the wider prison community to be fed. To incomers like Delaney himself, it seemed extraordinary. Only in Greenland would a convicted murderer still serving an active sentence be sent out into the community laden with knives and carrying a loaded gun.

For decades most Greenlanders had simply accepted it as a fact of life. But now that traditional acceptance was being tested more and more as the old notions of crime and punishment became stretched to what some were already regarding as breaking point. Which was perhaps epitomised in the silent figure of Kaju Olsen, at that moment maintaining his careful watch across water that was turning once again to ice.

The punishment of offenders.

The treatment meted out to those who transgressed.

How to deal with evil.

In old Greenlandic society, it had been simple. Disputes had been settled by singing. If anyone wanted to make a complaint against a neighbour, family member or friend, they would compose a song outlining their grievance and then challenge an opponent by announcing the time and place they intended to sing their composition.

An audience would assemble to listen to the two sides in the dispute. First, one party to the dispute sang while the other listened. Then the other party could present his or her song. This would continue until the audience decided on the merits of the respective cases by jeering the song that didn't find favour.

Things had moved on since then but there were many who still found the Greenlandic approach to crime and punishment idiosyncratic in the extreme. There were others who found it positively perverse.

Other countries had penal codes. Greenland had a Criminal Code. Other countries spoke of punishment. Greenlanders spoke of measures. It wasn't that punishment was actually abolished, as some critics of the Criminal Code had alleged. It was just that punishment was only one of the measures available to a court, largely due to the basic principles of that Criminal Code being founded on one of the oldest modes of conflict resolution: the Arctic Peace model.

Under that model, punishment wasn't determined by the severity of the offence. The principal consideration was the measure of correction considered most expedient to keep the criminal from committing any other crime. The underlying aim was always restorative, to return the criminal back to society and to restore that society back to a state where it could function normally once again.

Those visiting police officers had looked at Delaney as if he'd just been beamed down from some other planet as he'd attempted to explain his adopted country's very particular approach to justice. Delaney glanced at the latest visiting police officer at his side as the engine of the taxi continued to impotently idle, the rain now coming down harder outside. Maybe this latest arrival would also look at him in that exact same way if he tried to explain it, although – and he couldn't quite explain why – he doubted it. This particular officer already seemed different somehow.

Delaney looked back out of the window again. 'Never mind the criminal' had been the refrain. What about the victim? Never mind pouring all that effort into the miscreant and their rehabilitation. Why not just punish them in such a way that they or anyone like them who may be tempted to commit similar crimes in the future never do so again?

Which was one point of view. And one that was gaining traction inside the country now too, as crimes increased both in number and intensity. In the previous two years rape offences had increased by almost 50%, with drugs convictions following close behind. Only the previous day an editorial in one of the two national daily papers had railed against the rising crime rate, questioning again the effectiveness of the Criminal Code in dealing with what it was already beginning to call the 'new breed of criminal'.

Along with many others in the national force, Delaney doubted there was any new breed of criminal. Perhaps it was just that crime was simply being reported more widely now.

Dark deeds had always scarred this isolated land and Delaney's mind now drifted back again to that small house bolted onto rocks, the house they'd just left, and to Desna and Dorthe Kalia. Then Delaney looked out of the window at the gridlocked traffic once again.

And if he completed this new investigation, if he apprehended and incarcerated the person or persons who'd killed Imaneq Kalia, if Delaney found the person or persons who earlier had killed Kalia's daughter, would he then be standing on some ice cap at some point in the not-too-distant future as he'd previously stood with Kaju Olsen, watching as they raised their rifles too, completing a kill a few metres away across a channel of newly formed ice?

And what would that be?

Restorative justice?

A circle squared in an ancient system once more?

Or, as critics of his adopted country and that justice system were ever more vocally alleging, yet another example of a world gone mad?

Half an hour earlier and half a kilometre away, the girl responsible for the traffic chaos was standing outside the Home for Convicts, keeping herself at a deliberate distance from the rest of the callers that day.

Cars passed on the road just a metre or so away. From inside, drivers stared out at the Home, the questions embedded in their expressions silent, but still all too clear. What crime or crimes had been committed by those inside?

But the girl standing on the pavement, her head shrouded in a large, loose-fitting hoody, didn't take any notice of the passing stares. She just stared up in turn at the building before her.

The original Home for Convicts had been a small log house built next to the local Queen's Hospital and had previously been a sanatorium for tuberculosis patients. It had been given to the police in the 1950s to be used as a remand home. Initially it could only hold six prisoners, but then new premises were sourced, boosting prisoner numbers to eighteen. Some were held in secure cells but most were placed in rooms with no locks on the doors or bars on the windows, and most prisoners worked in the capital during the day on the understanding that they all returned to the Home at night.

In the last few years the Home had been enlarged again and the present capacity was now almost sixty. At the moment the Home was full, but not for much longer. Not if the girl in the loose-fitting hoody had anything to do with it.

The girl turned away from the Home, staring back at more drivers looking out at her in turn from the comfort of their hermetically sealed cocoons, mainly large SUVs.

In the past ten minutes at least fifty had passed. It didn't matter that no one could drive for even a few miles outside Nuuk. Even the insane amount of tax motorists had to pay for their vehicle each year didn't seem to matter. In a city of 16,000 people, there were still over 3,000 cars and that figure was rising almost daily. Even for a journey that would take less than five minutes on foot, the average Greenlander was still much more likely to drive.

The girl suddenly yelled across at one car in particular which was now idling by the traffic lights, a GMC with a young woman inside.

'What are you looking at?'

The young woman's head jerked back to the road as the girl moved towards her, dodging a posse of BMX bikes before hitting the passenger window with her knuckles. The lights fortuitously having changed, the young woman drove on, quickly. A couple of officers outside the Home looked over at the girl in the hoody warily as she stared after the fast-disappearing car, but none of the other visitors seemed to take much notice. Just another local lunatic.

Which was when the girl in the hoody saw the Jeep, its engine still running as its owner sweetened his coffee at the counter of a small coffee kiosk on the pavement.

Using the vehicle to keep herself concealed from the driver, the girl in the hoody moved across the road, swung her small frame into the cab, then flicked it into gear, hitting the accelerator pedal hard at the same time. The Jeep barrelled forward, its bull bars scoring a direct hit on the grey front door of the Home ahead. That flimsy barrier breached, the Jeep ploughed on, bringing down a supporting lintel at the front of the building and collapsing the front wall, now affording the passing traffic an infinitely more interesting sight than the few waiting visitors and milling officers that had been there just a few moments before.

One prisoner was exposed doing his morning sit-ups.

A guard was exposed viewing satellite porn.

And someone else was exposed too: someone in a room towards the rear of the now-partially demolished building, someone the young girl in the hoody knew only too well, even if the stunned prisoner in question had never seen her before in his life and didn't know her from the proverbial Adam.

But he would.

'Report of the autopsy.'

One hour later, their taxi having finally circumvented the sudden gridlock, Ros and Delaney were inside a squat, two-storey building that housed the local Police Headquarters.

Isaak Sandgreen, Delaney's senior officer, slid a single sheet of paper across the table. The pathologist had worked on Imaneq Kalia for the last few hours, after Cecilie had accompanied his body down to the capital the previous day. But Delaney barely glanced at it and neither did Ros. It was already only too obvious that Imaneq Kalia had died from injuries sustained during the most savage of beatings. The rather more salient point was why, and in what way it was related to the mysterious appearance of that new headstone on his daughter's grave.

Sandgreen had already asked Delaney if Dorthe Kalia had told them anything about the headstone, which she hadn't, of course. But that didn't mean her husband hadn't stumbled upon something – possibly the same something that had cost him his life. But that matter dispensed with, another loomed immediately in its wake.

'Desna Kalia.'

Delaney looked to his side at Ros as Sandgreen spoke again, his pulse quickening now.

They'd had victims of crimes resettled abroad for their own safety before, of course. Prior to Ros's arrival, the choice for Desna would have been obvious. She'd have been committed to the tender mercies of PET, the Danish Security and Intelligence Service, the body responsible for identifying, preventing and countering threats to freedom, democracy and Danish interests abroad – including, naturally enough given the special relationship that existed between the two countries, Greenland.

But Desna wasn't being taken into a protection programme in Denmark. She was being taken to the UK instead.

'So am I going to be told?'

Sandgreen looked at him. Ros didn't. Maybe she'd been anticipating the question.

'Told what?'

'What this is actually all about?'

Now Ros did turn towards him, her expression level and her eyes neutral.

'Desna might well be at risk. No, correction: she is at risk. So are many other witnesses we've taken into protection programmes over the past few years, the difference being we haven't had to parachute in an officer from a totally different force a couple of thousand miles away.'

Delaney nodded once more at Ros and Sandgreen.

'So I'll ask again. What aren't I being told?

Which was when there was a knock on the door and another officer appeared, a report in hand. Ros and Delaney were about to find out why their journey into the capital had been delayed that morning and why this case conference was taking place a good hour or so later than it should have.

The arriving officer swiftly relayed the news of the attack a short time previously on the Home for Convicts. Like prisons the world over, that particular institution had endured its fair share of attention from disgruntled relatives and the like, but in this attack the entire front of the House had been comprehensively destroyed. Several officers and inmates had been injured as walls and ceilings had given way. The petrol tank of the vehicle that had caused the damage had also subsequently exploded: whether that had been deliberately at the hands of its driver or as a result of the high-level impact wasn't yet known, but it had spread further panic and confusion.

But everyone had been accounted for, save for the sole occupant of one of the small cells sited towards the rear of the building, who now seemed to have disappeared. He could have simply taken his chance and escaped in the general confusion, but as this particular prisoner had been something of a model inmate during his various periods of incarceration up to that point, that seemed unlikely.

Delaney stared at the officer as she gave the escapee's name.
Tobias Lundblad.

The man whose chief claim to dubious fame – his various petty offences over the subsequent years notwithstanding – lay in his status as the last known person to see Alasie Kalia alive.

A man who, within a week or so of that new headstone appearing on Alasie's grave and within a few days of her father being savagely murdered, had suddenly disappeared.

Meanwhile down by the harbour a familiar scene was unfolding, the cause only too clear.

Heavy drinking had always been a curse in Greenland, despite the fact it was actually against the law to get drunk. It was a fact of local life that had been a source of considerable amusement to Ros on her sole previous trip, but the wording of the provision relating to alcohol in the Greenlandic Criminal Code was unequivocal.

If a person, intentionally or by gross negligence, becomes intoxicated or causes others to, thereby endangering the body or property of others, then he or she is to be prosecuted for abuse of alcohol.

As a lawyer, David Kleist would have been well aware of that, but it didn't seem to be making much difference. Kleist was stumbling around the Old Quarter near to the colonial harbour, barely able to put one foot in front of the other, saying little to the various passers-by he was currently crashing into. The little he was saying was making less and less sense, as the middle-aged waitress who'd managed to avoid his stumbling progress so far could see only too clearly.

That waitress, Antaria, didn't know him, but she'd already identified the type. Just another helpless, hopeless drunk, she reflected, as she wiped the tables outside the National Museum – albeit a well-dressed drunk, for a change.

Every day and every night of every week the same sight scarred the Old Quarter's bars and restaurants, and it was getting worse. It was a statistical fact, as both of the capital's local papers kept reminding their readers, that consumption of alcohol in Greenland was considerably higher than in just about every other European country. And comparisons with its closest neighbour were even more worrying. Consumption in the country of her birth was twice as high as that in Denmark.

But Antaria didn't need bare statistics to tell her that. Just sit on the harbour wall, in the nearby mall, or stand on any street and it was the same story. Sooner or later the drunks would congregate.

Antaria turned away as this latest one stumbled over a low kerb and crashed to his knees to the accompaniment of loud cheers and catcalls from a group of watching drinkers in a nearby bar. She could have gone over to help him up, and in her younger days maybe she would have done, but what was the point? He'd only fall down again.

The previous summer Antaria had been waiting for a ferry to take her to the island of Karrat. She'd been on a trip she'd long promised herself, to visit relatives she hadn't seen since the break-up of her marriage to a man who was now a woman. At the time, she'd burned inside with humiliation. She'd have infinitely preferred to have returned home one day to find some young woman in their marital bed rather than her husband trying on her dresses.

The trip was meant to be restorative, a chance to get away from everything and everyone, only the captain of the ferry that was supposed to take her away from it all had been drinking for three days without a break. Desperate to complete her journey and to see her impatiently waiting relatives, she'd attempted to wean him back to sobriety using the only food she had in her rucksack – Danish cheese, a few pieces of rye flatbread and a box of Californian raisins. But nothing roused him from his self-imposed stupor. He remained seated on a box of pallets by a small warehouse for a further three days, smoking a succession of cheroots and asking each and every one of the local girls who passed to marry him.

A clock struck inside the museum and Antaria looked past the well-dressed drunk and out over the water, forgetting about the country's issues with alcohol for a moment. The tide was now on the turn and within a few moments, courtesy of that receding tide, she'd be able to see the famous Sassuma Arnaa, the Mother of the Sea: a beautiful granite figure, soon to be visible above the surface of the water. The goddess was charged, so local legend had it, with watching over all animals that may be hunted or fished. If the Mother of the Sea wasn't satisfied with the way that prey was being pursued, she'd gather them all in her hair at the bottom of the ocean until there was nothing left for the hunters to trap or catch.

As the waters receded further, another loud cheer sounded behind her. Another group of drinkers in another bar had now spotted David Kleist and were urging him on as he attempted to reach the relative safety of the Hans Egede House a few metres away.

Antaria watched, disapproving again. She knew that Egede, a man who'd bequeathed more than his now overly-common surname to his adopted country, had always been something of a controversial figure in Greenland but she was still old-school enough to view him as a hero – an apostle, indeed. The founder of their capital city and the man more responsible than any other for awakening interest in the isolated country after centuries of indifference and neglect.

Antaria knew that to others he was viewed as a cultural tyrant, forbidding more than one family to live together under one roof – to take just one of his well-publicised initiatives – thereby destroying at a stroke the mutual support needed to hunt seal or pilot a kayak. In an attempt to turn native minds from the old ways to the new, he'd even turned the old Greenlandic word for spirit, *Toorianaarsuk*, into a swearword, but that made no sense to most Greenlanders anyway. Those sort of expressions were the province of those who wished to speak badly of others and native Greenlanders had always signified their disapproval by saying nothing.

But that still didn't mean his house should suffer the attentions of a drunk – and for a moment, as the drunk in question swayed just a metre or so away from the national institution, the waitress feared a very specific sort of attention. More than one of his less-than-illustrious predecessors had actually relieved themselves on that front door before now.

But then this one just fell spreadeagled on the ground, and the nearby group of drinkers cheered even more.

Antaria turned away from her now-cleaned table, went inside and forgot all about him.

Twelve hours later the tide had turned again and the Mother of the Sea was once more on full view.

Antaria, arriving for her new day's shift at the National Museum, paused once again and looked across at the ancient granite monument, taking her usual moment to savour the almost mystical sight. But this morning the shocked waitress wouldn't be savouring anything.

Antaria's precious Mother of the Sea hadn't entrapped any endangered animals in her hair overnight.

Just a drunk and now very dead solicitor.

15

R OS OPENED THE front door of her rented apartment.
When Ros had visited Greenland before, she'd been a
teenage runaway, living and sleeping wherever she could. This
time her living and sleeping arrangements were very different.
Her sense of acute inner turmoil was identical.

On arrival in the capital, Ros had been offered a house in
a residential district out near the airport, some five kilometres
or so from the centre of the capital; a building that had been
constructed in the traditional style and painted in one of the
country's three traditional colours: oxblood. She'd opted for
what had been seen by her bemused new colleagues as inferior
accommodation in central Nuuk itself. But Nuuk boasted the
best internet connection in the country, and so far as Ros was
concerned, that was the most important thing right now.

But there was another reason too. Something more nebulous.
A strange sensation she couldn't pin down at first, but which had
led her to opting for this functional and sparse accommodation
the moment she'd seen it.

'What's happening?'

Masters's face appeared before her a few moments later.
Behind him, Ros could see the rolling expanse of Green Park,
visible from the rear window of Masters's weekend apartment. As
always, Ros wondered briefly about the personal circumstances
of a man who maintained an apartment on one of the most
expensive streets in one of the most exclusive boroughs in one
of the costliest cities in the world, and all on a police officer's
salary. Then, and as always, she dismissed it. Just another puzzle

making up the conundrum that was her new, if temporary, senior officer in her new, if equally temporary, department.

'I've met Desna. We're making arrangements to transfer her back to the UK. Conor's already found a place for her.'

'You've not attempted any sort of debrief so far?'

Briefly, another image swam before Ros's eyes: the perennially forbidding and withdrawn Dorthe Kalia.

'Not yet.'

On the other end of the video link, Masters nodded, that line of enquiry dispensed with. Time to move on to what was always going to be the real matter of the moment.

'We've tracked a selection of CCTV images over the last couple of months.'

Ros hunched forward.

'And?'

'Emmanuel Ocon's been identified on at least six different CCTV images in the last week alone – four of them in Ilulissat, close to the site of the attack on Imaneq Kalia. But none, aside from the single image on Edwards's phone, that place him in any direct contact with Kalia or anyone else.'

Masters checked a report in front of him.

'On the last two occasions, the images place him in the capital.'

Masters paused.

'The last one within a few metres of your current apartment, in fact, though we lost track of him soon after that.'

Another chill assailed Ros but her face didn't betray her for an instant. She just looked out of a window towards a nearby bar that was just about to open for the night.

Emmanuel was close and Ros didn't need Masters to tell her that. She'd already sensed it.

Ros kept looking out onto the street. Crowds of people were already gathering outside the bar. One man in particular stood out among the crowd – Ros had seen him on her way inside a short time earlier. He was handsome with short-cropped hair, looked to be part-Danish, part-Inuit and was dancing around like Baryshnikov on speed. He'd blurted out to the passing Ros that he worked in a bakery just a few streets away but from the amused comments Ros picked up as she'd walked on, it seemed he'd just been released from a psychiatric clinic and was still on medication.

But now Ros didn't even see the wannabe-Baryshnikov. Now there was only one face she was seeing.

Somewhere out there, on those streets among those people, was the man who'd changed her life irrevocably, as well as somehow leading to the end of the lives of the remaining members of her family.

The man who may also have had something to do with irrevocably changing the life of Jo Edwards and ending the lives of her two small boys too.

Ros looked back at the screen.

'Has anything come up in the records?'

'Nothing, but we wouldn't expect it to.'

Ros stared at Masters's face on the screen, not remotely accepting that for a moment.

'If Emmanuel had been what we always believed him to be, if he really had been a police officer –'

Masters cut across, impatient.

'If Emmanuel had been the officer he'd always claimed to be, there'd be no record anyway – or certainly none we could access. You know how those things work as well as I do.'

Masters was being disingenuous. He knew that a hell of a lot better than she did.

Ros kept eyeing the face in front of her on the screen.

'Try finding any trace of your and Jukes's old department, you mean? There wouldn't be any record of that either?'

That wasn't Ros flying a kite. That was a cast-iron fact. In the wake of a rogue officer blowing up in all their faces almost a year before, Masters's old unit, which had specialised in running deep swimmers – undercover cops who would sometimes infiltrate organisations of interest for years – had been comprehensively airbrushed from history. So had the same happened when it came to Emmanuel?

Masters almost sounded bored.

'If he wasn't and he never had been the officer he'd always claimed to be, there'd be no reason for any record to exist in the first place. Either way, that was always going to be a dead end.'

Then a more impatient Masters hunched closer to his laptop screen.

'It's not the past that's the point and it's not the past that's the answer to all this, it's the here and now. It's where is he, it's who is he – as in who he really is – and what he's got to do with at least five past and present murders we know about, and maybe countless more besides?'

Ros and Masters talked for a few more moments before Masters cut the connection. Then Ros crossed over to the window again.

The bar across the street was fast becoming packed. Through the window she could see a barman – perhaps Chinese, maybe Japanese – who'd clearly perfected the art of tossing bottles through the air, creating bursts of alcohol-lit flame before expertly dispensing what looked like Kahlúa or maybe Sambuca into a whole array of tall glasses, most of which were being emptied as soon as they were filled. The music was at full volume, although no one seemed all that interested in dancing. Slumped bodies already littered the tables.

Ros looked up towards the sky. The mountains in the distance hung like ghostly sentinels and high above them the northern lights danced across the Arctic night.

But suddenly Ros wasn't seeing those ghostly sentinels or those near-comatose revellers. She wasn't even now thinking about Emmanuel. Somewhat to her surprise, Ros found her mind now running instead on the officer she'd been deputed to shadow: her fellow countryman, Delaney.

Ros knew about his history. That had been easy enough to establish. The failed paedophile sting that had ended his career in the UK was a matter of public as well as police record. What had been more difficult was getting any sort of handle on the man himself.

Partly, and as Ros was only too aware, that was because he seemed to keep himself determinedly to himself, just as she did. But partly it was something else – although what, she couldn't decide.

But then Ros turned away from the window, almost shaking away the sudden image that had floated in front of her eyes. She wasn't here to probe or ponder any of that.

She was here for one purpose and one only. And if Delaney really was something of a mystery, it wasn't the one that was obsessing her right now.

Meanwhile, that same night and a few miles away near his own rented home, Delaney did what he'd done each and every night for years.

Delaney walked.

It didn't matter where he might be living or what settlement he might be visiting, either on official business or – on the rare occasions when he actually took one – on holiday.

Wherever he was, Delaney walked.

These walks were usually solo outings, but occasionally he had company. A few years previously he'd been working on a case on a small island a short distance up from the coast from Cape Farewell. Each night he'd wander the whole of its length until one night, about a week or so into his stay, he attracted a small party of local children who began to follow him, perhaps scenting adventure of some sort. Delaney, the most unlikely of Pied Pipers, led them in a loop from his rented house down to the island's most easternmost point.

The fast-swelling procession first passed a whale rib stuck upright in the sand that had been there more years than even the oldest inhabitant could remember, on through the island's only proper village and past the *butik* – the small general shop or store – and then down onto a beach before returning all the way back to Delaney's house again.

On reaching journey's end, the children all stared at him in open bewilderment, the expression on their faces saying it all. Was that it? And when they realised that quite clearly was it, they melted away back into the darkness and the next night Delaney completed his circuit once again alone.

It was a ritual that had started years before in the dark days and even darker nights following the collapse of the paedophile sting. Delaney had been suspended immediately and even though the subsequent disciplinary hearing cleared him of any actual oversight, it hardly mattered. The subsequent inquiry revealed that the paedophiles in question had received a tip-off from somewhere deep inside the actual police team, that tip-off from a source unidentified then and still unidentified now, but that barely registered either. All that mattered to him was that an operation had gone badly wrong. On his watch, a small child had been abducted and then, as they subsequently discovered, killed.

Which was when his walks began. Delaney had retreated to a small seaside cottage, an out-of-season holiday let on the far western edge of west Wales, which was where he'd first acquired the name that followed him around for the next few years.

The Beachcomber.

As a description, it wasn't strictly accurate. He certainly wasn't scouring the local sands for anything of value. But maybe he'd already begun to unsettle those amongst whom he'd temporarily settled and the description comforted them somehow, seeming to give some sort of point or purpose to the wanderings of the strange solo figure they espied as the day dawned and as dusk fell, out on the distant beaches and headlands.

When he first came to Greenland, Delaney's new countrymen had been even more uncomfortable with the idea of a man who walked for no apparent purpose. Many would hover around whatever small house he'd rented, watching as he set off on one of his walks and remaining there until he returned, clearly relieved when he did so. The reason, he soon discovered, was simple. In old Inuit society, no one wandered off alone unless they were about to commit suicide. It all derived from a similarly ancient belief that solitude was a sign of unhappiness.

One evening, a week or so after he'd arrived in his newly adopted country, he'd been caught out by the tide. He hadn't been able to make it up off the beach to a small cliffside track, and was forced to take shelter at a house fronting the sands. The owners took in a fair number of waifs and strays in similar circumstances, particularly in the summer when visitors unfamiliar to the area would find themselves similarly marooned.

Delaney couldn't fault the welcome. The problem was the conversation. Over the previous year he'd become so used to his own company and that company alone that normal human contact was something of a trial. He sweated through two hours of small talk before the tide receded to the point where he could bolt back to his habitual solitude. From that night on, he'd always kept a watchful eye on the water.

Delaney was better at making conversation these days. He still didn't seek it out, although at least his neighbours now seemed to have accepted that. Certainly none of them called in on him as they'd occasionally done when he'd first moved there, asking how he was, if he needed anything – asking about anything and everything aside from the questions they really wanted to ask, which he would never have answered anyway.

What, actually, was he doing, and why?

On his latest walk, with the tide lapping at his feet, Delaney clambered up over some rocks to a path that led around the headland. A short distance along was a natural seat made out of more rocks thrown up by the sea. Delaney took his usual place on his makeshift bench and looked out over the distant horizon as the lapping water below him began to claim back the land.

All those years before, no one, let alone Delaney, could have predicted that he'd rebuild his life this way: beginning by fulfilling a long-cherished ambition to move to a country that had always fascinated him and continuing by his picking up the reins of his former career. Equally, no one, let alone Delaney, could have predicted that he'd find love and a family.

Some of his former colleagues would speculate, albeit well out of Delaney's hearing, that what happened next was a macabre kind of retribution. A life taken from him in exchange for a life that had been lost by him. In darker moments, Delaney had wondered the same himself.

Delaney's son Michael, known to friends and family as Mikey, had been killed just over three years before in an accident. Mikey had been thirteen. Back in Delaney's old home, a young boy's favoured method of transport would probably have been a mountain bike or skateboard but growing up in Sisimiut offered other possibilities – more specifically an ultra-cool and, as it proved, ultra-fast snow scooter. They didn't actually look particularly powerful but appearances were deceptive. The resulting cocktail of chance and circumstance was to prove catastrophic.

192

In one sense it was an all too familiar story, irrespective of geography or setting. Take one over-excited young teen, a winding track, a blind bend taken just that little bit too fast and the outcome was the sort of story you'd hear on any local news bulletin in any country virtually any night of the week, although those sort of bulletins usually got more animated by accidents that involved multiple deaths, preferably of innocent passers-by as well. This was all a little ordinary by comparison.

Delaney hadn't seen it as ordinary. Neither had Marie, his wife. Mikey was an only child – although even if he'd been one of a multitude of siblings, the sudden and unexpected death of a child would still have been well-nigh impossible to bear.

Up to that point, Sisimiut had been a good place to live and raise a family. It had been Marie's home before Delaney met her and from the moment he did, he couldn't imagine living anywhere else. Even his first impressions after flying in on the short flight from Kangerlussuaq were overwhelmingly favourable as he took his first deep breath of the clean and seemingly bone-dry air.

Like many other seemingly similar towns Delaney had journeyed to back then, it boasted a population of sled dogs that almost rivalled humans in terms of numbers, but it was much more than just a simple hunting settlement. Sisimiut was a cultural town too, a college town with a language school, as well as one devoted to building and construction and yet another hosting a Centre for Arctic Technology. But it was that clean, bone-dry air that had first captured him – which was all the more ironic, as within just a couple of days Delaney was literally fighting for what seemed to be his last breath.

On his first couple of days there, he'd followed the usual tourist trail. He'd taken a bus tour around the town, falling for the time-honoured trick played on the first-time visitor when a local shouted the magic word, *Aalirijuk!* – the traditional warning heralding a sighting of a so-called killer whale. He'd dived to the windows along with all the other gullible travellers, only to scan a completely empty sea. He'd visited the *braettet*, the town's local market, where fishermen and hunters sold wares including reindeer and Atlantic wolffish. He'd also dodged the improbable approach of Icelandic horses, trotting along the road from the airport, as well as marvelling at the sea eagles perched on the nearby mountain, Palasip Qaqqaa.

Then he'd then taken a trip down Aqqusinersuaq, the hill leading down to the harbour, to visit the artists' workshop at Umiasualivimmut in the former and still beautiful Royal Greenland Trade Warehouse. The air inside was thick with dust from burning narwhal teeth which one artist, a striking young woman, was drilling, sharpening and scraping to transform into bracelets.

But Delaney hadn't arrived just to take in the sights. He'd travelled to Sisimiut to take part in the one of the world's toughest cross-country endurance tests: the 160 km-long annual Arctic Circle Race. That year over a hundred participants had registered and all just about finished, including Delaney. That he did so was due to that striking-looking female artist. Two days later she was on hand to urge him along the last couple of kilometres of the gruelling course, despite his lungs feeling as if they were about to burst.

A still-gasping Delaney returned the favour as the artist, whose name he'd now established was Marie, also threatened to fall, close to the finishing line. Together they staggered and stumbled across and later that night they shared a congratulatory drink together. One week later they'd sailed out of the small settlement on their first fishing trip. Six months later they married and all these years later he was still there. So it was that Delaney arrived for one marathon and ended up staying for another.

In that time Delaney had raised a family and established himself in a career, two endeavours he would have regarded as fanciful all those years before when he left his home country to travel the world in general and the Arctic, principally Greenland, in particular. Delaney had once tentatively mentioned to an old geography teacher that he wanted to go on holiday there one day, only for the scornful teacher in question to tell him that no one holidayed in Greenland because there was nothing there.

Delaney had sunk back in his seat, cheeks burning as the mocking laughter of his classmates rang out around the classroom. But over the years Delaney had come to think perhaps he should thank rather than censure that teacher, in the unlikely event of ever seeing him again. He'd lit a spark that day by his derisive dismissal. A spark that changed a young boy's life.

Marie had fallen ill a month or so after Mikey died, and nothing the doctors could do seemed able to prevent what looked like an inevitable decline. They couldn't even properly diagnose what was wrong with her, at least in terms that made any sort of medical sense. But it all made perfect sense to Delaney. His wife's heart was broken. It was as simple as that. And with it her will to live.

One night, a few weeks before Marie died, Delaney was in the private room of a hospital that the medical insurance provided by his employers had arranged for her. A nurse had been trying to get Marie to eat something. Tiring of the nurse's now-constant entreaties, Delaney stepped in and lifted a spoon to his wife's lips, which was when – and with a strength that totally belied her now-wasted frame – Marie had grabbed Delaney's arm and lowered it back down onto the bed, as if they were arm-wrestling.

The nurse stared at her, frozen, unable to understand what was happening; but Delaney understood only too clearly. His wife was going to die because she had determined she would. And all the strength she had, of which he and the nurse had just had a fleeting glimpse, was now being directed inwards, was becoming focused on one thing and one thing only, her entire will bent on the task of destroying a life she'd come to despise.

A few days later, Marie was floating in and out of consciousness. The doctors had warned Delaney it wouldn't be much longer. But then suddenly, as a different nurse this time washed her emaciated body, she'd opened her eyes and looked straight at Delaney. For a moment as she did so and as he looked back at the wasted shell that had once been his vibrant wife, there was a silence that seemed to last forever. Then she told him that he'd killed their son.

The nurse's pitying expression as she looked back at the staring Delaney said it all. Marie's fevered mind was playing tricks on her. The hallucinations of a tortured soul about to pass over to the other side. And a short time later Marie did indeed breathe her last.

A short time after that, Delaney moved out of the family home in Sisimiut and relocated south to the larger, more anonymous capital of Nuuk: a place where he knew no one and no one knew him. The police, still his employers, had kept their distance throughout the duration of his wife's illness and they kept a similar distance for a few months after her death. Delaney guessed he was still being paid: he was able to pay his few bills, so he assumed money was coming in from somewhere. In that sense he was fortunate, although no one he knew could exactly describe him as lucky.

After another month or so he'd received a visit from a high-ranking colleague, not his then immediate senior officer but the Commissioner himself, no less. He had made the usual concerned and sympathetic noises about Delaney's health and state of mind. But then the real purpose of his visit emerged, as he tried to find out if Delaney had any intention of returning to his old home and his former job. Delaney wasn't pressed for an answer there and then, the Commissioner just left him to think about it for a week or so. After that he returned and Delaney tendered the resignation that had been expected all along.

But then the Commissioner told Delaney about a new post had just been created in what could be his new force if, understandably enough, he had decided he didn't want to return to his old one. Delaney would be looking at cases that had somehow slipped through the net, at investigations that had stalled for reasons other than the simple fact they'd remained unsolved for too long. They'd include the still unsolved disappearances of that ever-growing raft of young female Inuit teens. Maybe Delaney could be the man who'd finally lance that running sore. As well as taking in the length and breadth of the whole country, it could be among the most interesting work Delaney had undertaken since he'd started there, as the Commissioner had pointed out.

Even in his current withdrawn and isolated state, Delaney was well aware what was really behind all this. It was those stresses and strains currently bombarding the aeons-old Arctic Peace model again. Every day some newspaper editorial or career politician would be railing against its seeming inadequacy – and perhaps they had a point.

Only the previous week one of the capital's newspapers had published a list of sexual offences against minors that had been punished by measures that were now being deemed no punishment at all. One man found guilty of sexual intercourse with a ten-year-old girl had been fined 4,000 Danish Kroner. Another found guilty of sexual relations with two boys of six and eight years old had been fined the equivalent of two weeks' wages. On the same day a 32-year-old male in Eastern Greenland had been released back into the community after raping an intoxicated and unconscious 26-year-old woman.

In many towns in the country there still weren't even any jails. In his early days with the national force, Delaney had been sent to the far north to Uummannaq to familiarise himself with the work of some of his colleagues, who were manning one of the local police cutters. One night a small girl had been brought to the local children's home, having just witnessed her mother kill her father with a skinning knife. Badly shaken, the girl had been given hot drinks and a fresh nightgown and had been put to bed in a newly painted room with a view of the nearby mountains. The mother had been visited by the local police but hadn't been removed from the scene of the killing, firstly because there was nowhere to take her but secondly because it was felt there was no need. The local policeman who'd been overseeing Delaney's training told him that from that moment on the censorious looks of her neighbours would be prison enough.

But it wasn't just the landscape of crime that was changing. Violence was increasingly being turned inward as well as directed outward. Only the previous week and just a short distance away from Delaney's latest rented home, a young man, recently rejected by his girlfriend, had taken a gun and shot himself in front of one of the local police stations. The previous month another young male had hanged himself from a church bell tower. The week before that on his way into work, Delaney had followed a sled carrying a coffin containing the body of a young Inuit male being transported back home to Siorapaluk, one of the most isolated of the northernmost villages. He'd also shot himself, this time in front of a small party of schoolchildren.

But perhaps even more worrying was the manner in which these stories were now being traded amongst modern Greenlanders – almost casually, as if such incidents were simply becoming part of the fabric of daily life. Another recent article in one of the same newspapers had pointed out that while native Inuits had a long tradition of accepting suicide more equably than almost any other culture, there'd been a massive rise in recent years. The first spike had occurred after the end of the colonial era in the 1950s, with a second taking place after Greenland became the first Inuit nation to achieve Home Rule at the end of the 1970s.

What was happening to their country during this process of modernisation and change, the leader writer asked? Why was it producing so many fragile young men who saw death as the only way out? And was this yet more evidence of a country now at odds with itself?

So Delaney knew that his new posting wouldn't just be challenging and cover a large geographical area, it would be something of a public relations exercise as well. The creation of that sort of post would send out a clear message to newspapers, to politicians and to criminals – past and present – alike. No matter who you were, no matter what you'd done, no matter how long ago you might have done it, the law had a long and an unforgiving memory. And maybe then the much-criticised Criminal Code would be seen as not quite so toothless after all.

Once again, the Commissioner didn't press him for an answer immediately. Once again, he left him to think it over, promising to return in another week or so's time. Delaney saw him out, thinking that he could in fact have given him his answer there and then: another no.

But then something happened.

Delaney had returned home from one of his usual solitary walks. Night had fallen by the time the lights he'd left on inside his small rented house had come into view. Aside from those lights, the track leading to his house was dark. All he could hear was the distant sound of waves crashing onto the nearby shoreline.

On many similar walks before, it had felt as if he was completely alone in the world, but this time it hadn't. For the last few miles he'd had the curious sense that someone had been keeping him company. Close company, in fact.

He let himself inside and stood in the darkness for a moment or so, trying to work out why he might have been feeling that way. It wasn't anything he'd actually heard or seen. It just seemed to be some strange kind of instinct at work – but he'd learnt in the last twenty years not to dismiss that too lightly.

Delaney had finally turned in for the night, but after a few minutes had got up and gone back to his desk and switched on his computer again. He didn't know why. Maybe it was that same instinct at work again. Sure enough, he had one message from an address he didn't recognise, although it had somehow negotiated its way through his spam filter. There was nothing in the actual message but it did contain an attached document. When he opened the document, he found himself looking at just four simple words.

IT WASN'T AN ACCIDENT.

After a more than usually fitful sleep, he woke to find the message seemed to have deleted itself. He didn't know how that was even possible, but later some research led him to a programme that could cause a message to effectively self-destruct a specified time after being opened. He didn't know if it was still recorded somewhere on his hard drive and didn't bother trying to find out. Delaney also strongly suspected he wasn't going to be able to find out who'd sent it, and he was right.

Nothing happened for a while. No more anonymous messages arrived. Delaney logged the incident with the local police, but they put it down to some sort of prank, possibly by a malicious neighbour. Most of his neighbours, so far as Delaney was aware, didn't even know his name, but the fact he'd kept so much to himself could have intrigued someone or they could have seen his high-ranking visitor call and recognised him. Then all it would have needed was for someone to type in a couple of keywords and they'd have the whole story of the past year or so of his life before them on screen.

The oddest and most unsettling thing of all was the actual choice of words.

IT WASN'T AN ACCIDENT.

Delaney had heard those exact same words before, when his now-dead wife had accused him of killing their son. That was how their last conversation had started. She'd looked up at him from her bed, looked beyond the nurse who was attending to her and that was when she'd said it.

Another couple of days passed. No one looked at him oddly out on the tracks or streets. No fishermen nudged each other as he walked by. Life settled back to what passed for normal, in Delaney's universe at least.

The seasons were changing now. The nights were getting lighter. Delaney was staying out longer and longer. From four hours of daylight in December they'd soon be in June with some twenty hours of daylight instead, which always caused him a problem. For some reason returning home in the darkness felt right somehow. Any earlier and he felt he should be doing something, which only served to remind him he no longer had anything to do.

Coming back home along the narrow track again, he'd paused as he'd come across a party of teenagers taking advantage of a fresh and unseasonable fall of snow to make a sculpture of a giant penis. He'd moved on, but then paused once more, sensing something before he saw it. A bin bag he'd left outside for collection had been kicked over. That could have been caused by a stray dog sniffing around, but the bag wasn't torn as he would have expected and neither were its contents strewn all over the ground. Someone just seemed to have pushed it out of the way. The recently fallen snow was trampled all around the overturned bin bag too.

Delaney looked up, half-expecting to see some sort of message spray-painted on the side of the house. The last communication had teetered on the edge of the melodramatic, after all, but this time his mystery messenger had contented themselves with posting a note through the letterbox instead. The message was once again anonymous, its contents inscribed in thick, block capitals. And it was once again simple and to the point.

HE WASN'T THE TARGET.

After logging that with the local police too, Delaney didn't actually have to wait too long for the next message. Something – that same instinct once again, perhaps – was telling him it would probably be delivered via his home computer again, and he was right, only this time it came in the form of an instant message that popped up on the side of his screen. Needless to say, once again there was no way of identifying the sender.

This new message asked a simple question.

DO YOU WANT TO SEE YOUR SON'S KILLER?

Without thinking, Delaney typed back an immediate response.

Yes.

Delaney was directed to a website which appeared at first glance to be blank. But there was a space on the far right of the screen which seemed to contain something, a hidden image of some kind, detected by his mouse. Delaney clicked on the space and an image duly began to form. Even though a previous tenant had installed the latest high-speed connection, it still seemed to take forever. Or maybe that was just how it seemed to his understandably impatient eyes.

Slowly, Delaney began to pick out details. A track leading to what looked like a small settlement, some trampled snow, a small house at the end of that same track and a figure, initially indistinct, standing by a bin bag kicked over onto its side. The face of that initially indistinct figure took the longest to download but Delaney had already worked out who it was long before it assumed anything like its final shape.

Delaney remained in front of his computer, looking at a picture of himself outside his own rented house taken just a single day before. Underneath the stark image was a single word.

KILLER.

Then the image disintegrated as it wiped, he would discover seconds later, his hard drive.

Neat trick.

The Commissioner returned a day or so later to a pleasant surprise. Delaney was a talented officer and the force wanted to keep him. But the Commissioner, in common with most of Delaney's former colleagues, was already reconciled to the near certainty that he'd eke out the rest of his days living some half-life in a retreat similar to the one he was currently inhabiting. A shadow of the man he used to be, not even doing a pale imitation of the things he'd once done before.

But the Commissioner found a rather more focused individual on this latest visit. Delaney seemed positively energised, in fact. Delaney first showed him printed screenshots of the messages he'd received. Then he accepted the job offer that had been made that week or so previously, and asked when they'd like him to start.

16

Two days after the attack on the Home for Convicts and the disappearance or abduction of Tobias Lundblad, Ros was on a ferry approaching Ilulissat again. The ongoing inquiries into the murder of Imaneq Kalia were being handled by Delaney back in Police HQ, his department handling the case in light of its connection to Alasie Kalia's unsolved murder.

Delaney was also overseeing another possible development. The stonemason who'd installed the new headstone on Alasie Kalia's grave was travelling to Nuuk. He was bringing with him all the emails from the mystery benefactor who had ordered and paid for the work. The email address had proved to be untraceable, Dorthe Kalia was still maintaining her silence and the young Desna was proving similarly uncommunicative as she waited to be moved to her temporary home in the UK. But the stonemason was also bringing with him one possible lead.

A family making a visit to a recent grave in the same graveyard had taken a picture of Alasie's new headstone shortly after it had been installed. They liked the colour of the granite and the style of lettering and wanted to know if the stonemason could provide something similar to replace the temporary marker that had been placed on the grave of their own loved one.

At the side of the photo a figure could be seen, a single male who seemed to be looking down at the same headstone. He could have been simply passing through the graveyard, he could have been visiting another grave completely, and the stonemason had no idea who he was. In other words, it was the longest of long shots, but the stonemason had brought the photo with him just in case.

So while Delaney remained in the capital, Ros had volunteered to investigate Tobias Lundblad. Ostensibly, at least. Her primary purpose, as ever, lay elsewhere. Because if Lundblad had anything to do with Alasie's death, as local gossip had always strongly suggested, and if Emmanuel had anything to do with Imaneq's death, as that photo also strongly suggested, then was there a connection?

And if there was, then could that connection lead not only to Lundblad's whereabouts, but to Emmanuel's too?

In other words, it was probably the longest of long shots too, but Ros was heading back to Ilullisat anyway.

Just in case.

Before she'd set off, Ros had called into Delaney's office to try and build some bridges, but it was an attempt that had spectacularly, if perhaps predictably, failed. Delaney was still clearly deeply suspicious of the new arrival and still distrusted the official reason she was there in the first place. For her part, Ros couldn't blame him. If she'd been in Delaney's shoes, she'd have felt exactly the same. So she travelled down to the harbour and boarded the late-night coastal steamer instead.

Ros actually managed a half-decent night's sleep, gently rocked by the rolling sea outside, and woke to an azure sky and a landscape of tiny icebergs dusting the horizon. She also awoke to a change of air, and not for the first time tried to imagine what it must be like for those growing up in the far north to travel south, feeling the air quality deteriorate the further they went.

A few moments after the ferry had glided into the harbour, Ros was walking down the main street, passing the local *braettet* where local fishermen sold their catches and hunters bartered whatever they'd managed to capture in their traps. The cafés were packed with tourists, most whiling away the time while they waited for one of the many excursions on offer. The most popular seemed to be a midnight sail up to the ice cap, from which visitors would return with their very own piece of the thousand-year-old ice sheet packed away in a small freezer by the crew, before returning to hotels where they'd listen to that same ice crackle as it melted into their late-night drinks.

It was an expanding trade, and that wasn't solely due to the rest of the world discovering the attractions of a hitherto-unspoilt country. Some of it had been forced on the country too. Back in the 1960s the Danish boat-building industry had suffered a dramatic collapse. To help stimulate demand for their boats, the Danes had effectively forced many Greenlanders to give up hunting and take up fishing instead. When the worldwide fishing industry then went into recession in turn, many of those displaced hunters foundered. Tourism became a way of making up the shortfall.

Ros looked at life going on around her as she walked on. In truth, it had always been an uneasy lifestyle for many, and Ilulissat still bore all the hallmarks of a reluctantly modernised settlement, where a large proportion of the population were separated from the traditional way of life they had been more familiar with. The old ways and even older attitudes died hard, and sometimes didn't die at all. Only the previous week, according to a report in a local paper Ros had found on the ferry, a local nurse had been called out to the house of a man who'd kept his daughter in a cage for seven years. The girl was autistic and her father simply didn't know how to handle her. If he let her out, he feared she would run out onto the ice and drown. He wasn't bad, just fearful, but the girl had now grown up fearful too, hating her makeshift prison. So she kept trying to run away and he kept bringing her back.

Then Ros paused as her first port of call hove into view further down the street: a carpenter's workshop, two figures visible inside. One of them was a local man, Rasmus Broberg, who'd been an old schoolmate of Tobias Lundblad and a good friend of Alasie Kalia. Which yet again wasn't much of a connection, but again it was all she had.

As Ros drew closer, she could see through the clear glass of the front window the usual beaver shots of naked white women pinned up on the wall. A small pack of Greenlandic sled dogs were tethered outside, slightly smaller than the Alaskan husky but with the same shape of head and ears and the same upturned tail. But as Ros walked past there was no response. These dogs paid attention to those who fed them. No one else mattered.

Inside, the workshop was high-ceilinged. All around the walls, as well as the pictures of women, were workbenches on which a whole variety of sleds were being constructed. Ros stood for a moment in the doorway, drinking in the smell of the freshly cut wood. Neither of the two men, who both had bottles of Tuborg beer by their sides, looked up. Perhaps they'd already pigeonholed her as just another curious tourist.

Ros walked across and nodded down at the sled on which the nearest of the workmen, Broberg himself – a great bear of a man with reddish-blond hair – was working.

'Are these for Uummannaq?'

Broberg himself made no response, but the carpenter to his side looked up, surprised. Each district in Greenland had different styles of sleds, each serving a different purpose depending on their function and the time of year. Long sleds, up to eighteen feet long, were used in the spring to hunt narwhal when the sea ice was breaking up, while sleds for hunting seal in districts such as Uummannaq would be only six to eight feet long.

Ros bent to inspect the runners.

'And you use whole trees, yes?'

The second carpenter eyed her, growing impressed now as well as surprised. If Ros was a tourist, she was curiously well informed.

'We take them split in half and air-dried.'

Broberg eyed her as Ros put her hands on the carved handles, which were perfect for manoeuvring in the mountains

'From Denmark?'

'Norway.'

Which was the sum total of Ros's internet-sourced knowledge of sleds and sledging dredged from some hasty research on the ferry. She was hoping it might break the ice.

She was wrong.

'So what's this?'

Broberg spoke for the first whole time, still looking at Ros as if she was one of the town's resident rats.

'Chance to rehash all that shit you people wrote before?'

Ros stared, puzzled for a moment as Broberg nodded again.

'I saw you a few days ago –'

By his side, the second carpenter began to tense as comprehension also began to dawn for Ros.

'Up at the graveyard –'

Ros stepped in, quickly. She'd been accused of many things in the past but this was a stretch too far.

'I'm not a journalist.'

'So what are you?'

'A police officer.'

Which only made the temperature in that small workshop plunge even further.

'And what's all this to do with the police?'

What had a murder – a double murder, indeed – to do with the police?

Ros couldn't help blinking at that one.

'You've got the boy who killed Alasie. Lundblad. Not for that, maybe, but he's down in Nuuk in the Home for Convicts.'

Ros hesitated. Clearly news of the latest development involving Tobias Lundblad hadn't reached the town yet.

'I'm new to the case. I've been reading up a little. Getting myself up to speed.'

Ros, as casually as she could, began to take out the photo of Emmanuel, cropped from the Imaneq Kalia picture found on Tom Edwards's phone.

'We're looking for this man. There might be a connection.'

Did Broberg even glance at it? And was there any glimmer of recognition in his eyes if he did? Ros would replay that encounter time and again in the hours that followed, but she still couldn't decide. There was certainly no time to probe it then. Broberg was already moving towards the still-open door leading back out onto the street, shepherding Ros before him as he went.

As they emerged, one of the pack of dogs, its head marked by a distinctive patch of russet red and grey colouring and the leader by the look of him, raised himself from the ground. The dog moved closer to Ros, perhaps as she was now in the company of one of the pack's regular providers of food.

Ros, as another belated attempt to build already burnt bridges, held out her hand by way of a greeting but Broberg emitted a low warning whistle and the dog immediately slunk back onto the ground.

Ros looked down into the dog's now-frightened eyes for a moment, then moved on too.

Meanwhile, back in Nuuk, Sandgreen saw the light as he was putting out his own. A dim illumination along the corridor coming from Delaney's office, but he knew Delaney was down at the harbour right now, meeting the stonemason from Ilulissat.

Sandgreen trod carefully along the corridor. Intruders actually inside the local Police Headquarters were pretty well unheard-of, but the one thing Sandgreen had learnt in nearly thirty years of policing was that nothing should be taken for granted. He paused outside the office door, then pushed it open.

Bent over Delaney's desk, her long hair almost obscuring the file she was studying, was Cecilie.

Cecilie raised a lazy eye to look at the staring Sandgreen framed in the doorway, and an all too familiar feeling stole over him. It was ridiculous and Sandgreen knew it, but almost from the first day this particular new recruit had started, Cecilie had the ability to make him feel as if she was the boss and he the junior, usually just by dint of that same lazy stare.

Partly, he would have to concede, it was how most men felt in the company of exceptionally attractive women – and Cecilie was certainly that. Tongue-tied and foolish. As if they were star-struck teens all over again.

But something else was going on here too. Something he hadn't yet been able to pin down. Sandgreen wasn't a man to give in to the fanciful, but sometimes he felt as if she could almost peer inside minds somehow, read thoughts in some way. And for various reasons he really didn't want to explore too closely, he didn't want to give that disturbing notion too much credence.

For a moment Cecilie just kept contemplating him with that same stare. Then she bent her head back to her file. Sandgreen paused for a moment longer, still at a loss to know what to do or even say.

Then he turned as Delaney himself returned, a single grainy photograph in hand. It was the photo of the man seen standing in the graveyard near to Alasie Kalia's grave.

It meant nothing to Delaney and when he showed it to Sandgreen and Cecilie, it meant nothing to them either.

One hour later, after running it through all countrywide police records, it still meant nothing.

Laila Lundblad, Tobias's mother, wasn't hostile or incommunicative. She was the exact opposite.

She started talking about her missing son the moment Ros stepped into her house, a light burning in her eyes all the while. In her mind, the adult Tobias was quite clearly still the infant she'd always doted on, even if others viewed him differently. The suspicions all too volubly expressed to Ros by the carpenter with the flaming red hair were shared by a lot of people in Ilulissat and it didn't help that in the years since Alasie's killing, Tobias Lundblad had mired himself in all manner of other troubles.

Ros didn't know if Lundblad's father possessed the same animation in his voice when he talked about his son. She didn't see him, at least at the start. There was a small shed at the back of the house where he worked on his motorbike. It was old and needed a lot of attention, apparently.

'These are the reports, right from the very first day.'

Almost before she'd taken a seat, Ros found herself staring at a bound scrapbook. Each page contained a newspaper cutting neatly excised from the local paper, all dealing with the disappearance of Alasie Kalia and the subsequent discovery of her body. It was the kind of scrapbook a parent might keep for a child's progress through school. Laila Lundblad had used it to record a child's murder.

'There were lots of other reports I could have put in, but most of them were just using what was reported here, so there wasn't much point.'

Ros silently scanned the neat pages.

'At the back I've put all the letters we got, as well.'

Ros turned to a small but still significant bundle appended to the end of the scrapbook. Letter after letter pouring coruscating vitriol on the teenage Tobias, dismissing his story that he'd simply seen the young Alasie that fateful evening and then walked on.

'Some are just abuse, but there's a couple from people who'd known Tobias for years and who didn't believe for a moment he was capable of something like that.'

Ros broke in.

'But you kept them all, including the hate letters?'

'Shouldn't I have done?'

'Some people might have found them distressing.'

'And there's this letter too.'

Laila smoothly dodged that one.

'This was from someone who knew Tobias well.'

Briefly, Ros felt her heart quicken.

Emmanuel?

'She used to live down the hill.'

Ros's heartbeat began to slow back to its normal rate.

'Eva's her name, Eva Lennert. Her father was long-term sick: his skin used to peel all the time. He used to work up in the airbase and always blamed the bomber, but no one knew if it was that or something else.'

Laila didn't need to elaborate. The story was well known in Greenland. In 1968, an American B-52 bomber had crashed in Bylot Sound, just south of Thule Air Base. It was carrying four nuclear weapons. On impact, a quantity of plutonium had spilled from the plane, contaminating many of those working in and around the airbase at the time. There'd been no medical survey carried out to study the long-term effects of such exposure and no one had any real idea of the quantity of plutonium involved or the scale of the contamination either. But in the years since, the number of walking wounded had grown exponentially.

Laila took another letter out of the bundle but didn't hand it over immediately. She just looked towards the window with eyes that now seemed miles and several lifetimes away.

'Her letter came a few years later. They'd moved away soon after Alasie was killed – her father was deteriorating fast by then. Tobias didn't show it to me. He was in such a dark place at the time, I don't think he even read it. It was his way of dealing with it all. Closing himself down so no one could hurt him.'

Laila Lundblad reached out, an instinctive gesture, and patted a slumbering old dog that had taken up near-permanent residence by her chair.

'She told him she'd also seen Alasie on the day she was attacked.'

Ros had been about to try and return the conversation to the actual reason for her visit, but now looked with renewed interest at the letter Laila was holding but had still not handed over. This was something new.

'I haven't seen any deposition from an Eva Lennert in any of the case notes.'

'You won't. That's why she wrote to Tobias. She'd just been told to go away when she tried to say all this to Geisler – Hans Geisler, the policeman in charge back then. He thought she was making it up because Eva and Tobias were friends.'

Laila shook her head, firm.

'Eva had never been like that. She had a hard time of it growing up but her father brought her up properly, to know the difference between right and wrong.'

Then Eva paused and the dog at her feet tensed as the door opened behind her and a small, wiry man appeared. Ros nodded at Tobias's father by way of a tentative greeting but Arne Lundblad just spotted what he was looking for, a steel chisel hanging on a hook, retrieved it and headed back again. From outside, Ros next heard the sound of the chisel digging into metal as if Arne was now gouging great chunks out of the frame of his bike.

Laila handed over Eva's letter as if he'd never even been there. Ros had the feeling she did that a lot.

Ros looked at the scrawled scribbles on the page in front of her. Over the years she'd got into the habit of scanning statements quickly, but this one wasn't going to take that long anyway.

Eva had spoken about seeing Tobias talking to Alasie. Then she'd seen him walk away. The problem being that everything was shot through with all sorts of wild assertions – how sweet and innocent Tobias was, how he wouldn't hurt anyone, how it was ridiculous that anyone would think he would – all of which sounded like special pleading on the part of a blinkered if not positively biased and naive young girl.

But there was something else in her statement. According to Eva, she'd seen someone else. A man, waiting a short distance down the track. There was something familiar in the way he was standing, she also claimed, but her attention had been more on Tobias and Alasie. She didn't see the man directly approach Alasie, and when she looked back down the track after Tobias had walked away, both the mystery man and Alasie had vanished.

Ros stared at the letter. Unreliable and vague as it may be, it was still the first report she'd read from any eye witness reporting a sighting of anyone with Alasie Kalia that afternoon aside from Tobias Lundblad.

So why would it have been so comprehensively dismissed by the man leading the investigation at the time?

And why hadn't this sighting featured in any of the case notes she'd read since?

Then suddenly, Laila broke in again.

'I kept them so one day I can answer them.'

For a moment Ros looked up at her, puzzled. Then she realised Laila had spooled back to Ros's question of a few moments before about keeping the letters, the question Ros had assumed she hadn't even heard.

'Tobias didn't do it. I know he didn't, because he told me. I knew that was never going to be enough for some people round here, but it was for me.'

Laila shook a quick, bitter, glance towards the door in the direction of her absent husband. The sound of the chisel hitting metal had now been replaced by the sound of silence, which in its own way was even more deafening.

'One day I'm going to answer each and every one of these.'

Laila Lundblad flipped through the hate mail at the back of the scrapbook, letting the letters fall through her fingers like so much confetti.

'And I'm going to send them a picture of Tobias.'

Laila nodded back at her.

'Looking at Alasie's killer being led down to the cells.'

Before she left and as casually as she could, Ros had laid out the photo of Emmanuel before Laila, much as she'd done with the hostile and incommunicative Broberg.

But the face staring out at her from that cropped photograph quite obviously meant nothing to her. And Emmanuel's name, when Ros cautiously broached that too, equally clearly meant nothing too. Then again, Ros had no guarantee that name wasn't one of many that Emmanuel might have used over the years.

Ros retraced her steps back down towards the harbour. She'd got precisely nowhere and had achieved nothing. She checked her watch. And there was still three hours to kill before she could catch the return ferry.

So Ros next dived into a nearby small house that had once been a family home, climbed the narrow stairs of the restored and preserved building and looked out from a window in a library on the first floor.

The house in question, now a museum, had been home to the Arctic explorer Knud Rasmussen and Ros was standing right now where Rasmussen himself must have stood so many times in the past as he looked out over the icebergs, waiting for the ocean to freeze over so he could set out with his dogs.

Born towards the end of the nineteenth century, Rasmussen – who was half Dane, half Eskimo – had grown up enthralled by his grandmother's stories of seal hunting, of song and drum dances and of tales of giants and spirits who dwelt on the ice.

Conventional schooling always held little appeal for him. From the earliest age, Rasmussen seemed to know that his real education was going to come not from schoolteachers or from books, but from the mouths of returning hunters, their sleds loaded with whale, seal and walrus.

But at the age of twelve, disaster struck the putative explorer. His father, a pastor, was transferred by his Church back to his own home in Denmark and Rasmussen swopped his icy paradise for what seemed to him to be a flat and rainswept hell. All through his teens the pull of the country of his birth fought a constant war with his newly adopted home, but finally Rasmussen found his way back when he was invited by the captain of a sailing ship to join what would be the young boy's first exploratory expedition to West Greenland. Metaphorical and probably literal wild horses couldn't have stopped him. So began a life that would be spent discovering and recording lives that would otherwise have been forever lost.

Ros wandered around the small museum. Up to that point, few had attempted anything like it. Greenland and its inhabitants had been little more than historical and geographical curios to most travellers, an interest that had occasionally assumed the most grotesque of forms. In one of the most extreme instances of cultural barbarism anyone could or would wish to remember, at the start of the twentieth century the American explorer Robert Peary had brought an Inuit father and son to New York to be paraded as living specimens before a generation of curious eyes in the American Museum of Natural History.

Ros moved back to the window, looking out again over the bay at the bergs and the howling dogs. Maybe what Rasmussen had done all those years before was all she'd ever wanted to do, and maybe that was why he and his life's work fascinated her. Create a true record of the lives of otherwise forgotten souls, a record that would stand the test of time.

Ros remained in silent contemplation for a few moments longer. Then she retraced her steps back down the winding stairs again.

A few moments later Ros passed the red-haired carpenter's workshop again.

Broberg and his companion stopped work as they saw her though the large front window. They didn't come out this time, but they did turn and stare. At first Ros imagined their hard stares were sending out the same silent, hostile signal as before, but then she realised there was another reason for their sudden scrutiny as she saw a rust-coloured patch just outside the window itself. At the same time, she saw that the pack of dogs were all now huddled to one side of the door.

Ros paused, unsure what she was actually seeing at first. But then she saw the dog, or at least what remained of the dog. At the same time, she recognised what was left of the distinctive russet red and grey colouring.

It was the dog who'd had the temerity to get up as Ros approached, the one who had responded to her hand stretched out in that instinctive greeting, before cowering back at the command of its provider and protector. Only this dog wouldn't be springing up again. And its protector and provider had obviously turned into something far removed from that too.

The dog was laid out on its back, paws stretched out crucifixion-style, nails from the workshop hammered into them, its fur sliced from crotch to neck and its inner organs strewn over the surrounding snow. Later, the rest of the dogs would be allowed to approach and feast on the remains of their former companion, but for now they'd been held back in that silent huddle, their freshly killed companion lying just a short distance away as a warning. An all too visible testament to the folly of engaging with those who should not be approached.

Ros looked down at the eviscerated dog for a moment longer as the eyes of the carpenters remained on her. Then she turned and walked on towards the harbour, the soft, almost inaudible, whimpers of the surviving dogs following her as she did so.

One hour later as Ros was waiting in the harbour for the ferry to take her back to the capital, she received a text from Sandgreen.

There'd been another killing.

Ros watched Delaney as he handed out the different reports, much as Masters had handed out those different reports on Tom Edwards back in that café in Cardiff – which was already beginning to seem like a lifetime ago.

Ros opened the first of them, staring at the face that appeared before her – the face of another bereaved soul.

First, Dorthe Kalia in Ilulissat.

Now Louise Andersen in Nuuk.

And once again, there it was. Once more the same phenomenon manifested itself. It was as if Ros had actually been there. As if she herself had directly witnessed all she was now reading.

'Why didn't you go with her?'

The young girl stared back at the adult standing a few inches away, and she was scared. She'd had adults shout at her before but that was for things she understood, like not putting her toys away or spilling her drink or getting her new school shoes scuffed when she'd been told not to go and play out in them, but this wasn't that sort of shouting. This was something else.

It didn't help that there were two strangers in the room as well, two police officers, another dislocating element in an already dislocated setting.

'We were just playing.'

'She wasn't playing, she wasn't even there.'

Then Louise stopped, aware even in her current torment that she was going too far. Part of her wanted to scoop the anxious little girl up into her arms, whisper soothing words of comfort as she would have done with her own child, soothe the terror lines that were now creasing her small face, telling her it was fine, that everything would work out, like everything always did.

Up to now, anyway.

The other part of her, the mother in her – Tia's mother – wanted to shake the stupid little thing to within an inch of her life until she told her where her own little girl had gone, because right now she was the only living soul who might be able to lift this nightmare from their heads.

Maybe – it was a desperate hope, Louise already knew – by suddenly confessing they were still playing some extended game of hide and seek, that all this was some kind of misjudged joke on the part of two six-year-old little girls; because the alternative was too awful to contemplate.

That her daughter, her precious only daughter, really had wandered off all by herself to change a skirt that had become muddied after a fall. That she'd come out of the field in which she'd been playing with her small friends and had then walked a short distance, only fifty metres or so, back towards home. But that had been three hours ago, and Tia still hadn't arrived. And her increasingly frantic mother had retraced the steps she'd taken a hundred times since, but of the small six year old with the muddied dress, there'd been absolutely no sign.

Tia's small companion, the child Louise was frantically interrogating, was the only one of her friends to see her actually leave. The little girl was trying her best, she really was – she could see this was important, even if she didn't know quite know why, so she screwed up her eyes in concentration, trying even at her young age to make sense of all she was being asked. All she really wanted was her mother, who had been alerted to what seemed to have happened and was racing back from work, but for now there was just Tia's mother and these two strangers, who were also trying to sound calm but were obviously anything but.

'She said she'd be back in a minute. She told me not to start the game again until she'd changed her dress.'

Then Tia's friend paused, her face suddenly creasing in injured complaint.

'She said she'd bring us lollies.'

Momentarily a picture flashed through Louise's mind: four ice lollies made that very morning by her daughter and herself, set into ice in the freezer compartment of their fridge. One for Tia – the red one, her favourite – and the others in different colours for her daughter to dispense to friends as she saw fit.

'But she didn't come back.'

Tia's young friend stared up at the adult, her blue eyes accusing now.

'And she didn't bring the lollies.'

And as Louise stared at her, the young mother's heart broke in two. She'd read about it in cheap novels, but she'd never believed it could actually happen – but it did, right there and then, and it happened the moment she looked into the eyes of an aggrieved little girl and realised she was telling the truth.

Because while that same little girl might join in with a misplaced tease, while she might keep playing a game way beyond the point at which anyone older than her small circle could possibly regard it as fun, she could never, ever, fake her obvious distress at not receiving her promised lolly.

Meaning the little girl was telling the truth.

Louise's beloved daughter Tia had indeed set off to walk back home, but had somehow never got there.

Cecilie joined them as Ros leafed through more reports as, now, did a grim-faced Sandgreen who had brought with him the initial findings of the police pathologist.

The small body of Tia Andersen had been found a couple of days later courtesy of a dogcatcher who'd come to Nuuk in disgrace. Previously the dogcatcher had lived in the far north of the country in the isolated communities around Qaanaaq until he'd screwed up, and big-time too. A major expedition had been planned by a few local hunters who'd intended to head over to the Humboldt Glacier, a vast stretch of frozen ice that stretched right to the edge of the ocean at Kane Basin. It was a trip that would take them at least a month to complete each way, but it was a trip that thanks to the dogcatcher was destined never even to be embarked on.

The dogcatcher was supposed to have vaccinated their dogs. But that was meant to take place three days into what became a five-day drinking session and the dogcatcher simply forgot. By the time he came out of his alcohol-induced miasma, distemper was already spreading through the pack with no way to stop it. Briefly the hunters contemplated setting off with the dogs that had not yet fallen ill, but twenty dogs died in just the first night, eighteen the next. Soon the hunters had only four dogs left between them and the trip was abandoned. The shamefaced dogcatcher left the very next day to carve out an equally precarious living patrolling the outlying districts of the capital, shooting any stray dogs he could find.

It had been out on one of his regular patrols that he'd seen it. A flash to his left as something copper-brown in colour darted past. He caught a glimpse of a fox, something in its mouth as it made its escape across a nearby road. A speeding vehicle blared its horn as it crossed its path, perhaps in anger, possibly in admiration. Foxes were a common sight in that part of the world but this one seemed to be a particularly fine, well-fed example.

The dogcatcher turned back from the road, stopping as he now saw what the fox had been feasting on. And where previously his normal working routine had just been its usual source of mild irritation, now it became something else. All of a sudden it became a nightmare in which he'd become enmeshed.

It also became a story he'd repeat to colleagues, friends and even casual acquaintances for months to come.

But first – his most immediate priority – it was a story he was going to have to repeat time and again to the local police.

Delaney picked up the pathologist's report. He'd taken personal charge of all that had followed. The routine was one that would have played out in any country anywhere in the world after any similar discovery, but that didn't make what followed any the less harrowing.

The closing of the road.

The painstaking efforts of various scene-of-crime officers as they collated the gruesome evidence.

The careful collection of different parts of a human body that couldn't be formally identified until they'd been returned to the pathology lab, but which everyone already knew for certain were the remains of a local six-year-old girl.

And, despite the frantic efforts of those local police to keep her away from the unholy resting place of a daughter whose body had been torn into pieces by that well-fed fox, a visit to the site by the frantic mother just a short time after the dogcatcher's discovery only served to confirm that.

An ever-grimmer Delaney personally led all that happened next too. The little CCTV evidence that had been gathered so far was checked. Eye witness accounts, mainly from motorists who had travelled that route over the last day or so, were investigated. Selected vehicles were identified as being of possible interest.

But then, as he began scanning the latest report that Sandgreen had just handed to them all, everything else was wiped so far as Delaney was concerned.

Delaney's disbelieving eyes took in the report of the speaker cable fashioned into ties, securing Tia's hand to that of her captor.

His ever more disbelieving eyes also took in the report of the thin smear of superglue that had clamped her lips together.

Already knowing what he was going to see, Delaney next took in the pathologist's initial report testifying to the high level of alcopops in the small girl's system, presumably the means whereby she'd been pacified prior to her attack.

And now Delaney wasn't seeing pictures of Tia anymore. Now Delaney was seeing pictures of another small child from twenty years before being led away from an adventure playground some two thousand or so miles away. The country was different, the setting was different but in all other respects it was like stepping back in time.

Tia's murder was an almost carbon copy of the killing of the small child that had ended his career in the UK all those years before. Delaney had been haunted by the memory of that tragic killing ever since.

Now, it seemed, it had literally come back to haunt him.

Delaney looked across the room at Ros, who was looking back at him. He could see instantly that she'd made the same connection too, but he could see more than that. He now saw his own confusion and bewilderment reflected back in her eyes as well.

Delaney left the briefing room a few moments later. Ros followed, as did Cecilie, who could also now quite clearly see that something was seriously wrong. But as Delaney came out into the fresher air outside Police Headquarters, a woman approached.

'He was going to some conference somewhere.'

Delaney stopped, as did Ros and Cecilie, all three officers staring at a young woman with similar blue/grey eyes to Cecilie herself, a small girl by her side who was staring, unblinking, up at them.

'That's what they said.'

The young woman stopped, looking across the water at an old colonial-style house, a long-established Nuuk landmark, the name of the business – *Mathiassen & Co., Attorneys at Law* – picked out in discreet lettering on a board outside.

'I didn't even know he was going till the night before and that was odd in itself: he never did anything last-minute. It was a standing joke – if we wanted a takeaway at the weekend, he'd be looking at the menu from the Wednesday before.'

The young woman stopped as Delaney just kept staring at her, realising that she wasn't actually making any sense.

'My name's Nivi Kleist. My husband, David –'

The young woman stopped. By her side, the young girl switched her unblinking stare onto her mother, who massaged her daughter's shoulder in an instinctive gesture of reassurance.

Ros was about to step in. They were in the middle of a murder inquiry. Whatever this young woman was talking about, this wasn't exactly the time and place to pursue it, but Nivi ploughed on, almost as if she realised she only had a few moments to say what she had to say and couldn't waste a moment.

'He'd been to conferences before, of course he had – and he'd travel too – he had clients to see; some here, some in different towns up and down the coast – the practice covers a large area. But he never got there, never even set off. He just went off drinking, they said – but he wouldn't do that. I know David: he just wouldn't.'

Dimly, for Cecilie, Ros and Delaney, the memory of a recent report began to coalesce: a local solicitor, a drunken trawl round the bars down in the harbour.

His body fished out of the water a few hours later.

Ros laid a cautious hand on Nivi's arm, still trying to divert her, but she didn't even seem to see her. Nivi just looked back across the water towards the large colonial-style house again.

'And I've found these files among his things – things he'd never told me about, things he'd never talked about – I don't understand why he'd be looking at stuff like that.'

Then Nivi stopped as she saw her small daughter still staring up at her. Nivi hesitated a moment, clearly not wanting to go into this in front of her, then she slipped a file into Delaney's hand, followed by a photo.

'Look, please – I have to understand.'

Nivi turned to head away with her daughter.

'Something's not right.'

Delaney looked down at the photo almost involuntarily, which was when for the second time in the last few moments, he froze. At the same time something of a miracle happened, because the fate of Tia Andersen and its macabre echoes were – momentarily at least – wiped from his mind.

The stonemason's grainy still of the figure standing near to Alasie Kalia's new headstone still hadn't thrown up any matches in police records in Nuuk or anywhere else.

It still meant nothing to the stonemason in Illulissat, nor to anyone he'd shown it to in the town.

But it meant something to Delaney now.

Delaney raised his head as Cecilie moved to his side and stared down at the same photo, realisation dawning on her now too.

The figure in the graveyard was the same figure in the photo now before them.

The drunken solicitor who'd drowned in the nearby harbour a few days before: David Kleist.

*S*HE WAS PERFECTION.
  I actually remember thinking that.

And my biggest regret, among so many others, was that I never told her.

But she knew it, in the way I'd trace the contours of her back with my fingers, in the way I'd stare into those eyes that held my stare as so few before had dared. In the way my voice always sounded as if it was a stranger's whenever I talked to her.

I didn't even want her to go back that day, despite everything we still had to do. I just wanted to forget everything; to close that door, shut out the rest of the world, let it just be the two of us – there, in that room, together, forever.

But I'd sent her back. Because we had to finish this. We'd both come too far and travelled too long for either of us to stop now.

And she'd smiled as I said that to her, smiled at the words she too had needed to hear, the words that were giving her the strength to do what she needed to do now too.

Swiftly, she'd leant forward and kissed me lightly on the lips.

Then she'd turned and, without looking back once, closed the door behind her.

If I'd known that was to be the last time we'd be alone together, I'd have curled myself into a foetal ball and howled to the skies.

But I didn't. All that was to come.

So for a moment I just lay back on the bed, staring up at the ceiling, that single tattoo in the middle of her back, just down from her recent branding, back before my eyes.

Then I rose and crossed to the phone.

Like Tyra, I now had work to do.

PART THREE

'PINIARTORSUAQ'

THE GREAT HUNTER

Ros SEATED HERSELF in front of her MacBook laptop. She was expecting another Skype call from Masters. Outside the streets were still quiet, the evening yet to get under way. Inside her mind was racing.

A debrief with Delaney following the exchange with Nivi Kleist had further laid bare the similarities between the murder of Tia Andersen and the murder that had ended his career in the UK. All logic dictated it had to be a grisly coincidence.

Ros looked out of the window, unseeing. Just as all logic dictated that the death of David Kleist could have nothing to do with his equally inexplicable appearance at the graveside of Alasie Kalia. A call to his widow in the aftermath of them all seeing that photo had confirmed that Nivi had no idea he'd made that trip and had no idea why he should have visited the grave. To the best of her knowledge, she was unaware of any connection at all between her late husband and a schoolgirl murdered more than twenty years ago.

But he had been there. That photo was incontrovertible. And now David Kleist was dead.

Just as Tia was now dead, having suffered a carbon copy of the fate of another child, also murdered over twenty years before.

Ros kept looking out of the window with those unseeing eyes. The shadowy figure of Emmanuel, a few grainy sightings aside, remained obstinately out of reach. But his presence still seeped into the very air around her. All that had happened both immediately before and since she'd arrived told her so.

The violent deaths of Steven and Callum Edwards, the murder of Imaneq Kalia, maybe even the potentially mysterious death of David Kleist and the brutal savagery meted out to the small Tia Andersen – logic may dictate one thing, but Ros better than most knew how unreliable simple logic could be. There'd been no logic in her sister's murder all those years before either.

How Emmanuel was connected to all those seemingly unrelated deaths, she still had no idea. What part he'd played in them, she also didn't know. But he was connected. He had played some part. Every instinct she possessed – instincts she'd come to trust without question – told her that. There were dots here to be joined.

But as she remained in front of her computer, staring at the unblinking screen, she was still as far away from connecting those dots as she'd ever been.

A couple of hours previously, Ros and Delaney had checked out his widow's concerns regarding David Kleist's movements on the day of his death with his employer, the present-day owner of Mathiassen & Co., Attorneys at Law, Martin Mathiassen. Cecilie, at her own insistence, had come along too.

Mathiassen had greeted them with old-world courtesy as he stood at the door of that elegant colonial house fringing the water. He was a tall, slightly patrician-looking man with a shock of white hair and looked to be around fifty, although it was difficult to age him exactly.

Mathiassen immediately also extended old-world hospitality, from a large drinks tray set on a sideboard that ran almost the whole length of the far wall of the office, then listened impassively as Delaney declined the offer and outlined Nivi's concerns.

Then Mathiassen expressed his own.

'We liked him. Everyone in the office did. David was a hard-working, popular member of the team and what happened to him was a great shock – all the more so as it seemed totally out of character.'

Mathiassen paused.

'The character we knew, anyway.'

Mathiassen hesitated again.

'We'd already begun to get the impression something was wrong, though.'

Mathiassen struggled for a moment.

'A month before he died, he told one of the partners he had to go to a conference. In Nanortalik. It was a two-day trip: fly into the heliport one day, fly out the next.'

'Nanortalik?' Delaney broke in, and Mathiassen nodded, picking up the query in his voice immediately.

Nanortalik was Greenland's southernmost town, located in amongst some of the country's most picturesque fjords. They were renowned for what some refer to as its 'natural skyscrapers' – the sheer, craggy peaks dotted all around Tasermiut Fjord, Pamialluk and the unique Prince Christian Sound. The region stretched from the island of Qeqertarsuaq over Cape Farewell to the 60 km-long Lindenow Fjord on its eastern coast, totalling over 15,000 square metres. Around 2,200 people lived there, working mainly in seal hunting and fishing, living in the small town, five outlying settlements and a number of sheep farms and worshipping in a small wooden church that dated from the early part of the twentieth century. The town's name meant 'place of polar bears', testament to the steady stream of them that would pass through the town in the summer, together with the pack ice from the Arctic Ocean.

It was not known for its conferences, legal or otherwise.

Mathiassen opened a desk drawer, extracting a slim cardboard file from inside.

'Then we found this among the documents on his office computer. It deals with the enforced chemical castration of sex offenders, including a case study on a procedure that actually took place in the former Soviet Union as well as details on exactly how that might be done, not only by those in the medical profession but by laymen as well.'

Mathiassen retrieved another sheet of paper.

'This deals with the identification of a 'criminal gene' at birth, enabling anyone who might be interested – the police or laymen again – to build up a database of likely criminals before the criminal in question has even been suckled.'

Cecilie broke in.

'Was David Kleist working on a case connected with the abuse, sexual or otherwise, of young children?'

Mathiassen just looked at her for a moment almost as if he was registering her presence for the first time. Perhaps he was. The silence stretched for a few moments longer as he kept looking at her, almost as if he vaguely recognised her from somewhere.

'We did find some files relating to that on his computer here. We wondered if they might be exercises of some kind. One of our senior partners initiated something similar years ago. His argument was that simulating controversial cases sharpened the intellectual reflexes and responses, recreated the cut and thrust of debate our colleagues enjoyed – or perhaps endured – at college and returned them to the day-to-day fray in a keener, more cutting frame of mind.'

Mathiassen shook his head.

'Total nonsense of course, but it was something of a company tradition at one time, and my father indulged it.'

Ros followed his look towards a portrait on the wall: it depicted an older version of the man currently before them, sporting the same shock of white hair, against a background that looked vaguely familiar.

Mathiassen nodded.

'That's him. Long dead now, sadly.'

Ros kept scanning the background.

'And that was painted in – ?'

But then suddenly Ros stopped as she recognised it.

'Ilulissat.'

Mathiassen smiled, nodded again.

'Where the practice started.'

A photo in a silver frame on the sideboard below the portrait showed the same older man again, but this time posed in front of a group of smiling children.

'That was something of a passion of his too. The local choir.'

Mathiassen eyed Delaney again.

'No, I can think of no work-related reason why David Kleist should have amassed this sort of material on either his home or his work computers. Even if they were just exercises of some kind.'

Mathiassen grimaced.

'They still seem pretty sick to me.'

Out of the corner of her eye, Ros caught Cecilie staring back at him, level and cold.

Back in her rented apartment, Ros looked up as her MacBook beeped with an incoming call alert.

She reached out and hit a key on the keyboard. But it wasn't Masters's face that swam before her.

Monobrow nodded back at her, cheerily, instead.

'Do you believe in Father Christmas?'

Ros stared back as Monobrow nodded behind him. Now she could see he was in her own apartment, the concierge behind him once again, maintaining his usual, long-suffering, watching brief, the video call having come from his number now she looked properly at the display, and redirected from her iPhone.

'Whoever built these apartments must do. I've just found a survey a so-called Specialist Timber and Damp Surveyor put in your kitchen drawer.'

Monobrow snorted.

'Know what a Specialist Timber and Damp Surveyor is?'

Ros couldn't help herself again. She was still just staring at his eyebrows.

Monobrow snorted again as he tapped the offending report.

'Well he's not any sort of real surveyor, for a start – he's a commission salesman.'

Monobrow hunched forward, his eyebrows now filling even more of the screen.

'This joker's sole purpose in life is to sell you timber treatment. For that he gets about 25% commission for a load of useless chemicals. Then he gets someone in to inject them into the walls, cutting him another 15%. Then he gets someone to replaster the wall and pockets about 10% of whatever they charge you for that. And for what?'

Monobrow's high-pitched voice was now scaling the upper heights of incredulity.

'To inject a water-based chemical into a supposedly wet wall and then expect it to somehow dry out.'

Ros tore her eyes away from the dense bush of hair scarring her caller's forehead, and checked the Skype message log at the side of the screen.

No incoming call from Masters as yet.

'And because so many people are brainwashed into believing all this, he gets a steady income from peddling it and the chemical companies make millions in profits.'

Monobrow's eyebrows nodded back at Ros again.

'Know what I'd do?'

In truth Ros couldn't have cared less, but she already had an all too familiar sinking feeling she was going to find out.

'Get the phone numbers of all the Timber and Damp companies I can find. Look them up, read the wording of their guarantees, then ask them whether they cover condensation damage in their guarantees.'

Monobrow hunched closer to the screen, nodding at her.

'Now that really would send them running for the hills.'

Ros cut across, finally speaking for the very first time.

'What do you want?'

Monobrow stopped.

'What?'

'Why have you called me?'

Monobrow looked back at her, puzzled for a moment as if he couldn't quite remember himself, then his expression cleared and he nodded towards the far wall of the kitchen.

'I've sorted out a date for the work to be done. I've put it on the calendar.'

'I don't have a calendar.'

Monobrow grinned.

'You do now. I've left one for you. I've left one for every resident in the block.'

The concierge, now looking ever more hard-pressed and long-suffering, cut in from behind.

'It won't take more than a few hours apparently, but I wanted to let you know in case you were back by then.'

The concierge shot a quick, harassed glance sideways at Monobrow.

'Or you wanted to be out while he was doing the work.'

Monobrow, now standing by the calendar with a red ring around the date, held up the leaflet from the damp course company he'd retrieved from Ros's kitchen drawer.

'Do you want to keep this?'

Ros shrugged.

'I didn't even know I had it.'

'I'll take it with me then.'

Monobrow smiled, grim.

'I'm presenting a paper next month at our trade convention. This sort of stuff is grist to the mill.'

But Ros wasn't looking at him any more. She was looking at the thin red ring encircling the date on that small calendar tacked up above one of the worktops.

For a moment Ros just stared at the date, rooted. For that moment she was back in the hallway of her father's small house, staring at the numbers picked out in his blood on the wall.

Ros kept staring. This was another simple, if macabre, coincidence. All logic once again dictated it had to be.

But the date that had been ringed for Monobrow's return and the date spelt out in blood on that hallway wall were one and the same.

Ros remained in front of her computer for a good few more moments. Outside, the different sounds on the street were growing more clamorous by the moment. But none were more clamorous than the sounds filling the silent space inside her head right now.

She took a deep breath, almost physically shaking herself as she did so. Then she turned back to her computer and opened up a different window before typing in the name and the only potential new avenue of inquiry Laila Lundblad had given her during their interview.

Eva Lennert.

Tobias Lundblad's old childhood friend and, seemingly, his only childhood champion.

M ASTERS WASN'T DESTINED to make his Skype call to Ros
that day.

He'd taken another phone call just one hour previously. He hadn't told anyone in Murder Squad what it was about or what his caller had said to him. He just climbed into his Bentley and pointed the bonnet of the six-litre behemoth towards the busy feeder road that led to the remand facility inside the capital's Victorian prison.

Partly because he didn't want to think about the phone call he'd just received, and partly because he couldn't help thinking about it, Masters let his mind run on Ros as he drove. To his mild unease, he found it happening more and more these days. Partly that was just the simple curiosity he'd felt ever since their paths had first crossed, which had only increased since he'd understood more about her background in the last year. Partly it was because he also didn't know what to do about it.

If what he was experiencing was pure and simple attraction then maybe he could have consummated or excised it, in the case of the former by asking her out for a drink, with a refusal condemning him to the latter.

There was another option, of course, which was to do absolutely nothing. Which was what he'd done up to now and strongly suspected he'd do from that point on too – which, in the life of a man always renowned for his determinedly decisive action, was something of a new experience and an unwelcome one at that.

Masters parked in the multi-storey opposite the prison and walked across to the Visitor's Centre. Holding up his hands for the obligatory rub down and check with a metal detector, he barely registered the passive drugs dog who gave him an equally disinterested sniff. He also barely registered the sudden commotion that broke out as another visitor believed, mistakenly, that she was being asked to remove her religious headwear. He didn't even take in the large posters advertising the prison's new amenity: a restaurant actually inside the prison itself, open to the public and staffed by the inmates.

Masters just followed his guide for the day, his mind not on the security procedures or the attractions or otherwise of the newly opened restaurant, or even on his upcoming interview with the family murderer, Tom Edwards.

Masters's mind, once again, was running on Ros.

It wasn't just attraction, although Masters was honest enough to admit that was at least part of it. All he knew was that for reasons he was at one and the same time excited and reluctant to explore, Ros fascinated him – and that wasn't simply to do with all he'd recently discovered about her. For her part, he didn't think Ros remotely realised that, which of course only added to the fascination.

Masters stared, unseeing, at the depressingly dull corridors as they walked on. He was also sufficiently self-aware to realise that fascination was probably obvious to anyone else who cared to take an interest in the way he would studiously try and ignore her every time their paths crossed. But he really didn't want to think about that, and so he didn't.

A door opened before him and Masters was ushered into an interview room where the pale killer with the mousey hair and the watery eyes was already waiting for him.

Tom Edwards's duty brief was with him, but neither he nor Edwards nor Masters were destined to remain there for long.

Within another two minutes the three men were down in the prison kitchens.

Masters had checked before he'd even set off from Police HQ that they weren't being used at that time. He'd also checked that the cleaning staff had finished for the day, which meant he had Tom Edwards exactly where he wanted him for everything he now had to say.

'What's that, do you suppose?'

It was about the first thing Masters had said after leading the two men out of the interview room, and Edwards's brief followed Masters's look across the kitchen floor. They were standing by a large metal door, presumably to a freezer room for the prison's fresh meat and fish. Masters had seen it on one of his previous visits and had always known it would come in useful one day.

For his part, Tom Edwards barely glanced at it, barely indeed even seemed to register where he was or who was with him. He'd completely closed down, in fact, after his first interview with Masters, and had remained that way ever since. Which was what this was all about.

The kitchen.

That freezer.

Masters was about to open him up again.

Masters yanked open the door. Then he turned back and with one swift movement locked his right hand around the brief's left arm. Under a second later the brief was inside, the door firmly locked from the outside.

Masters turned back to Tom Edwards and was gratified to now see something other than the near catatonic stonewall withdrawal that had been on sole show so far flecking his prisoner's eyes.

And as he realised there was now just himself and Masters, alone in that prison kitchen.

'Are you familiar with the works of Cicero, Mr Edwards?'

Edwards just stared back at him as Masters began to pace the spotless tiled floor of the kitchen.

'Roman orator and statesman, some say the greatest Roman orator that ever lived. Although not the greatest statesman: my vote on that count goes to Augustus.'

As Edwards kept staring, Masters paced some more.

'Christian or given name, Marcus Tullius; murdered on 7 December 43 BC, although I understand CE is now more commonly used amongst scholars, hunted down by lackeys of Mark Antony – hired assassins who finally caught up with him in his old age and slit his throat.'

From the freezer behind him came the sound of muffled cries as Edwards's brief attempted to muster what protest he could against his totally illegal incarceration.

'After his death they hacked off his head and hands and sent them to Mark Antony and his wife Fulvia as proof that the deed had been done. When the parcel arrived, Antony ordered that the remnants be displayed in the Forum, nailed to the spot in fact where Cicero had delivered many of his devastating tirades, but not before Fulvia had taken the head on her lap, pulled out the tongue and stabbed it with a pin taken from her hair.'

Masters paused.

'A telling choice of both weapon and target, because in rending his tongue with her hairpin, she was of course attacking the very faculty that had come to define Cicero's power.'

Edwards finally spoke.

'What the fuck is this?'

A bewildered intervention which was treated in exactly the same way as his brief's frantic cries from inside the freezer.

Masters just ignored them both.

'*Vixere*. That was my first introduction to him. A single word I couldn't get out of my mind when I first heard it – although some might argue that *vixerunt* might be a more accurate translation, but as *vixere* and *vixerunt* are simply alternative forms of the perfect tense third person plural and there's no difference in grammar or sense either way, then let's put pedantry to one side for now, shall we?'

Masters moved closer. Edwards wasn't the most educated or even intelligent of men. He'd never heard of the subject of Masters's current diatribe. But what he lacked in intelligence, – both conventional and clearly emotional too, if the actions he'd taken against his two sons were anything to go by – he made up for in instinct. The same instinct that was telling him his life had never been in more danger than it was right now.

'That single word was shouted down to the crowds outside the Roman Forum just after the death of Lucius Catilina, the one incident more than any that was to dog Cicero, not just in his life but to this day.'

Masters smiled briefly at his one-man audience, who wasn't smiling at all.

'And if any more proof of that were needed, just look at the two of us. Still talking about him even now.'

From inside the freezer, the cries were beginning to sound louder, more panicked.

'Catilina was a young aristocrat, frustrated by his failure to win election to the political office he thought his due, so he decided to take an alternative route to riches by plotting a revolutionary uprising.'

The still uncomprehending Edwards wasn't looking at anything else but Masters's eyes boring down into his own. The whole world had shrunk down to just the two of them, everything and everyone else excluded.

'Cicero drove him out of the city, rounded up the remaining conspirators and put them to death without trial. As they were dispatched, Cicero called out just that one word to the crowds waiting in and outside the Forum – *vixere*, which literally meant *they have lived*, which was another way of course of saying, *they're dead.*'

Edwards tried to cut in again, the sound of his solicitor hitting the inside of the freezer echoing louder all the time.

'What are you doing?'

But Masters just rolled on as if he hadn't even heard him, which was actually perfectly possible. More than one of his colleagues had testified to Masters almost going into some sort of trance when he was off on one of his extended soliloquies.

Others, Ros among them, didn't believe a word of it. In her book, Masters was never anything but totally calculated, always in total control.

'Those judicial killings instantly became something of a cause célèbre. Yes, a state of emergency had been declared, yes, there was a perceived and active threat to the very heart of the body politic, but what exactly should even a state of emergency permit a state to do? How far, for example, was it ever legitimate for a constitutional government to suspend the constitutional rights of its people? It made Cicero's colleagues in the Forum extremely uneasy and it actually handed his enemies the opportunity they'd been seeking for years to act against him, by not only killing him but knocking down his house in Rome and replacing it with a shrine to the goddess Liberty.'

Masters leant closer, his face now just inches from his unlikely and even more unwilling new Classics scholar.

'But there were more fundamental questions for Cicero, because quite a few contemporary commentators even wondered exactly how much of a threat to the state the young Catilina actually posed.'

Masters started pacing again.

'Cicero was a self-made politician. He had no aristocratic connections and only a precarious place in the top rank of the Roman elite, amid families who claimed a direct line back to the age of Romulus. Julius Caesar, for example, could apparently trace his lineage back to Aeneas and the goddess Venus herself.

244

So to secure his position, Cicero needed to make a splash. An outstanding military victory against some threatening barbarian enemy perhaps, but Cicero was no soldier. So he needed to save the state in some other way.'

Edwards tensed. Something told him that whatever game was being played here, and whatever the fuck Masters was actually talking about, that game was now approaching its end.

'So was Lucius Catilina and the Catiline conspiracy if not an invention, then an opportunity? Was that simply a means to a greater end, and was Catilina himself simple collateral damage?'

Masters nodded at him.

'Why did you kill your solicitor, Mr Edwards?'

Edwards blinked back.

'What?

'What was it, pure and simple blood lust? Having killed once, did you feel impelled somehow to do it again?'

Edwards stared back at him, one thought only now hammering through what was fast becoming his overheated brain.

Was Masters actually insane? He wasn't to know it, but many had also pondered that exact same notion before him, including many of Masters's own colleagues.

'That's not true –'

Masters just cupped his hand to his ear.

'Listen, Mr Edwards. Just listen, and from across the centuries, if you listen closely enough, you'll hear the plaintive cry of Catilina also insisting he's done nothing wrong, that the crimes of which he's accused are simply an invention on the part of his persecutors.'

Masters shrugged, eyed him almost pityingly.

'But Catilina didn't write the records.'

Masters nodded at him once more.

'As you won't get to write any record of what's taken place in this room.'

Masters began to pace again.

'From the moment I left you in the company of your brief to reflect on the statement you wished to make after the news I'd just broken to you.'

Less than a metre or so away across that tiled floor, Edwards now began to still.

'To the moment I returned – too late, to my eternal regret, to prevent the callous killing of a totally innocent and well-respected fellow-professional by a prisoner clearly tormented by guilt and grief.'

Edwards just kept staring at him.

'What news?'

From inside the freezer, the ever more sporadic blows on the locked door from Edwards's brief had stopped, incipient hypothermia perhaps beginning to rob him of any further ability to protest his confinement.

Masters once again didn't reply, just flicked open his phone case and summoned up the photo that had kick-started Ros's current journey: that of Emmanuel with Imaneq Kalia.

'Who's this?'

Edwards didn't even look at it.

'I said, what news?'

The next moment Edwards had little choice to look at it as his neck was constricted into a headlock.

Masters repeated his question.

'Who?'

Edwards gasped some more as Masters increased his grip on his neck and he finally took in the image before him.

From the freezer came a dull thump, possibly as his brief finally slumped to the floor.

'Where did you meet him?'

Edwards gasped.

'I've never met him.'

'So why is his photo on your fucking phone?'

Masters leant closer, his eyes now all Edwards could see.

'What happened, Mr Edwards?'

Edwards just kept staring back at him.

'What happened in your sad little life that put an inadequate little fucker like you in this man's orbit?'

Edwards's breathing was now coming in great rattling gasps.

'There was some trouble.'

Edwards gasped again.

'When I was in the Army.'

Masters nodded.

He'd guessed that much himself.

'And he sorted it for you – that was the deal: he sorted it and from that moment he had you, yes?'

Edwards's voice was now little more than a wheezing, suffocating whisper.

'How many more times, I don't even know who he is.'

Masters stared at him. He'd really have expected to have broken Edwards's fall-back story by now.

'So who did sort this trouble for you?'

Strange rattling noises were now coming from Edwards's throat. Masters leant closer.

'I said, who?'

Edwards told him.

And that was the moment.

The moment that changed everything.

Masters just stared back at Edwards, slowly releasing his grip as he did so. Edwards himself slipped to the floor, massaging his throat, trying to force air down inside his still-constricted windpipe. Masters didn't even see him. All he saw was a face summoned by the name Edwards had just uttered.

Masters remained in the same state of near-suspended animation for a moment longer.

Ros's past had comprehensively caught up with her a few days before. Now it seemed Masters's past had just caught up with him too.

Masters remained silent for a moment longer. Then, still without speaking, he left the kitchen and the still-gasping Edwards without saying another word, as the sound of guards approaching along the corridor grew louder.

Masters exited the prison and climbed back into his Bentley, remaining stock still for a moment longer again, his mind still full of that name he'd just heard and the images it had conjured.

He pressed a button on the central console in front of him and a low rumble sounded. Picking up his mobile, he sent a quick text to the Prison Governor and to the solicitor he'd just 'imprisoned', thanking them both for their part in the charade he'd just staged. Both had been equally sickened by the actions of a man who could kill his two small boys like that, and both had been more than happy to let Masters to conduct that latest interview in his own idiosyncratic way.

Then Masters selected a gear, but before he drove away, he realised that he still hadn't enlightened Edwards as to the official reason for his visit that day – and after the bombshell he'd just endured, he certainly wasn't going to now.

He'd let the Prison Governor tell Tom Edwards in his own good time that his grieving wife Jo had given up the unequal struggle to maintain any sort of interest in life any more, and had killed herself that very morning.

L AILA LUNDBLAD HAD been reluctant to put Ros in direct touch with her son's old friend; a reluctance that puzzled Ros at the start, given that Eva's testimony about spotting the mystery figure on the track immediately after she'd seen Lundblad and Alasie Kalia was the closest thing Laila's family had to fresh evidence.

So Ros made the approach herself.

She drove out along a single-track road that led from Nuuk to the outlying district of Qinngorput. Her destination was a small rented house in a small cluster of similar houses, painted like its neighbours in blue with windows stretching floor to ceiling. Ros's online searches had revealed it to be the present day address of Eva Lennert. And a short time later, Laila's reluctance to introduce them was becoming a little more understandable.

Eva had actually left Ilulissat some years before, but her move seemed to have nothing to do with Lundblad or his mother. And she'd had little or no contact with any of her old friends or contacts since she'd left. That part of her life, her one letter to Laila aside, seemed to be well and truly over so far as she was concerned.

Ros's further and necessarily hasty online checks on Eva revealed that she'd initially settled in the now-demolished Block P on arriving in the capital. Ros passed the land it had previously occupied on her way. From her previous visit she could still recall the locals who would gather at either end, look all the way up the five stories to its roof, look down its 200 m length and shake their heads at the grotesque dislocation between its setting and scale – and no wonder.

The whole edifice had seemed to Ros to have materialised as if by some macabre sleight of hand, crammed in among the more traditional single-gabled dwellings from some other galaxy somewhere, although initially its notoriety had actually made it an unlikely tourist attraction too. In its early days, travellers would actually make a special trip to see a housing complex dubbed as one of the most depressing in the world, and not even a defiant work of art on one of the windowless, concrete end walls – a four-storey-high red and white Greenlandic flag created by a local artist and sewn from hundreds of articles of discarded clothing with the help of local schoolchildren – had ever made it anything else.

'Vicious little bastard.'

Ros stared at Eva as she dragged on the first of many cigarettes.

'It was only a matter of time.'

Ros kept staring as Eva shrugged.

'Scum always rises to the surface. What else do you expect?'

The smoke from Eva's cigarette broke against the far wall as Ros kept staring at her.

Eva shrugged.

'It's all I heard. All the time I was up there. Everyone said it too, not just the police. The only place for Tobias from the moment he was born was inside.'

Behind, in the next room, a mobile phone rang. But Eva paid it no heed, just plunged on with her story – the phone stopping after just a couple of rings, the call presumably diverted to her answer service.

'Every time I tried to say something, when I tried to point out that Tobias really wasn't like that, I was just shouted down. So I stopped.'

'Shouted down by who?'

'I told you. Everyone.'

Ros persisted.

'In particular?'

'That officer, the one in charge.'

Eva lit another cigarette.

'He was the main one, I suppose.'

Ros didn't need to supply the name but she did anyway. Just to be 100% sure.

'Geisler?'

Eva nodded back. In the next room the mobile rang again before, presumably, being diverted to the answer service again.

Ros hunched closer.

'The figure – the one you saw on the path after seeing Tobias and Alasie –'

Eva cut across.

'I didn't see any figure.'

Ros stared at her again.

'That's what he told me. Geisler. I didn't see anyone. That never happened. There was never anyone there.'

Eva shook her head.

'I was thirteen, for fuck's sake. What could I say?'

The brooding Eva paused for a moment and dragged on her cigarette, her mind totally back there now, in her home town with her old childhood friend.

In the next room, the phone began ringing for a third time. Again, it was the same pattern. Eva ignored it and after just a couple of rings her the answer service cut in.

As it did so, Ros looked round, now taking in a radio playing softly in the corner as well as an incense stick in a holder with a notepad next to it. As well as a discreet but still visible small glass container with what looked a dozen or so condoms inside.

And now Ros began to put a few connections together, including Laila's Lundblad's reluctance to broker any actual meeting between herself and Eva, and those near incessant phone calls.

'And you've no idea where Tobias might be now?'

Eva shook her head.

'I don't know if I'd even recognise him.'

Ros looked at her, curious.

'Is that why you got away?'

And now Eva hesitated.

'All that happened?'

Eve hesitated some more.

'Not just that.'

The young woman lit another cigarette, having taken just one drag from the previous one, now discarded.

Ros looked at her as Eva hesitated again, struggling for a moment longer.

'Something happened to me. Something bad. Didn't Laila tell you?'

Ros shook her head.

Eva struggled again. In the next room the phone rang once more. In her hand, her latest and still untouched cigarette was burning down towards her fingers.

'We'd all been in this bar. The whole town – all the kids, anyway. I met this boy – well, man, I suppose. Early twenties, something like that. I'd never seen him before.'

Eva paused, the red tip of her cigarette getting closer to her fingers all the while.

'We danced. Drank. Scored. Then he took me outside, lit this pipe with all these crystals inside. Pressed it up to my lips.'

Eva shuddered.

'I'd never felt anything like it before. Never felt so awake – so alive – so happy, I suppose. The next thing I knew, he'd ripped my skirt off. I tried fighting him off but he smashed me up against the wall. He finished in seconds but before he went, he injected me with something. After that, nothing else mattered. All I could see were those crystals.'

Eva paused again, looked at the radio, the incense holder, the notepad, the condoms.

'All I wanted to do after that was get away.'

Then suddenly there was a ring on the bell outside. Eva hesitated another moment, but then she checked her watch, looked back at Ros, already clearly regretting opening up to her like that.

'That's all I can tell you.'

Ros hesitated, then nodded back and stood. But Eva cut across as she began to head towards the front hallway.

'There's a side door.'

Ros looked back as Eva nodded behind her.

'Can you use that?'

Ros hesitated a moment longer again, then nodded back once more. Ros had never met Hans Geisler but by all accounts he was a well-respected and now retired senior police officer. She really shouldn't take the testimony of a small-time out-of-town prostitute over a figure like that.

But she'd seen the light shining in Eva's eyes.

And she believed every single word she'd said.

But then, just before she reached the door, Ros paused and looked back.

'Are you sure you can't remember?'

'What?'

'The man – the one you saw talking to Alasie?'

Eva kept looking at her.

'Was there anything about him at all?'

Ros took a photo out of her bag. It was the third time she'd shown it to a potential witness. On the first two occasions she'd been met by indifference and incomprehension.

But this time Eva nodded back immediately.

'Yeah. That's him.'

Ros looked down at the photo of Emmanuel, then turned away as the doorbell rang once more. Ros emerged from the side door of Eva's small house a few moments later, just catching a single glimpse of a furtive face heading in through the front.

On the drive back to the capital, Ros took a phone call from Masters, who told her about Jo.

For the next few moments, Ros's mind simply emptied. She didn't think about anything or anyone. And when a figure finally did swim before her eyes, it wasn't the one she'd have expected to see.

Ros's mind was suddenly filled with someone she hadn't thought about for years: a young Greenlander called Malik Olsen. A young man who, in ways neither he nor she realised at the time, changed her life.

Malik had actually prompted Ros's previous visit to his home country. At the time Greenland seemed to be just another of the countries she'd trawled as a teenager as she'd wandered around the world more or less aimlessly, or so it had seemed to her back then. In actuality and as she'd come to understand later, it was all part of the same seemingly ceaseless quest that she was following at the time, as she searched for her place in a world in which everyone else seemed to already have found theirs.

Ros had found one such place in a small square in Amsterdam, just before she'd made that first trip to the land of the frozen North. On her arrival in that city, she'd moved around the usual canals and cannabis cafés as all around her milled stag parties and sex tourists. But then, by total chance, she'd walked into a small piece of heaven, a refuge housed in a small courtyard.

The various houses sited there had originally been a sanctuary for the Begijntjes, a Catholic sisterhood who lived like nuns although they took no monastic vows. The sisterhood had long gone but the tall houses were still grouped around a small square which contained a well-maintained garden. Amsterdam's oldest house, Het Houten Huis, was also sited there. No traffic noise intruded, augmenting the otherworldly atmosphere.

On that first visit to the former sanctuary, Ros simply settled herself on a small bench and stayed there till nightfall, undisturbed by the curious or concerned. On her various trips back to the city since, Ros had always returned. It was almost as if she'd adopted that small and curious retreat in some way. But it was more than that, because unlike many of the places she'd visited as a sole traveller back then, Ros always felt as if it had adopted her too.

It was there that Ros had also come across Malik, whose name in Greenlandic meant 'wave'. Malik wasn't an aimless traveller like Ros, but a lawyer sent by his company on a training tour of different branches of their company in northern Europe and beyond. He'd already visited Denmark and the UK and was travelling on to America. In one of his coat pockets he carried an electronic notebook, into which he'd commit thoughts regarding the different branches of the law firms he visited. But in his other pocket, he carried a stone.

Malik had a girlfriend back home in Greenland called Paninnguaq. Her name translated as 'sweet little daughter'. They'd grown up together as children and had been inseparable ever since. Many of Malik's friends and family, and possibly even Paninnguaq herself, had seen this trip as something of a test, and a make-or-break test at that. Maybe his employers had too.

Would Malik's eyes be dazzled by the wider world he encountered? Would he return home changed beyond recognition by his new experiences, and would his old relationship survive all that? Would he indeed return at all? In the six months he was going to be away, would he simply meet someone else and forget her? Or would Paninnguaq, who was something of a beauty from the pictures the shyly smiling Malik showed Ros, forget about him instead?

Before Malik left home, he'd picked up the small stone. Nothing special, just an ordinary stone he found in the snow. He told Paninnguaq that he'd keep it with him and think about her every time he held it in his hand. And when he returned home he'd show her that exact same stone and then they'd marry.

That stone travelled with Malik everywhere. He took it through Customs in all the countries he visited, hiding it each time so no inquisitive official would find it, because he didn't dare risk it being confiscated. On his visit to America he'd had to hide it in his mouth when he was being patted down by immigration officials. By such subterfuges he'd kept that keepsake safe as he promised, and when he went home all those months later, he took that exact same stone out of his pocket and showed it to his childhood sweetheart and they married two weeks later.

Ros had kept in touch with Malik since their very first meeting, journeying with him vicariously on his travels as he kept her company on hers. Two souls in transit, one with a fixed point in view, the other with none. When Malik had returned home, he'd emailed her a photo of his childhood sweetheart, now his fiancé, holding the stone along with an invitation to their upcoming wedding, if she would like to visit his country.

One week later Ros travelled to Copenhagen and managed to secure passage on a steamer. She spent almost the entire journey on deck, not even feeling the deepening cold. As they approached land, Ros remained on the open deck, listening to the sound of the water breaking on the shore in the distance and watching lights sparkle in the settlements ahead. A cry suddenly sounded high above and Ros looked up to see a white-tailed eagle, or *nattoralik*, to give the striking creature its Greenlandic name: the country's largest breeding bird. As Ros kept watching, the eagle dived into the water, bringing up a prime cod, its main sustenance along with char – although it wasn't, apparently, averse to carrion or other sea birds such as eider.

Two days later Ros stood next to Malik as he pledged himself to his new bride in a ceremony unlike any Ros had ever witnessed. There weren't any rings exchanged, although Paninnguaq did carry Malik's small stone in her hand all the while. In one of the simplest and most affecting set of vows Ros had heard before or since, all the young couple did was to make the old Inuit promise to each other to live so as not to injure each other's minds.

Two days later and still nursing a hangover from the extended Greenlandic celebrations that followed, Ros had stood on a nearby dock dwarfed by a ramshackle collection of buildings clad in corrugated iron and painted blue. As ever, she cut a solitary figure. The lights of another small settlement could be seen in the distance: the last remnants of the Moravian mission of Lichtenfels, established in another inlet of the same island by the pioneer Matthäus Stach and four families from New Herrnhut. Ros stood there for over an hour, once again savouring the sights and sounds all around her.

Ros next travelled to Qeqertarsuatsiaat, a settlement originally known as Fiskenæsset when it was first established back in the eighteenth century. Little more than an extended village, the settlement lay approximately 150 km south of Nuuk and its new Greenlandic name meant almost literally 'the quite large island'. The various tourist bodies tasked with selling the country to the growing number of curious tourists often penned purple prose about Greenland's natural treasures, but in the case of Qeqertarsuatsiaat that wasn't just patriotic hyperbole. Back in the 1960s, deposits of corundum were discovered in the area. There are better known as rubies in the jewellery trade, though if the impurities causing their colour were more blue than red, they are sapphires. The deposits were particularly large in the nearby Aappaluttoq and Kigutilik mountains, with the quality of the rubies sourced from those two locations on a par with the best in the world.

Ros, a lone and undisturbed presence once again, walked from the harbour to an old school which was now closed to pupils but still open to visitors. Inside the building there was a picture of the Danish King and Queen on the wall and old exercise books still stacked neatly on a collection of desks, all arranged in straight lines and all facing the front. A clock on the wall showed 9.25, assembly time in most Greenlandic schools.

But all the time Ros was moving seemingly aimlessly from place to place, she was doing what she always did. She was thinking without thinking, which she was finally coming to understand was why she'd actually made that trip in the first place. At key moments earlier in her life she'd done it before and now she was doing it again, surrendering herself to a process that had no real name in the country of her birth but which did have a name in Greenland: *qarrtsiluni*.

The literal translation was 'waiting for something to burst'. Ros had experienced the sensation a few times before in a life scarred by events no eyes should see. It described the moment when a thought was hovering just on the edge of consciousness while refusing to solidify into any sort of coherent shape. At one time, when she was a small and largely confused young child, Ros would pursue it like a hunter stalking a kill, only for it to recede ever further into the mist. Now she waited, often travelling as she did so, letting the thought come to her instead; well aware from past experience that it would remain obstinately out of reach if she even dared to approach it head-on.

So Ros paced the dock again as the men finished their loading and unloading, looking at the small settlement across the water where families had made homes and dreamt of better lives for themselves and their children, and waited, hoping she wouldn't have to wait too long. She didn't.

One week later, Ros was back home in the UK – or at least back in the city that had housed the latest in a series of homes, none of which had been any sort of home at all. She was with the latest in what seemed back then to be a constant succession of protection officers.

Which was when the strangest thing happened. Sitting in the foyer of the anonymous hotel that hosted their meeting, with business-type guests working all around them, Ros suddenly asked the protection officer a question she didn't even know was in her mind, but a question that had been forming ever since that solo walk on a dockside a couple of thousand miles away in Qeqertarsuatsiaat. It was the end of the process that had started back there. Ros's moment of *qarrtsiluni*.

Was there ever an instance, Ros wanted to know, and could it ever happen, that someone growing up inside a protection programme could become a protection officer themselves? If the protection officer sitting opposite her was surprised by the question, he didn't show it. He just looked at her for a moment, a smile beginning to play on his lips. Then he'd told Ros that not only could it happen, but perhaps it already had.

Years later Ros would wonder if that was more prophecy or prediction than anything else, but it didn't matter anyway. From that moment on her career path was defined. Ros joined the Protection Unit as a new recruit a few years later and so began a new journey, trying to understand in the lives of others something about her own life and own experience. Along the way she reinvented herself again, taken up her posting, erasing all trace of her past life, aside from the name she'd been assigned and a few sundry other details held on only the most secret of records, and working with colleagues who knew nothing about her save the few facts about herself she chose to present.

And now her new life and calling had led her back once again, back to the country where that new life had effectively begun.

On the trail of a man connected to ending her old life and the lives of the rest of her forever-fractured family.

And a man who definitely had some part to play in the death of a totally innocent young mother called Jo.

Ros pulled up outside her small apartment in the capital, left her car and walked down to the harbour, where she seated herself on a bench looking out over the stretch of water where David Kleist had also breathed his last.

And then and only then did she finally let her mind run on the young woman she'd always known in her heart of heart would end things this way. Ros remained there for what felt like hours but was probably only a few minutes, now seeing again what Jo would have seen nearly all of her waking moments after it happened: the bodies of her two dead boys.

Then Ros stood to resume her search, but as she turned she saw Delaney, newly arrived behind her.

'Desna's heading to the airport right now.'

Delaney paced the harbour. The hapless Family Liaison Officer, Amy Manson, had finally been pressed into useful service and was accompanying the small child back to a safe house currently being prepared for her by Conor.

'But you're still here – you're not with her and you're not going anywhere, so that's one story shot down in flames, isn't it? You're not any sort of escort and you're not any sort of protector or babysitter. For all I know, you're not part of any sort of protection programme at all.'

Ros hadn't known Delaney long but she'd never seen the normally calm and composed officer like this before. Delaney was raging, which maybe could be expected. The murder of the small child, Tia, had taken its toll on all of them.

Time and again Ros had seen it in her own unit and in Murder Squad. An outlet had to be found, and often it was an officer's own colleagues who bore the brunt, followed closely by that officer's own family. No wonder the divorce rate among police officers was twice the national average.

But there was something else here too and Ros could see that as well. Something beside a more than usually sickening case. Something else that had seriously destabilised him.

'And why are you so fixated on just one of Imaneq Kalia's attackers, for fuck's sake? He's the only one you ever ask about. Why? Who the fuck is he and why out of all the people in that photo is he so fucking important?'

In his position, Ros would have asked all Delaney's ever more agitated questions too. In one sense, of course, she was in Delaney's position. She also had a million questions of her own, and as yet no answers.

So for the time being, the imperturbable Ros simply trotted out the mantra she'd clung to since she'd arrived.

She was escort and shadow, she insisted.

She was escort to Desna, albeit by proxy right now, and shadow the investigation into the murder of Imaneq Kalia.

The man Delaney was referring to was just one suspect among many in that case, but he was also a person of interest to the police back in the UK on a number of other inquiries which may be related and may not.

And at the end of all that, Ros told him about the next interview she was now going to undertake: with Hans Geisler, the man who'd handled the initial investigation into the murder of Alasie Kalia and the man who, according to one witness she'd just interviewed, seemed to have discounted at least one piece of potentially key information at the time.

Delaney looked at her for a long, long moment.

For that moment Ros fully expected him to blow once again, but he didn't.

Delaney just told her he was coming along too.

22

A COUPLE OF hours later, Ros and Delaney arrived in the town of Uummannaq courtesy of another hitched ride on another Twin Otter.

The officers wandered around Uummannaq all morning, asking everyone they came across if they knew of any boats either coming in from the island around fifty miles to the northwest or about to head out there. The island in question was called Ubekendt Ejland, which translated literally as 'Unknown Island'. As its name implied, it was mostly uninhabited. There was just the one village on the island, Illorsuit, which was sited on its north-eastern coast and was home to a population that had never numbered more than just a few hundred souls.

Almost a hundred years before, the village had become home to the famed American painter Rockwell Kent, who had been shipwrecked there on a voyage from Nuuk to Copenhagen. Kent had salvaged his paints and brushes from the wreckage and spent the next couple of months painting and falling in love with the Greenlandic landscape and several Greenlandic women, mostly at the same time, and recording his exploits, artistic and otherwise, in a series of journals. Now the island was home to Hans Geisler, the police officer who'd led the failed investigation into the murder of Alasie Kalia.

An hour after disembarking from the Twin Otter, Ros and Delaney had a stroke of luck. Down by the harbour a couple of drinkers, just about the right side of comatose, told them a fisherman was coming in from Illorsuit in the next hour or so. He made the trip twice a week to drop off his excess catch, always returning the same day. Sure enough, a short time later a forty-foot ketch glided into view, its two-cylinder diesel engine drumming out a not-altogether-healthy sound.

The officers approached the boat's owner, a tall fisherman in his late fifties, as he tied the boat to the end of the pier. The fisherman spoke only Greenlandic but he seemed to understand what they wanted, probably because he agreed to several similar requests each month. With no commercial ferry plying the fifty miles from Uummannaq to Illorsuit he could probably have made a useful income providing a sporadic taxi service, but in those parts that would have been called Danish thinking.

The fisherman waited until they'd been joined by a crew member, who took the helm while the tall fisherman lowered himself into a skiff and, complete with rifle, rowed out among what soon became an almost unbroken horizon of icebergs to kill seal, sending thousands of resting fulmars high up into the sky as he powered through them.

At the end of the Uummannaq Fjord they turned north and the new crew member, his hands dripping grease from the helm, offered Ros a hunk of dried seal from a previous trip. An hour later the fisherman returned in his skiff with another recently killed example. For another two hours the only sound was the slow, uneven drumming from the boat's engine until, in the perpetual daylight, Unknown Island came into view with its stark, snow-covered high peak and the dark cliff barrier that formed its western shore.

A short time later, Ros and Delaney were outside the biggest and brightest house in the small bay. At one time it had probably been the Colonial Master's house, but it now belonged to a retired policeman who barely responded to Ros or Delaney's sudden presence, just nodded at a small skiff out in the bay instead.

'I was going to collect some tern eggs.'

Hans Geisler nodded back at them.

'We can talk on the way.'

Ros and Delaney hesitated, but only for a moment, the ground rules clearly being established from the start. Geisler wasn't going to be overly obstructive to two younger colleagues from what for him was now very much a former life. But he wasn't going to make it easy for them either. If Ros or Delaney wanted any sort of exchange, it was going to be on his terms and having come all this way to do that, they didn't have too much choice but to fall in line.

As Ros and Geisler were following Delaney down to the skiff, Cecilie was standing alone on a headland looking out over a small collection of houses below.

Out on the water a ferry had just pulled out of the nearby harbour and was making its way back to Nuuk – the same ferry Cecilie had boarded and which had brought her down to the small town of Paamiut.

Paamiut translated as 'Residents of the Estuary', the whole settlement lying on a peninsula with inland mountains towering over the houses beneath. It had always been an isolated locale, but now and again the occasional cruise ship would dock and curious sightseers would spend the day looking at the local church, the building of which had been inspired by a Norwegian stave church, some timing their visits to take in one of the concerts given by the local choir. Some of the more intrepid souls might take a trip with some of the local fishermen to look for whales or to fish for trout or redfish, and some even more intrepid souls might even head out with a local hunter to trap and kill reindeer.

But what most visitors would remember most of all about Paamiut was the fog that would form almost in an instant: a dense, swirling mass created by the northern winds coming in over the ice, which created in turn alternate currents of warm and cold air.

However, lately those fogs had become a lot less frequent. While visitors had welcomed that, the townspeople were already growing concerned. It was the same concern that had Cecilie had seen on the faces of residents back in Ilulissat a couple of years before when the sun, expected on its usual day in the middle of January, ending the customary month and a half of winter darkness, actually arrived in that most westerly town in Greenland two full days before, prompting confused – if not positively alarmed – gatherings on street corners and in all the town's café's and bars.

The mysterious sunrise that unexpected day didn't confuse the scientists who'd been monitoring the sun's activity in and around Greenland for years, although it did alarm them.

Average temperatures in the whole of Greenland, so those same scientists told anyone who cared to listen, had risen by over three degrees above the average in just the one single year. And now the sun had risen early too, which was nothing to do with any offence that might have been caused to any of the watching gods, as some of the older inhabitants were already darkly alleging, but everything to do with the lower height of the melting icecaps allowing the sun's light to penetrate through to the town that much earlier. As the ice sinks in the sky, those same scientists tried to explain, so does the horizon, creating the illusion that the sun has risen early. Which was an explanation, but not one many of those huddled on those street corners or in those cafés or bars actually welcomed all that much, perhaps because they all knew what it meant.

Already other strange tales had surfaced. If you stood on a glacier out in Disko Bay, far from where the bergs actually calved with their customary loud crack, you'd hear a strange background murmur, an almost ceaseless whispering that appeared to come from nowhere but which was actually the sound of meltwater rushing down through fissures in the ice below.

Meaning everywhere you looked, it was the same story. Everything was getting warmer, however improbable that might seem to visitors staring out over a polar landscape. Meaning everything, at some elemental level, was wrong and growing more so by the passing moment.

Cecilie stayed there, looking out over the water, for a few moments longer.

Ten minutes later she was in a bare room.

One minute after that she cried out in pain and her body slumped forward, but she didn't fall to the floor.

The ties securing her arms and legs made sure of that.

Ros and Delaney walked with Geisler over sand mixed with seal bones towards a wooden boardwalk where children from the settlement were playing. Some of the more enterprising ones approached Ros and rattled off questions, one of them asking her about America. Ros was briefly tempted to stop and point out that she came from a country as far removed from America geographically as their own, but by then Geisler was already in the skiff and it was time to go.

Their destination was a group of tiny islands that appeared only as dots on even detailed maps of the area. They were inhabited by thousands of seabirds called Arctic terns that came all the way from the Antarctic in the summer to lay their eggs. Geisler's trip was part foraging but part local tradition too. Most inhabitants of the island took trips such as this on a regular basis at this time of the year, mainly to break up days that were really nights and vice versa, as the unending light could easily induce a kind of cabin fever. With no clear division between waking and sleeping, the body became sluggish all too quickly, the mind a blank miasma.

Paninnguaq, Ros's old friend's bride, once told her that when she lived for any extended time above the Arctic Circle, she'd settle into the pattern of eating four or five meals a day, with the main meal at one or two in the morning. Then she'd rest between five and nine later that same morning. The routine helped, but darkness still seemed an opulent luxury, an indulgence to be craved, a reward still months away.

After a few more moments, Ros saw a cove ahead with another fishing boat already anchored just off the shore. Another much younger man and some children were gathered around a smoking turf fire. The young man rose, wary, as Geisler's craft berthed. His eyes never left Ros and Delaney the whole time they were approaching.

Geisler made only the very briefest of introductions.

'My son, Salik.'

Geisler didn't bother introducing the officers at all. There was no need. News of their visit had clearly circulated in advance and seemed as welcome to the son as it was to his father. Not that Ros and Delaney were alone in being an unwelcome presence right now. Above the three men's heads, the sky was already a cauldron of circling, shrieking terns, incandescent with rage that their sanctuary should be invaded in this way and already more than fearful as to what might happen next.

Those terns had travelled over 22,000 miles to reach that spot. The partners they had chosen and bonded with would be their partners for life. All of which meant that each individual tern had invested a great deal in the eggs they'd produced and did not appreciate intruders. Especially intruders with such malevolent intent such as these.

Geisler nodded at his son and they moved away from the shore, the children following. Ignoring the protesting terns wheeling over their heads, they began to scan the grass, looking for small, olive-coloured eggs, most speckled brown. Within moments they'd found hundreds. The children collected them into sacks while the terns dived at them in impotent fury, desperate to save what would have been their offspring, but the collecting continued undeterred.

This was the only time of the year the inhabitants of Illorsuit would eat eggs, which were usually considered a rare delicacy. Within a few minutes, the first of the batches had been taken back to the boat, where they were boiled in its tiny galley. The children, working together, popped the first of the boiled eggs from the pan and rolled them onto plates before one of them was offered to Ros. She cracked the olive shell on a nearby stone, then peeled it and popped the small marble-shaped egg into her mouth. It was strongly-flavoured, most closely resembling a duck's egg in texture and taste. Above their heads, flocks of terns continued to mill, growing ever more maddened all the while.

Still barely a word had been exchanged but then, suddenly, Salik rounded on them.

'Just six months he was away, the first time my father sent him down.'

Ros and Delaney stared back at the young man.

'And you know the first thing he did when he got back? Went out and bought himself a motorbike.'

Delaney listened with a sinking heart. He'd heard variations on the same aggrieved complaint many times since he'd first arrived in the country.

'We'd see him from the window, riding it up and down, making sure everyone could see it.'

Ros glanced at Delaney. Even in the short time she'd been there, she'd heard it too. It was that eons-old debate once again.

Tobias Lundblad had actually been a model prisoner on the first occasion he'd served time in the Home for Convicts in Aasiaat, where he'd been sent. He did all the tasks that were expected of him and never missed a single day of the various work placements to which he was assigned. For that, and like all convicted prisoners, he was paid a wage. Out of those wages a deduction would have been made for board and lodgings and Lundblad would have been given a small amount of pocket money. Any excess would have been paid into an account held on his behalf and administered by the Home staff, who also made sure that any debts to the State, damages and fines would be cleared.

But Lundblad, being that model prisoner, didn't incur any debts or fines. And the wages he earned would have been commensurate with those paid to the workers around him. So like many other convicts before him and many to come after him too, a surplus was accumulated and Greenlandic law was quite simple in regards to what happened then.

The convict would be given that money on release, the intention being that it should go towards re-establishing them back in their former community. It was a laudable intention, but the effect was often more unfortunate. When a convict arrived back, bringing with him a brand new pick-up truck or the most modern fishing vessel in his home town, it often aroused astonishment and worse among the other members of that same community, who would never have been able to save so much by living a law-abiding life.

Lundblad hadn't returned with a modern fishing vessel, although had his crime been more serious on that occasion and his incarceration longer, then he might have. Ros looked back from a silent Delaney to Geisler's son, Salik. He'd clearly still returned with enough to ruffle many a local feather.

'Do you know his age when he first got in trouble? Fifteen!'

The young man stared at them in disbelief.

'And you come up here, telling us my father was wrong.'

Geisler himself still hadn't spoken. His mind seemed a million miles away and his eyes fixed on a very different place.

But Salik was still just looking at Delaney. And his eyes seemed fixed on a distant landscape now too.

'They always say it, don't they?

Delaney looked back at him.

'They always say there's a case that haunts you.'

Ros looked across at Delaney, stilling as she saw the same tormented look she'd seen on the steps of the Police Headquarters steal once again across his eyes.

Clearly either Salik or his father had done their homework as regards at least one of their visitors.

Salik nodded at the staring Delaney again.

'And for the rest of your life, for the rest of your career, all you do is hound and persecute others.'

Delaney just looked back at him, the image he'd carried for over twenty years, the image which had so recently returned courtesy of another similar and savage killing, in front of his eyes again now too.

That single, sunny day; that park; the angelic little five year old about to be visited by devils.

'Try and exorcise the ghost.'

Geisler himself still hadn't spoken. For a moment Ros wondered if he was going to speak again at all. His eyes still seemed fixed on somewhere else completely, but Ros still had no idea where that might be.

But then, slowly, he reached into his pocket. The next second a gun materialised in the retired officer's hand.

Bizarrely, and despite the clear and overwhelmingly present danger, Ros still registered the make and model. At her side and by the expression on his face, Delaney recognised it too.

It was a US Army-issue Colt .45 pistol.

The same make and model of pistol that had killed Alasie Kalia all those years before.

The man in the mask behind Cecilie raised a wooden paddle and brought it down hard again on her back.

Cecilie bucked fiercely under the fresh blow. The man waited a moment, watching, but then she gave a slight nod, her silent signal clear.

Do it again.

Cecilie closed her eyes and waited for the next blow to land. Her silent companion still hadn't said a word. He also hadn't remarked on the many abrasions and scars he could see covering her back, a collection that would only increase with each of her visits. He never would. It was what she paid him for. His discretion, as well as his ability to inflict the most intense pain. So far he'd managed to achieve both.

The paddle landed on the small of her back once more and Cecilie bucked again, losing her footing momentarily but then regaining it. Gritting her teeth for a moment, she paused, then gave the same silent nod she'd given before. The man behind her stood motionless for a moment, waiting to see if she was going to change her mind – this had been an unusually strenuous session – but Cecilie gave no further signal, just braced herself for the blow to land.

All the time she waited for the impact, one thought kept racing through her brain.

She so wanted this to work, she really did.

She so wanted this to drive everything else away.

One hour later her latest session was over and Cecilie knew for a fact that nothing had been driven away. In her heart of hearts, she'd always known it.

The time was fast approaching when only one thing would do that and for the very first time – since this whole crazy enterprise had started – she had at least the glimmer of an idea of how to do that too.

Cecilie looked out beyond that small room, beyond the punishment she endured, at the face now swimming before her.

The face she was seeing almost constantly now.

The face coming into ever sharper focus every time that paddle landed in the very centre of her back.

With a strength that belied his slight frame, Geisler had chopped at the back of Ros's calf with the butt of the gun, collapsing her onto the floor before placing his bended knee in the middle of her back.

Now that gun was resting against Ros's ear and at any moment she was now expecting the sudden flash of noise and light that would be the very last sensation she would experience – in this world, at least.

And for a moment, and despite the danger she was now in – or perhaps because of it – her mind suddenly wandered. Images of her family, of Braith and of Di, flashed in front of her eyes.

So was this to be the moment? The moment she might see them all once more? The moment she might open her eyes again to find them waiting for her on the other side?

Which was when the pressure on Ros's back eased. She sensed rather than saw Geisler wheel round. Ros twisted her head to see Geisler give a silent signal to his son to look after Delaney. For the first time, Ros saw a gun also now in Salik's hand, trained on her staring fellow officer. Then Geisler hauled Ros to her feet and captor and captive began to set off away from the small harbour up into the nearby hills.

She felt the pressure from the gun on her back all the way. Until they moved out of sight of both Delaney and Salik, at least. Then Geisler stopped. Ros looked round, still unsure if the next thing she'd experience would be the blinding flash of a bullet.

But she didn't. Ros saw tears beginning to course down the old man's face.

For a moment Ros just stared at Geisler, who was still holding the gun. For a moment longer, the old man still didn't speak. Then, suddenly, Geisler started talking about his son.

Geisler told Ros all about a motor accident Salik had been involved in some twenty or so years before. He told her how it had been touch and go for weeks. That their local hospital had told him they could do little but wait and hope. Geisler could still remember only too acutely the blind panic that had enveloped him.

For much of this sudden outburst, it was as if Ros wasn't even there. But then Geisler looked directly back at her.

'I'd have done anything. Anything at all. To get my son the help he needed.'

Which was when Ros spoke for the first time since Geisler had brought her to her knees in that small harbour.

'Which was when you met Emmanuel.'

It wasn't a question but a statement. It was also the very first time she'd done it. The very first time she'd actually said that name out loud since she'd arrived in the country.

Ros held Geisler's stare as he just stared back at her in turn. And for that moment, it was as if she was looking into Tom Edwards's eyes again.

She saw the same bitter, intense regret she'd seen in Edwards. The same mourning for a life that should have been lived, a life that now never would be lived. That fork in the road that should never, ever, have been taken.

Then Ros stopped as she saw Geisler lift the gun.

A single gunshot sounded.

A few moments later a silent Ros and Delaney just watched as Hans Geisler's son, now weeping soundlessly, cradled his father's dead body in his arms.

23

As Ros and Delaney were staring at Hans Geisler's lifeless body and as Cecilie was returning from Paamiut to Nuuk, Tobias Lundblad was doing what he always did.

The last known person to see Alasie Kalia alive was doing what he actually did most days at that time, in fact, because he had little choice.

Lundblad was staring at the time traveller.

He'd first seen the creature on his second day there. It was a caterpillar caught in a curious limbo right now, which was maybe why he'd first noticed it. Its body was suspended in a frozen stasis for nine months of each year, when the temperature dipped below freezing. A few days previously the temperature had risen and it had begun to thaw out. But Lundblad knew the cold would soon return and the thawing process would stop, meaning the time traveller would revert back to its frozen state – all of which meant its development from egg to butterfly may take years.

Maybe he'd be there to see that final flourish, he had no way of knowing. He'd been there for what already seemed like months, if not years.

But his thoughts weren't only dominated by that one silent companion. It was his other equally silent companion that obsessed him much more. And in the last few days he'd begun to wonder about her.

There was something about the way she moved. A sway of the hips as she put down his food, the angle her arm described as she placed the tray on the floor. It triggered something, and last night he thought he'd identified just what that might be.

Had that been her?

All those weeks before his latest misdemeanour had seen him locked up again?

The seemingly innocent exchange that had taken place out on the beach that day – was that seemingly innocent encounter not so innocent after all?

'I heard about the headstone.'

Lundblad had been working on his boat. A young woman had passed, stopping to watch him at work. Within moments it had been established that she came from his old home town and a few moments later they were talking about the new development in the Alasie Kalia case. The case that had defined his life.

'You must have been surprised.'

Lundblad looked out over the sands, old familiar ghosts dancing on the horizon before him. But he'd shaken his head.

'Actually, no.'

The young woman had looked at him, puzzled at that, but Lundblad had just shrugged.

'I always knew he'd have to break cover one day.'

Lundblad shook his head again.

'How can you live like that, knowing what you did – looking at children growing up, at girls becoming mothers; knowing that one girl will never do that, that some child will never be born and it's all down to you, that you're responsible?'

A note of wonder crept into his voice.

'I don't care how much of a monster you are, there must always be a time – late at night, early in the morning, when you're walking along a beach, maybe – one moment when it's all going to come along and ambush you.'

Then Lundblad had paused. All this was so long ago now, but it was a past as real as the present and it was the same questions still demanding answers everyone remained unable to supply.

'The police at the time.'

Tobias paused again, a residue of bitterness now clouding his eyes.

'All those questions: did I go straight home, did I go anywhere else, did anyone else see me, had I ever had a gun, had I ever even seen a gun, did I like Alasie? Over and over again, for hours.'

Tobias shook his head again.

'When they finally let me go, I thought that was the end. My mother told me I had to just forget it all – I was just in the wrong place at the wrong time, that's all; I wasn't the one who'd done anything wrong, she knew that and I knew that – and she was right, but it didn't make any difference.'

Lundblad looked out over the water again as, a metre or so away, the young woman's eyes never left his face.

'I left school a couple of years later and became a postman. I didn't last long: it was the worst sort of work I could have gone into, given what had happened. Day by day, every day of the year, I was coming up against everyone who'd ever known me, everyone who'd ever known Alasie, and every time I could see that same question in all their eyes.'

Tobias tailed off, but only for a moment.

'"Was it you?" It didn't matter what the police said, they still asked. "Did you do it, did you follow her back up that track that day, did you do that to her?"'

Then all of a sudden Lundblad seemed to veer off on an unexpected tangent.

'A year after it happened, while I was still in school, we had someone come in. He was supposed to give us advice on what to do once we left. He took a look at my books, checked some of my results, then he told my teacher I should think about going to college – there was one opening up the next year. I was bright, he said, I had potential. So I went home and told my mother and she did what all mothers would do, I suppose: she went out and told all her friends and our neighbours. It's what parents do, right? They can't help it, boasting about their children.'

Lundblad paused.

'It was only the one neighbour, I think. Just one spiteful old soul. I didn't even know who it was, my mother wouldn't say, but I know what she said.'

His young companion's eyes still hadn't left Lundblad's face.

'She said she knew I was bright. Everyone did. I must be, I'd fooled all those police officers all those years, hadn't I?'

Lundblad paused another moment, then shrugged.

'I lost interest in school after that. Didn't want to give anyone any more ammunition, I suppose. So I left the first chance I got and became a postman, and when I got sick of all the grief I got doing that, I left the town and started working for Sirius in Daneborg.'

The young woman knew the area and she knew the organisation. And she could imagine only too well the life Lundblad must have lived up there. Sirius was responsible for delivering mail in some of the most desolate regions in the world – when it was possible to deliver mail, at least. There would be none even attempted between November and March. During the rest of the year the mail would be delivered perhaps fifteen to twenty times, distributed among the twelve to fourteen military personnel that were stationed there, spread out over nine hundred thousand square kilometres, an area more than twenty times the area of Denmark. On leaving Ilulissat, Tobias Lundblad had certainly embraced isolation.

'The way it follows you around.'

Tobias looked out over the water with eyes that now seemed a million miles away.

'Even when you had nothing to do with what happened. The way it changes things for you, even when it's nothing at all to do with you.'

Tobias paused again.

'All going back to one afternoon after school when I nodded at a girl on her way home and never saw her again.'

Then Tobias had stood and turned and, with the eyes of the young woman still on him, walked back to his small boat.

Back in his room that was more of a cell than anything he'd previously endured in the Home for Convicts, the door now opened in front of him, light spilling onto the trapped time traveller, which was now in the process of returning to its frozen state once again.

The same indistinct figure, head shrouded in a shapeless hoody, moved in, carrying food on a tray. Then she did what she'd done ever since he'd been dragged from the scene of one incarceration to another: just put the tray down on the floor in front of him and made to exit.

But as she reached the door, and perhaps emboldened by the new memory of that exchange out on the beach, Tobias suddenly yelled at her.

'What do you want?'

The figure paused, momentarily, in the doorway.

'Why are you doing this?'

Then the indistinct figure pressed on and did what she'd also done ever since she'd brought him here, dazed and injured. She moved to close the door behind her and Tobias heard what he always heard: just the sound of fading footsteps by way of a reply.

F OR THE WHOLE of the night that followed his prison kitchen interrogation of Tom Edwards, Masters had paced his exclusive apartment bolthole in St James, assessing options, debating his next move.

Then he'd acted.

It hadn't been easy tracking down the first of his new targets and pressuring him to turn up, and it had proved – perhaps understandably – massively problematic persuading the second of those targets to attend as well.

But Masters had done it. And the first of those targets was now sitting across his desk from him and he was looking at that face again.

The face of pure evil.

Which was when the door opened and the second of the day's unwilling guests wheeled himself inside.

A day earlier Masters had been in the air. No one in Masters's department knew where he was going and no one asked. The few officers who'd seen him prior to his latest unexplained absence could see only too clearly he was a man on a mission right now, and they were right.

Ros had journeyed two thousand miles to attempt to confront a face from a dim and distant past. Masters was about to travel just a few hundred miles to confront a face from a much more recent past. Those two confrontations, as Masters was already beginning to suspect, would turn out to be linked in ways neither he nor Ros could possibly have anticipated even just a few days before.

A few hours later the twin-engined aircraft shuddered in the buffeting wind as it came in low over Nissen huts on the airfield below. A new ferry terminal seemed to shimmer in the distance. Ten minutes later Masters was being driven in a taxi on the long straight road towards the small Scottish town of Stornoway on the Isle of Lewis. Half an hour later again he was in a whitewashed cottage, which was the latest in a whole series of temporary homes for the woman inside.

The woman who'd known as well as anyone the name that Tom Edwards had confided in Masters. A name he would never in a million lifetimes have expected Edwards to know. And the name of a woman – if all Edwards was saying was correct – who'd been intimately linked to the man in the photo from Edwards's phone. The photo Masters was now showing to her.

Kirino hardly gave the photo a second glance. She didn't need to. The recognition was immediate and it was absolute.

'He was the one.'

Masters stared at her. At one time Kirino had been live-in companion to the man who had always epitomised pure evil so far as Masters was concerned. The man who would face him across his desk less than 24 hours later: a Ukrainian gangster known only by the single name of Yaroslav. The man responsible for the killing of one of Masters's own police officers and the butchery of that officer's pregnant wife.

Kirino looked back up at him.

'The one Tyra was seeing.'

Masters kept staring back at her.

When Kirino could see that Yaroslav was growing tired of her – and that a replacement was already on the scene – she'd decided to get out, but not before securing a strictly unofficial little pay-out of her own in the shape of drugs scammed from her soon-to-be-former lover and concealed in a hollowed-out compartment in one of her brand new Jimmy Choo platforms.

It had proved to be a costly mistake. It had also cost her the lower part of her right leg, as Yaroslav had smashed the door of his upmarket 4x4 against it time and again by way of a punishment, until he'd virtually severed it just below the knee. That had precipitated her flight into the protection programme, where she'd been asked to join forces with that replacement herself to testify against their joint former boyfriend.

Until everyone realised that replacement was playing something of a double game.

Masters looked at her.

'When she was with Yaroslav.'

Kirino shuddered.

'I only caught a glimpse of him once. Outside the club. He picked her up one night around the corner and I saw them kiss. That was all I wanted to see too. I couldn't believe it. What a crazy bitch – cheating on that psycho.'

Masters looked down at the photo of Emmanuel again.

Tyra – Tyra Rhea to give her her full name – had been a cop. She'd gone undercover, or so they all believed at the time, to bring down Yaroslav. But Tyra had turned out to be playing a double game and she'd paid the price. In her case that price was being immolated alive in a burning furnace.

Ros's old boss in the Protection Unit, Jukes, had told him that Tyra had been seeing someone apart from Yaroslav shortly after she'd entered the protection programme but no one had ever been able to trace the brave soul in question. No one, indeed, had ever been able to categorically establish he even existed. Like so much of what Tyra had told them back then, he could even have been a fiction, a cover story to mask something else.

Masters kept staring at the photo, then looked back at the now-silent Kirino.

But Kirino didn't even seem to see him. The face on that photo, the sight of Masters and all he'd brought with him – she was lost now in her own never-to-be-forgotten pictures of the past. Memories of real-life events that were going to condemn her to a life of moving from one house to another, dwellings that never could be and never would be homes. Outside, the temperature was dipping all the time, but Kirino didn't notice. She was lost, another victim of still-raw memories that would never loosen their grip.

The second of that day's arrivals had expected many things to ambush him.

The sights and sounds of his old police unit.

Some of the still familiar faces.

What Donovan Banks didn't expect to ambush him was a mug adorned with the crest of Leyton Orient football club.

Banks had forgotten about Murder Squad's esoteric collection of football mugs till that moment. It was possible he'd have forgotten about them entirely, had it not been for a solicitous secretary who'd just ferried in a coffee to the Head of Murder Squad sitting opposite him right now.

Then Banks saw it. The mug. The football crest. And all of a sudden he was back again: back in his old life, doing the things he used to do, things denied him forever by his now broken body.

The things denied him by that same man sitting opposite, not even looking at the mug in front of him with the crest of Leyton Orient; just looking at him instead.

Which was when Banks had looked Masters full in the face for the first time since he'd wheeled himself in. When he looked at the man responsible for that downfall, the man who had dominated his every waking thought ever since. The man who had held the power of life and death over him that day and had exercised that power in the most chilling way imaginable as he'd suspended him over that sheer drop before releasing his grip, condemning Banks to that seconds-long fall all the way down to the concrete walkway below, and to the apology of a life he now inhabited.

But the man – and the sudden thought was heady, inspiring almost, and for a moment the realisation actually took Banks's breath away – who actually held no power at all over him now.

Which was when Masters finally spoke, putting a photo of a now-dead officer on the desk in front of him as he did so.

'I want to talk to you about Tyra.'

In a different world and time maybe Masters would have stayed silent, let Banks make the running. It was a tactic that had served him well in the past. But Banks had been there, had been an almost constant presence throughout much of that joint past, so that was always going to be a doomed tactic anyway.

Banks just looked at him. He hadn't even looked at the face in the photo now staring back at them.

By his side, Yaroslav couldn't look at anything else.

'She's dead, or don't you remember?

Banks looked at the staring Yaroslav at his side.

'She had an accident.'

Banks nodded down at his wheelchair as he picked up Masters's coffee mug, turning it round to examine the football crest all the more closely, almost as if it was a beacon guiding him to the safety of some distant shore.

'The same time I had mine –'

Which was when Banks stopped looking at the football mug. The hand that had suddenly shot out and grabbed his throat claimed his attention rather more urgently.

Banks looked back at Masters. In a different world and time, he might have been terrified beyond measure: he'd seen the sort of rough justice his former senior officer was capable of meting out at first hand. He'd had nightmares in the past at the prospect of such treatment being inflicted on him. But he was no longer the man he'd been back then and these weren't those times.

Banks just spat at the man before him, defiant.

'What are you going to do?'

Banks spat again, sheer effort of will forcing the words past his constricted windpipe.

'Take me up onto the roof? Drop me over the other side all the way down to the water if I don't say any more?'

Banks's gasped words were more and more agonised, but his tone was ever more triumphant.

'Do it. Take me up there and just fucking do it.'

Banks leant closer, his face now just a matter of inches from his former and present persecutor.

'You'll be doing me a fucking favour.'

Masters slowly released his grip, stared across the interview desk. He'd genuinely forgotten what a cocksure, arrogant little shit his former DS had been. Then again, perhaps he'd had good reason. He'd certainly fooled Masters for long enough.

'There's no difference, is there? You and her. You're both just the same, fucking with people, fucking with minds – and don't even begin to tell me what you did was different, that you were doing it for the greater fucking good.'

Banks held Masters's stare.

'Didn't do anyone too much good in the end, did it? I was there, remember?'

Masters stayed silent.

'You used to collect willing souls like – what was her name, Clare? Anya? Whatever the fuck she called herself when you ran her. Tyra recruited damaged ones. In the end it doesn't make much difference though, you're both fucking collectors and if anyone fucks up they get a knock on the door from you both.'

Banks looked down at his broken body, his useless legs.

'I know which one I'd rather get.'

By his side, Yaroslav, who hardly seemed to have heard any of that, reached out and picked up the photo still on the table. It was the first time he'd seen that face for three years – a face he'd never stopped seeing in his mind's eye for one single day.

Which was when it happened. If Masters had to describe the phenomenon, he'd have said it was like watching a personality collapse in on itself. Yaroslav's shoulders sagged at the same time as his mind seemed to collapse too. He curled shaking fingers around the photo of the woman he knew as Tyra and Masters knew without a shadow of a doubt that he wouldn't have let go of it if Masters had trained a blowtorch on his hands.

Masters also knew that he'd made something of a miscalculation in showing him that photo of Tyra upfront. He'd seen it many times over during what had been a long and turbulent career. Hate builds criminal empires over years, but love destroys them in a heartbeat. Yaroslav had opened himself up to the woman they'd all known as Tyra, had opened his heart in a way he'd never done before and would never do again. And now this was all he had left, a single photograph and the memory of a ghost.

Which meant he was useless so far as Masters's present purpose was concerned, but that still left Banks. And if Masters had even the slightest lingering doubt that Banks might not be connected to the real paymaster behind the subterfuge that had led to his literal and metaphorical fall, he was about to have that doubt well and truly vanquished.

Banks snaked out a hand and picked up another item from the file in front of Masters: the calendar left in Ros's apartment by the ventilation engineer. It had been reported to Masters by Ros herself and collected by him in case there was some connection – and that single date ringed in red, now less than two days away, was clearly visible.

Banks didn't say a word for a moment, just laid it down before them.

Then he nodded at the man across the interview desk.

'Don't you understand yet?'

Banks looked at the photo of Tyra again.

'They never counted. None of them, not like Tyra did.'

Masters just kept staring at him as, across the desk, Banks almost smiled.

Almost, but not quite.

'He'd have left Ros alone. Even when she joined the force, even when she went into the programme he put her in in the first fucking place, it meant nothing: why should it?'

Banks nodded back down at the photo of Tyra, still face up on the table.

'But you did it, didn't you? Took away from him the only woman he ever loved.'

Banks looked back at Masters.

'So it's all he's wanted. Ever since.'

Then Banks nodded at him.

'To do the same to you.'

I WATCHED HER *that day as she headed for that final, fateful meeting.*

She looked exactly what she was. A woman totally on top of her game – and for good reason, because she was. Because this was the moment. Her moment. The moment everything would come together. The moment – long delayed but much-anticipated – when the endgame would finally play out.

I kept watching as she strode along the side of Atlantic Wharf, deliberately taking the path closest to the water. I knew what she was doing. That route would take her longer than taking a left by the new County Hall and heading past the fast-food outlets before coming up to the large glass-fronted building on the edge of the Wharf itself, but Tyra didn't care.

Because today she wanted to savour each and every moment. She wanted to postpone the inevitable gratification. It was going to be pretty intense as it was and maybe she was being greedy, wanting to milk it even more. But that's what she was, and she always saw little to apologise for in that either. She wanted more and so she achieved more. End of story.

But then, regretfully – and once again you could almost see it – she cut up from the water. It was time now to walk into that building, to take the lift to the top floor, to let herself into the apartment overlooking the old docks and the new Bay.

Time for the third piece in the jigsaw to be slotted into place.

First, there'd been the Ukrainian. She'd set about ensnaring him with a dedication that had left him little choice but to submit.

Then there'd been her own department, and little did they know it, but they'd all been played to perfection too.

But they would. They'd all know it. In roughly thirty seconds time when she walked in through that door.

I stood to follow her inside.

Which is when everything went wrong.

Horribly, tragically wrong.

PART FOUR

GOTHIC SILHOUETTES

2 6

R OS WAS LOST.
She felt as if she was going round in ever-increasing circles, each cycle in the orbit seeming to take her further and further away from a quarry who seemed to be moving further away from her in turn.

And that was probably with good reason.

Because she was.

It didn't help her current and overpowering sense of landlocked stasis that she and Delaney arrived back in Nuuk on Greenland's National Day. The celebration dated from the day in 2009 when the country had assumed self-determination and Greenlanders were finally recognised as a separate nation under international law. Denmark may still maintain control of foreign affairs and defence, but to most Greenlanders it was still a crucial step along the road to full independence, meaning everyone was in holiday mode. Making Ros's sense of acute dislocation even more disorientating.

Sandgreen wasn't in holiday mode. He'd demanded to see Ros and Delaney in Police Headquarters the moment they'd arrived back. The subsequent interview was short and to the point as a grim Sandgreen listed the mayhem they'd all witnessed in the previous few days.

Imaneq Kalia had been murdered.

Tia Andersen had similarly been brutally murdered.

A long-standing suspect in another notorious and unsolved murder, Tobias Lundblad, had disappeared or more probably had been abducted.

And now a retired police officer had committed suicide.

In Sandgreen's perhaps understandable view, even just that last item alone questioned not only Delaney's professional competence, it also made Ros's continuing stay in their country untenable. Sandgreen's conclusion was swift and it was irrevocable.

Delaney was to be suspended pending inquiries and Ros was to be sent back to her rented flat to pack for what would be as early a flight as possible back to the UK.

Ros exited the building a short time after her effective dismissal by Sandgreen, by which time there were at least a couple of thousand people outside the City Hall, all waiting for the official start of National Day.

Neither she or Delaney spoke as they separated. Sandgreen had said everything that had to be said, and neither officer could disagree with any of it, so there was nothing more to add.

Ros didn't go straight home. She dived into a nearby cinema instead, needing time and space to think. She expected the usual mind-numbing Hollywood blockbuster to be up on screen, giving her ample time to do that much needed thinking.

But as it happened, Ros stumbled on something different.

This film was a local production and the actors were non-professionals, largely teenagers recruited from a home for neglected Inuit children, and local seal hunters. The film was in Greenlandic with Danish subtitles but it was easy enough to follow. The story concerned a young boy named Inuk.

Inuk was sixteen years old and lived in Nuuk with his alcoholic mother and violent stepfather, and had already been involved in several clashes with the local police and Social Services. Then, one day after the half-frozen boy was pulled out of an abandoned car, a decision was made to send him north to a children's home on a tiny island in the middle of the sea. There Inuk met Ikuma, a local polar bear hunter, haunted by a troubled past.

Slowly, an alliance formed and Inuk and Ikuma set off on a seal-hunting trip. So began a road movie without roads, focusing on characters adrift in a strange and unfamiliar world.

So it was that Ros went into that cinema hoping to empty her mind so she might better work out what do next, but spent those two hours watching characters attempting to build a future out of the shattered remnants of the past.

Meanwhile, Delaney headed down to the harbour. A few moments later, as he was sitting in one of the local bars, he looked up as a great shout suddenly sounded from another bar opposite, where a group of excited men were staring down towards the water. A moment later and with the men now gesturing and pointing at it, he saw a polar bear break the surface of the water.

Delaney kept watching, his face darkening as he did so. The bear had featured in the local papers for the last couple of days. The animal was hungry but in days gone by would simply have been driven back to the wild. But people in the area – and not just tourists but native Greenlanders who really should have known better – had encouraged its approach by feeding it scraps from the boats that were moored around the harbour or from the increasing number of restaurant tables lining the harbour walls. The owners of some of the local eateries, Café Tuap and Igaffik in particular had done their best, but food from customers had still ended up in the water to be pounced on by the circling bear.

Delaney looked to the side of the avid watchers. The bear was coming closer to the shore all the while and Delaney could now see the hunter who had been tasked with killing the emboldened animal before it came any nearer.

Across the harbour he could see yet more drunken locals, all still in full holiday mode, all still sourcing food for the hungry animal from neighbouring boats and cafés.

As the hunter took aim, Delaney suddenly saw him.

Delaney stared out across the harbour. Even from a good few hundred metres away, Delaney recognised the slight stoop in his posture, a characteristic common to all the men in his late wife's family, accentuated now by the way he was shifting from foot to foot nervously. As if his father-in-law was already debating with himself the wisdom of making a final approach.

Delaney hesitated too as he kept taking in the still-distant figure. As with anything to do with his former life and his father-in-law, Niels, Delaney's mind seemed to simply freeze. But then, as he took the deepest of breaths and made to move towards him, Niels just turned and walked away.

Behind him a single shot rang out, but Delaney didn't even register it.

He didn't see the giant paw that came out of the water which boiled, briefly, red all around it.

He also didn't see the polar bear, which could now be seen sinking beneath the surface as the now quietened spectators looked on.

All Delaney saw was the space on the other side of the harbour that his father-in-law had just vacated.

As Ros was watching the local film and Delaney was staring at the sudden apparition that vanished almost as quickly, Desna Kalia was landing in the UK.

The young girl had expected lots of things to spook her. The different sounds, the different sights, the crowded streets, the strange clothes, the unaccustomed temperature and the odd smells. But in truth, all that just washed over her; perhaps because many of those same images had already been fed into her subconscious from countless television programmes and films. As she rode from the airport to her new home, something else transfixed her instead.

Desna glanced quickly at the protection officer seated at her side, who had introduced himself just by his given name of Conor. She knew that she must seem as if she'd simply closed down, and maybe no wonder. It had been a long series of flights from her home town and she'd passed through a bewildering number of different landscapes while fleeing the horrors that had provoked her sudden and enforced departure.

But that wasn't the reason for her almost complete and catatonic withdrawal. What had completely ambushed her to the point of robbing her of all speech right now were the trees.

Desna had seen pictures of them, of course. Everyone in her home country had. But like everyone else in her home country – everyone who'd never travelled outside it anyway – she'd never actually seen one for herself till now.

They'd learnt about them in school. She knew all about the common beech and the smooth-leaved elm as well as her favourite, the juniper. She knew from those same school lessons that the juniper thrived on chalk moorland, that its bark was grey-brown and peeled with age and that its small, needle-like leaves were green with broad silver bands on the inner side, curving to a sharp, prickly point. She also knew that mature junipers could reach a height of over ten metres and some could live for over two hundred years.

Desna knew too that the common juniper was dioecious, meaning male and female flowers grow on separate trees, with male flowers being small, yellow and globular, growing in leaf axils near the tip of twigs. She also knew that they provided dense cover for nesting birds such as the goldcrest, and in more northern areas, for black grouse. It was also the food plant for many species of moth, such as the juniper carpet moth and the juniper pug, as well as birds like the fieldfare and mistle thrush.

But what made this tree her favourite of all was the fact it was a deterrent against the devil. It was hung over doorways on the eve of May Day as well as being burnt on Halloween to ward off evil spirits.

Desna kept looking out of the window, hoping to see one, but she didn't – which confirmed all she'd also read about its recent decline. No one knew exactly what was sparking it, all they did know was that for some reason, the species was starting to experience difficulty regenerating. She'd printed off a whole list of possible reasons for that from the internet and on the flight over to the UK had been reading her way through them one by one.

An hour or so later, she made the call. It was pre-arranged: she'd been told she could make a call at the same time each day, and this was the first of them. And Desna just couldn't help it. She could have talked about anything – about home, about the police and their investigations, even about Alasie's new and still puzzling headstone – but out it all came instead: all the different trees she'd seen, the individual descriptions of them spilling out in a seemingly unstoppable torrent.

On the other end of the line, the woman just listened.

And suddenly it was as if she was back there.

Back in their old home, not a lot younger than Desna was now, listening to her older sister in turn talking about the latest project she was doing in school: plunging herself into whatever new enthusiasm had claimed her, always doing that little bit extra, as her smiling teachers knew she always would.

Which was when it happened.

When the careful game she'd been playing up to now suddenly became impossible to maintain. When she knew she simply had to act and act right now, irrespective of the consequences.

And all it had taken was one overexcited child talking about a tree.

MASTERS HAD FILLED in most of the gaps, but there was just one last piece to slot into place. So before he set off after Ros, he made one last call and arranged one final meeting.

Tom Edwards sported the same mousey hair. The same blank eyes peered out from underneath the nondescript fringe. But he'd changed almost beyond recognition since Jo's suicide, Masters could see that at a glance. He could but hope Edwards would take the opportunity he was now being offered to act on it.

If Edwards had been surprised by this new summons to the Murder Squad offices, he hadn't shown it. If he'd been alarmed, he didn't show that either. Perhaps because any nightmare Masters could now summon up for him would always be superseded by an even worse one.

A small suburban house, a simple cushion and the dead bodies of two small children lying in their upstairs beds.

But suddenly, and before Masters could even ask his opening question, Edwards spoke.

'Not here.'

Masters glanced around the interview room, pausing for a moment. Then he looked back at Edwards and stood, indicating to Edwards to stand now too.

'She was fourteen.'

Ten minutes later, Masters and Edwards were on a newly constructed towpath skirting the water of the Bay.

Now it was Edwards's turn to see something in Masters's eyes. Because Masters knew. Edwards could see it in those eyes, focused now on him alone.

Masters knew all this already. And Edwards was right. Masters did indeed already know this story. He'd dredged it up in its every sorry detail after that interview, or perhaps more accurately interrogation, in that prison kitchen, but he still wanted to hear it from Edwards's own lips.

'It's all her mother had kept saying to us.'

Masters just kept staring.

'She kept saying it over and over, every time she looked at us, every time we all looked at her. It must have been one of the few English words she knew: over and over, out it'd come – *fourteen* – *fourteen* –'

Edwards paused.

'As if it was some sort of code or something. Something she could say that would keep her daughter away from harm.'

Masters stayed silent as Edwards tailed off and a hunted look occupied more and more of that mousey face.

'It was just talk, that's what we all thought.'

Edwards turned watery eyes back on Masters.

'How the fuck we were to know he was serious?'

From the dredging exercise he'd undertaken, Masters now knew that Tom Edwards had been part of a small detachment of solders stationed just outside Mosul.

He also now knew that across the street from the checkpoint manned by Edwards and two other soldiers was a modest two-bedroomed house owned by a family of two boys, one girl, a mother who worked in a local store and a father who worked an almost-barren strip of nearby land. The boys were six and nine. The girl was fourteen.

And he also now knew that one of Edwards's fellow soldiers, a then twenty-something obvious sociopath called Ben Holland, had become obsessed with the young girl he'd see each day, helping her mother and father with the household chores across the street.

Sweat was now running freely down Edwards's forehead.

'She'd started carrying water back to the house in a bucket, there was a problem with the pipes. When she spilled some, he told us we should help. Fix the pipes or something. Show them that we weren't the animals they all thought we were.'

Masters conjured up again in his mind the file he'd left lying on the desk in his office. The father, Yusef, had dreamt that one day all his children would go to college in the west. It was a dream that was to perish along with those children that hot, alcohol-fuelled day.

'The two boys ran in after us. The father was out – I suppose they thought they were being the men of the house or something. It was funny in a way, these small kids, standing up against us. One of them wasn't even fazed when Holland took out his gun. We still thought it was just part of some stupid game he was playing. Then Holland did it. He pulled the trigger. Blew the boy's brains out.'

What had happened next wasn't totally clear to Masters. Did Edwards and the other soldier participate in the atrocities that followed or were they simply too traumatised by what their companion had done to prevent them? All the investigating officers knew for sure was that the other boy was also killed, as was the mother, who had dashed in at the sound of the first gunshot. The fourteen-year-old girl had tried to get away to alert her father, but had been grabbed by Holland.

'She kept trying to keep her legs closed, and she was saying all sorts of stuff to him, to all of us, in Arabic, but he wouldn't listen – not to her, not to us, not to anyone. He just held her down and forced himself inside her.'

Edwards paused.

'Then when he finished, he shot her too.'

What followed was the all too familiar cover-up. The explanation on the part of the soldiers led by Holland that was anything but an explanation. The story trotted out to the disbelieving and grief-stricken father that it all been the work of Sunni insurgents. An explanation and a story that shouldn't have stood up for a second, so why had it?

Edwards turned those same mousey eyes on Masters. The resolve that had propelled him so far was now almost visibly draining away. Now he was fast returning to the cowed, malleable figure he must have presented in that small house a few metres from that checkpoint. The figure he'd attempted to keep at bay by constructing his perfect family, ruling it with that rod of iron and perfecting his DIY.

Tom Edwards did indeed have one massive skeleton in his past. A skeleton that had been airbrushed out of existence, officially at least. Unofficially it had just lain dormant. A favour waiting to be called in.

Three squaddies, one a certified sociopath. All now in a lifetime's debt, a debt that must have been called in that night. There was no other reason why Edwards should have snapped like that. The Sword of Damocles must suddenly have fallen.

But that wasn't what was interesting Masters right now. All that was part of a past that couldn't now be altered. It was the future and the immediate future Masters was much more interested in.

'So who called you?'

Edwards hesitated.

'Holland.'

'And he wanted what, exactly?'

Edwards struggled a moment longer. But he was way beyond any sort of genuine resistance right now and he knew it.

'First, to make sure you saw it.'

'Saw what?'

'That photo. That man you keep talking about.'

'Emmanuel?'

Edwards nodded.

'Keep it on my phone, he said. And my computer. Don't draw attention to it. He said you'd find it sooner or later.'

Masters kept staring at him. Now he had confirmation they were being well and truly played. What he still didn't know yet was for what purpose.

'Then?'

Edwards shook his head.

'I don't know. I never found out. The next thing –'

Edwards cracked.

'I'd done it – my boys –'

Edwards looked out over the water. Then he turned those same mousey eyes on Masters, hunted and fearful. Guilty and tormented. In other words, easy prey.

'It was never going to end. Ever. And even if it did end for me, even if I just walked off the nearest cliff so they couldn't reach me any more, it still wouldn't have ended: they'd made that clear time and again. They'd just have gone for the next in line – they'd have gone for Steven or Callum instead.'

Edwards looked back at Masters.

'I was theirs. Bought and sold. And so were my boys.'

Briefly, another image flashed in front of Masters's eyes of another soul mortgaged to the past, but in Ros's case there was no culpability involved. Unlike Tom Edwards, she was blameless – but it made little difference. The effects were the same.

'There was no other way. Nothing else I could do. It was the only way I could set them free.'

It was a refrain Edwards must have rehearsed to himself a thousand times, but then suddenly he hesitated.

'Get him.'

Masters looked back at him.

This time Edwards held his stare.

'Whatever else you do. Get Holland. Take him down.'

Then Edwards handed Masters a photo. Masters stared at the picture before him. Edwards and some old Army pals. Including the obvious leader of the group, posed right in the middle of them all, his arms around his acolytes.

Masters kept staring. For once his much-fabled gift of intuition seemed to have deserted him.

Because the name of the man staring back out at him from the very centre of that photo wasn't Holland.

Or at least that wasn't the name he was using now.

Masters kept staring at the face in the photo as the ghost of a smile almost flecked Edwards's features. Then Edwards swung one leg after the other over the rope that separated the pathway from the surging waters and dropped over the side.

Back on the walkway Masters watched for a moment as Edwards slipped under the water, attempting again to end – as he'd always intended to – his miserable, unlamented little life.

Then Masters moved forward, though not out of any belated sense of fellow-feeling or compassion.

He had one last task for Tom Edwards to perform.

After that, Masters would happily push him under those grey waters himself.

Ros was booked to leave on the evening flight, but a couple of hours before it was due to depart, she received an unexpected call.

A short time later she was sitting in an igloo, though this particular igloo wasn't made out of ice. This one had been constructed using an aluminium frame. In common with other igloos, it did boast a place to sleep and a place to sit and even some cooking facilities, but unlike any other igloo Ros had ever seen, this one boasted a bathroom. It also boasted an uninterrupted view across to the sea, which looked as if it was almost within touching distance.

Delaney was waiting for Ros when she arrived. The igloo where he was waiting had once been home to the Icelandic singer Björk. She'd come for a three-night stay once and had ended up staying several weeks. Ros could immediately understand why as she took in the view, not to mention the smell of grilled catfish wafting across from the nearby hotel restaurant, a branch of the Brasserie Takanna.

But neither the view nor food seemed to be on Delaney's mind. Unsettled by that unexpected appearance from his father in law, unsure whether it might be related in any way to the persecution he'd been enduring, further unsure whether that was anything to do with the stonewall in their current investigations he and Ros had experienced since she arrived in the country, Delaney had wanted to talk to her before she left, maybe in some last-ditch attempt to try and make some sort of sense of it all.

'The whole thing started just before I took up this post.'

Delaney stopped for a moment, looking wracked.

'I couldn't put it together – still can't. It just seemed to be stuff that was happening that made no sense.'

Delaney rolled on.

'I still don't know who's doing it. I don't know why. But it has to be something to do with Alasie and Imaneq, because I'm the only one – before you came, anyway – the only one who's digging into all that.'

Ros listened as Delaney went through the whole story.

The computer.

Those messages.

The all too obvious campaign of persecution.

She could have reciprocated with similar confidences of her own. She could have told her companion all about the dead Braith and her murdered father. She could have told Delaney the real reason she was in Greenland. She could have told him about Emmanuel and shown him the various photos she'd brought with her from the UK featuring the different sightings of him in and around Nuuk and elsewhere.

She could have tried using him as an independent and impartial ear. She could have tried to sound him out regarding the role Emmanuel might be playing here, because she still didn't know exactly what that was. Was he instigator or innocent? Main agent or bit part player? On the side of the angels looking to bring down devils, as she'd always previously believed? Or was he firmly on the dark side himself, and maybe always had been?

But she didn't get chance to rehearse any of that.

Because Dorthe Kalia suddenly appeared behind Delaney.

Delaney wheeled round, following a rooted Ros's sudden fixed stare, both officers now transfixed for a moment at the sight of the very last person either would have expected to see right now.

Dorthe looked back at them in turn, also not speaking for a moment. When she did, it was to utter just two simple words.

'Help her.'

Ros and Delaney kept staring.

'Help my daughter.'

Dorthe faltered.

'Before I lose her too.'

Ros's eyes flashed wide in alarm. Had Conor been trying to reach her, maybe while she was in the cinema watching that film or here in this fucking igloo?

'What's happened to Desna?'

But Dorthe shook her head.

'Not Desna.'

Then Dorthe glanced, almost involuntarily, out across the water towards the harbour in the distance.

And all of a sudden Ros wasn't seeing Dorthe any longer.

All Ros was now seeing was Cecilie, sitting in Martin Mathiassen's office all those days before.

Martin Mathiassen frequented quite a few bars down by the old harbour, the scene of the shooting of that polar bear just a few hours before.

The bars changed, as did the clientele drinking in them, but one thing almost always stayed the same. Despite knowing most of the people in most of those bars – he was a well-known and respected local figure after all – Mathiassen almost always drank on his own. Maybe because people largely left him alone.

But not that evening. Sitting at his usual spot, he sensed it before he actually saw anything. Something in the way the atoms rearranged themselves in the atmosphere, perhaps. Or maybe just some almost forgotten instinct somewhere deep inside, stirring back into life.

Mathiassen half-turned on his seat, then stopped. Standing in the doorway was a young woman, staring across the room towards him. And as he looked back at her, she held his stare

– something he could scarcely credit at first. But the more he stared, the more convinced he was.

The young woman was actually eyeing him, and him alone, of all the people in that bar that evening – including, it had to be said, a lot of much younger men. She was eyeing him coolly, admittedly, but that only added sparkle to what looked like some kind of definite intent in her eyes.

And the more he kept looking at her, the more he could see that there was more than a hint of promise in there too.

Then, suddenly, he placed her. And now he grew even more intrigued, because his interest had been sparked by this young woman the first time they'd met, and not just because there seemed to be something faintly familiar about her.

There was just something in the way she'd seemed to be studying him back then too.

As she was very definitely studying him now.

Across the bar, Cecilie may have been looking at him, but all she was actually seeing were trees.

As the excited voice sounded again in her ears, she actually saw everything Desna was describing: that common beech, that smooth-leaved elm, and above all, above everything else, that juniper tree. The tree that thrived on chalk moorland with a grey-brown bark, which had small needle-like leaves that were green with broad silver bands on the inner side and which curved to a sharp, prickly point.

And Cecilie kept looking across the bar at the white-haired man as she heard that same young voice in her ear now telling her that the juniper was the tree of choice to ward off evil spirits.

And then suddenly she had to blink back quick tears as she heard once again the animated young voice telling her that mature junipers could reach a height of over ten metres and that some could live for well over two hundred years, because that was when it happened. When that voice now mixed with that other voice once again: the voice of that other child whom she'd idolised when she was young herself.

Even now, all these years later, as Cecilie closed her eyes each night trying to summon a sleep that rarely came, she'd hear that same voice, the words spilling out of her mouth in a torrent, telling their mother all about this school project or that assignment, making clear the extra work she intended to put in to make sure it was going to be the very best it could possibly be, the best she could possibly make it, like she always did.

The young Cecilie, at that time known as Sika, used to stare at the older Alasie, hardly understanding a word she was saying, in truth, but knowing one thing for certain nevertheless.

When she grew up, she silently vowed, she was going to be just like her sister.

One hour later and Mathiassen couldn't believe his luck.

He was lying face up on his bed. Above him he watched a ceiling fan slowly rotate. From the bathroom just across the small corridor he could hear taps being run but his unexpected guest didn't seem to have undressed yet. Or if she had, she'd kept on her high heels because he could now hear them clacking on the parquet floor as she made her way back across the small landing to him.

Mathiassen leant back on the bed and smiled. In truth, he had been more than a touch fearful that maybe he'd be a little too inhibited when it came to a moment like this. With a divorce more than twenty years behind him, it had been a long time, after all. But listening to the sound of those approaching high heels, he felt an all too familiar stirring begin to develop and smiled wider.

Then the door opened and the young woman walked back in, something he couldn't quite make out at first in her hand.

Ten minutes later, Mathiassen was fighting for air inside a tight-fitting mask. The blow that had temporarily winded him had been delivered expertly enough, but the shock of the sudden and unexpected attack would probably have disabled him anyway. Then he was rendered as helpless as a babe in arms as his assailant slipped that mask over his head and secured his unprotesting arms and legs with the shackles she'd also brought in with her, shackles that now restrained him.

For a moment, a desperate thought illuminated his reeling brain. Maybe this was some sort of game being initiated by the kinky bitch? Maybe in her world this passed for some kind of foreplay? Then Mathiassen felt his stomach muscles scream in pain as another blow landed and he realised only too clearly that this was no game. He was in trouble.

Suddenly Mathiassen couldn't breathe, and that wasn't just because of the mask pressing against his nose and mouth. Suddenly he was terrified. What had begun as a totally unexpected but highly welcome chance seduction had turned into something that actually smelt of evil – he couldn't describe it any other way.

And what was this crazed young woman saying to him all the time? Mathiassen simply didn't know. Now and again he picked up the odd stray word here and there, but it all still made no sense. In fact he feared he really must be hallucinating right now, perhaps because of the unfamiliar and excruciating pain flooding his body, because the only thing he could pick out were some stray descriptions of – of all things – different trees.

Then Cecilie leant closer. Swiftly, she let him know that she was less than impressed by his performance so far in responding to all she was saying. Another equally swift blow to his genitals cemented the admonition. A gasping Mathiassen, now in even less of a position to mount a protest, felt himself being yanked to his still-shackled feet by a woman who clearly possessed a great deal more strength than might have been suggested by her slight frame.

In between now-violent retches, Mathiassen managed just the one question.

'What are you doing?'

Cecilie paused for a moment and looked back at him.

Then she leant close to the wheezing solicitor and whispered in his ear, telling him exactly what she was doing and what she was now going to do.

Which was when Mathiassen realised something.

He thought he'd been terrified before but he hadn't, because now he understood how real terror felt.

Which was when Cecilie leant closer and spoke again, and Mathiassen realised something else.

There was only one thing he could do now to stop this. Cecilie had just made that all too clear.

Outside the upmarket apartment in the centre of Nuuk, Ros and Delaney stared at the security lock that secured Martin Mathiassen's front door.

Both officers could see at a glance that it was state of the art and that it was going to take some considerable force to breach it. But fortunately that considerable force was close at hand.

Ros looked round, stilling as she saw a Toyota Land Cruiser parked nearby, similar to the one – according to the police report – that had virtually demolished the Home for Convicts the day she'd arrived in Nuuk. Moving across the road, Ros flashed her warrant card at the startled owner before climbing into the driver's seat, Delaney following her into the vehicle.

Martin Mathiassen was quite clearly not the only one to have been fooled by Cecilie. They'd all been duped by her. That recent recruit to the national police force was very much not the simple, uncomplicated junior officer she'd originally seemed.

Dorthe had told them that she'd spirited the young Cecilie away immediately after her elder sister's murder, desperate that she too shouldn't join the roll call of innocence lost. She was only just over four when that had happened to Alasie and it had always been Dorthe's intention that her daughter should simply forget who she was and should never find out the truth about what had happened to her original family.

But Cecilie had never forgotten. And from the time she had attained Alasie's age, she'd dedicated her life to finding out the truth behind her sister's murder, the murder that had precipitated her own enforced expulsion from her old family home. From that moment Cecilie had lived a life that was hidden in order to try and expose more hidden lives and an unsolved murder.

And what better way to investigate any kind of murder than from inside the police?

Ros felt Delaney tense beside her as she started the engine and selected a gear.

Less than one minute later, Mathiassen's front door, secured by that state of the art security lock, was in pieces on the floor as the bull bars of the Land Cruiser forced it from its hinges.

Dimly, Mathiassen heard the crash sound below.

For a moment he heard nothing else, and for that moment he wondered if he'd been hearing things, conjuring yet more terrors to add to the actual ones he was currently enduring. There'd been silence for the few moments before that loud crash too, a silence that was more terrifying – if such a thing was possible – than all that had gone before.

Then Mathiassen moaned softly as a faint whirr sounded from across the room. Because he knew that sound. More importantly he knew what it meant. It was the sound of a life ending, the life he'd been bequeathed. The life he'd fought to maintain against sometimes overpowering odds.

Then Mathiassen heard something else, which was the sound of running feet approaching up the stairs.

A moment later, Delaney and Ros walked in on a scene of unparalleled brutality.

Or, as Cecilie herself would later point out, a scene of almost unparalleled brutality. In her view – and in the view of her family too, no doubt – the brutality meted out to the infinitely more innocent Alasie Kalia would have far eclipsed any of this.

Delaney took in the tortured figure on the bed and his junior officer sitting calmly by his side, an unmarked DVD case in her hands. For her part, Cecilie didn't even acknowledge the now staring, rooted figures of Ros and Delaney. Her gamble, in her eyes, had paid off. She might not have the man she'd hunted all those years, but she had the next best thing. And she had something else too.

Cecilie crossed to a state-of-the-art media system and outsize monitor that lined one whole wall of Mathiassen's bedroom and pressed the play button, the DVD from that unmarked case already loaded inside.

On the bed, Mathiassen moaned again as images pervaded the room and sound began to be heard, but no one took any notice. He was now an irrelevance, a sideshow.

All eyes were on the images that were now filling that outsize screen, and this time Ros wasn't going to need any of her fabled empathetic identification.

This time everything was on that screen for everyone to see.

The camera was set at the eye level of a child. The pictures were grainy, the colours bleaching now. In a few more years everything would have merged into a milky grey, but for now it was easy enough to pick out what was happening.

The girl was staring round the room as if she'd just landed on a different planet, and no wonder. When would she ever in her life before have seen a room full of naked adult men, all looking at her own naked body, massaging their private parts as they did so, a few of the bolder ones already reaching out scrabbling fingers towards her?

One held up his erect penis to her face and her eyes widened even more. She simply did not know what to do with it, and her clear bewilderment caused considerable merriment in the room, which only increased her bewilderment even more.

But she'd learn.

Soon enough.

As a voice off-screen made clear.

The men on the screen were drinking, most sipping champagne as befitted what was clearly a special occasion. The deflowering of an innocent was, after all, always something to be marked.

But there was a problem. The small girl was just a touch too immobile and several of the men were starting to complain. Another stepped forward and tied a rubber strap around her arm. With the vein suitably swollen, a needle was inserted. The girl simply kept staring straight ahead, almost as if she could already see what would eventually happen to her and was already welcoming it. Anything would have to be better than this.

The small girl sank to the floor. For a brief moment she seemed to be trying to cover her ears and eyes with her hands, trying to blot out all that was happening, but her limbs wouldn't respond properly. She started to shiver with cold, despite the fact it was clearly hot inside the room, as attested by the sweat glistening on the rolls of fat on all the men around her.

'What's happening?'

That same voice spoke again.

'I said, what's happening?'

Then the man, sporting a shock of white hair, was seen pushing through the thickening throng of naked males. It was the man whose portrait Ros, Delaney and Cecilie had seen hanging on the wall of Mathiassen's office.

He grabbed the young girl's unresisting wrist, checking her pulse, then swore loudly at the man who'd injected her.

'How much did you give her?'

Another equally panicked voice responded.

'The usual, just the usual.'

The man with the shock of white hair, who was still holding the girl's wrist, swore again, ever more agitated.

'She's dying, she's fucking dying.'

There was silence for a moment, then a babble of near-hysterical voices broke out, but then that same voice cut across once again, silencing them.

'OK, OK, listen.'

The small girl was now on the floor, slipping all the while from one life to another, from a vision of hell to eternal oblivion. As she did so, that same voice spoke once more, confident as ever, in charge as always.

'This is what we do.'

The man with the shock of white hair stretched out an elegant hand for a nearby phone. Within moments the connection was made. Within a few more moments the man who would resolve this would be there, as he had been before. As he always would be.

But then his voice stopped, light suddenly flooding the room as a door opened. Almost involuntarily, the man operating the camera and recording the dying girl swung round and captured another young girl standing in the open doorway, staring in stunned silence at the scene before her.

Then that same voice spoke again.

'Who the fuck is that?'

At the open door, Alasie Kalia just kept staring in at them.

Back in his now fetid bedroom, Martin Mathiassen was still shackled and splayed out on the bed.

Cecilie was staring at her older sister on the screen, the sister she carried around in her head in her every waking moment. The burden that led directly to the lie she lived daily. Leading to the punishment she inflicted on herself to try to atone.

But Ros wasn't staring at the young, clearly terrified – and soon to be dead – Alasie Kalia. Because all of a sudden Cecilie's quest and Ros's seemed to have fused into one, as Ros stared at the man who'd just appeared behind Alasie on screen, the man summoned by the figure with the shock of white hair.

Back on the bed, Mathiassen moaned again, although more softly this time. Because deep down, some part of him actually welcomed all this. He'd spent a lifetime covering up for his father, only now it was over. And despite everything, relief began to flood through him that he wouldn't have to do it any more.

Ros hardly even saw him or anyone right now. She was still staring at the man now conferring in a low urgent voice with Mathiassen's father, nodding across at the drugged and comatose young girl as he did so, and then back at the rooted Alasie.

Back on the bed, Mathiassen followed her look. If he could have done what Tom Edwards had attempted to do, could have risen from that bed, walked outside and slipped into the water out in that harbour and let it wash him away, then he would. But he couldn't and he knew it.

But as he kept looking across at Ros, still staring at that new arrival on the screen, an idea began to form. For generations, Mathiassen and his family had been the ultimate survivors. And maybe he could still survive this.

Mathiassen gasped out a series of numbers. The three officers stared back at him, none of it making any sense at first, but then Ros realised.

Mathiassen was giving them coordinates.

Mathiassen was looking directly now at Ros, and no one else. 'That's where you'll find him.'

Ros punched the coordinates into her phone. Those coordinates corresponded to a small island off the coast nearby, connected to the mainland by a causeway.

Ros stared at the location on the screen in front of her for a moment, everything else forgotten, then she looked back at the figure still with Martin Mathiassen Senior on the screen.

Maybe – just maybe – they finally had Emmanuel in their sights.

Ros, Delaney and Cecilie had never thought they'd ever feel any sort of affection for Sandgreen.

Sandgreen was old-school and proud of it – although 'Neanderthal' might have been a more apt description. He came originally from Qaanaaq in the far North, just a few hundred kilometres from the Pole, a town that had reminded Ros of a Nordic fishing village when she'd previously visited it, with its colourful, steep-pitched houses and well-maintained dirt streets. It also boasted the world's most northernmost football pitch, ploughed off the sea ice.

The whole place was isolated and very, very small. Ros didn't subscribe to the view that backwaters necessarily produced backward-looking residents, but in the short time she'd been in Greenland, Sandgreen had given her pause for thought.

In Sandgreen's world, women were best seen and not heard, along with children until they reached the age of majority. Immigrants from overseas were better off back there, and as for some relatively new union that had been set up to look after the interests of gay police officers, Sandgreen's bulging eyes almost imploded into the rest of his jowly face at just the thought of it. But Ros had definitely warmed to the man in the last hour.

Protocol dictated they all now wait for a SWAT team from Denmark. That same protocol dictated the procedures that would need to be followed both before and after that team's arrival, and the risk assessments that would need to be put in place. Ros wouldn't quite have been collecting her state pension once all those individual hurdles had been cleared, but it would be a close-run thing.

Ros had little appetite for that sort of red tape. A grim Masters had arrived from the UK an hour or so previously and he'd made it clear that neither did he. Both Delaney and Cecilie seemed of the same mind too. Sandgreen was the only potential obstacle in preventing an immediate hit on what seemed to be Emmanuel's hideout, and as he stared at the officers assembled before him, Ros was already wondering about employing Cecilie's clear talent for incapacitating unwelcome opposition.

Then Sandgreen suddenly turned and headed for a door at the far end of his office. Opening it, he brought out a selection of weapons: not only the usual hunting rifles and skinning knives, but also semi-automatic carbines and ballistic vests, along with well over sixty rounds of ammunition per carbine.

For once even Masters seemed lost for words, as Sandgreen handed him one of the carbines and spoke for almost the first time since Masters had arrived.

'Let's get the fucker.'

But ten minutes later Ros discovered that Sandgreen's call to arms wasn't actually to include her.

Sandgreen had commandeered an outsize Wrangler Jeep. Supplies were being loaded into it, ready to cross the causeway at low tide. Ros could almost feel her heart pounding inside her chest at the thought of finally coming face to face with the man who'd virtually defined her whole life – as well as uncovering the full truth about him and all he had or had not done.

Which was when, with an equally disbelieving Delaney, Cecilie and Sandgreen looking on, Masters had caught her arm and shaken his head.

'You're not coming.'

Ros stared at him. For a moment she was actually amused. What was this, some sort of sick joke?

'It's what he wants.'

Still, all Ros felt was amusement. Even if that was the case – and it was one hell of an *if* – how did they imagine they were going to stop her?

Swiftly, anticipating and decoding her all too obvious expression, Masters outlined all he'd learnt from the sadly still-alive and very much unlamented Donovan Banks.

If Banks was right – if that's what this was really all about, if this whole enterprise had been some sort of elaborate revenge kick; a trap – then they had to fight fire with fire and respond in kind.

So that's what they were now going to do. Set a trap in turn.

But then Masters hesitated. Because there was something else as well.

'And look at the date.'

Masters snaked out his wrist in front of her. A Breitling Navitimer wristwatch– what else? – displayed that day's date. And as Ros stared at it, she felt all her previous defiant amusement begin to evaporate.

Half an hour later, Masters, Delaney, Cecilie and Sandgreen set off in the Jeep to apprehend and arrest Emmanuel Ocon, while Ros stayed behind.

Two hours before that and an hour before Masters's arrival, Ros, Cecilie and Delaney had been closeted with Martin Mathiassen in a side ward in the capital's Queen Ingrid's Hospital.

Incredible as it seemed to Cecilie in particular, the patrician Mathiassen still looked as if nothing could touch him. As if neither he nor his family were ordinary mortals to be judged by the standards of others. As if whatever they did, no one had the right to bring them to book.

Which was presumably why, as Delaney pointed out to him within moments of that interview commencing, Mathiassen had attempted to thwart Delaney's new investigation into Alasie's murder by targeting Delaney himself with those computer messages. Creating a false version of reality to try and send him further into the form of madness he had inhabited after his wife's death.

Mathiassen didn't reply. For a moment Ros didn't think he would. Then he looked up and spoke for the first and only time.

'I protected my father. I concealed his crimes. I disguised some of his worst excesses, occasionally passing them off as academic exercises and inventing others to cover the trail. All that is true.'

Then Mathiassen nodded at the watching Delaney.

'But I know nothing about any campaign of persecution against you.'

Ros and Cecilie both looked at Delaney, puzzled. That had actually seemed to come from the heart. But Delaney just eyed Mathiassen back levelly, clearly not buying it for a moment.

Then Mathiassen cast down his eyes. Which was how he stayed. Immobile and frozen. He'd done as much as he was going to. He'd given away his father and he'd handed them Emmanuel's present location. The rest was down to Delaney, Ros and the other officers.

But Mathiassen's involvement wasn't completely over. Unbeknown to the white-haired solicitor, he had one more role to play.

Masters kept watch on the causeway.

Sure enough, and as they'd all expected, a 4x4 made the journey from the small island to the mainland as soon as the ebbing tide permitted. Masters and the other officers had hidden their vehicle away from the road behind some thick bushes, but Masters still caught a clear glimpse of at least three men: hired muscle, probably of Danish extraction. He didn't need to follow them to know where they were going.

They were heading for Ros. Today – the date shown to Ros on Masters's watch – was the much-trailed day of her execution. That final part of a decades-old mission complete, they'd probably decamp to the airport, leaving their paymaster to reflect on a long-anticipated task accomplished at last.

So Ros had been left behind as a sacrificial lamb, tempting that hired muscle away from their lair. Which was when Masters and the rest of the officers would move in.

Not that all the officers were too happy about it.

'I don't like it.'

Cecilie had been uneasy, and volubly so, all the way over to the causeway. If Delaney and Sandgreen shared those concerns, they didn't show it.

'She'll be protected.'

A frustrated Cecilie looked back at Masters.

'A detachment of officers will be inside and outside her apartment at all times.'

'Something could still go wrong.'

Masters, calm, trotted out the mantra.

'She won't be at risk.'

'You can't know that, not for sure.'

Then Cecilie stopped as the causeway hove into view.

Along with Ros herself.

And now Cecilie understood. Ros wouldn't be at risk because she wouldn't be there. There would be a sacrificial lamb waiting inside that apartment, but it wouldn't be her, it would be Mathiassen. The scanners those goons would undoubtedly be using would still reveal a human presence inside that small apartment, just not the one they were expecting.

Mathiassen should still be safe enough, but there were always risks, just as there was always the possibility of some kind of collateral damage.

Just ask Alasie Kalia.

Masters looked at Ros, the patrician solicitor wiped from his mind. No way would she not have been in at the kill and he knew it, no matter the risks. If he'd been among the ranks of those desperate and damned who indulged in the ancient sport of betting, he'd have staked his beloved Bentley on Ros refusing to absent herself from this showdown.

Besides, for the next stage in this extended gamble to play out as they wanted it to, it was essential that she did not.

Masters looked back at the exposed causeway, the 4x4 now long gone. He just hoped they'd gambled correctly. They'd done what they'd set out to do, constructing a trap inside a trap and making sure that even among the officers involved, everything was on the basis of need to know.

But would it work?

The small island loomed before them.

The steep banks on all sides made any sort of approach difficult from the water, so the causeway really was the only realistic way in or out.

The same scanners that would be being used right now to identify a human presence in Ros's apartment had already been employed by the officers in turn to identify a single human presence, currently in a small shack on the island.

They couldn't positively identify that single human presence as Emmanuel. But it would be him, Ros was as sure of that as she'd ever been of anything in her life before. She was finally closing in on her lifelong quarry, and even if she couldn't explain how, she still knew it.

The officers approached the causeway, singly and silently. The water to each side was black and mirror-like. The night was still, the air cold, the moon full. One by one they made it across without any sign they'd been spotted or any warning being raised. Dimly ahead a faint path could be seen, tyre tracks scarring the soil. At the end of that track they could just make out the faint outline of a small building. Smoke pooled lazily from a chimney set to one side.

The approaching Ros felt her heart rate quicken again, then – equally quickly – she took the deepest of breaths, consciously calming herself until her heart rate slowed to something approximating normal. More than anything right now, she needed to stay focused. From the anxious but determined faces around her, she could see her companions all felt the same.

Masters gave a silent signal. As one, the officers donned their night goggles. Suddenly the world became bathed in an almost eerie green, illuminating the shack ahead so now Ros could make out the very knots in its wooden walls. Inside, and just visible through a frosted window, a shape flitted across her vision. Ros looked at Masters, who looked back at her.

And then suddenly, and from out of nowhere, she heard her late eldest sister's voice once more. And she saw Di too, meeting her as a child and their parents as well, outside the church that had just hosted Braith's funeral, urgently telling them all that she'd discovered about the man she'd met and fallen in love with, a man she now knew was a hero undercover cop. A tearful Di had insisted over and over, before the accompanying and increasingly alarmed police officers could spirit her away, that she hadn't married a bad man.

Ros looked towards the small wooden shack again, her face setting, ever more determined to find out the truth.

Which was when she suddenly saw something else.

On the rocks all around them, now revealed by the night goggles, she saw rigging. Looking round in increasing panic, she saw that rigging supported a whole array of miniature wireless cameras. Jerking her head to the side, she next saw the unmistakable outline of a motion sensor, and looking back towards the causeway – and now also revealed by the night goggles – she could see similar rigging stretched across the rocks that lined its short length.

Ros looked back at Masters, the expression on his face making it clear he'd spotted the same thing. Their careful and silent approach had counted for nothing. They'd been tracked all the way.

Masters hissed a two word instruction to the other officers, all three still oblivious to anything amiss.

'Fall back.'

But it was already too late. As Delaney, Cecilie and Sandgreen stared back at him, their night goggles swinging his way, the sudden roar of a 4x4 was heard, approaching back along the causeway, the vehicle slewing to a halt in the very centre of the only way onto and off that small island, blocking any escape. Dark figures, still unmistakably Danish somehow, poured from the doors of the vehicle as they burst open.

The next second the shooting started. Delaney fell.

Masters, Cecilie and Sandgreen returned fire, all bolting for the relative safety of some more rocks lining the path as they did so. But Ros ran in a different direction. Courtesy of her night goggles, she'd just seen a dim figure slip from the shack and make for a snow scooter parked at the side of the property. Emmanuel, the ever-elusive Emmanuel, was taking advantage of the gun battle now raging outside to again make his escape.

The snow scooter fired into life and Emmanuel gunned the engine, intending presumably to roar back towards the causeway, past the fighting officers, and steer the vehicle along the narrow path that had been left for him by that slewed 4x4.

But he didn't get there. The small slight police officer who launched herself at him a moment later made sure of that. Ros and the unbalanced Emmanuel hit the unforgiving ground hard, rolling and rolling on the slippery surface, both scrabbling for a grip that never came.

Emmanuel hit the water first, Ros a second later, the cold sucking the air from both their lungs. For that moment, Emmanuel's face was clearly exposed in the moonlight, making identification certain. In that moment too, had Ros been so minded, she could have picked up one of the rocks lining the bank and smashed it into Emmanuel's head, sending him to the oblivion to which he seemed to have consigned so many others, including the totally innocent members of her own family.

But Ros wanted answers. She wanted to make some twisted sense out of all that had happened to her in what was still her short life. And so Ros grabbed the gasping Emmanuel instead.

For a moment the sensation was eerie. Impossible almost. To be in actual physical contact with him after all this time felt other-worldly somehow. But that only lasted seconds as Ros began to steer the winded Emmanuel back towards the shore.

Which was when Emmanuel's hand snaked for her throat, at the same time as his leg lashed out at her hip. Both connected at the same time, the leg landing a glancing blow but the hand finding a secure grip. His fingers began squeezing her windpipe. Ros lashed out in turn, connecting with Emmanuel's left eye. His grip loosened momentarily, enough for Ros to take a gasping breath before she saw the silver glint of the knife being whipped from his jacket pocket. The next second Ros dodged the first of the lunges which, if it had landed, would have virtually separated her head from her shoulders.

Ros brought up her head, and smashed it into Emmanuel's cheek. She felt the splintering of bone and heard an anguished yell that sounded somehow close and distant at the same time. She felt his grip on her throat slacken for an instant and she yanked out her hand, felt it fill with a large clump of thick hair, and readied herself for another attempt to steer her quarry back to the bank – hoping against hope that maybe Masters had seen the struggle and could help reel him in.

But then suddenly everything went black.

Ros was now under water and Emmanuel's hands were keeping her under the surface. Time and again she attempted to kick upwards, but his renewed grip was like iron. Emmanuel snaked his legs around her neck, using her as a human buoy, levering himself up, keeping his head above the surface, forcing Ros's head ever-deeper down into the blackness.

Which was when she actually did see them. And not just in her mind's eye – now they were actually before her eyes too. Ros saw her family: she saw her elder sister, Braith, murdered all those years before; she saw her other sister, Di, also gunned down years later; and she saw her mother, who had died shortly after that of a broken heart.

And then she saw her father, the last of the line to fall. Or at least the last of the line till now.

Which was impossible and Ros knew it. And not only was it impossible, it didn't change a thing. There was no supernatural springing from beyond the grave, no actual physical intervention that, miracle-like, was going to rescue her from the oblivion into which she was fast being sent.

But there was still something in all their eyes. Some message that only she could read: a recognition that each of them, in their moment of greatest danger, had frozen somehow, had allowed themselves to fall in their different ways and had allowed evil to prevail. It was as if they were willing Ros not to do the same.

But no strength of will could deny the laws of physics.

Ros's body had been deprived of oxygen for too long already. Her strength, already depleted, was failing fast. And Emmanuel's grip remained like iron.

Ros sank down into the blackness, sensing rather than feeling Emmanuel loosening his grip on her as she did so. All sound faded away, all sensation fading with it.

Then there was silence.

WHAT HAPPENED TO *Banks was clear enough. I saw him go over the side of that tenth-floor balcony myself.*

But where was Tyra?

For a while – as more police arrived and as the net spread further and further out from that same tenth-floor apartment – I thought she had to have got away. Or had gone to ground somewhere.

Then I saw the fire engines, and the ambulances. I saw one of the firemen ascend to the roof and open up what looked like a refuse shaft.

Then I saw him turn and retch, violently, all over the roof tiles.

Which was when I saw someone else, standing by the entrance to the apartment block. Masters joined her a few moments later.

But it was Ros and Ros alone I was watching now.

No one ever came back. It was the unwritten rule, the unspoken mantra. But there she was. After everything that happened. Still standing. Still moving on.

As time passed, I had wondered if it had all been down to her age. Maybe she seemed to carry no scars because she simply had no memory. All that had happened that day and since had simply been blanked.

Even later, when she joined the protection unit, the unit she'd lived inside all her life, alarm bells didn't really start to ring – at least at first. And when they did, the solution seemed simple. Another killing, the father this time. A final warning written on a suburban wall.

But even that didn't stop her and I had to confess to developing a sneaking, if grudging, respect. I think Tyra sensed it back then too. Maybe she felt the same.

To rise above all that had happened to her, and to be now running the very unit to which as a child she'd been condemned – that really did take something. I didn't know exactly what that something was, but it definitely provoked that grudging respect.

But that day outside that apartment, as Masters leant close, talking to her ever more urgently, I stared at that alabaster face. It was still betraying absolutely no emotion.

Maybe it was my way of sublimating grief. Of deflecting loss. It didn't work, of course: that grief washed over me in waves soon enough, and that loss twisted me inside out.

But I always knew that one day it would happen. That one day we'd meet up again, because she wouldn't rest until we did.

And then it would play out.

Everything that had started all those years before.

And finally, it would end.

PART FIVE

THE COLD DARKNESS

M ASTERS STARED STRAIGHT ahead, not looking right or left, not even seeming to notice the order of service that had been thrust into his hand as he entered the small crematorium.

Conor stood to Masters's left. Behind them were two men Conor didn't recognise, but Masters had seen one of them before. He was the long-suffering concierge who had negotiated Ros her exclusive solo space after fielding a thousand and one complaints from other residents, infuriated by her idiosyncratic parking, and who had let him in to pick up the calendar with that fateful date ringed in red.

The other was a strange-looking individual whose eyebrows met in the middle. His connection with Ros was unclear and neither Masters or Conor were in the mood to work out what that connection might be.

Masters suffered in silence through the anonymous service, which comprised just hymns and a short reading. There were no eulogies and no friends came forward to offer any anecdotes about the soul to whom they were currently bidding farewell. Ros had no friends, in that close sense anyway. And there were no anecdotes.

She had died in the same way she'd lived.

A mystery.

Masters wasn't a man usually given to introspection, which was why the sensation that had assailed him ever since Ros's death felt so strange. Because standing on that bank by that black water on that distant shore, scanning the surface ever more desperately for a figure that was quite clearly destined never to reappear, barely registering in the distance the disappearing sound of a snow scooter as Emmanuel presumably made his escape, Masters had experienced something he'd never experienced before.

Yes, he felt horror at the fate that seemed to have now ensnared his often puzzling colleague; a woman he knew without a shadow of a doubt would be absolutely irreplaceable so far as he was concerned, in ways he still didn't understand and knew he never would.

And yes, he felt grief a short time later as dawn broke and her body was spotted, washed up on the rocks on the south side of that small island. But on that night and during the long days that had followed, Masters also realised exactly why he'd become a police officer in the first place.

It wasn't to apply the law, or to ensure that rules were observed or order maintained. It was so much simpler than that. For a determinedly unconventional officer, it was for the most conventional of reasons in the end. He'd become a police officer in order to keep people safe.

Only when it mattered – as in really mattered – he hadn't done that. Had he?

Masters had looked out over the black, mirror-like water. And for the rest of his life, Masters knew he would forensically replay the events of that night, dissecting his each and every action – knowing that at each and every turn if he'd just done this differently, had that thought just a second sooner, acted in that different way just that little bit more quickly, then maybe he could have prevented what had happened.

And even if he hadn't managed ultimately to prevent the fate that had been sealed for Ros, maybe he could at least have bought her a little more time. If she'd had to die, if that really had been the inescapable end the gods had ordained for her, then at least he could have made sure she did so knowing a little more about the truth behind her life.

The service ended and Masters moved with the rest of the congregation to a rear door where a few floral bouquets were on display, including one from his own Unit as well as one from the Protection Unit to which Ros had dedicated virtually the whole of her short adult life. There was going to be a small wake in a nearby pub, but Masters wasn't attending. He had one final task to perform instead.

Masters waited another half hour until a crematorium assistant appeared at the far end of a well-manicured garden, a small parcel in his hand. Masters took personal charge of the final remains of the finest officer he'd ever met or ever would meet, and then drove to the airport.

It would take three changes of planes, but finally Masters would arrive in the place he knew would have been Ros's own choice for her last resting place on Earth.

A majestic and lonely setting for a majestic and lonely young woman.

Delaney, his injuries patched up as well as the hospital could manage for now, saw again him the next morning.

The same lone figure now standing on the edge of the track that led from Delaney's house down to the shore. The same slight stoop in his posture, accentuated by the way he was shifting from foot to foot once more.

This time Delaney approached, and this time his father-in-law didn't turn and walk away. Niels just looked at him for a moment instead. For that moment there was silence. Then the old man spoke.

'All those walks.'

Delaney looked at him.

'I've seen you. Watched you.'

Delaney kept staring. This was news to him.

'All that time, all by yourself.'

Niels nodded at him.

'So what's all that? A chance to think?'

Then Niels nodded at him again.

'Or an excuse not to?'

Delaney kept looking at the old man, who held his stare.

At exactly the same time, another tortured soul was also making a pilgrimage.

Cecilie, Dorthe and Desna Kalia – Desna recently returned from the UK – were standing before Alasie's grave. Nivi Kleist, David Kleist's widow, was there too. A puzzle was about to be solved, and a reputation restored.

Nivi had come across some old bank statements a few days before, as she was going through more of her late husband's effects. One debit in particular, withdrawn some months previously, stood out: a withdrawal made out for cash. But it was a strange amount, nothing like the amounts her husband usually took out.

It was Cecilie who had made the connection. And now Cecilie, her mother, her sister and Nivi looked at the new headstone sparkling in the spring sunshine. Because the amount David Kleist had withdrawn was exactly the same as the amount paid anonymously to the stonemason who had erected it.

Cecilie had checked with the stonemason and found it was Martin Mathiassen Senior's firm who'd put up the original headstone. It had been paid for by the law firm as a gesture of sympathy to a local family, tragically bereaved.

Cecilie looked across at Nivi, who was staring down at the headstone. It meant David Kleist had completely unwittingly signed his own death warrant. If his wife had been able to work out who had paid for that replacement headstone, then Martin Mathiassen Junior would certainly have been able to work it out too.

And if Nivi had been able to work out what was behind it, then he would certainly have been able to do that as well.

From there it would have been a short step to that fateful night in the old Colonial Harbour and the present head of the law practice shedding crocodile tears over yet another local tragedy.

Nivi smiled a smile that was no smile at all.

'It must have stuck in David's throat, I suppose. The very people responsible for Alasie's death paying to put up her headstone. So he dug into his own pocket and arranged to have another one put up instead.'

Nivi looked up at Cecilie, Desna and Dorthe.

'That was David for you.'

Out in the bay another iceberg calved, with its trademark great crash. None of them even registered it.

'Always did know his right from his wrong.'

Which was an answer to one outstanding question. But Dorthe needed more. And for that she had to make another journey down to the capital in Nuuk.

Later that same evening, Delaney lit one candle. Niels lit another. Outside the house, lights were coming on and soon the horizon would be lit up like a Christmas tree. But inside Delaney's rented house, the only illumination came from those two candles.

Ghosts exist, Delaney knew that now. Not the ghosts of horror fiction, the spectral beings of nightmares, but definitely the souls of those departed, carried around in the hearts and minds of those left behind.

As exorcisms went, it wasn't exactly the most dramatic. There were no muttered incantations while a kindly-disposed cleric splashed holy water in the background. There were just two people in a small house, locked in a past they'd both been unable to resolve.

Perhaps Delaney and Niels hadn't been able to do that because they needed this moment of joint communion to do so. For the last few years, all they'd done was cling on to what had been lost, becoming lost themselves. In the last few days Delaney had seen only too clearly the damage something like that could cause. What happened when the past corroded the present.

That evening there were no words, just those candles flickering in the darkness. The two men watched as the candles burned down and then, just before they extinguished, Delaney leant forward and blew his out. His companion did the same. Then they remained seated, in silence, the smoke from the candles vaporising as it broke on the ceiling.

Niels left a while later with an agreement that they'd meet again and soon – an agreement they both knew they'd keep. They'd bidden their ghosts goodbye now and from that moment on maybe they could both look forward, not back.

But first there was one more ghost to bid on its way. And as his father-in-law left, Delaney looked down at the text that had arrived in the previous half hour from Cecilie.

Dorthe Kalia would be arriving in Nuuk the next morning.

That next morning, Sandgreen was standing outside the newly rebuilt Home for Convicts. Standing to the side of him was Laila Lundblad, recently arrived from Ilulissat.

Both Sandgreen and Laila endured the same curious stares from passing motorists. The faces might change, but the ritual never altered and probably never would. But for one of those faces that day at least, the world had shifted on its axis.

In the wake of his arrest, Martin Mathiassen had sworn a statement finally and totally clearing Tobias Lundblad from any involvement in the murder of Alasie Kalia and implicating his late father. At the same time Lundblad himself had suddenly reappeared, after being released from a locked room in a remote house some 30 kilometres or so from his original place of incarceration.

The mystery behind Tobias's forced abduction from the Home they were standing outside had still not been solved. At least not officially. Sandgreen had his own suspicions as to just who was behind all that, but as he had no wish to name one of his own officers as chief suspect, he kept those suspicions firmly to himself. Sandgreen also shrewdly suspected that Cecilie's intention in abducting Lundblad had been to pressure him into confessing that he'd had something to do with Alasie's murder after all. But once again, Sandgreen was keeping that firmly to himself too.

Lundblad had been returned to the Home to collect the few possessions that had been kept there for him, but he was coming back out again almost immediately. In the light of all that had happened to him recently, his remaining sentence for his latest minor crime had been swiftly rescinded.

'I always knew, you know'.

Sandgreen looked across at Laila.

'That he didn't do it.'

Sandgreen kept looking at her. Lundblad's determined mother had indeed faced down all her doubters and was now about to get her reward. Her fabled scrapbook would now be concluded with the final entry she'd always craved too: a front-page local newspaper article stating once and for all that Tobias Lundblad had been exonerated of the crime for which he'd been under suspicion for decades.

'But that's what it's all about, isn't it? Keeping the faith?'

Laila tensed as the door to the Home for Convicts opened and a flurry of activity began as reporters moved nearer and photographers began to take pictures. Then Tobias himself appeared, smiling shyly, those few possessions in hand, giving the press the shot they'd assembled to record.

For a moment, Laila's face illuminated. There was no other word for it. It wasn't a smile so much as some flame that had lit inside and was now almost literally suffusing her. Laila made to move towards her son, but then she paused one last time, looking back at the hovering Sandgreen.

'Things really are never best left alone are they?'

Laila nodded at him.

'But I don't suppose that's something you'd understand?'

A puzzled Sandgreen watched her head away, towards her waiting son.

Sandgreen kept watching as she took him in her arms, giving the assembled photographers another picture for her scrapbook. He really didn't know whether she'd just been talking about herself and her family.

Or whether Laila Lundblad had just issued some kind of veiled warning instead.

There was only one thing that Dorthe Kalia had ever wanted.

An explanation, and as full and frank an explanation as possible.

A reason or reasons, however twisted and incomprehensible they might be, that would go some way at least to understanding why the man she married and the daughter she had borne him were no longer alive.

That was why she'd arrived in Nuuk that morning. Cecilie had requested that Delaney meet her to try and provide that full and frank explanation, and Delaney had had no hesitation in agreeing.

As Delaney was still on sick leave, the meeting took place away from Police Headquarters in his rented house, the scene of that unofficial exorcism the night before. Cecilie seated herself next to her mother, Delaney opposite them both. Now the two women were together, Delaney could see the clear resemblance

– which wasn't just physical, but something deeper, more elemental, somehow. There was just something in the eyes. A shared experience producing the same kind of woman, perhaps. Contained and guarded.

For a moment an image flitted before Delaney's eyes of another woman he'd come to know only recently, a young woman now lost who had possessed that same quality too.

Then Delaney took a deep breath.

'This is what we know so far. It's fair to say we're still piecing together the full picture because some elements are still not 100% clear. But we're pretty sure we've now got most of the story in place.'

Delaney struggled, trying now to organise his thoughts.

'So far as Alasie is concerned, she seems to have just been in the wrong place at the wrong time. That's tied into a wider investigation which is still ongoing, and a figure who's evaded us as yet.'

Delaney paused again. All this had been difficult enough for him to take in, and he didn't have the emotional investment that Dorthe and her daughter quite clearly had in this story. Which was going to make what they were about to hear even more difficult to absorb.

One second later, Delaney found it even more difficult to organise his thoughts as the door opened behind them, and a man he'd last seen just outside Mosul seated himself opposite.

Then the new arrival nodded at him.

'Hello, Holland.'

Delaney stared back at Tom Edwards, but that wasn't the last of the shocks in store for him that morning.

A moment later, Ros appeared behind Edwards and seated herself next to him.

O N THE OTHER side of the glass, watching Ros and Cecilie face him in the interview room in Police Headquarters in Nuuk, Masters had to concede that Delaney had played it well.

Had it not been for a few tiny miscalculations on his part, he might have continued to get away with it too.

The first of those miscalculations had taken place those few nights before on that island, when he'd gone down just that second too early in that exchange of gunfire. That fractional moment just before the first shot had sounded and not after, as if he knew just what was about to happen.

Because he did.

Masters kept looking at him. His second miscalculation had been to lay the persecution he'd seemingly suffered at Mathiassen's door. All Ros and Cecilie's instincts in the subsequent hospital interview with the white-haired solicitor had proved correct. Mathiassen genuinely knew nothing about that. It had all been part of the same smoke and mirrors.

But his biggest mistake of all was believing Tom Edwards would never betray him, that he'd forever remain too scared to do so. After Delaney took away from the mousey little man, wittingly or unwittingly, everything that made his life worth living, Edwards simply didn't care.

'Tia Andersen.'

Across the desk from her in the interview room, Delaney looked up at Ros. Of all the names he might have imagined he'd be confronted with right now, that of the small murdered girl was clearly the last one he expected. But on the other side of the glass, it was exactly what Masters would have expected. The possible sacrifice of an innocent would always be the very first priority for Ros.

Delaney hesitated a moment, then shook his head.

'That was nothing to do with me.'

Then Delaney hesitated again as both women just continued staring at him.

'Take a look at that dogcatcher. The one who's been telling the story about finding her. He's always been the first name in that frame for me.'

But Cecilie cut across, not buying any of it for a moment.

'Those ties? The superglue?'

Delaney hesitated yet again and Ros answered for him.

'That was just part of the picture, right?'

Cecilie kept staring at him too.

On the other side of the glass, Masters nodded. Ros had worked it out, as had he. Take an unrelated crime and make it look as if it's part of the same persecution. Make sure any inquisitive eyes keep looking elsewhere.

Once again Delaney didn't reply, but he didn't need to.

Across the table, Ros eyed him once more, another name now on her lips.

'Michael.'

The beginnings of an uncharacteristic – or at least unfaked – agitation began to exhibit themselves.

'I didn't kill my son.'

'But you killed your wife.'

On the other side of the glass, Masters kept watching as Delaney fell silent once again.

Once Delaney's story had begun unravelling, the facts had been relatively easy to piece together. Initially, everyone had bought it. A cop on the tragic wrong end of a disastrous police sting leaves his home force. After a time he finally finds work in a different country. It had happened before and would happen again. The difference, as everyone now knew, was that this cop had instigated the failure of that original sting himself.

As everyone also now knew, he'd reinvented himself in the interim as a squaddie called Holland, before reverting back to his original identity. How many other identities he'd assumed was another question currently being probed.

All they knew for certain was that Delaney was a deep swimmer, although in exactly the opposite sense to the traditional moles that Masters had known before and had indeed run himself in dim, distant and much-regretted days in the past.

Working side by side with paymasters still to be tracked or traced, Delaney had infiltrated the police, in the UK and elsewhere. At a certain point his wife had uncovered the truth about the man she'd married, perhaps because Delaney had been genuinely destabilised by the death of their son and become careless. And she'd paid the price.

Masters looked through the glass that divided them at Cecilie. It meant that the national police force in Greenland had had two imposters, in a sense. Though Delaney had been using his position with evil intent, whereas Cecilie was fighting a rather more righteous fight.

Cecilie herself now stepped in, her own agenda and that rather more righteous fight very much in her mind.

'Alasie.'

Delaney looked back at her.

'That happened years before I even got here.'

'But you knew about it. You knew Geisler killed the investigation because he'd been bought off?'

Cecilie paused.

'Just as you knew Alasie had been killed to save Martin Mathiassen's father?'

Delaney hesitated as Cecilie kept those steel grey/blue eyes trained on him.

342

'And my father?'

Delaney still didn't reply. Again, he didn't need to. They'd already established that he'd recruited the Danes who had administered that savage beating to Imaneq Kalia that night. It had been intended as a warning not to follow up on his concerns about Alasie's headstone. But it had gone wrong.

More questions bombarded Delaney, but they only acted now to drive him further into an ever more inpenetrable shell.

Was the whole rape incident in Iraq just a cover? A ploy to recruit a handful of carefully picked squaddies, including Tom Edwards? Human currency to be brought back into circulation at a later date?

What was Delaney's relationship to the trade whose existence had been the object of hushed rumour in the country for years, if not decades? That steady stream of young Inuit girls apparently being spirited abroad, the trade that had partly provoked Dorthe Kalia's panicked exile of her middle daughter, Cecilie, lest she fall prey to the same forces that Dorthe believed had killed her older sister?

For Ros, there was just one question above all others. But every time she attempted to turn the interrogation back to Emmanuel, Delaney retreated further inside that shell.

And as the ultimately frustrating and abortive interview continued, pictures suddenly began to dance before Ros's eyes.

A single shot blasting from the barrel of a standard police-issue handgun.

Delaney's body crashing into the water, staining it red.

The predators out in the bay already picking up the scent.

Ros stepping into the water and pushing at him with her foot, sending Delaney's body out towards them to be consumed in its entirety within minutes.

Ros standing on the shore, watching Delaney's body sink down to oblivion.

But none of that happened. That might have been justice – and real justice too, some would say. But this was also Greenland. And it wasn't Greenlandic justice.

In a few moments' time Delaney would be led away into a prison that had no doors on the cells and no bars on the windows. From there he'd be taken to a courtroom where the full story would be exposed, after which he'd be taken back to that prison with no doors on the cells and no bars on the windows, which he'd leave each day to work in the community and to which he'd return each night.

Ros glanced at the silent Cecilie at her side. It might sound like the crazed definition of total madness to some, and maybe it was, but it was also the way of this ancient land. And if Cecilie could accept it, then Ros could too.

But on the other side of the glass, Masters kept eyeing Delaney.

Ros walked out of the Police Headquarters and headed down to the harbour.

She was still lost, in truth. Delaney might now have been exposed and his true nature laid bare, but her original quarry remained maddeningly elusive, his true nature still opaque.

All of which meant that with Delaney remaining resolutely silent regarding Emmanuel, Ros was no further on in the quest that had brought her to Greenland in the first place. The same questions remained unresolved.

Was Emmanuel some over-arching mastermind, the very mention of whose name immediately cowed subordinates such as Delaney into silence?

Or was Delaney trying to work out Emmanuel himself and his silence simply an attempt to buy himself time to do that?

Was Emmanuel really the figure he'd presented all those years before – the figure Di had clung to both in her mind and that one time in actuality when they were finally, only too briefly, reunited? A man dealing with devils in order to defeat them?

Or was that yet another fiction on the part of a man who'd sloughed so many skins over the years?

Was Emmanuel actually an instigator, in other words, or could he still possibly be – despite everything – some sort of infiltrator instead?

Either of those incarnations was still just about conceivable. Even his ultimately doomed attempt to silence Ros for good in their apparent fight to the death out in that freezing water didn't automatically condemn him one way or the other. Emmanuel had been playing a role for decades. Along the way there would have been a lot of casualties by way of collateral damage, as Ros already knew only too well. It still left the question as to whether those casualties had been sacrificed in what might be called the greater good, or whether that was yet another smokescreen on the part of a master illusionist.

Ros kept walking, a soul still adrift.

But not for much longer.

33

Two days later and back in his office in Murder Squad in the UK, Masters looked at the screen in front of him.

He read his letter through just the once, then printed it out. It was short but to the point and it said all he wanted to say.

Then Masters stood, leaving his resignation letter behind him on his desk, and walked out of the door.

As Masters was walking out on his old life, Ros was looking out of an aircraft window as the plane began its descent over the Massif Central.

An announcement sounded over the tannoy to say that they'd be on the ground in Marseilles in twenty minutes, and the captain was as good as his word.

Thirty minutes later, having been fast-tracked through Customs by Masters's counterpart in the Police Nationale in Marseilles, Ros was on the airport train into the city, having declined the offer of a taxi. The narrow, tortuous streets radiating from one of the most cosmopolitan ports in one of the most cosmopolitan cities on the planet were always a hive of insane activity, making the task of navigating them by car even more of a nightmare.

Ros looked out as she passed the Porte d'Aix, which looked like a smaller version of the Arc de Triomphe, before arriving at the horseshoe-shaped harbour, crowded as ever with the unrigged masts of what looked like thousands of berthed sailing boats. From there it was a swift walk to the old quarter of the town and another maze of narrow, sloping streets and neighbourhood bars; all filled, so it seemed, with North African gangsters. A short walk across La Canebière, the city's main commercial thoroughfare, then took her to the main office of the man who had sanctioned her fast track through Customs.

'This way.'

Gilles Ferard, that high-ranking counterpart, didn't waste time in greetings. He nodded towards the door, not even offering his visitor a coffee or a Gitane. He just wanted to get this particular officer and all she'd come to do away from his office and his jurisdiction as quickly as possible.

Ferard led Ros back towards the aquamarine Mediterranean, stopping as they reached a *tabac,* a small shop selling cigarettes and tobacco, with a flat above it.

The temperature was now rising as the sun climbed ever higher in the sky, and the sounds of the city percolated all around her.

But Ros didn't notice the heat or the clamorous sounds competing out on the street. She just stared at the windows of that upstairs flat.

For everything Masters had in mind – this final roll of the dice – there had only ever been one candidate.

It wasn't just that Yaroslav was the embodiment of pure evil. It was his very personal connection to the very particular quarry Masters had in mind. So for the second time in as many weeks, Masters steeled himself for another exchange with a man he'd hoped never in his life to see again.

The irony was that Yaroslav didn't actually see himself as evil. In fact he'd actually saved the life of a young girl once in his teens – an act that was witnessed by many children and adults in his home village back in what had been the old Ukrainian Soviet Socialist Republic.

The young girl in question was playing by the bank of a river. Part of the bank gave way and she fell into the water and, screaming for her life, she'd been washed downstream. The young Yaroslav saw the fear on the other children's faces, even on the faces of some of the adults. They knew they'd risk almost certain death themselves by plunging into that torrent and that knowledge robbed them of a resolve they would have liked, in calmer and braver moments, to think they possessed.

Yaroslav plunged in. Without thinking. Totally uncaring of the consequences – and they were potentially severe.

His first reaction was one of total shock at the temperature of the water, a sensation he'd not experienced on even the coldest nights of the year, sleeping under thin blankets in the house he shared with his mother and father. The second was a determination he didn't know was in him to retrieve the girl from the icy grip of that river and deliver her back to the bank where the villagers were now staring and pointing, where her mother was now screaming and where her father was yelling impotently, while the young girl's smaller siblings whimpered in fear.

A tree, almost collapsed into the water, gave him the opportunity. He'd managed to get a hand on the girl and with his other hand he reached out and grabbed a bent branch as they catapulted past. For a moment he thought the tree might give way under the sudden pressure, its roots already struggling to hold fast onto the crumbling bank.

But it held, and his hand held firm on the branch. At the same time, he made sure to keep hold of the small girl, who wasn't screaming anymore – perhaps because she'd given up, the bitter cold convincing her small body that she may as well submit to the inevitable.

Yaroslav felt hands reach him as he held on in the water. One pair of hands took the girl, others helped him back to the bank too. The girl was rushed into the local hospital, where she was treated for a few minor cuts and bruises as well as hypothermia.

After being similarly checked over, Yaroslav was returned home, where – for the rest of that day, that week, that month; indeed for the rest of the time he stayed in his home village – he was treated as a hero.

Yaroslav killed for the first time a year later. A traveller had called; little more than a beggar, in truth. He made an appearance most years and was tolerated for a time before the community tired of feeding and sheltering him and he moved on.

Yaroslav had watched the traveller with a strange sensation building inside him. He'd saved one life, so how to explain the overpowering desire now to take another? He couldn't, but the feeling grew ever more overwhelming.

Then one morning a thought popped into his head. Maybe this was his reward in some way. Maybe because he'd committed a good act, he was now allowed an act that was not so good. Maybe that was the way the world worked.

Yaroslav didn't bother exploring the somewhat dubious logic. He just acted on it that very night. He slipped up behind the traveller as he was bathing in the nearby river, the self-same river from which Yaroslav had saved the child. He grabbed his head and held it under the water until the traveller stopped struggling and was dead.

Then he simply released his grip and let the traveller float downstream, where his unresisting body bumped a few times on some overhanging trees as well as a nearby bridge, before moving out of sight around a bend in the river and heading out to sea.

Yaroslav didn't know if the body was ever found. No one reported the man missing when he didn't turn up at any of the houses he usually visited or when he didn't appear at his usual begging place in the village square. So Yaroslav's first murder went unrecorded and unpunished, which he took as a sign from the gods that his actions had some sort of celestial blessing.

Meaning there'd always been a dichotomy inside Yaroslav. He'd always felt he held an angel and a devil inside him. For the vast majority of the time the devil dominated, but the angel did come calling at times as well.

As it did when he first laid eyes on a young woman called Tyra, and lost his heart to her along the way.

So when Masters pushed a photograph across the table towrds him and identified the man in that photo as the one who had turned his beloved Tyra away from him, he felt his heart start to pound.

And when Masters slid another photo across the table featuring a different man, this one in combat fatigues, and told him this man could lead them to him, Yaroslav's heart began to pound even louder.

Unlike the heart belonging to the man in question, the ex-soldier and unconvicted rapist and murderer once known as Ben Holland, in fact born James Delaney, which stopped pounding around two hours into one of the most extended torture sessions even Yaroslav had ever initiated.

But not before Delaney had told the determined Ukrainian all he needed to know.

Less than one hour after landing at the city's airport, Ros looked up as the door opened in front of her. The man currently living in that small flat above a neighbourhood *tabac* had just walked in, a couple of shopping bags in his hand.

Emmanuel stood motionless in the doorway for a moment, looking back at her.

Which, in the end, was all it took. Even watching Emmanuel on that monitor liaising with a panicked Mathiassen Senior all those years before, Ros still hadn't been able to definitively read the game he might be playing. But that one single look told her. That simple shared moment.

Ros had arrived with a million questions. But now she was here, almost all of them simply disappeared. Everything Ros had rehearsed on that plane ride, every scenario she'd played out in advance in her mind: all of a sudden, they were all redundant.

Across the room, Emmanuel kept staring at her. If he was surprised to see Ros, he didn't show it – and she wouldn't have expected him to. She couldn't explain why, but once again, maybe she didn't have to. This was the man who had tracked the course of her entire life, the man who'd shaped and moulded it and the man who had been at either the back or the front of her mind for almost every moment of that life too. She'd carried him around with her much as Cecilie had carried around her older sister.

This was also the man she knew she'd still be thinking about when he was no longer in her life or anyone else's. She was and always would be caught in the web he'd first started to spin over twenty years before, and nothing could now change that.

At the same time, Ros also realised just why she'd been maintaining that seemingly endless inner debate about him. Because she'd been clinging onto some last vestige of hope that in the end her story would contain within it some semblance of honour. That there was a point to all that had happened to them; a reason for all they'd endured.

Ros kept looking at him. But if the vast majority of her questions were now redundant, it didn't mean there wasn't still some unfinished business.

Finally, she spoke. The first of the only three questions she now needed to ask.

'Did she ever mean anything?'

Emmanuel just kept looking at her for a moment.

'Di?'

Emmanuel stayed silent.

'Did she ever mean anything at all?'

Maybe he could have just turned round and walked back out again. But again, both he and Ros knew he wouldn't. The gun she was holding made sure of that.

Emmanuel shook his head.

'No.'

Ros nodded back.

One question down, two more to go.

'She was picked out because she was ordinary? Because there was nothing remarkable about her, about any of us? She – we – were all just the perfect cover?'

Now Emmanuel nodded.

'Yes.'

One final question to go.

'There are a dozen other Di's out there too, aren't there? Maybe more? A dozen families just like us: people you've latched on to each time you've reinvented yourself? Cover stories in whatever new fiction you'd just created in order to do whatever it was you had to do next?'

Emmanuel just looked back at her for another moment. There was no need for an answer. Ros could see it in his eyes.

Emmanuel himself had probably forgotten by now which particular illusion he was attempting to perpetuate when he came across the innocent Di on that holiday beach in the Indian Ocean. He probably couldn't now recall the specific twisted charade he'd been acting out at the time or maybe even the paymasters he'd been working for at the time. It didn't matter. They didn't matter. Ros and her family had just been bit-part players in some larger conspiracy they were never intended to know anything about.

For a moment Ros wondered if he was even going to say

another single word. But Emmanuel, to his dubious credit, seemed to know he owed her a final response, at least.

'Yes.'

Out on the street below, the waiting Ferard received a one-word text enquiry from Masters.

The next second he heard the single gunshot ring out from the flat above.

Ferard sent his confirmatory response, which was the same single word that Masters had sent, albeit without the accompanying question mark.

Yes.

Then he nodded across the street to two of his waiting men to begin the clear-up.

Back outside the Murder Squad office and sitting in his Bentley, Masters looked at the text on his phone screen.

Then he looked out across the water. Within the next few hours, Delaney and Emmanuel's bodies would be found. Yaroslav's involvement would be laid bare and Masters wasn't going to extricate himself from that by pleading extra attendance at his weekly chess club.

He pressed the start button and the engine in front of him rumbled into life.

The truth was, the end of the road had been approaching for some time now. It could have come courtesy of any one of a number of souls he'd damaged, sometimes terminally, during the course of a long and eventful career.

Masters was just pleased the end of that road had arrived this way. At least with Emmanuel, he could feel he'd gone out on something of a high.

Masters remained where he was for a moment longer, then he put his car into gear and drove away into a future unknown.

EPILOGUE

34

Ros ARRIVED BACK in Greenland three days later. She left her rented apartment the following morning to find three Leviathans blocking her path.

Ros stared at three highly modified Toyota Land Cruisers, which a team of eight hardcore adventurers, as the local press had described them, were planning to drive from Nuuk to Isortoq, a distance of nearly five hundred miles across Greenland's ice cap. The vehicles had just been offloaded from a ferry inbound from Iceland, where they'd been especially adapted for the trip.

Laid out by the side of the outsize trucks were the supplies that would sustain the adventurers for the duration of their trip, including a trailer, six 55-gallon drums of diesel, crevasse ramps, spare parts for the vehicles and enough food and water to last for up to fourteen days.

To the side of the extensive and impressive display and on the edge of the fast-swelling crowd, Ros also saw an old Inuit hunter, looking on in blank bemusement.

Ros had talked to him before. He'd embarked on similar expeditions in the past, armed with just a dogsled, a harpoon and – that most vital of all equipment on an extended hunting trip – a sewing kit. Old folklore still recounted the fate of the members of one past expedition who forgot to take along their sewing kits and eventually died from exposure as they had no way to repair torn clothes. Even the smallest hole would kill you, which the ill-fated expedition members discovered as the cold seeped in.

On his last trip, the old hunter told Ros, he'd been ambushed by a blizzard. The wind turned into a storm and the storm into a gale. Soon he couldn't breathe so he stopped at a large rock for shelter, while his dogs waited patiently at his side for instruction. With little or no chance of building a snow hut, he'd dug a hole in the snow. Crawling inside, he pulled the sled over his head – as his dogs settled on the raging snow outside – and slept. He'd have been better taking the dogs in with him for warmth.

When the hunter awoke, he found he'd lost all feeling in his feet. He tried to dig himself out but his hands next started to freeze. During his ever more impotent digging, his beard froze to the side of the sled. When he finally summoned the strength to pull it away, much of the skin on his chin came away too.

The hunter was saved by a call of nature. He felt a stabbing pain in his stomach and moments later passed a stool. And an idea was born with it. Saving it in his hands, he exposed it to the elements and, before it froze, fashioned the stool into a small makeshift shovel. Using his own now-frozen excrement, he then dug himself out and was reunited with his dogs, who were still waiting for him a short distance away from a shelter that had threatened to become his tomb.

The old hunter stared at the extraordinary trappings of the modern-day expedition before him for a moment longer, then turned away. As he did so, he caught Ros's eye, his silent glance saying it all. Somehow he doubted any of these modern-day adventurers would be called on in the course of the next fourteen days to shape their shit into a shovel.

Ros watched him walk away, then she turned and walked away too, through the old quarter where the famous/infamous Hans Egede statue still took pride of place, passing a red wooden cathedral, the National Museum and a red and yellow teacher-training college as well as Egede's yellow house itself.

She stopped for a moment in the small harbour, looking across at the Sassuma Arnaa. A local artist was playing a guitar. Then she turned again and didn't stop until she was at the top of a nearby hilltop. All around her were thousands and thousands of dandelions, lining the steep hill leading down to the port.

Ros lay down and suddenly, out of nowhere and as if she was in the middle of some sort of out-of-body experience, she saw an image of herself, thousands of miles from the land of her birth, on the edge of the Arctic Circle, lying on a golden hill.

Later that same day again, just before the light finally faded, Ros was alone in a saddle valley, guarded by granite. Above her head, and fringed by the cliff that contained it, lay a shallow lake: all that remained of what was once a thousand-foot-deep slab of ice. Now there was no ice, just a waterfall that ran down into a fjord. Downstream from that, a creek meandered through boulders covered with lichen, before the water dried up completely.

But the water lines on the rocks could still be seen: three of them, and all distinct. The top line was almost white, the second a dark, smoky brown and the third almost resembled copper.

But that's all there was there now, just sand and rock.

And that fading light and silence.

Ros kept looking round. When the last drop of water finally drained from this valley into the ocean, it wouldn't refill. It would be yet another spot on the map where evidence of ice could be found, but not the ice itself.

Ros reached into the bag she was carrying and took out the urns she'd brought out with her from the UK, remains finally sourced from different resting places that had been no resting places at all. Now perhaps they would be.

Ros scattered the ashes of her different family members on the ground. Turning that patch of ground into yet another spot on the planet where evidence of life could be found, but not the life itself.

Then Ros looked round, a peace beginning to settle on her. Maybe – and despite her initial reservations concerning the treatment of Delaney – in Greenland at least, the old Arctic Peace model had worked after all. It was only since being there that a circle had been squared, a form of restorative justice achieved. Something that had steadfastly eluded her everywhere else.

Maybe that was also part of the reason she was staying here now too. Ros had no idea what she'd do and no idea where this new life in her new country might lead her. But she felt as if she'd finally taken at least the first step in finding out.

Like Masters before her in a different country, Ros remained where she was for a few moments longer. Then she turned and walked away.

ACKNOWLEDGEMENTS

The *Shelter* series of novels began in 2013 with the publication of *Gimme Shelter*, continued with *Secret Shelter* in 2015 and now concludes with *Shelter Me*. There are several people I want to thank for enabling me to write Ros's story, tracking her from a small child to adulthood.

Lefi Gruffudd and Garmon Gruffudd have backed this series from the start and I'm enormously grateful to them and to the whole team at Y Lolfa over the years, including Eirian Jones, Branwen Rhys Dafydd, Fflur Arwel, Eifion Jenkins and Gwenllian Jones. Special thanks also to Carolyn Hodges, who is an inspirational editor.

I would like to record my debt to various writers who have been crucial to this final novel in the sequence in particular, with their insights into the extraordinary country of Greenland where much of the story is set. These include Gretel Ehrlich, Niviaq Korneliussen, Peter Stark and Knud Rasmussen.

I would also like to thank the various professionals who have advised me on many aspects of the witness protection programme, but I'm not allowed to name them. I'd nevertheless like to record my gratitude for their invaluable assistance.

Rob Gittins
June 2020

Also by the author:

'Visceral, strongly visual and beautifully structured... powerful, quirky characters.'
Andrew Taylor, Winner, Crime Writers' Association Cartier Diamond Dagger

Gimme Shelter

———

ROB GITTINS

£8.95 (pb)
£17.95 (hb)

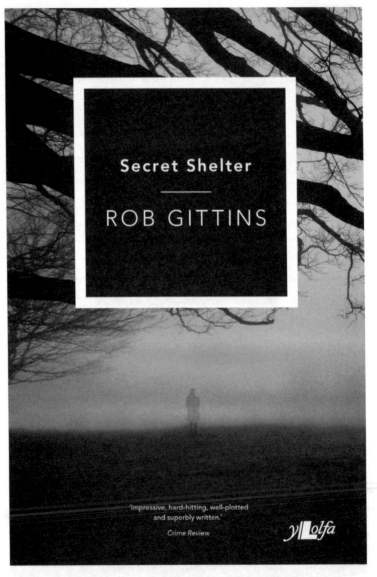

Secret Shelter

—

ROB GITTINS

'Impressive, hard-hitting, well-plotted
and superbly written.'

Crime Review

y Lolfa

£8.95 (pb)
£17.95 (hb)

Dylan Thomas's last days – and someone's watching...

THE POET &
THE PRIVATE EYE

ROB GITTINS

£8.95 (pb)

ROB
GITTINS

INVESTIGATING
MR WAKEFIELD

'A superb, unsettling book, both culturally
significant and beautifully written.'

Jeni Williams

y Lolfa

£8.99 (pb)

ROB
GITTINS
HEAR THE ECHO

y Lolfa

CAFÉ · ICE-CREAM PARLOUR

CARINI'S

Two strong Welsh-Italian women...
separated by a lifetime, linked forever

£8.99 (pb)
£17.99 (hb)